Survival

Book Two in the Fire & Ice Series

By

Karen Payton Holt

Copyright - Karen Payton Holt: 2018

All rights reserved

No part of this publication may be reproduced, stored in a retrieval system, or transmitted, in any form or by any means without prior written permission of the author, except for 'brief quotations' as part of articles of critique or review.

No part of this publication may be circulated in any form of binding or cover other than that in which it is published.

The story is a work of fiction.

All characters in this book are fictitious and any resemblance to real persons, living or dead, is purely coincidental.

Think 'Twilight' meets 'Game of Thrones', with a dark twist, and you are in the right mindset to enter the world of Fire & Ice.

AVAILABLE NOW:

BOOK ONE in the Series:

Fire & Ice: Awakening

Available in Paperback on Amazon

Paperback and Hardback available in bookstores:
A5 Paperback ISBN 978-1-9996614-0-3
Hardback ISBN 978-1-9996614-1-0
FREE on Amazon Kindle Unlimited

This is **BOOK TWO** in the Series:

Fire & Ice: Survival

Available in Paperback on Amazon

Paperback and Hardback available in bookstores:
A5 Paperback ISBN 978-1-9996614-2-7
Hardback ISBN 978-1-9996614-3-4
FREE on Amazon Kindle Unlimited

Watch This Space, up VERY soon,

Fire & Ice Prequel: Death of Connor Sanderson

Available in Paperback on Amazon

Paperback and Hardback available in bookstores:
A5 Paperback ISBN 978-1-9996614-8-9
Hardback ISBN 978-1-9996614-9-6
FREE on Amazon Kindle Unlimited

Three upcoming releases are:

BOOK THREE: Earth Walker

BOOK FOUR: Heart of Stone

BOOK FIVE: Invasion

For the latest news on the publishing dates visit my websites:

karenpaytonholt.com

Karen Payton Holt on Facebook.

@karenpaytonholt on TWITTER.

This is the start of our epic journey, and I hope you enjoy the book.

Please share your thoughts and feelings in reviews – this is my second novel and I welcome your support.

I dedicate this novel to the two people who believed in me.

They drove me forward, and, at times, gave me a much-needed kick up the posterior.

This is for my mum, Sylvia, and my friend of forty years, Steve.

Chapter 1

Doctor Connor kept the three humans in sight as they walked in single file through the woods. He swallowed down the venom which flooded his mouth when a gust of wind rattling through the leaves buffeted their scent into his face.

Hell, they are downwind. Connor peeled off and swept the immediate area, until, where the trees were thickest, he stopped. If he had a beating heart it would have been in his mouth while he listened for others of his kind. This part of the woods was not a favorite haunt for the London Vampire Hive, but there was always the possibility of a lone hunter exploring further afield.

Connor's black garb blended into the shadow, and standing motionless brought its reward. The nocturnal scrabbling of the woodland creatures filled the air once more, believing the danger had passed.

They were the perfect barometer. If a vampire approached, warm blooded prey instinctively froze or went to ground.

Connor listened to the humans' distant lumbering with growing ease. They were almost at the meeting point eight miles out, and Greg could take it from there. *He is human, but the toughest specimen I've ever come across.*

He shot a glance at his watch. *Five a.m.* There were three hours left of the frosty winter's night. Being unseen by humans was easy, for it was just a matter of stealth and speed, but when it came to his own kind, invisibility was more about smoke and mirrors. Connor's vigil would last until dawn drove his brethren back into the shaded streets of the city. *Until I know the humans are safe, I need the smokescreen of behaving like a vampire.*

Resigned to delivering a performance, and looking as though he was in the woods to hunt, he took a deep vampire breath to scent the air and chose a promising trajectory. He darted off between the trees. Skimming through the maze of rough bark in an effortless weaving motion, he picked out a path between obstacles as though the jet black on charcoal landscape was bathed in full sunlight.

He was not hungry, except for sight of his Rebekah; to enfold her in his arms, delight in the pounding of her human heart, and feel the rushing tide of her adrenalin-drenched blood tingling beneath his aching kiss. *For that, I am ravenous.*

Connor eased his powerful shoulders in frustration. The fabric of his shirt creaked as the threads fought to stay bonded over rock-hard muscles moving beneath firm skin. He hated hunting fully clothed, but the moonlight on his stark white complexion would be a beacon to other vampires. Stripping to a bare chest would be an invitation to hunt as a pack, and company was certainly not what he wanted.

Tonight, he was playing the part of Doctor Connor, the dedicated surgeon, feeding on the run before returning to pull a double shift back at the vampire hospital. *A far cry from my human days of saving life and limb. Now, it is just sun scorched vampire limbs.*

It was not always possible to hunt prey which offered exhilaration. Pumas and tigers could be found in the vampire safari park of Dartmoor, only three hundred miles away. But, sometimes, when a vampire could not spare the half hour it would take to get there and back, the deer herds roaming in the woodlands of the English countryside offered an acceptable substitute.

Connor stood stock still, and despite himself, saliva flooded his mouth as he listened to a snuffling sound – the brushed-velvet snout of a male roe deer tore leaves from the shrubbery.

He moved fast, and in a devastating blow which snapped the deer's foreleg, Connor's marble-hard chest slammed into its side. He snatched his prey out of the air in mid leap and crushed it to the ground, compressing the softly packed woodland floor into a biting mattress of sharp stones and twigs.

This is no time for finesse. Connor closed a fist around the muzzle, shoved the deer's chin up until he heard the tendons in its neck snap, and then tore out its throat. Blood gushed into the back of his own throat as the agitated heart rate reached a frenzied peak before the blood pressure died away.

As he rose to his feet, the blood smeared across his bone-white skin settled in the hollows beneath his cheekbones, dressing his striking features in a macabre mask. Connor lifted his chin and embraced the tingle skittering through his limbs. The warm blood pooling in his lungs and stomach rampaged along his arterial system, swelling his vampire tissue to the point of saturation. He set off again, riding the wave of knowledge that he owed his formidable strength to a mortal frame which was turned when at its peak of physical fitness.

Connor's powerful fully fed stride took him a half mile through the woodlands in an instant. He followed the lullaby of rushing water playing over moss covered rocks to where a brook meandered through the trees. Without pause, he waded fully clothed into the tumbling waters. Falling to his knees and cupping his hands, he rinsed the stains of the hunt from his skin. The fast-moving current beat his clothes against his hard body, releasing the blood in dark billowing clouds to race away downstream.

Loping back through the undergrowth, he scraped his hands through sleek, wet, black hair. River water poured from his clothes. *I am clean, at least.* Knowing that once Greg had settled Leizle and Thomas in the new shelter, he would have double-timed it back through the familiar terrain alone, Connor headed out to meet him at the rendezvous.

The chilled air was motionless as the woodlands thickened. The leaves of the canopy barely shuffled in the oppressive silence which accompanied Connor's controlled movement. He carved a path towards the small chapel, and the pressure inside his chest eased when glints of the granite-gray structure flashed between the black picket of towering tree trunks. *This time tomorrow, they will all be safe.*

Finding the chapel had been a blessing, and even Connor could barely believe his luck. *It is perfect.* Living on the knife edge of an impending attack from Vampire Councilor Serge and his guardsmen had taken its toll on the humans. So, finding a temporary hiding place while he and Julian excavated an approximation of their old eco-town dwelling, was a gift from God. *Strange, that vampires and God should be on the same side.* Creases etched into

Connor's perfect twenty-four-year-old face as, for a moment, he smiled.

Inevitably, the catacombs beneath the chapel were eerie; the chambers provided the resting place to mounds of intricately placed bleached skulls and bones. Nothing could be done to render them anything less than terrible.

Connor had erected wooden screens over the arched entryways, but the humans still knew the remains were there.

Thankfully, Rebekah's Uncle Harry had stepped up to the mark. He succeeded in managing the danger of jittery human heartbeats, making sure the group took their modified beta-blockers and applied pheromone suppressant spray on a strict regimen.

The crumbling facade of the chapel came into view, and Connor heard slow measured breathing before his preternatural sight combed the shadows and discerned the outline of a human shape. *Greg's back.* Connor took comfort from the mountain of human muscle standing guard.

Rebekah's group had survived the pandemic which wiped out most of the human race, but few could anticipate that they would face worse than that. But, Uncle Harry had seen the vampire invasion coming. Being a biochemist, his talent for innovation had extended to modifying drugs to alter human physiology. It gave the refugees a fighting chance of remaining undetected by the keen senses of vampires. But, when acting fast and getting out of London became crucial, Greg's contribution had been make or break. *That was where Greg had excelled.*

Once vampires broke cover, it took only weeks for the vampire councils to round up the dwindling human population and imprison them on the farms. Vampires siphoned the humans for blood, pushing their bone marrow to its limit of replenishment and introducing them to a state of perpetual exhaustion. *With the release of death taken from them, hell has arrived on earth.*

As he burst through the tree line, Connor directed his steely gaze into the darkest corner of the chapel portico from where Greg gave him the thumbs up signal. Arriving beside him in a hurricane of damp air which stirred a crackling storm of dried leaves around their ankles, Connor stared intently back out over the graveyard.

"You're very wet. Don't tell me, you've been eating fish?" Greg said, deadpan.

Connor chuckled. "Funny. I see you made good time. Leizle and Thomas didn't give you any trouble?"

Greg shook his head. "They knew they had to go next. Even with the pheromone suppressants, we can't risk a scent trail of *five* people. They know that. And as Rebekah said, they'll see her again tomorrow."

"And the new eco-shelter? Do you think it will stand up to the winter?"

"It's small." Greg smiled. "But, I dare say it will feel like home in no time." He lifted an eyebrow and assessed Connor's profile. "You and your friend have constructed in two days what it took us a decade to achieve, thank you."

Connor shrugged. "It helps when the workers never tire and can keep going for forty hours without pause, and of course-"

Greg waited expectantly.

"We vampires actually understand the concept of quiet."

Greg rummaged around for a sarcastic response, but in the end, muttered, "Touché."

Connor considered the upheaval of the last few days. Although, the new eco-shelter location was eighteen miles away from the first, it was not further from London. Since the community had scouted the area for fifteen years, leaving a familiar stamping ground altogether, would be foolish. So, the move took them in an arc, from the south, to southeast of the city. *The human farm and vampire hunting grounds are both west of London, so it's a calculated risk.*

The safe house, situated south of the River Thames in Clapham, remained a secure place to gather. From there the group could forage inside the city and gather supplies and fuel, all as before. *And I can keep an eye on Rebekah and protect her.* Moving the equipment from the old eco-shelter to the new, was accomplished with Julian's help. *It would have been exhausting for the nineteen humans. They were better off keeping calm and staying hidden.*

The three main communal caverns were dug out beneath the rolling swells of the North Downs of Kent, and the successive undulation of hills offered the chance to expand, in time. With Julian's help – and he turned out to be surprisingly willing in that – building had progressed quickly.

The soundproofed chamber housing the generators was a feat of vampire engineering. The exhaust system vented out to the inside of a hollow tree trunk deep inside the woodlands, where the odors of methane and carbon dioxide formed part of the naturally occurring rich cocktail of nature's decay. The generator chamber was already operational, harnessing water power and kinetic energy, and the hot water pipes salvaged from the old eco-town had been reworked to fit into the new space. Tapping into an underground spring, Connor had dug a well inside a small cave which fed water into the kitchen cavern, and the still to be completed hospital chamber. *It's all looking good.*

"As soon as we are settled, I'll take one of the guys and let Seth know we have moved." Greg frowned.

"Finding he was still out there must have been a pleasant surprise," Connor said, thinking of his own close friendship with Principal Julian. "It's good to know someone is watching your back again."

"It makes life easier," Greg replied. Both men had served as Royal Marines and backing each other up was second nature.

Resting a hand on Greg's shoulder, Connor said, "Are you sure Seth wouldn't understand your situation?"

"That I am fraternizing with the enemy? No offence."

"None taken." Connor grinned.

"No, it's best this way. We came back together by chance, but after fifteen years our paths are set. He has his group of humans to protect, and I have mine, plus a vampire invasion to evade."

Connor let the silence hang.

"You were human once. When Seth and I were in the Marines, a platoon had to get the balance right. Enough men to become a team and support each other, but not so many that clashes of personalities cause unrest." Greg took a deep breath. "*Our small group works well as a unit. It seems foolish to risk it falling apart.*"

The link between the two camps of human survivors was tenuous, but comforting. And they were only twenty miles away, which was a two-day hike in an easterly direction.

When London became besieged by vampires, Greg scouted out the surrounding terrain. He established early on, that with a network of vampire hives cropping up throughout England, Europe, and probably the rest of the world, survival was a matter of hiding, not running.

The funeral pyres of those who died in the pandemic had laid a haze over the London skyline, and the humans captured and taken to the farms had little hope of finding old friends. Seth and Greg each thought the other was dead.

"Seth agrees it is best not to put all our eggs in one basket. We can back each other up in a fight. And the less he knows about you, the better."

"I guess you know him best." Connor let the subject drop.

Humans prefer familiarity, so for Rebekah's group, it made sense to replicate the environment of their previous hideout. *As far as possible, anyway. After all, it has worked for them, up until now. Their fifteen years of liberty probably would've stretched into decades, had their luck not run out.* Connor was relieved he had Greg to rely on. *Even a vampire can't be in two places at one time.*

Cold was the biggest enemy right now. Greg's cold-climate survival training helped *him*; the ability to lower his metabolic rate to where his body conserved fuel and warmth was his forte. Surviving underground in the labyrinth of stone catacombs for three days, even wearing extreme weather clothing, had pushed most to their limit. *And the mental stress – there are only so many whispered conversations and games of checkers the human mind can cope with.*

Connor shook his head in wonder. *I'm still not sure how I got myself into this.* Amusement danced around his lips at the realization he had known Rebekah only a few weeks. In that short time, she had turned his life upside down.

She was the reason he stumbled across the eco-community. A blow to the head had led to their fated encounter in the hospital. Her suppressed human physiology had thrown him when he had swept into the room, intent on examining a female *vampire* for hardening; the tissue damage most common in vampires. He was distracted by the burning sensation in his nasal lining, but too busy being a 'doctor' to pay attention.

Connor grinned wryly. These things mocked him now. *How did I not know instantly? Because she's a fighter, that's how.* When she regained consciousness, she had held her nerve, relying on the smokescreen of beta blockers and pheromone suppressants. *And she almost pulled it off, too.* She had very nearly escaped before the pieces fell into place.

A sudden overwhelming need to fill his heart with the sight of her delicate features landed a sledgehammer blow to his chest. He closed his eyes for a moment, and hunted out the delicate scent of her which rode the currents of the night air. *First, I must do one last patrol.* But as his gut wrenched and his mouth flooded with saliva, another realization drove disappointment through him. *Grave sleep, I'll have to wait awhile longer.*

He had already inspected the mausoleum in the chapel cemetery where he would confine himself before he unleashed the bloodlust of grave sleep. Using it saved him a trip back into London, to the hospital, where vampires used the secure confinement of cadaver drawers. Harming another vampire in grave sleep had the equivalence of first degree murder in vampire culture, and Principal Julian delivered harsh penalties to those stupid enough to offend. *Luckily for me, Julian is on my side.*

"Hey, Greg, tell Rebekah I need to sleep first. But I'll come and find her soon."

Greg nodded. "We will clean up camp and make ready to move out. We'll bury the food scraps and garbage out in the woods while you are gone. But don't worry, we'll be careful."

"Make it within the hour, the vampires will have finished harvesting crops by then, and some may still fancy a snack before the sun comes up." Connor glanced at the cloud-cluttered purple night sky and added, "It's set to be a dull day, though. And I don't have to tell *you* vampires are out there twenty-four-seven. I think you were the first to discover that sun and shadow limits us, not night and day."

"We'll be ready when you give the word," said Greg. "You'd better get going."

He's right, let's take one thing at a time. Phase two is almost complete. Inside the chapel, only three humans remained, Greg, Oscar, and his Rebekah. The rest had safely made the ten-mile trip to the new eco-shelter, with Greg escorting and Connor running interference. And, even though they were still underground, the caverns, dug out of packed earth and lined with rocks made from clay, retained heat. *Unlike the church.*

The new habitat was warmer by several degrees, which made the difference between living and dying.

Waving farewell, Connor reeled around and vanished into the night to satisfy himself all was well in the woods before he surrendered control to the psychopath inside his head for grave sleep.

Rebekah's group of humans, at least, knew more about vampire sleep requirements.

Vampires had perfected a state of permanent awareness, but brain tissue did not rehydrate spontaneously like muscle fiber – and three cerebral sleep centers had evolved. When opening the floodgates to hydrate the chosen compartment of the brain, inhibitions tumbled down, and the appetites contained inside took over. *Our problem lies in wrestling with the triple personality disorder unleashed to run riot.*

Connor's gray eyes glinted with pleasure. *Of course, the relaxation of revival sleep has been my salvation.* The brain center which reduced vampire stress levels released an inmate who gentled his touch, and tempered the movement of every sinew. In that state, when his body hungered for hers, he could touch Rebekah and not break bones. He had still to master the bruising, but he was happy to spend decades getting that right.

The surrounding woods were clear, and Connor's control was crumbling. It was never a good idea for him to think of Rebekah when grave sleep was calling. As he crossed the graveyard, the three sluggish heartbeats echoed through the walls of the chapel in a mesmerizing rhythm. *It would be so easy to give in to temptation.*

Resolutely shutting down the thought, he entered the mausoleum.

He effortlessly moved aside a boulder almost as tall as his six-foot three-inch height, and a rusted wrought iron gate groaned in protest when he pushed it open. The stone steps leading into the dank, dark space below were slick with lichen and rainwater. In winter, they would become sheets of black ice. Connor's boots barely skimmed the surface as he glided down and came to rest on the flagstone floor. Lifting a square grate at his feet, he descended to the dark subterranean chamber of the crypt.

If he was only releasing the volatile aggressive drunkard of rapacious sleep, just closing the metal gate and lying out on the stone altar in the room above would be enough. *Or stand in the corner like a stone statue as I did on many occasions when vampires were still in hiding from humans.*

Sadly, he had seen humans die when a vampire, thinking he could withstand the fragrant blush of blood fumes when a human passed by, found his control fractured. *And the human newspapers reported one more horrific murder.*

The vampire council existed even then. *Jack the Ripper and The Butcher both risked exposing us as monsters and suffered the penalty.* Jack's psychosis had earned him death – Connor's fingers twitched as he remembered the kill, out in the dark London streets.

The Butcher was not so lucky.

His body was condemned to petrify until it resembled granite, but he was fed enough human blood to retain brain function; he had an eternity to think over his crimes. He remained the most infamous resident in the London Hive's vampire internment facility. *Julian's twelve-decade reign as principal is certainly hard line. Though, the crimes are different now.*

Connor was committing the one – threatening the food supply – which carried the harshest penalty. By keeping a group of humans out of Human Farm Factory Eight, he risked the same fate as The Butcher. He had the grace to feel guilty about sucking Julian into this, too. *But it is too late now.*

"So, let's get this done." Delving into his pocket, Connor pulled out two vials of human blood, flipped the lids, and downed the contents.

It was the last piece in the puzzle of vampire survival. The vampire brain could not function on animal blood alone. Those who tried it, refusing to relinquish their lone hunter status, suffered vampire dementia. The vital daily dose of human blood forced vampires into tending to the needs of humans on the farm, and subjected them all to visiting the hospital blood dispensary to collect their rations.

Like lions without teeth, vampires were victims, too.

With a wry grin, Connor pushed aside the lid of the sarcophagus and lay down inside. The heavy stone brushed his chest as gripping the rough surface, he dug his fingernails in and excavated a shower of stone chips. He dragged it across and settled it back into place.

Connor's body jolted into spasm as the human blood pooling in his throat filtered into his carotid artery and entered his cerebral cortex. The stone coffin shook, showering gravel down from the plinth onto the hard floor as the seams grated with the force of his muscle spasms. He grimaced. Summoning iron will and digging deep, he reined in each sinew and locked his cramped limbs in place.

Deathly stillness settled like a lead weight onto his chest. Bloodlust drew his lips back, baring his teeth, and the growl rattling in the back of his throat splattered flecks of blood on the underside of the closed sarcophagus lid, mere inches from his snarling muzzle.

Chapter 2

Rebekah heard the muffled approach of feet padded with animal-skin, and disappointment settled on her shoulders. *Connor is never that noisy.* Greg's footfall scuffed along the polished stone floor of the catacomb passageway until, eventually, the candlelight danced his shadow over the walls.

Focusing on something other than Connor, Rebekah sighed in relief, knowing Greg's return meant one thing. "Leizle and Thomas made it, then?" she whispered, smiling warmly.

Entering the chamber, Greg shouldered his shadow aside and filled the doorway. "They did," he said, lowering his utility belt carefully onto the ground at his feet.

"Of course, they did, lass. Did you ever doubt it?" said Oscar.

Rebekah pulled an 'are you kidding me?' face, and said, "This is Thomas we're talking about, master of huge cock-ups. He's tested Connor's patience before."

"Well, maybe turning seventeen has made the difference."

"I don't think so," muttered Greg, "I almost slapped a gag over his mouth. He's got no idea how to be quiet."

Rebekah shot Oscar a smug look. She had known Thomas since he was two, and Leizle since she was three years old. Rebekah, herself, had been a dazed and confused six-year-old when Uncle Harry told her human society had ended. For her, looking out for them had helped make sense of a strange new world. Fifteen years on, they were like a brother and sister to her, but, at twenty-one, she felt more like their mother at times.

"But they are both safe?"

"Oh, yes," said Greg wryly, "mission accomplished, and Connor is glad we are on the last run."

Rebekah darted a hopeful glance over Greg's shoulder.

"He's here, but he has to sleep," he said, as he eased his kit-bag from his back and rubbed a palm over the dark stubble on his chin. His keen eyes alighted briefly on Rebekah until he gathered her nod of understanding. *Sleeping was vampire code for 'steer well clear'.*

"I'm sure he won't be long, lass. Anyhow, we've got chores to fill the time," said Oscar with forced enthusiasm. He jerked his head to indicate the zip-lock plastic bags of garbage and food scraps. "We've got those to get rid of, and the roasting pit needs damping down and emptying. But for now, eat up."

Rebekah took the plate he held out and made a show of forcing down slices of pit-roasted rabbit and jacket potato. The meat was succulent, having been slow roasted in a terracotta pot buried beneath glowing coal embers. Connor had rigged up the oven inside an empty stone sarcophagus. This was no time for misplaced sensibilities; after all, vampires not being able to smell the meat was far more important than the relocation of a long-dead relative.

Connor was an efficient fire starter, generating heat by rolling a thick twig between his palms until it burst into flames in his hand, setting alight the bed of kindling, and then fueling the fire with nuggets of coal. Dragging the stone lid almost into place, he fanned the flames with a tireless constant flow of vampire breath. Once the fire was ablaze, the potatoes and meat sealed inside the cook pots were buried in the hot coals, and the sarcophagus lid closed, trapping the heat, extinguishing the flames, and containing the smell.

They could only eat hot meals at certain times, when vampires were either harvesting and planting crops to feed the humans on the farm complex, or attending council sessions in London, but Connor was always on hand to shift the four-inch thick heavy stone slab aside, and from there, Oscar came into his own.

Oscar had fed them for fifteen years in the old eco-town, and making something out of nothing much, was his forte. But even though the spice-marinade cooked rabbit fell from the bone and was delicious, all Rebekah tasted was sawdust.

A dart of color danced across her vision, and a vise closed over her skull. "Great," she muttered. *A headache, just what I need.*

The heated stone of the sarcophagus warmed the chamber, and suddenly Rebekah craved cold, refreshing cold, against her skin. Pulling the collar of her shirt open offered no relief and nausea swilled in her stomach. Connor's cool touch would have been her idea of heaven about now.

"Are you ok, Rebekah?" Oscar plucked her plate from her fingers and peered into her pale face.

The blonde feathered strands of her hair suddenly felt like a heated cap, and sweat broke out on her brow. "It's just too warm in here," she whispered. A dull cast to her gaze ruined the impact of a reassuring smile. "I'll be fine." *And I will. I fought off a vampire in the woods, and faced Connor's anger without flinching. I'm made of sterner stuff than this.* On a stronger voice, she said, "I'm fine, and we've got chores to do, remember?"

Greg exchanged glances with Oscar and shrugged. Checking his watch, he said briskly, "Connor said, within the hour."

Moving in coordinated silence, the three of them filled black duffle bags with zip-lock pouches of clothes too wet to salvage, and food scraps and vegetable peelings, setting aside the cooked meat wrapped in candle wax-coated muslin cloths which sealed in the smell.

Straightening and shouldering the heaviest of the bags, Greg cast a final glance around the catacomb chamber. "Ready?" His voice rumbled with excitement.

Rebekah swallowed when her stomach performed another somersault. *Nerves are good.*

She shoved her walking boots into the deer-hide covers which would deaden the echo of her footfalls to a whisper, and followed Oscar and Greg out along the roughly hewn stone passageway. Leaving the candlelight behind, she followed the dancing beam of Greg's flashlight, knowing that if it disappeared around the bend up ahead, she would be plunged into darkness.

Mounting the steps and emerging into the chapel above, Rebekah welcomed the draft of cool night air brushing over her clammy forehead, and the cotton-wool fog cleared from her thoughts. Hitching her backpack higher, she copied Greg and Oscar as they pulled their boots free from the deer skins, and emerged to cross the graveyard.

On the other side of the railings marking the boundary of the chapel grounds, Oscar pushed a nylon cord into Rebekah's hand, and with sure fingers, she depressed the trigger on the clamp at her waist and slipped the loop over the metal clasp. Yanking hard on the rope, signaling she was ready, they set off into the woods, tethered together.

The bite of frost in the air fanned her damp hair and chilled her scalp, and Rebekah pulled her hood tighter around her face, gasping when turning her head sliced pain across her vision once more.

"Rebekah?" Greg's urgent tone was barely a whisper.

His dirt-smeared, camouflaged face loomed before her as he waited for an answer.

Rebekah shook her head gingerly. Pointing skyward, drawing a circle in the air and jabbing her thumb back over her shoulder, she indicated her return to the chapel.

Greg frowned, held up three fingers to communicate the thirty minutes they expected the trip to take, and unclipped her rope from her belt.

As she turned back, focusing on the black silhouette of the chapel spire rising above the trees, the dancing lights in her vision confirmed it was the right decision. Stumbling blindly through the woods, she would have put them all in danger.

The metal railings surrounding the chapel glinted in the gloom, and the moonlight breaking from behind a cloud, cast the marble facade of the mausoleum, where Connor slept, into stark relief. Without thought, Rebekah found herself drawn there, and before the voice of reason could tell her to go back, she slipped through the rusted gate Connor had left propped open. *I won't stay. I just want to be close to him for a moment.* Digging into her pocket, she popped two more beta-blockers into her mouth, even though her heart rate was already sluggish in her chest. *It can't hurt.*

Moving carefully down the steps into the altar space, Rebekah found the iron grate in the floor. Using both hands, she pulled on it, fighting against the thick moss clinging to its edges. It shifted suddenly, her blood pressure peaked, and the headache unleashed a sparkling shower of pain. She cringed, preparing for the death knell

Fire and Ice: Survival

clang of iron on stone when the grate slipped from her grasp, and breathed a sigh of relief when the blanket of moss muffled the clang to a dull thump.

It's too late to turn back now. Putting aside the voice arguing with that, Rebekah descended into the crypt. Though the black shadows thickened, she could still make out the hulking shape of the sarcophagus elevated to waist height, commanding the space from its plinth.

A shiver rattled through her as she realized that Oscar's makeshift oven in the catacombs obviously offered more warmth than she thought. But the idea of spending half an hour alone inside the chapel was not appealing. Her five-foot six-inch height suddenly seemed too tall for her sluggish heart to cope with, so, she found an alcove and folded gratefully down into it. Drawing her knees up inside the tent made by her oilskin coat, she curled around the ball of heat of the warm meal inside her belly. She rested her pounding head back on the wall, closing her eyes as energy drained away, and, as she drew comfort from Connor being nearby, the heavy shroud of sleep crept in.

<><><>

The burning fuse-wire of heat raced through the neuron pathways inside Connor's brain and, gradually, he pushed back the crimson curtain of blood which clung to his mind. The stone weight inside his chest eased as he drove the breath from his lungs, and his eyes snapped open.

He surfaced slowly from the resting semi-conscious state. Waiting for the waves of ecstasy to ebb, his stomach a hard wall and his groin tight where a scent of Rebekah still filled his nostrils, he smiled in anticipation. Dreaming of her was a permanent feature of sleep now, but this dream seemed more vibrant. *I can almost taste her scent.*

As he moved the age-pitted coffin lid aside, the grinding of the rough stone vibrated through his body. His fingers curled around the edge of the slab, he held it steady on the seesaw pivot point until his feet touched the floor, and then, pushed it smoothly back into place. *I never know when I may need it again.*

He now understood the elder vampires in London who shunned the stainless-steel cadaver drawers of the morgue, preferring to seek out mausoleums as places more fitting to their status. *Grave sleep was certainly more vivid than I expected.*

Leaving the crypt, he dragged the grate in the floor across, swept out of the arched doorway, closed the gate, and pushed the boulder back into place. Swooping between the crumbling array of neglected headstones, he approached the chapel, and melted into shadow as he slipped inside. In habitual deathly silence, he approached the altar at the rear, and passed through the heavy oak door behind it.

Connor descended into the bowels of the building and moved briskly along the underground passageway.

He knew it was empty before he reached the cavern; its sweeping domed ceiling marked it as the central chamber of the catacombs, its walls now punctuated by the wooden screens which hid the human remains from view. But, for him, the air was laden with calcium-flavored fragments. He laid his cold palm on the warm stone of the sarcophagus oven, idly scoring grooves into its surface as he ran through Greg's words.

They must still be out burying the evidence of the camp. Oscar and Greg were both formidable in size, although, Oscar was closer to a bear than Greg's rhinoceros tough mass. *Rebekah should be safe.*

Connor made his way back up through the chapel and waited inside the embrace of the portico. An indolent leaning statue, he rested his shoulder against the wall, stillness creeping over him as his senses scoured the woodlands. A frown etched into his face when he heard approaching footsteps and counted only two sets of everything. He grimly absorbed the heightened stress levels rattling around inside the humans. Their adrenalin-pumped heartbeats were still inclined to race, but then, it had been only two days since their last fight for survival.

Greg and Oscar emerged from the wood, and as Connor moved forward into the moonlight, the stark anger on his face froze their half-smiles of welcome.

Connor's gaze cut a path through the trees behind them, searching for her face and her slender, graceful frame. "Where is Rebekah?"

"She's here, waiting for you." Oscar's tone vibrated with sudden nerves. "Isn't she?"

"No." Connor shot the word into the dark.

His vampire perceptions went into overdrive as he relived past events. The weeks he had known her were marked by anguish. Her flesh had been almost as cold as his, the night she nearly died of hypothermia, lost out in the woods trying to rescue Thomas. And then, his heart clenched anew as the lingering threat of the rogue vampire they had failed to track down reared as a specter in his mind. His enemy had left his scent when he had laid a hand on her during the last battle at the old eco-town, and creeping suspicion struck fear into Connor. *Has she been captured? Did he track us, and I missed it?* He knew he had not missed anything, but nothing else made sense.

Greg's words struck a chord of reason in Connor's brain. "She's got a headache. We were only twenty yards out before she came back. She's here somewhere. Hiding maybe, because she's here alone?"

"Hiding?" An elusive feeling laced tendrils of doubt through his mind. *I am missing something.* Closing his eyes, Connor tried to get inside that stubborn head of hers. Like a thunderbolt strike, a sudden surge of electrical activity arced through the atmosphere and his body jolted. He could smell the static charge as her brain raced through the tunnels of a nightmare, and, as if his gaze could bore through earth and stone, he zeroed in on her depressed heartbeat and cold skin as though he was standing next to her. And in the next moment, he was.

He swiped away the boulder which sealed the mausoleum, sending it crashing to one side, pulled the wrought iron gate from its hinges, and buckled the rusted grate in the floor in his haste to drop down into the crypt and pull her freezing body up into his arms.

"Damn it, Rebekah," he murmured, as the micro tremors racing through her gave him an insight into a mind gripped in the horror of a night terror. Her lips were gray, and her capillaries were gossamer strands of purple lace tinting her clammy skin blue. Connor was already moving, rifling through the options he had available to warm her, because that was all that mattered. *The nightmare may even be the delirium of her cold body crying out for help.*

◇◇◇

Rebekah's throat ached, and electric-white sparks arcing across a black velvet sky crowded her vision. Her mouth gaped as grief tumbled rocks of ice into her chest.

She forced her eyes open to look down at the limp weight of the baby in her arms, Connor's influence was clearly written in the stark contrast of her milk-white skin and jet-black hair, her head resting back and her mouth, an open pink bud, hanging wide.

"Don't touch her!" she howled, the words inside her head screaming, and not the croak which barely escaped her dry throat. Rebekah glared into Connor's impassive face. "Don't touch her," she whispered vehemently, squeezing the soft body to her chest. She ached for a sigh of protest from the tiny throat; something to cling to that the baby was not dead.

Why she was so scared of Connor, she didn't know, but she felt sure that if she lost her grip on this tiny body, she would never hold it again.

His hands, even colder than the glacial chill inside her, closed over her shoulders and shocked her back to awareness.

"The baby's not dead," Connor's voice whispered, the tone dull and empty as he pulled in a harsh breath. "She will never die, it's not over." He dropped his hands and held them out, waiting for her to pass the baby to him. "It's never over for us," he added simply.

Rebekah looked down again into the infant's still features, muscle tone slack. "Don't let her die," she wailed, watching helplessly as his hands scooped up the tiny body and bore it away. "Please, save her. Save her," she breathed, hugging her own body and seeing only blackness as she squeezed her eyelids tightly closed.

A thick silence settled and dread gripped the base of her skull. As she strained to listen, a rhythmic, moist suckling sound pulsed through the stillness and dragged her gaze up. She had to see. The smell of soured milk on his breath as his jaws tore into new-born flesh curdled her stomach and nausea engulfed her.

The vampire holding her baby was no longer Connor. Wavy black hair framed features which were sharp with spite, and deep-set predatory eyes bored into hers as he bared his teeth in a grimace of satisfaction. Blood made every tooth appear dark red, and pooled along his slackened lower lip. Understanding struck Rebekah in the chest, taking her breath away.

Her fist clenched in her sleep, as if she once again held the knife that had been all she had to protect herself the last time she looked into that face. Connor had arrived and the vampire ran, but the zealous cast to his features when her blade had skidded over the polished marble of his stomach muscles returned to haunt her, more and more.

A viselike grip of fear closed around her throat... and she woke up sobbing.

"Sh... it's okay, it's okay." Connor's soothing tone pierced the terror and melted the scene from her mind as his warm arms pulled her back into his body. "It's okay, honey, you're safe, you're safe."

They were alone in the warm cavernous space beneath the chapel. She was lying on her side on a padded bedroll with Connor's body, his *warm* body, fitted seductively into the curve of her spine, beneath a soft fleecy blanket. Rebekah's breath scratched at her parched throat. she took comfort from his embrace, running her palm over the sinews on his forearm draped across her chest, and then she noticed the ashen cast to his skin. A frown chased across her features. Running her fingertips over the satin-clad iron of his smooth muscle was a familiar feeling, but this time her hands became covered in carbon dust.

"You're hot again?" She smiled weakly.

"Well, if you could stop trying to freeze your ass off."

"What happened?" She reached back and ran her fingers through his wet hair.

Connor's tone was grim. "You put me through hell, again, literally, this time."

Rebekah thought she had dreamed that part, too. The image of the sarcophagus lid slipping back, and the glow of coal embers flaring to life as Connor climbed out, had felt surreal to her terror trapped mind. His silhouette, framed in a flickering orange halo as he walked towards her, with his skin dressed in a gray sheen of ash from the fire, had taken the familiar and dressed it in awestruck wonder.

"You were in Oscar's oven?"

"I had to be creative. But you know, you don't have to try and kill yourself every time you want hot sex." Connor growled playfully. "How about we make it an anniversary thing?"

"I'm sorry, I just wanted to be close to you." Her voice cracked, and the tremor of relief wiped the smile from his face.

"But, you had a nightmare?" he asked.

Rebekah nodded slowly.

"Are you going to tell me?" he murmured gently.

She pulled his arm in tighter around her chest. "Not right now. I need to get my head around it."

Moving up onto his elbow, Connor turned her face to his. Looking into her eyes, he found confusion, with their usual spark extinguished. "But it was bad?" He felt her chin nudge his fingers when she nodded again.

"Alright, I will wait." He subsided back and held her again. "Try and sleep, while you can."

He settled down to wait for her to fall asleep with his mind in turmoil. When in the throes of the nightmare, she had cried out his name, and he needed to know what demons he was fighting.

Rebekah rubbed her chin, tracing the tender areas left by his touch. He was as gentle as he could be, but there would always be battle scars. Even though he sank into revival sleep whenever they were together, he dusted her skin in bruises, bruises which Rebekah bore with joy in her heart.

His body simmered as he immersed himself into the tranquil waters of revival sleep. His warm fingertips traced over the hot spots on her skin, leaving streaks of charcoal in their wake. His hand drifted down over her tummy as he pulled her gently against him, melting the nightmare and stirring fire in her belly. Rebekah's pulse quickened as his hands moved, and erasing the vista of horror inside her head suddenly seemed simple when she turned in his arms.

Connor's eyes glinted in the dim candlelight. He was awake, as always, and stone still, as always, until Rebekah put her palm on his cheek and whispered, "Love me."

He drowned in her scent, savoring the honey accented odor washing over him. A smile settled on his face as he reveled in the pain of resisting, of not biting into her soft skin and drinking his fill. Scorching hunger abraded his throat and burned a trail down inside to fill his raw chest. He tortured himself further, resting his bared teeth on her carotid artery and feeling the echo of her tantalizing heartbeat. As venom flooded his mouth, he leaned in to kiss her, deep revival sleep washing relaxation through his muscles, and for him, it was as if he waded through water, with every gesture slow and controlled.

"Love me, Connor." Rebekah closed the space between them, stroking her thigh up over his and pressing into his hard, smooth chest. The citrus spice of his kiss was a familiar pleasure which transformed the simmering heat in her stomach into a burning hunger of the flesh, of the human kind.

"I will. I do," he whispered.

He molded his hands to her body and moved his lips gently over hers. Contentment swelled inside him that she was still his, and the dread in her voice, from her dream, had not filled her heart. She was still his Rebekah.

But, her agonized voice nibbled at his consciousness. He would ask her again, but for now, he needed every ounce of control. Rolling onto his back and taking her with him, his touch played over her body as her breasts brushed his skin every time she moved. His hooded gaze devoured her rapt expression, the heavy bouquet of her scent settled in his gut, and he locked down his muscles as her thighs framed his hips and he filled her.

The flush on her skin entranced him and she felt deliciously warm to his touch. The shudders racing through her, and the heat pooling in his groin, sliced satisfaction though his core.

As she bit her lip, smothering her gasping breath, he surged up and kissed her. Tasting her excitement, his own body ached to join hers in rapture.

Rolling her over onto the padded bedroll, his body was tight with regret as he pulled away at the very moment when he wanted to stay. His sure touch stroked inside her and a snarl of triumph tightened his face as he tumbled her clamoring body over the edge once more. He savored every tremor, embracing the storm of vibrations which rocked through him, too, as her breathless sighs whispered in the air.

Afterwards, Connor held her tucked into his side, feeling satisfaction that she was relaxed and at peace. He stayed tuned in to her body, and the only trembles he detected in her slight frame were those he had built inside her as he made love to her. The taint of fear in her scent had gone.

"I wish you could stay, you know, until..." Rebekah murmured.

Connor dropped a kiss onto her hair. "You know the score honey. I am in suspended animation. Not dead so much as frozen in time. The risk of pregnancy is non-negotiable. I'm a doctor, and I won't gamble, Rebekah, not even on long shots." Melancholy dragged through every line of his body as he said quietly, "That night, I made a mistake. Saving you from hypothermia in the woods, and then, risking your life, all in the same moment was idiotic."

It was barely three weeks ago, and his joy at having her back was still tinged with guilt. It was the *only* time that his emotions had overwhelmed him, and, unable to hold back, he had poured his seed into her. "I'm not playing with fire again."

"Apparently, you are," said Rebekah mischievously, "Oh, no, that's right, it was submerging yourself in boiling water until you were a man-sized storage heater, that time."

Connor growled. "Don't mess with me, young lady. My living hell is no joke."

"Talking about living hell." Rebekah craned her neck to look into his face. "When do you have to leave?"

"Tomorrow night, you will all be safely installed in the new eco-shelter. Although Julian has bought me a few days by telling Charles, the vampire who runs the blood dispensary, that I'm at the Bristol Hive operating on a human with appendicitis, I'm still expected to show up at the hospital soon."

Connor would return to London and keep up the pretense that nothing had changed for him since Rebekah. He was still a doctor, and Councilor Serge's relentless hounding would continue on as always, of that he was sure.

Charles bought the appendix explanation easily. There were so few vampires who could cut into human flesh and not succumb to their hunger.

Connor possessed a rare ability; to slam his vocal chords shut, isolate his lungs, and minimize the effects of the odor of human blood. Even without his plastic mask pressed tightly over his features, he could resist that lure. Maybe it was because he was a surgeon when he was human. He'd spent his vampire years haunting battlefields throughout the last century, delivering his own brand of triage.

He handpicked and trained every vampire intern who worked on the human farm, but he had yet to find one who could master their bloodlust without using revival sleep, suspending their breathing behind the form-fitting plastic face masks, and ensuring they were first fully fed first. *And even then, there have been accidents.*

"In any event, thanks to Julian, no one has been looking for me, or wondering why Anthony is doing the rounds at the hospital on his own. I have a day or two to settle you all in before I have to face Serge again."

Rebekah laid her cheek on Connor's silent chest and trailed her fingers over his sculpted torso, tracing patterns in the sheen of carbon which accented every ridge.

"Rebekah." His low tone was a speculative warning. "Spit it out. What are you plotting?"

She took a deep breath, and her words rushed out before she could stop them. "Greg and Harry are planning a trip into London to pick up the supplies you stashed at the safe house. I'm going, too."

Connor's chest rumbled as he chuckled. "Of course you are. Why would I expect anything else?" His cool fingertip tilted her chin and his serious gray gaze raked over her determined features. "I have already spoken to Greg. You will all wait a couple of weeks, *at least*, and I will make sure you get home. I won't rest, not knowing if you made it back safely. Understood?"

The relief blossoming on her face told him all he needed. "Understood," she said solemnly.

"Now, go to sleep." Connor anchored her fingers to stop them wandering into dangerous territory, and closed his own eyes.

Chapter 3

Connor played out the deception and approached London from the northwest as though he was returning from the Bristol Hive. It was not ideal, because it meant detouring from the usual route through the woodlands south of London, which passed by where the human traitor, Douglas, was buried. The body was twelve feet underground, preserving the venom locked inside his desiccated tissue. It was the evidence he and Principal Julian held against the vampire who had slipped through their fingers, and whom they hoped would surface again.

The advantage, however, was that he could stop off at Julian's West London home in the leafy suburb of Richmond. He hurtled across Kew Bridge. The tumbling gray waters of the River Thames were a fair reflection of his mood as he wondered if Julian had uncovered any news on Douglas' killer. *He is definitely a fly in the ointment.*

Connor announced his arrival at the house by skidding to a halt and scattering the gravel of the driveway up over the immaculate facade, just to annoy his fastidious friend.

On cue, the heavy oak door swung wide and Julian glowered at him, icy annoyance glittering in his green eyes. "Connor." He greeted him stiffly and turned away, leaving the door open.

Following him into the house, Connor matched Julian's stride along the wide hallway. Once inside the study, he sank into an old brown leather chair which creaked under the dense weight of his bones.

"Any news?"

"Nothing yet." Julian shook his head as he sat down behind his Victorian desk and rested his elbows on the sage green leather covering its surface.

The two friends had not been alone together since the clean up after the final battle at the eco-town. Their gambit of luring Councilor Serge's attacking guardsmen into the underground habitat, at the same moment as they smuggled the humans out through an emergency exit tunnel, had gone according to plan.

The eight guardsmen had met their deaths at Connor and Julians' hands, and they had felt secure until Connor had caught the scent of Rebekah's panic attack. Typical of the chaos which hounded Rebekah, she had not made it to the safety of the burrows, the hiding spaces dug out beneath the woodland floor. Connor had reached her in time to scare off the rogue vampire before he could kill Rebekah. At least, that was the preferred scenario to Connor's mind. A more sinister motive for him leaving her unharmed did not bear thinking about.

"I have his scent," said Julian soberly. "It is still early days. If he shows up in the hive, then he'll be charged with threatening the food supply. Douglas' body is preserved, and we just have to play the waiting game."

The body would condemn the vampire to the certain death of internment where he would keep company, indefinitely, with other vampire offenders in Storage Facility Eight. *We are in good shape.*

"So, for now, I will carry on doing fly-pasts of the grave site to make sure it remains unmolested," said Connor.

Douglas' death released Rebekah from a forced marriage to a husband who tried to rape her, but in the same moment, it had revealed a more dangerous threat. Connor smiled as irritation warmed into pleasure. *It was poetic justice for betraying his own kind, and if he had not run, I would have ended the scumbag's life myself.*

"Play Serge's game for a while. Keep your enemies close," Julian said thoughtfully. "I'm sure you'll bump into him at the hospital. If I know Serge, he will be unavoidable."

◇◇◇

A couple of weeks later, Connor suppressed a wry grin as he faced yet another showdown with the councilor. *Julian was right.*

Serge had been hard on Connor's heels every day since his return to London, and today's encounter was tediously familiar. Connor tapped into his genuine irritation at the constant pollutant of Councilor Serge encroaching on his territory. Connor was venting quite convincingly, his glowering anger all the more potent when set against the stark white backdrop of the walls of his hospital, a place where he felt completely at home and in control.

"Bloody baby-sitting service." A growl rumbled in Connor's throat. "I'm a surgeon, for God's sake." His pewter-gray eyes flashed as they bored into the yellowed reptilian stare of Serge.

It was an arresting tableau; Connor, his chiseled features pulled into a sneer, his black hair ragged where he had shoved his fingers through it, and a granite-hard regard, staring down at the aged, feeble gray-haired figure of Councilor Serge.

Serge's dry cheeks folded into a grin.

"My time could be better spent." Connor's anger spat the words and snapped his jaw shut, clamping sculpted lips firmly closed.

"Now, Doctor Connor," said Serge, "we all have to pull our weight. Or are you too good for us now?" He oozed satisfaction at Connor's apparent annoyance, his smile revealing a portcullis of yellowed teeth which lost the battle of holding back his saliva.

"With respect, Councilor Serge, I already have the blood dispensary delivery to attend to." Connor's sneering tone trickled icy sweetness. "Allowing Charles to go hunting on Dartmoor today was shortsighted, and I don't see why Anthony can't release the vampires sleeping in the morgue. The morgue attendant has been in grave sleep for four hours already, he'll be surfacing very soon."

"I would prefer that you see to it."

Serge was making Connor's life as difficult as possible. Having failed, yet again, to make his charges against Connor stick, in court, he took pleasure in haunting the hospital and treating Connor as an errand boy. *A councilor trumps a doctor.*

"Very well," said Connor, and yanking his white coat straight, he strode away. Out of Serge's sight, on his way to the morgue, Connor grinned. He was enjoying the pantomime. *If it keeps Serge occupied, thinking he is getting under my skin, I'm okay with that.*

In truth, my life was built on far tougher experiences than Serge could ever imagine. I'm used to blood drenched battlegrounds, from the First World War through to Vietnam. Connor was not a sadist, but he had enjoyed the anonymity of the smokescreen of perpetual human deaths. *This is a picnic in comparison.*

His youthful twenty-four-year-old face was distractingly handsome, but the century of wisdom in his eyes had a knife edge of fatalistic acceptance. In 1910, the time he was turned, vampires came to terms with what they had become, one way or another. In some ways, Connor pitied the vampires of this new spoon-fed society. They were hunters without prey. As a result, they lacked the conditions needed to hone survival skills, and their intellect was blunt and unimaginative.

Connor shook his head in amusement. *Vampires with any sense keep their personal histories to themselves.* Serge had no idea how futile his attempts at irritating Connor were. As a recent vampire, *Serge's* intellect was blunt. But Connor's was as sharp as the scalpel he wielded.

In this new order, he was hailed as the surgeon essential to human survival. *I enjoy effortless control around humans, with one obvious exception, Rebekah.* Her presence had hit him in the chest like a sledgehammer and hot-wired a path to all his pain sensors. Connor remembered it with masochistic pleasure, and today his confrontation with Serge was spiced with impatience.

He grinned as he tuned into her deliciously moist heartbeat. It warmed his chest to feel her vibrant presence nearby. She was in London. She had dosed up on beta-blockers, and her signature was a muted canter, easily missed with the 'white noise' of the farm cattle nearby. Pheromone suppressant spray reduced the risks further, so anticipation overwhelmed his concerns. *I will see her soon.*

He would check on the vampires locked down in the morgue because it suited him to do so. *And then continue on out of the side exit of the hospital, and go to her.*

Almost a month had passed since Serge's last attempt to haul Connor up in front of the council, thanks to Julian. *If councilors trumped doctors, then principals were higher than both.* Serge had to get through him, before any charges against Connor would be taken seriously. *Serge does not help his own cause.* He had cried wolf too many times.

Serge was so sure all he lacked was proof that Connor was protecting a human, and his desire to see the doctor condemned consumed him. His frustration gave him an air of desperation, and the man was unpredictable. *Julian's ear to the ground is keeping us ahead in the game, and my own constant needling, of course, makes it hard for him to reason.* Connor was enjoying the battle of wits.

He moved along the corridors sweeping aside doors, not caring when they bounced from the walls in protest. Of course, Julian's interests were keener now, his nineteenth century repression gave the illusion of imperviousness, but Connor knew better. *I wonder, if he knew how miserable his pretended indifference is making Leizle, would he unbend or resist harder?*

"What the hell?"

As he rounded the last corner, the shrieking noise of metal trolleys crashing against walls urged him forward. Breaking into a vampire run, he unlocked the morgue doors and swept through them in less than the two seconds it took to think about it.

He swung into action, unhesitating. A stainless steel-lined door of a cadaver vault hung open, and a vampire careened around the room, scrambling as if hunting an invisible prey. Connor grabbed his shoulders from behind, hooked his fingers under the collar bones and swung the vampire through the air, landing him heavily on the sliding bed of the cadaver drawer. With a sharp kick, Connor drove the drawer home and snapped the catch into place.

"What the hell?" he breathed again, with a frown.

The vampire – his pupils distended to oil-black pools of hunger – was in grave sleep. *So much for the morgue being a safe method of confinement. They can't get out until someone releases them.* "So, what happened here?" he muttered.

Connor had locked them in himself. *So, I can't blame Anthony for this one.* He had watched them drink the vials of blood he handed over. In the confines of their locked morgue drawer, each surrendered willingly to grave sleep, knowing they would wake refreshed and still in one piece. *That's the theory anyway.* An ironic grin hovered before it shifted to puzzlement again.

This was the baby-sitting service Connor had referred to, the feeding, locking up, and eventual release of vampires who needed grave sleep. "So how did one escape?" Connor mused, taking in the devastation the vampire had wreaked.

In a blur of movement, he began to gather the metal autopsy tools scattered across the floor. As his fingers closed over a heavy bone saw, still useful, even on vampires, a physical reaction stabbed through his preoccupation. His stomach churned as a cloying scent stung his nose, and, even as his mind registered it, the sluggish heartbeat he detected suddenly picked up pace.

His eyes darted unerringly to the spot where the metallic scent of blood drew the compass needle in his head, and he was sure. *The laundry basket.* Blood specks on white linen were the final piece in the puzzle of his unease. He crossed the room, plunged his hand inside the linen hamper and pulled – tempering the inescapable force – on the arm that his fingers closed around. *I want answers, and humans with broken bones are not too good at talking.*

"Ouch!"

The girl emerging like a bedraggled rabbit from a hat was slight, and her bruised neck and shoulders were covered in reddened arcs left by vampire teeth. *A human pet?* It explained the depressed heartbeat which he almost missed. Vampire venom slowed the heart rate and this pale girl looked more drained than could be healthy. Her blonde hair was matted, unwashed for weeks by Connor's reckoning, and the terror in her blue eyes did not bode well for the answers he wanted. The pupils had flooded them to black. *And her face is almost as white as mine.*

"What the hell are you doing in here?" Connor grunted as he lowered the girl to her feet, holding her shoulders for a second until he trusted her balance.

She flinched at his explosion of words, and he stepped back and studied her with annoyance.

A breeze eddying over his skin drew his gaze, and following the logical chain of events provided some answers. The fire exit door

Fire and Ice: Survival

was unsecured. *That would be how she got in.* He stared at the newly replenished chiller cabinet which stored vials of human blood. *They camouflaged her scent. If she hadn't cut herself, she might have gone undetected altogether. That just leaves the 'what', the 'who' and the 'why'. Easy.* A memory troubled him. He felt sure he had seen her before.

But where? "What are you doing here?" said Connor. He probed the turbulent pools of fear in her gaze and ran through his options. *Which one will get to the bottom of this?*

"I need help. I escaped and I need help," the girl whispered.

On an exasperated breath, Connor stepped in and caught the girl as a vibration trembled through her, signalling the collapse which would have sent her to the floor if he had not been there.

That's just great! He hoisted her up into his arms. Rebekah, alone in the safe house, loomed in his mind. He just needed this girl out of his way. He shouldered the morgue doors open and headed for the surgical wing where the six beds he used for his patients were empty. *I just hope she comes round quickly.*

◇◇◇

Her arms swung uncomfortably, her wrist bone making contact with the doctor's flexing thigh as his stride ate up the distance of the corridor. Emily's mind raced through her story. They had met before. *Will he remember me?* It was important that he did.

Her court appearance was seared into her memory. She was not sure Doctor Connor found the event as memorable, but her life depended upon it.

Councilor Serge had paraded her around the vampire court as evidence in an effort to convince the jurors Doctor Connor kept a human as a pet. She *was* a vampire's pet, but *that* vampire had secured immunity from prosecution in return for relinquishing her into the custody of Councilor Serge. And so, her nightmare began. The attempt to frame the doctor failed when the results of bite and venom tests cleared him of the allegation.

Serge would set her free if she discovered the location of the human nest the doctor was protecting. Having looked into his fiercely intense eyes and felt the full force of his disapproval, she was filled with doubt. The weight of the task settled like concrete in her heart.

The cramped muscles in her neck burned, and remaining rag-doll limp prevented her from thinking. *About anything but the stomach muscles rippling along my side and his biceps flexing.*

The waltzing movement of his gait left her stomach behind when Connor whisked around and shouldered his way through a door. Her limbs swung in convincing abandon as she found it was not hard to trust him. *Why?* Peeping through veiled lashes, she watched a deserted room sway within her field of vision, and a bed loomed. The woozy feeling was real, so her disorientation would not be entirely pretense.

Connor laid her down on the narrow bed, not roughly, but with little care. Emily dug deep to hang onto her relaxed state while he eased his arms out from beneath her and his fingers found the pulse in her wrist.

"Malnutrition is only a stone's throw away," he muttered. "Who is this waif?"

Knowing she could not wait any longer, partly because the awkwardly folded arm underneath her was losing feeling, and because she could not fool him now she was the focus of his attention, Emily groaned, coming round convincingly. Hoping that her acting was up to par, her eyelids fluttered open and she let the ceiling drift out of focus. She allowed a second to elapse and then scrabbled, with apparent terror, up the bed. Cowering, she hugged her knees. The trembling of her crouched body began as an act but soon became a reality when his probing gray stare traveled over her.

Fear and Emily were well acquainted; he had taken up residence many years ago and his touch told her she was still alive, and that she was still fighting. Looking at the doctor did the same thing, but it spawned a different kind of sensation in her stomach.

Connor reared at her burst of energy. Fierce concentration cast shadows over his face as realization dawned. Indicating her fragile frame and hunched shoulders, he said, "Ah, the waif. You're the girl from the courtroom." His expression was serious. "So, you *are* a vampire's pet," he muttered as he automatically reached out and placed a Band Aid over the deep scratch she had put in her knee when scrabbling into the linen basket.

Emily found herself wondering if his touch, had she felt it, would have given her the same jolt of shock that his face had. The perfection of it arrested her breathing and occupied the space inside her head where her thoughts should be. *Pay attention, he's asking questions.*

"I won't hurt you, but what do you mean by escaped?" His gentle tone could not mask the impatience in his penetrating gaze. "You've had a shock, I know, but-"

"My vampire, others came. Wearing uniforms. To search the house. He released me to hide in the yard. He had no choice. He threatened me, said he would find me if I ran, please help me." Emily forced the words to tumble out. She was terrified, but because she needed him to believe the lie. He remembered her, but that was not enough.

"Where? Which vampire?"

The white of his coat and black of his hair lost focus and loomed larger in the magnifying-blur of tears, and Emily realized she was really crying. "He hurts me." Her voice dropped to a pained whisper. "He gets angry. I saw my chance and I took it."

Connor looked skeptical for a moment longer, but as her trembling fingers moved her matted hair aside, his eyes raked over her skin. She wanted to hide, knowing that her hunched shoulders were marred with clusters of fresh angry skin lesions and dried bite wounds.

As Connor absorbed her injuries, Emily's flesh crawled.

Her skin tingled with the nightmares etched into it, as though she was back there now. Serge's cackle formed the bedrock of her disgust; the wrinkled dry skin on his face, his yellowed eyes alight with excitement, and the cold wet flaccid lips he pressed to her flesh made her insides churn, even now.

"You have been on the farm for four weeks, you look too healthy," Serge had said. "Doctor Connor has seen battered, discarded humans." His grin was sickly. "Before the shortage, vampires were less, careful. They went too far and broke bones. At the very least, he'll expect fresh wounds. You need to be convincing."

She had spent four years being unable to sleep, not knowing when her vampire, Jonathan, would reappear, so for Emily, the weeks on the human farm had come as a relief. Her master's visits had always been traumatic. The best she could hope for was a bite, which lasted a long time if his mood was sensual. At his approach, terror squeezed her heart. *But I never let him know how scared I was. I learned the hard way that it excited him.* Emily suspected he exercised more care than he would like. *If I was easy to replace, I don't think I'd be here now.*

It was not all lies. The uniformed vampires had arrived at the house, but it was her owner, Jonathan, who had left.

Serge appeared as a hideous apparition which overwhelmed her stunned human sight. His cold clasp on her shoulder had frozen her blood where it touched. She was a kid again, and the boogyman had teeth and drank your blood if you made a noise.

The human farm is a picnic compared to life as a pet, being in a dormitory is better than being locked in a cell alone, with my fears circling like vultures. Even the concentration camp-like processions to the siphoning sheds, drinking iron-infused pureed vegetable concoctions which often left her feeling sick for hours afterwards, and being marched back to the enclosure, all on endless repeat, was a welcome routine. *Although being tired made talking an effort, at least I belonged to a group.*

Connor registered her distaste to his inspection of her body and took it personally.

He held his hands up. "I won't hurt you," he repeated, "But you can't stay here. Look, you can trust me." He cocked his head, showing her different angles of his face. "Do you remember me? From the courtroom a few weeks ago?"

"Yes," she whispered, relieved. *Now I can pretend to trust him.* She tried not to think of the warm curling sensation she felt inside when she was in his arms while she dutifully studied his earnest expression.

"What is your name?" Connor asked.

"Annabelle," said Emily. *Operation Annabelle.*

Connor's head jerked. "Really? You weren't pretending for the court hearing, then." He shifted uncomfortably. It was the name he had plucked from thin air to protect Rebekah's identity, and he did not like the coincidence.

Emily released her trapped breath as he finally inclined his head and his tight features relaxed. His rejection was not something she wanted to contemplate.

Chapter 4

Julian's handsome features were tranquil and every bronze-colored hair on his head was in place. He was the epitome of relaxation, however, the fabric of his knitted shirt pulling tight across his tense shoulders told a different story. His simmering annoyance spilled over and he paced the floor of his study.

Connor kept his eyes fixed on a point over the mantelpiece – every time Julian spoke, he came to a stop there, and it was easier than tracking his friend's pinball machine circuit of the room.

Julian recognized Annabelle the moment Connor reminded him. "The fact that Serge also knows Annabelle just makes this sanctuary idea dangerous and reckless. After all the work we have put in? For Lord's sake, Connor, the dust in the new eco-shelter tunnels has barely settled." Julian said the words, even though, staring at Connor's set expression, he knew it was no good.

"She needs help. Yes, she was part of Serge's game in court." Connor's eyes glinted with steely resolve. "If we don't help her and give her a chance at freedom, then we are no better than him."

"Very well. Go," said Julian, "talk to Rebekah. If you can persuade her…" He snorted.

When he reached the door, Connor turned around. "It's been weeks now. I'm beginning to think we were right the first time. The vampire was nothing to do with the attack. He was just traveling through and Rebekah's scent in the woods drew him in. It *was* a lure, after all. We just caught one more victim than we expected."

Julian summoned a smile. "It's certainly looking that way."

"It explains why Serge is riding me so hard. He stinks of frustration." Connor smiled tightly. "With all his guardsmen lying dead, it fits."

"I'll keep my eyes open. Serge is not that good of an actor. If he knows anything, he will gloat." Julian threw Connor a jaundiced glance. "As for this girl, you better get going, talk to Rebekah, and get yourself back here."

Connor nodded sharply and burst into movement.

As the breeze of his departure whisked the papers on his desk, Julian resigned himself to a long night. The only good thing to come out of this was that he had no difficulty resisting Annabelle's aroma. It was sweet, and, clearly, his taste was more spice. *Leizle-flavored, in fact.* So, having a human girl thrown at him did not always result in obsession. *That's good, isn't it?*

With a human-like sigh, he entered the sitting room and turned to look into the girl's face. Her hair was blond underneath the grease, and a circle of azure blue in her eyes stopped the black pools of dread flooding her gaze.

I doubt Connor will be rushing back from his talk with Rebekah. It's going to be a long night. Making the best of it, Julian offered water, and, since his newfound association with humans called for him to expect the unexpected, he offered tinned peaches.

"Vampires don't cook, I'm afraid," he said. "Sit down, Annabelle. Doctor Connor will be gone quite a while."

"I'm fine." However, her trembling legs said otherwise.

"Please, sit down, you look tired."

The rhythmic sound of panicked breathing rushing in and out of her lungs caught his attention and held it. After nearly two-hundred years of indulging in the real thing, like an alcoholic with fifteen years on the wagon under his belt, he was not immune to temptation. Resisting the pull of the adrenalin-scented pulse throbbing in her throat clutched at his tendons, stiffening his movement.

"I'm going to my study for a moment, but please, relax. Sit." He smiled as best he could, and then, he was gone.

Inside the book-lined room, this time, he locked himself in. Resentment rumbled a growl inside his throat. "Rap-sleep," Julian muttered, giving himself an order.

Usually, he had the freedom of the lone wolf, but today, he felt more like the wolf tucked up in grandmother's bed waiting for Red Riding Hood to cross his path. *Damn Connor.* His ordered existence was shot to hell. *I can't even schedule my sleep cycles anymore; why the hell can't he clean up his own mess?*

Rap-sleep. He could resist Annabelle, but the tension burning in his tendons told him that could change if he didn't rehydrate the brain center where desire and anger vied for release. *I'm irritated with Connor, so anger would most likely win, but that girl would survive neither one.*

He took three vials of blood from his pocket, only two of which were human, although, as principal of the vampire council, his allocation was twice that. He shared Connor's distaste for it, now, although they had never spoken about it. The intensity of his feelings blindsided him when he admitted why he felt that way. *Leizle. I wish I didn't know where she was now. Resisting my own Red Riding Hood would be so much easier if I had no clue where grandmother lived.*

Julian heaved a silent sigh, enjoying the feeling of air expanding his intercostals and easing the pressure inside. He closed his eyes as if taking unpleasant medicine, and downed each vial of blood in quick succession.

Lying out on a couch, he prepared for the rush of sensation. Pain was part of being a vampire – an inevitable side-effect of the compulsion to feed – but he did not have to let it control him. Julian's muscles locked down, primed, but not allowed to release the energy as propulsion and to act out his dreams.

What he hadn't expected when his eyes closed was that Leizle would be the dream he had to resist. Her grubby and dirt-streaked face, as he had seen it countless times over the last two weeks, appeared like a siren call. As the old eco-town was being deconstructed, he felt compelled to seek her out, watching over her without her knowing it.

He was there to supervize the dismantling of the eco-town pipework. Securing tarpaulin fabric around each numbered and tagged bundle was a four-man job which he could do alone, with an arm tied behind his back. And that was how he felt most of the time. He was tying ropes into knots and yanking on them until they were tight. He didn't expect to feel like ropes had wrapped around his heart, bitten in, and bound him to her.

Fire and Ice: Survival

He grinned in his sleep. He could have performed every task at the eco-shelter unaided, but Connor and he left some jobs for human hands, to occupy them. Like therapy offered in a mental ward, taking everything away would have left them bouncing off the walls. *Funny, how I always ended up helping out on* her *shift.*

"But no good can come of it," he whispered.

The contorted muscles of his rigid face showed anguish as hydration forced burning tendrils into his capillaries. A red-hot migraine washed through his cerebral cortex, hunting out the rap-sleep center inside his brain, and as the pressure increased, his dreams of Leizle pulled him through it. In his mind, wish fulfilment raged as she ran her hands down his torso and plucked at his pants. His body flushed as her warm fingers closed around him.

When his eyes opened, he clung to the waves of pleasure, and, as they ebbed, he groaned. Dragging his palm down over his face, he swung around and sat up. The physical discomfort, before he mentally washed his body in a cold shower of common sense, made him grin.

"Damn it, she's only seventeen," Julian muttered decisively. *No good can come of it.*

As a young man in Georgian England, he had been disgusted by Britain's involvement in the slave trade and had lobbied in opposition. He could remember his satisfaction when, in 1807, he stood on the dock, knowing that the slave ship he watched setting sail from Liverpool was the last. *I valued freedom then, but I lost sight of it.* Human farming was merely another form of slavery but, two-hundred years on, his humanity had dulled to a faint echo.

"Until Leizle." *She has made me ask questions again.*

But one thing he did know… *I will not take away freedom she has yet to discover.* He could not talk about love and feelings. He did not even kiss his mortal wife until they were already married. *So I'll leave her be, to become a mother, a wife, and be all she should be, without my hand chilling her bones.* Every element of human and vampire existence was in turmoil. *Like the sides of a tossed coin, who knows who will end up on top?*

In the sitting room, on the other side of the hallway, when she realized Julian really was gone, Emily sank back into the cushions. Alone for the first moment in the longest time, she, too, was fighting demons. She feared that Connor may not return, and that his woman would talk him out of the rescue plan. *Whoever she is. Serge made it clear that there is someone.* Her mission could be over before it begun.

If I fail, I won't be allowed to return to the farm. Serge's protégé, the general, was a vampire with deceptively soft features, wavy black hair and a psychotic air. He planned to follow the scent trail of her primed, unwashed body. Leaving nothing to chance, they also expected her to lay a physical trail en route to the human nest. Emily's gut told her that the general's idea of retribution would be far worse than Jonathan's anger.

The general's face when his muzzle rubbed over her skin, the snake-like flicker of his tongue collecting her taste, and his bruising grip as he stared into her terror-stretched eyes, were all burned into her consciousness. Blinking would have meant losing sight of him for a moment, and she finally understood the frozen terror of prey, petrified, and not knowing from where the strike would come. Fear agreed with her on this. *His clutches would tear me apart.*

◇◇◇

The square mile known as the City of London, north of the River Thames, was the heart of the hive, and few vampires, because of their daily trips to the blood dispensary, gave a thought to settling on the south bank.

Vampire traffic extended from the west, where the human farm was situated, to the London docklands in the east, where vast warehouses stored the food shipped in from other hives as part of a bartering system. The super-tanker nomads were pallid brethren looked down upon by terrestrial vampire communities, but, as a vital link between Europe and Britain, their contribution to the dietary variety of the humans was invaluable.

Their presence on the streets always caused a ripple of discomfort as they headed into London to visit the hospital and collect the dues for their bounty in human blood quotas. On his way to see Rebekah, Connor noticed the thirty-strong crew skirting Hyde Park. He was grateful for the disruption to the clear thinking of the hive members who watched them closely, as though the nomads carried a disease they were frightened of catching.

He made a quick diversion across the park and hit the sidewalk running.

His head ruled his heart as he zigzagged back and forth across the river, covering his tracks and keeping his ears and eyes open as he covered the miles which would eventually take him to the suburb of Clapham.

Connor finally crossed Vauxhall Bridge and hurtled along the streets until he stood in darkness on the sidewalk outside the safe house, savoring the moment when he would see her face. She was so close he could almost taste her. He flexed his ribcage to take in a deep draft of air. Annabelle, Julian, and the past hours, were overwritten in one entrancing beat of the heart he loved. He closed his eyes and filled his senses with Rebekah.

He smiled as her slow breathing and even pulse told him she was sleeping, as he knew she would be. He contemplated waiting for her to wake, but he could not do that. Before he had time to decide, her peach flushed complexion filled his thoughts and galvanized him into action.

Gliding up the wide stone steps and closing his hand on the outsized Victorian doorknob, he entered with effortless stealth. The thick strip of pale carpet glowed like a guiding path running the length of the hallway, and the mirrors caught a fleeting glimmer of his ethereal presence when he whisked along it. Bypassing the sparsely furnished kitchen, he arrived in the reception room at the rear of the house where solid oak floorboards were too hefty to creak. *And they provide another barrier for sounds and odors.* Connor lifted an appreciative brow as he took in the row of thick moccasin slippers. It was reassuring to see complacency had not crept in. Greg drilled it into them all, silence at all costs.

Apart from the motorcycles, that is. Thanks to Connor, the group knew when it was safest to travel. Vampire dawn came before the real dawn, and after they had finished working overnight, planting and harvesting crops to feed their human cattle. It was the moment when night was ending, and the sky was rose-tinted with promise, but early morning mist diffused the sun's rays and made it safe for vampires to enjoy the muted colors of the day-lit world without care.

That was also when a few vampires drove cars, slowly, reacquainting themselves with the wonder of what was once considered efficient transportation. They drove cars down memory lane at twenty miles an hour, just for the fun of it.

However, motorcycles they rode at hair-raising speeds, pushing themselves to a limit which they could never reach. Their heightened senses were merely stirred to amusement, assured, that *if* they collided with a tree – not that their preternatural senses would ever allow that to happen – it would be the tree that disintegrated. They would walk away from the gnarled wreckage unscathed. It was also when the humans, with care and imagination, could slip through the net.

He instinctively razed his glance across the grubby window panes facing out over the potholed unkempt lawns, and satisfied himself that Rebekah's motorcycle was hidden from view inside the overgrown summer house at the bottom of the garden.

Connor crossed to the square hatchway cut into the floor, and moments later, he was inside the basement.

Looking down at her sleeping form, he anticipated drowning in the warm pools of her eyes, willing the delicate lids to open and reveal her inner thoughts to his hungry gaze. *I'll immerse myself in her joy before I tell her about Annabelle. Selfish, but I want her heart to sing before I have to weigh it down with my words.*

Where Rebekah laid out on one of the beds with the basement hatch closed, only the moonlight filtering through the grimy glass in the sidewalk-level window saved it from pitch black. London had a different rhythm to the eco-shelter, passing an evening reading and talking here was out of the question, once darkness fell there was only sleep or... *making love.* A half-smile tugged at Connor's lips at the thought.

He sat on the wooden bench and rested back against the wall, tracing his fingertips absently over the fist-sized 'missing lump', the puzzle piece of which he had gouged out and ground to dust in his palm the night he first met her.

Was it only weeks ago? And yet, the last twelve decades were a gray landscape of experience compared to the technicolor world in which he now existed. He watched her chest rise and fall, and timed his own pretend breathing to hers. Panting helped diffuse the insanity clamoring inside him, and in the battle of thinking and feeling, thinking gave up the fight. *Love.* Strange that he recognized it, because he never got to experience it during his twenty-four mortal years; Lavinia was an unfulfilled hope which had remained locked inside him – a beacon of his own humanity that he had loved her enough to leave her. *But now? I have it for an eternity if I want it, if Rebekah wants it.*

He had embraced the relaxed state of revival sleep when still outside on the sidewalk. He had downed his daily dose of human blood, although his nose wrinkled in distaste that it came from a captive human, and at the taste. Until Rebekah, he had never tasted blood which saturated him in desire. A vial of blood was like water to her mulled wine. *But, I have fed, and I'll be able to resist biting a little easier.*

He gauged his control. The searing pain swelling his tissue and wrenching his stomach when he drew in her honey-thick scent were only terrible today. His fingers ached to touch her and his body sang in anticipation, so at last, he slipped into her bed and pulled her back into his chest. As she sighed, he sucked the candied breath in and locked it inside like a smoker taking a hit.

"You're cold," she mumbled. Reaching back to run her fingers through the silken mass of his hair, she smiled sleepily. "I knew you'd come."

"Well to be fair..." He kissed her shoulder and ran his chilled palm over her stomach. "You're toasty warm." He chuckled. Any guilt he felt at covering her in goose bumps was chased away by the moist pool he found when his fingertips dipped between her thighs. "I could get some friction going if it would help," he murmured against her neck, and smiled when she turned and lifted her face for his kiss.

Closing his lips over her soft mouth, citrus scented venom flooded his throat and he growled. Sinking deeper into revival sleep, he moved his palms over her contours, stroking her thigh and savoring her enveloping warmth as he eased himself inside.

"Or maybe I'll just steal a bit of your heat," he said as his body thickened to fill her, driving the air from her lungs on a sigh as he moved. If his life had depended upon him coming up with a sentence which made any sense at that moment, he would gladly have died.

<><><>

Rebekah sat cross legged on the low trestle bed, facing Connor. The trailing hem of her silk shirt covered her modesty, but the ivory skin of her slender, naked thighs were almost Connor's undoing. The shaft of light from the high level window slanted across her face, casting dark crescents over her cheekbones as she studied the crackers which she demolished with gusto. Her blond feathered hair was a burnished halo, and Connor gathered every image and stored it inside his mind as adoration.

He was deliciously distracted by the way she licked butter from her thumb. Her warm brown glances were laced with satisfaction he had put there, and his regret that he could not be with her in their final moment was transitory. *I still feel her pleasure resonate through the fibers of my body.*

Shaking his head to clear it, reluctant to let the real world in, Connor finally drew in the breath he needed to speak of Annabelle. "Rebekah." He waited for her to look at him. He knew she was replaying their time together, in part, because it flooded his own mind every time he caught sight of a new bruise, and because her erratic heartbeat swelled whenever she smiled.

"I found a girl. She needs somewhere to hide." Leaning forward, he captured Rebekah's free hand and folded her fingers into his. "She needs your help."

"Found her?" A frown tugged at her delicately arched brows. "Where could you have found her... did you find her?" she said quietly. Withdrawing from him, her lashes veiled her eyes and her fingers stiffened until he let them slip from his grasp.

"She was hiding in the hospital last night. She was in the courtroom a few weeks back as a witness for Serge."

When she looked at him, Connor instantly regretted spoiling their moment, watching the warmth of her thoughts cool to a stagnant pool of worry. He added, "She was a vampire pet, and I don't think she knew what hit her. Serge's attentions were terrifying, I'm sure."

"How do you know she is what she seems?" she asked on a dry whisper.

Connor paused to consider. He didn't like the Annabelle coincidence. *I came up with the name, but her having the same name is not a crime.* He dropped the last cause for concern into the mix. "Her name is Annabelle."

Rebekah's chin jerked up. "Annabelle?"

He nodded. "I know, but yes, Annabelle. She's frail and covered in vampire bites. Battered and bruised." Connor, knowing how even Rebekah suffered bruises at his touch, hoped the list would pave the way to tolerance. "All I really know is her weakened physical state fits with her story," he said quietly. He caught hold of her hand again and stroked his thumb over the agitated pulse in her wrist, in a soothing circular motion. "She shows signs of long-term abuse. Her *scars* are real, Rebekah, but I understand if you can't help."

His intent gaze filled in the blanks. He knew Leizle had shared the horror of her experiences on the human farm. *I just have to wait for her to realize that she could not wish that on Annabelle.*

"Where is she now?" Rebekah asked on a sigh, unbending a little.

He laughed gently. "Julian's."

Rebekah slanted a stern look across at him. "Connor. You've got to stop torturing him. And what about Leizle? He may not be interested in her, but she'll be mortified if she finds out you are putting temptation his way." She snorted in a most unladylike fashion. "I know he doesn't care for humans, but let's not tempt fate."

Connor disagreed. *Leizle is Julian's Achilles' heel, he just doesn't know it yet.* He was just grateful for the decisive spark in her eyes as she squeezed his fingers.

"How do we get her to the eco-shelter safely?" asked Rebekah.

"Thank you." He turned her hand and raised her palm to his lips. Dipping into the pooled heat of warm nectar, he endured the branding of her skin on his kiss and smiled. "She will be grateful, I know it." *I know she wants to run from this. Fifteen years of bonding has forged their community, and letting a stranger in must feel like opening a can of worms best left closed.*

"How will we get her there?" Rebekah was trying to inject some enthusiasm.

"We'll use a couple of motorcycles and wait until vampire dawn," said Connor. "Julian and I know the country lanes better than most, and if you are up for a hurtling fairground ride, you'll be in safe hands." He ran his fingertip down her cheek, the exhilaration in his gaze dampened with reassurance as he said, "For us, danger is just a dream, we are beyond defying death. But, we can use that to get you and Annabelle out of London fast".

Rebekah stared at him. "Are you sure it's worth the risk? After all, we've only felt secure for a week or so, and Serge has no clue where we are."

Connor knew the new eco-shelter was beginning to feel like home again, and in wanting it back the way it was, changes were hard to accept. "What choice is there? Deliver her to the farm, or let her fend for herself? I don't have all the answers, Rebekah. I only know what I can't do."

"Are you sure it's safe, that she is safe?" Rebekah whispered.

And, even as he answered, "Yes.", a clutch of uncertainty tightened his nape.

◇◇◇

When Connor arrived back at the Richmond house, what Julian heard robbed him of speech. All he could do was glower. The plan of escape did not meet with his approval, and Connor's neutral expression irritated him more. *He knows my anger will blow itself out, and he's right.* He was waiting for Julian to admit that there was no other solution.

"Sorry?" ventured Connor.

"Really. You think that covers it?" Julian's scowl allowed his sarcasm to drip. "And a mad motorcycle dash through the early dawn, do you really think that's wise?"

Both vampires were shut away in Julian's study, yet again, and even though vampires didn't need to move, Julian was fast developing the habit of pacing. He carved a circling path into the thick pile of the carpet, not taking his eyes from his friend's face. "What do you know about her? Really?"

"One thing I know is that her fear is real, she stinks of it." His frown was fierce. "And you cannot fake a bloodstream that's fighting to find the strength to replenish. She's been bled at an unhealthy rate, she's suffered much more than being siphoned."

Julian shook his head. "I still don't like it."

"Neither do I." Connor jerked his chin, indicating where Annabelle sat on the other side of the wall. "You've seen her. She may have been a convenience in Serge's plot, but you can't seriously be suggesting we give her back to her owner?"

Julian stopped pacing.

"You're right, Julian, we *are* taking a risk. But Rebekah has opened a door." Connor dropped down onto a chair which creaked alarmingly beneath the dense mass of his body, stabbing a hand through his black hair as he said, "It was easier when they were just cattle." He glanced up at Julian. "Bet you're glad you're not inside *my* head, huh?"

Julian satisfied himself with glaring.

"The safe options are easy, give her back to her owner, take her to the farm, or release her outside the city."

An image of Leizle's terrified face, as he had seen it in his courtroom nudged every argument of Julian's into touch. "Damn it, Connor, stop playing Devil's advocate. I give in, but you can't keep picking up strays."

Connor bristled. "I wouldn't call Rebekah a stray. She changed everything. I had no idea how boring the last one hundred years had been." He expanded his lungs and puffed out his frustration. "Surely you understand that, now."

Julian refused to be diverted from the matter in hand. "Connor, if Annabelle ends up in the farm, it's not so bad, compared to the life she had." *It's worth one more try.* However, his heart was no longer in it.

"Mmm, not so bad? Very humane, I thought, and the insemination of forty human females." Connor sneered. "How many pregnancies were there?"

"None, thank God. And the story is the same throughout the other hives, so I have some leverage at last." Julian took an exasperated breath. "I held Serge off as long as I could. The Hybrid Project was always going to proceed, even if only to prove it would fail." He arched a brow. *There is always an upside.* "You should be glad. At least, you know now that vampires and humans are not compatible."

"You held him off barely weeks. That was as long as you could manage?"

Julian held his hands up in apology, swallowing the comments which would drive a wedge between them. *-I held him off for months, before that, but these last few weeks you've been too preoccupied to see that blocking every move Serge makes will arouse suspicion, and put us all in jeopardy. I had to concede something.-* Instead, he said calmly, "It is done. Serge has run his experiment and now it's done."

"Until he thinks of another sick scheme."

Julian met Connor's skeptical eye. "I am not going to let that happen."

"You let the hybrid fiasco happen." Connor growled gently. "What's next, Principal?"

Julian ignored the knot of frustration in his chest and allowed Connor to vent. He knew the danger of impregnating Rebekah lived as a spectre inside his friend's mind. But now, it had melted away, and the selfish benefit of the Hybrid Project would sit ill with Connor. *Guilt is never easy to assuage.*

Julian ground his teeth. "We are going to die if they die, you *know* that."

"I would turn Rebekah, and have us both die together, rather than sit back and watch the widespread torture of humans," Connor breathed.

"It won't come to that." Julian's green eyes flashed. "You know me better than that. I'm pushing hard for a compromise, *free range farming.*" He circled the room, easing the tension which urged him to give Connor a good shaking. "One step at a time, Connor, but humans forming social groups would be a step in the right direction."

Although vampires moved quickly on a physical plane, on the conceptual one they lacked urgency. *We are immortal and used to having all the time in the world to think things through.* Pushing the crisis of human mortality to the fore was proving harder than he expected. But Connor's next words pulled him back and reminded him that humans were actually their own worst enemy.

"Unless they have an egomaniac like Douglas in their midst." Connor cast a jaundiced look at Julian. "Too many men and too few women will always make the scum rise to the top." He suddenly grinned as the thought of Douglas' doughy fleshed carcass buried in the woods brought him a flush of pleasure. "If it weren't for the fact that the vampire who killed Douglas came close enough to Rebekah to leave his scent on her skin, my joy would be complete."

Julian gave Connor a long 'I'm doing my best, give me a break' look.

"Okay, truce," muttered Connor, "I have to leave Annabelle with you for another hour." He chuckled when Julian glared. "Serge informed me the storage facility has some stage-two's awaiting my attention." Connor turned on his most sincere expression. "I told him I'd be only too happy to deal with the matter at once, if only to annoy the hell out of him."

Connor rose from his seat and appeared abruptly in front of Julian. Cocking his head, he said, "And then, the mad motorcycle dash will commence." Connor's glance said, 'You up for it?'.

Julian thumped him on the arm. "Remind me again, why on earth am I friends with you?"

From the other room, Emily heard the mumbling voices. The speech was too fast for her ears, but the animation and colorful tones of the interaction was unmistakable. She sank slowly downwards, until she sat huddled on the floor. She thought vampires were indifferent and sadistic, but she knew better now.

An emotional kaleidoscope of expressions passed over her face, beginning with the tightness of dread, softening to hope and swinging back to horror, again. "I'm here to destroy them. Oh God." Emily dug her nails into clenched hands. Staying still was hard as each thought chased another around the circuit. "Him, really, Doctor Connor. And he has a woman, a human woman. So, he can't be a monster." Emily wrapped her arms around her middle, cradling her stomach as envy settled like hot coals inside her. "How would that feel, to be his woman?" she whispered.

Chapter 5

Storage Facility Eight was a stark name which suited the colossal gray granite structure positioned on the bank of the River Thames. It overlooked the estuary like a vulture perched in a concrete nest. The walls glistened in the moonlight as the crashing waves of high tide cascaded up the edifice. Connor sighed, pulled up the collar of his greatcoat and resigned himself to a drenching.

Councilor Serge's prod to make Connor visit today to pronounce vampire deaths was far from urgent. *He was merely flexing his muscles as a councilor. After all, he has precious little of those on his bony body.* Connor grinned at his own joke.

Vampires in stage-one were immobilized by muscle relaxant and restraints, and they would pass, without Connor's assistance on to stage-two within twenty four hours. Connor was reminded of the quote 'abandon hope all ye who enter here', because that most accurately described the purpose of this facility. You crossed Principal Julian at your peril. *He is not inclined towards weakness.*

Those vampires in stage-two could be maintained in the state of locked-in syndrome for many decades. A daily dose of blood, syringed into nose or mouth, fed them with just enough to retain brain function. It meant, although trapped inside a concrete body, the condemned spent every second considering their crimes in full.

Connor's routine visit was due, but the timetabling of it was never written in stone. *Not unless I'm preparing The Butcher for his annual outing.* He had his uses, as the ultimate deterrent which ensured others toed the vampire council's line. The Butcher's killing rampage was brought to an end by his internment in a mausoleum in London's Kensal Green Cemetery in 1919. When vampires became the dominant species, he was brought out of anonymity, to become the very first inmate in the purpose-built vampire penitentiary. *More than ninety years, and Julian is still not inclined to deliver him from his suffering.* Connor shook his head, reminding himself to stay on his friend's good side.

Most are sent here by Julian through sentencing at the council and the remainder are medical emergencies beyond saving. So, my hand is here, too. Connor had pretended to be irritated at Serge's patronizing reminder, as would be expected, but once he conceded, with sugar sweet compliance, he wasted no time in getting there.

He entered the large gray airless building. It reminded him of the stale musk of the Egyptian pyramids, filled with the heavy heat which made him sweat when he was human. The steel lined door closed with barely a whisper behind him, plunging him into unrelenting darkness.

Connor closed his eyes, and channeled his keen sense of hearing. When the change in the echo of his footfall told him he had arrived in the reception chamber, he stopped walking and unhooked a flashlight from an alcove carved into the wall.

He flipped the switch and the token infusion of a weak amber beam lifted black shadow to crystal clear vampire vision. The blurred arc of light pushed feebly at the darkness and a warden instantly stepped forward. *It is like a tomb.* The stillness of each warden resembled a stone effigy, and their charges were unable to move.

"Doctor Connor," said the warden, his dusty vocal chords creaking from disuse.

"Warden James." Connor nodded encouragingly as a frown etched lines into the vampire's middle aged face. Warden James took his responsibilities seriously, and Connor liked that about him. "Is there a problem?"

"Not a problem, just something I've not encountered before." The warden stroked a thoughtful hand over his chin, and a musty odor enveloped him as he disturbed the dust from his clothes.

"How many stages of graveling am I here to diagnose?" Being direct was expected.

"We have nine inmates in the stage-one chamber. They have been starved of blood, and their tissue has begun to harden, but for three, the graveling is slow." The warden registered Connor's inquiring glance. "Like gelatine hardening in jelly, they remain... well, soft."

"Let's take a look."

Connor set off at a brisk walk, the torch swinging in time with his footfall. He knew the way, and within minutes, he was surveying the row of inmates. Each vampire resided inside a container resembling a steel funerary box, and metal restraints secured the bodies, although they were essentially comatose.

He moved along the line, stopping at each open coffin shell, reaching in to prod their muscles, peel back sticky eyelids, stare into blown pupils, and bark his verdict at the warden.

"Here are the three soft ones," the warden said, urgently.

Connor pressed firmly on the first inmate's shoulder, and this time, the surface moved like the skin on a rice pudding. *It's not a pleasant way to go. As fluid loss approaches crisis point, muscles become spastic, skin shrivels, vision fades, and delirium sets in. Once the fluid loss exceeds fifteen percent it's irreversible.*

"How long have you had them? I can't smell the muscle relaxant," Connor said. A condemned vampire was given no chance to fight back.

"Almost three days." The warden flipped the catch on a steel band so Connor could bare the chest.

He pinched the skin on the sternum. "They should be about thirty percent desiccated by now." He levered the jaw open, leaned in to sample the breath that drifted into the air, and then looked up at the warden. "Their last meal was human blood. That slows down the dehydration process initially." As he walked away, he said, "You can move them down to stage-two in eight hours."

They had hung onto the golden hours of stage-one for a little longer, but they had passed the crucial fifteen percent threshold, and there would be no going back. Not even the drastic measure of a one-hundred-percent human blood infusion would help them now. And with human blood being so precious, no vampire was worth that.

Connor's pronouncements moved the vampires down through the levels of the storage facility, where the humane crushing of their skull was the final act. But, only after they had served sentences extending into decades would they earn that release.

"Any stage-three inmates to witness?" Connor hoped not, witnessing the crushing of skulls took time he would rather not spend today.

"Five," said the warden.

"Let's go." Connor suppressed a sigh. He had no choice, being the doctor of record. For him, ordering skull crushes would never be routine, even though they represented an end to suffering. *Julian will have to cope with Annabelle's presence awhile longer.*

"Has The Butcher been fed today?" asked Connor.

"Yes, sir."

"Good. He's still with us and fully aware?"

"Of course, Doctor Connor. Principal Julian's sentence has another fifty years to run. I take very good care of him, I'm not losing him to insanity."

Connor nodded decisively. "I know that you do."

Getting the dosage right was crucial, and Connor sometimes chose to deliver it himself, inserting the syringe needle between The Butcher's dried cracked lips and administering a precisely measured ten milliliter ration of blood. The blood would pool in his throat and wick quickly up the dried-out carotid arteries to spread insidiously through the straw-like texture of his brain, and, in witnessing the flash of excitement in his eyes, Connor knew The Butcher still suffered. That was what Principal Julian's sentence demanded.

Connor remembered looking for that same response in Vampire Vlad, another long term resident of the facility. No one knew his real name – he had remained stubbornly silent throughout his trial, and the nickname, meant to rile him into protest, had become the joke which stuck. It was a decade ago, now, but he could still remember the feeling of vertigo as he stared into Vlad's eyes, and the blown pupils had almost swallowed his soul.

It was Connor who had persuaded Julian that Vampire Vlad's psychosis had advanced beyond the stage of awareness, to where he no longer experienced meaningful recollections. He had gnawed away the inside of his cheek muscles in his craving for blood, and delivering the final release was, in Connor's opinion, the humane thing to do.

He had been the only one in the death chamber with Vlad. Usually, three or four vampires would be prepared to meet their final end, with Connor directing the ceremony and synchronizing the movements of the attendant executioners. In an act of kindness, they all met death in precisely the same moment.

Connor, alone, had taken responsibility for Vlad's execution. He had placed the C-clamp over the crown of Vlad's head, bracketing his skull snugly between two six-inch steel plates. He remembered using far more strength than necessary when he gripped the T-bar of the handle, whipped the screw into action and Vlad's skull imploded with a violent crack, in keeping with his depraved butchery, as the two plates slammed together. *It seemed kinder.*

The blast of the bone dust blown into Connor's face was a sensation he would never forget, and neither was the eerie silence after the shuffling particles had come to rest.

Connor followed Warden James down the polished granite slope into the bowels of the building. The familiar rumble of the River Thames thundering past vibrated through the floor. The polished steel walls glistened with moisture as the temperature dropped. The resemblance to an iceberg, with eighty percent of the building buried underground, was no accident. Sluice gates were opened at high tide and the river's tumbling current jet-washed the death chamber and swept away the vampire remains.

The enormous double steel doors loomed in front of them for a moment, before they swished silently open, dragging the blade of a rubber seal over the smooth marble floor.

Descending through the containment levels to the death chamber was the hardest part of being the hive's doctor of record. *There is no one to pass the buck to.* Without warning, the burden suffocated him as he longed for the carefree days when the onus of dishing out death did not rest upon his shoulders.

He suddenly missed Malachi's guidance. His skeletal features with the sparse covering of wispy hair were the thing of children's nightmares, but he was Connor's maker. His dead fish scale-colored eyes glistened with the sheen of mother-of-pearl, and his waxy skin had the aroma of dry parchment, but his brain was lightning fast.

Malachi had left Egypt, where he lived for thousands of years, in pursuit of his twin brother. Numu had left a trail of bodies across Africa, and up through Europe, and when Connor became his victim and had been left for dead, Malachi saved him by turning him into a vampire.

It had taken a while for Connor to feel grateful.

Together, they finally hunted down Numu, and Connor was forced into killing him. Malachi had spent almost a decade in London until his yearning for Egypt had driven him to leave.

I wonder what he is doing now? He had not thought of Malachi for half a century.

He occasionally missed the feeling of having someone who could empathize without words. Connor never knew if it was because he was thousands of years old, or because Malachi had turned him, but he had been able to read Connor's mind and fill his head with sights and sounds which were not his own experiences.

But, one decade out of a hundred years was a fragile transparency rather than a reach out and grab it memory for Connor. His recollections of Malachi slipped away as he entered the death chamber and surveyed the five vampires laid out on stone tables.

Connor pulled a key from his pocket and opened the steel door to a walk-in safe. Taking clamps down from their metal hooks, he checked that each one was oiled and fit for use. He dropped the third clamp into the reject crate as a cloudy residue of bone dust coated his fingers, and then moved onto the next.

The warden took those that met with Connor's approval and gave one to each of the five attendant executioners. Their charges lay staring at the ceiling as though they were already dead, but every vampire in the chamber knew better. *Would this be my fate, but for Julian's intervention?*

Once the prisoners were prepared and the clamps expertly fitted, the kindest thing was to proceed quickly. Connor nodded and the attending executioners took up their positions. With his hand held aloft, he commanded their attention. "On my count, gentlemen."

"Go forth into the comfort of oblivion, your sins are forgiven." The vampires offered the time-honored blessing.

Connor murmured, reverently, "Three, two, one."

At the count of 'one', each vampire drove the tungsten steel discs together and crushed the victims' skulls.

◇◇◇

While Connor was smothered in darkness, with his sinuses shrinking as the calcium-rich dust of crushed skulls inevitably wended its way inside them, across London, a calculating Sebastian was trespassing on his terrain.

Keeping a low profile was a frustrating necessity Sebastian was tired of. He traversed the hospital corridors, heading for the morgue. *I can pick up Emily's scent from there and find out which direction she went in.*

As Councilor Serge's general, Sebastian enjoyed power. Knowledge was that, but gathering this small crumb was of little consolation to him, now. His hazel eyes were muddy with anger. *For one week I knew where the humans were hiding. One damn week, and then he moved them.*

He had enjoyed looking Serge in the eye and faking regret that the ambush had robbed them of their informant, Douglas. He could still taste Douglas' fear and damp flesh, and it still curdled his stomach when he remembered the fragrant contrast of Connor's woman. *If only I had taken her when I had my chance.* Thinking himself superior, demotion back into the ranks of the ignorant was unacceptable.

Protecting his knowledge like a precious jewel, he kept it close and enjoyed its beauty. Of course, Connor's woman was the jewel he imagined he was holding, stroking her skin and feeling her warmth. *Eight attacking vampire guardsmen were slaughtered, I killed Douglas, and yet, I am back at square one.*

It was a bitter memory, the moment when he finally gave in to the temptation to return to the spot where this compulsion had ignited his senses, and found they were gone.

The sadist in Sebastian had risked all. Connor's woman excited him, and the scent of her fear was intoxicating. There were so many other shades of pain he would like her to experience. She was a succulent reason to pursue the human group.

She fought me. She used every ounce of her strength, but even hammering the knife home with a stone had only succeeded in branding him. Sebastian's fingertips traced the groove carved across his stomach. The scored line, glistening like a vein in marble, extended in an ascending arc over his hipbone. He smiled, his set teeth barely containing the saliva flooding into his mouth as he relived the moment.

He wanted everything Doctor Connor owned. *I want a slice of his life and she is the most enticing part of it.*

Sebastian's visit to the hospital marked the beginning of phase two of the plan conceived by Councilor Serge, although the seed was planted in Serge's mind by Sebastian himself.

Seeds were also a feature of the plan in which Emily would lead them to the human nest. Sebastian grinned. They had given her poppy seeds to scatter at intervals throughout the journey. The black pods, barely a millimetre in size, were indigenous to the meadows, but *not* found in the woodlands of Kent. Their subtle scent would become more pungent when they absorbed the moisture of the woodland floor, and it would be easy enough for Sebastian to pick up the trail. *Connor will not detect their odor when they are scattered, but following on later, I'll have no difficulty.*

Sebastian knew Connor was signing off on stage-three skull crushes at Storage Facility Eight, and he even knew that there were five. Therefore, he had half an hour to imagine walking these corridors in Connor's shoes. *Emily has followed orders so far, and things are progressing nicely; releasing the vampire in the morgue had been risky. But we needed the knight in shining armor complex. Connor saved her, so he feels responsible, and the doctor is absurdly predictable where humans are concerned. He has gone soft.*

Joining the flow of vampire bodies moving purposefully towards the blood dispensary, Sebastian adopted the same concentrated, unwavering expression and fell into step. *I've arrived at a busy time, so much the better.*

His view was obscured by the broad shoulders of a thirty strong clustered group marching in the unison of vampires who spend all their time working in harmony. Super-tanker nomads might as well be emblazoned across the back of the grimy fabric of their coats.

The seafaring vampires were here to collect their dues. They existed outside the laws of vampire society, living in their own floating community. Sebastian despised them. It stung that he could not be sure that their unfettered existence was not, in actual fact, in some way preferable.

Little was known about them, except that they transported crops grown by vampires for the humans on the farms from one continent to another. Their night time hours were spent unloading massive containers at the docks onto fleets of transporter trucks. Then, they delivered the cargo to each hive's human farm facility. They brought in food which could not be grown locally, and were paid by each hive in blood. They were eerily silent. Rumor had it that they were inbred, and when they were turned, each vampire had fed from the other, and a telepathic connection ran like a current between them.

Sebastian saw only the bluish, waxy toned skin which had clearly not seen even cloud-filtered rays of light in decades, and wondered at their strangely tribal existence. He instinctively dropped back, allowing other vampires to crowd into the space. *Just in case they can read others' minds, too.* Sebastian had a lot to lose.

The entrance to the morgue came into view, and he gained in confidence as sidestepping through the doors, he entered the coldly clinical room. At first glance, things were in order, however, a closer inspection told a different tale. The autopsy tools were on a trolley, but flicking back the cloth cover revealed they had been dumped onto the tray rather than set out in order. The bulging laundry hampers were lined up, but the unwashed linen from one had been regurgitated onto the floor.

The brownish specks on the linen told the story, and the scent of Emily's blood teased his nostrils. *So, this was her hiding place.* Sebastian gripped the edge of the sheet and tore off a blood-splattered sample. He buried it deep inside his pocket as a reminder of her scent, if needed.

The merest whisper of vampire movement snapped his head around, directing his attention to the far end of the room.

"I'll be with you in a moment," a voice called out.

Before Isaac, the morgue attendant, rounded the corner of the tall bank of locked cadaver drawers and came into view, Sebastian slipped out through the doors again.

He strolled along the corridor, embracing the growing feeling of complacency, until he came face to face with Anthony. *Ah, the surgical assistant.*

"Can I help you?" Anthony asked abruptly.

Sebastian's smile was automatic as he searched for an appropriate lie. Anthony would have no clue who he was, but being seen was a glitch, nonetheless. "Oh, sorry, I'm lost."

Suspicion focused Anthony's attention on the intruder. "This is a private wing. Please leave." Anthony's hands curled into fists, and his usual warm demeanor plummeted to ice cold.

Sebastian nodded in quick apology, and, deciding that the sooner he left, the better, he walked away.

Watching him go, Anthony resolved to talk to Doctor Connor if he saw the vampire again. He was less blinkered these days. Wandering the surgical corridors was not a usual activity for any vampire. Blood fumes alone were enough to upset the control of some. Anthony was offended on Connor's behalf. *This is Doctor Connor's territory, so what was he doing here?*

The wavy black hair and boyish face could not mask the calculating glint in the muddy-green hazel eyes. Anthony doubted that he ever got lost.

Anthony had finally woken up to the idea that Connor was more than just a doctor; he had scruples which bred enemies.

Fire and Ice: Survival

Since Doctor Connor's clash with Councilor Serge over the Human Breeding Project, Anthony had detected a restlessness in him. *A human girl died and I became part of a plan that I still do not fully understand.*

Vampires have time on our side, but finding a mentor who's willing to forgive my mistakes, four decades on, is rare. Most would have pulled him up in front of the council for his failings and suggested he was better suited to farming. *Doctor Connor has more than earned my loyalty.*

Anthony sensed his mentor was in danger, and he worried about that.

Chapter 6

Keeping vigil in the sitting room with his charge, Julian studied Annabelle's reflection in the mirror because looking directly at her pinched features made her fragile frame tense up.

Connor has been gone longer than I expected. Julian's curiosity ran through the list of possible delays, and he was left with one thought. *Connor is a pain in the ass.* His disarming expression disguised the urgent need to get moving. The breakneck speed of a motorcycle ride would be a welcome release after the effort of standing still in the room for so long.

Annabelle sat huddled on the couch, rubbing her arms and convincing herself that it was only the cold which made her shiver.

They were having a standoff of sorts, and Julian felt he was winning.

His battle was resisting the histamine aroma the arm rubbing released as a fragrant cloud. *Interesting that her scent is tarragon.* His nostrils flared as the enticing hint of anise tingled inside them. It was a sweet smell, also known as dragon-wort, thought to be able to fend off snakes and dragons. Julian's smile was ironic. *That should keep her safe, hmmm?* Clamping his throat muscles tight created an airlock in his lungs, so it was only his nose that stung. Julian's smile widened. *No contest, if I took a step closer, she would run a mile.*

The sound of a motorcycle pulling up outside signaled that the waiting was over. *Should I be glad about that?* As the hope that Rebekah had not let Connor talk her round faded, he was not so sure. He opened the front door, his roaming vision piercing the darkness beyond his boundary to make sure Connor was the only vampire out there. Looking over his shoulder was becoming second nature. Finally, he directed a skeptical look at his friend. *About time.*

Connor was standing on the sidewalk beside a motorcycle. He raked his hands through his black hair and released a cloud of bone-

Fire and Ice: Survival

dust which hung in the air for a moment before settling onto his broad shoulders. And then he sneezed.

The calcium-laden odor plumed into the air, and all became clear.

"You had some stage-threes to proclaim, then?"

"Five." Connor grimaced. "It's later than I wanted."

Julian jerked his head to indicate the trail bike parked up at the curb, the cooling engine ticking like a deathwatch beetle.

"We're off-roading?"

"Through the woods. I thought it would be safer, given that dawn is not so far off." Connor lifted a brow in enquiry. "See you in ten minutes, south of the Thames? We'll head out through Swanley. The street lamps there gave up a few years back.

Julian nodded. "Sure, it's overgrown now, anyhow. Sounds good." Casting a bemused glance at the scattering of stars above, he added, "But we have plenty of time before dawn."

Connor's lips twitched in amusement as he threw a bundle containing two jackets at Julian's head. "Let's just say, humans have a way of throwing a spanner in the works. You'd better cover up."

With a final salute, Connor headed off into the shadows on foot, intent on collecting his own off-road motorcycle, and Rebekah.

Julian watched him disappear before shrugging into the larger of the leather jackets and pulling on the gloves he found in the pockets.

Returning through the house, he entered the sitting room, and even though he remembered to stop and wait for her sluggish human vision to catch up, the girl still jumped when he materialized in front of her.

"It is time to go," he said, when she finally focused on his face.

"With Doctor Connor?" Her pleading eyes strained to see past his bulk.

"You *can* trust me, will have to trust me, Annabelle. Doctor Connor and Rebekah are meeting us, but we have to get moving."

He tossed the black weatherproof jacket to her and she caught it.

"Let's go," he said.

She put on the coat, zipping it up to her chin as she followed him out into the damp night.

Julian was aware his ten minutes were ticking by. *Connor will be wondering where we are.* He mounted the motorcycle and held out his hand.

"I don't-" began Annabelle.

"Sure, you do," he said, cutting off her protest. With a firm tug on her jacket, he pulled her up onto the seat behind him.

"Hold tight," he muttered.

Seconds later, Julian raced over wet tarmac with an anxious girl clinging to his back. He scoffed at Connor's assessment. *Dawn is an hour away, at least.*

Her grip tightened as he opened the throttle, kicking a few more horses into action, and the motorcycle surged forward. The leather jacket smothering his skin creaked when he flexed his shoulders, and he wondered again if it was really necessary.

He glanced skyward as he cranked the motorcycle over to take the bend onto the ring road which led onto Vauxhall Bridge. They crossed the River Thames. The oil-black waters glistened with moonlit slivers as though a shoal of a thousand silver fish played beneath its turbulent skin. "We have plenty of time," he muttered.

Julian revised that assertion a short time later when, for the fourth time, he skidded the motorcycle to a halt as Annabelle again cried out that she was going to be sick. It was not a plea he could ignore.

While she slipped from her perch behind him and staggered to lean against a tree, Connor pulled up alongside. Julian envied him his composure, as Rebekah dismounted to see if she could comfort Annabelle.

He shrugged impatiently. *It has nothing to do with the chance of seeing Leizle again. And it looks like Connor was right, maybe we won't make it before dawn.*

The sky's palette was two shades lighter. Dawn's fingers were preparing to unfurl, spread her pearl-tinted span, and gather the dark cloak of night into her grasp. Softened skin was a weakness vampires could ill afford. *Juggling the covering/uncovering thing is difficult.* But right now, Julian felt like a child forced to wear an itching jumper, and his skin protested at the unusual confinement.

"Are you okay now, Annabelle? There is no need to be afraid," coaxed Rebekah. Although, her own anxiety showed in her eyes, and her outward display of concern did her credit as she comforted the girl's huddled figure.

Rebekah was not fooling Julian. *None of us are happy. Having Annabelle here is a huge risk.* He watched closely, and his discomfort grew as the pantomime unfolded.

"I'm sorry, I just feel sick." Annabelle bent over double, lowering to her haunches and placing her palms on the ground as she groaned. "Maybe if I rode with Doctor Connor," she muttered.

Jealousy cramped Rebekah's features, but she shot an enquiring glance at Connor.

With a studied expression of calm, he said, "It's worth a try. We should get going."

Julian felt the knife twist in Rebekah just as surely as if he had seen the flash of a blade. He wanted to tell her Connor was acting, too. *He would much rather keep Rebekah with him, he just needs to get this journey done.*

Rebekah moved first, swinging herself up behind Julian and nodding firmly.

Setting off once again, Julian rode in Connor's slipstream, focusing on the girl riding pillion on the bike in front, with her arms clasped firmly around his friend's solid frame. The heavy shadow of the tree canopy offered the illusion of safety, but still Connor pushed the engine revs to screaming banshee proportions. His aversion to sunlight was ingrained, and Julian, too, wanted the journey over. *For Rebekah's sake.*

Surrendering her place to Annabelle had cost a lot. Rebekah's disquiet was clear in the death-grip which encircled his waist, and he could almost feel her pounding heart inside his own chest. *I know Connor would not hurt her for the world, but, damn, this is harsh.*

They raced the approaching dawn, and Julian's mood became more grim. His own motorcycle surged forward as he tapped his foot carefully through the gears, his sure fingers pumping the clutch and twisting the throttle with restraint – metal was a delicate material in his hands – as he acknowledged the creeping feeling that Connor had been played.

The final hundred yards over a carpet of potholed grass clattered the teeth of all four riders. Connor slewed his motorcycle into the mouth of the tunnel, parked in the darkest corner, and cut the engine. Giving Rebekah and Annabelle time to gather their senses, Connor and Julian sat still with their boots planted on the ground and held the motorcycles steady. The shimmering heat radiating from the cooling engines enveloped them all, and vampire eyes met, each accepting that they had cut this one fine. Connor nodded tersely, shouldering the blame for the delay.

The silence was thick with relief, both human and vampire.

They walked through the newly hewn tunnels towards the meeting chamber. It was at the center of the eco-shelter – which was configured like a spider – although only six tunnels led out to other areas. It was a smaller habitat than the one they had left behind, but large enough to accommodate the group of twenty humans comfortably.

Bringing up the rear, Julian was glad to see Connor held Rebekah's hand and fought to match her slower stride.

As the group emerged from the tunnel, Oscar stepped forward, and, seeing the windswept, grimy face of a strange girl, his astonishment erupted. "What on earth?"

"We had to move fast. There wasn't time to plan." Connor's tone was quiet.

"I'm not sure Greg will be happy," said Oscar, "but, he's out in the field, right now."

"You should have asked us, Connor." Harry had grown thinner over the last few weeks. His eyes still begged forgiveness every time he looked at Rebekah. He had almost allowed Douglas to destroy everything he held dear, and he was indebted to Connor in so many ways, but he was still the head of the eco-shelter. "We should have taken a vote on this."

Connor nodded. "I know, Harry."

Fire and Ice: Survival

Harry's rheumy eyes glistened in the candlelight as he met Connor's sober acknowledgement. Mollified, he nodded slowly. "I guess one more mouth to feed is not a disaster. Welcome-?"

Harry looked at Connor when their visitor remained silent, hiding her face behind the curtain of tangled hair.

"Annabelle," said Connor, ignoring the anxious glance Rebekah sent his way.

Harry nodded. "Annabelle. I'll go and measure out her beta-blockers." He briefly embraced Rebekah before moving away, his mind already preoccupied with the polystyrene-lined crates stacked in his hospital chamber which contained the eco-shelter inhabitants' healthcare regime, and the chemicals he would use when his laboratory was finally up and running.

Oscar lightened the mood.

"I'm sure you are all hungry." He swamped Rebekah in a bear hug for a moment. "I better see what I can rustle up, eh?"

Rebekah smiled warmly, knowing that Oscar rarely delivered anything less than perfection.

As Oscar left the cavern, Thomas ran forward to greet them.

"You're back." Thomas hugged Rebekah, too, a wide grin illuminating his face. He was seventeen now, much too old to be her son, but Rebekah squeezed him back with maternal fervor. Saving him from youthful recklessness had forged a bond which also encompassed Connor.

He turned to Connor and nodded shyly, the hero worship shining in his eyes.

Julian hung back. He was searching the tunnel entrances for her small frame, for eyes as green as his, a stubborn jaw and chestnut hair. And there she was. *Leizle.*

A breeze ruffled her short, flame-shot locks, and regret hit him in the chest. His fingers twitched as though he could feel the weight of her thick braid in his palm. He remembered the texture of the copper bright filaments when his blade had cut through the woven strands and he had walked away without a word of kindness.

That was the last time they had been alone together, and the last time he had looked into her face. The pain he had seen in her eyes still stung.

It was necessary, to prevent Serge looking for her. But did I need to be so cruel? Julian knew that in guarding himself against her, he had handled her heart roughly, and now, it was too late to expect her forgiveness.

He tugged her scent into his chest in short hits, gently, as though stepping into icy water. He gauged his control, gripping it tightly, lest he let his desire show.

His life was already altered, and empty without her, but his imagination tortured him. If his fingers traced her flesh, if he tasted her and lost himself in her warmth, he would not survive if she rejected him. He knew Connor would tell him the pain was worth the pleasure, but he was scared his reserved manner would leave her feeling unloved and drive her away.

But, he still found himself drifting towards her, unable to resist her plea to his heart. The rich autumn tones of her hair enhanced the translucence of her skin, but lilac shadows beneath her eyes drained the radiance from her face, and twisted the knife. *I hurt her.*

"Your hair." He reached out to move the silken strands over his fingertips as he looked into her eyes. "I'm sorry," he whispered.

Leizle stared at him. The shards of jade in her gaze reflected her agony, and her feelings flooded into his mind. He knew she feared he would not let her in. His chest heaved as he inhaled deeply and the muscles in his jaw worked. *She is right.*

She sighed with the weight of that knowledge, and Julian's mouth flooded with moisture. He wanted to pull her close, dip into her mouth to steal that sad breath, and return it to her as pleasure. But instead, he dropped his hand to his side, and before the diamond fragments on her lashes could cluster into tears, he nodded once and strode from the cavern.

His leaving was a blur which left her reeling as he simply vanished. For once, he cursed his preternatural hearing when her words reverberated inside his head as she whispered, "I don't want his pity. I wish I'd never met him."

The last word remained strangled in her throat, and he almost went back... almost.

◇◇◇

Rebekah released Thomas, and stepping back, she drew the other girl forward. "Annabelle, this is Thomas."

"Hi," said Thomas, blushing as he held out his hand. Clearly struck dumb by her pretty features and made awkward by his attraction, he cleared his throat and shuffled his feet.

Annabelle edged closer to Connor's side as she met Thomas' shy gaze. "Hi," she said, glancing up again at Connor, as if drawing on his strength and seeking his approval.

Connor suppressed a smile, enjoying Thomas' discomfort, until he heard Rebekah's sharp intake of breath. It ionized the air around him with a current of emotions he didn't recognize. Her heart clenched as if punctured by the bite of a venomous snake, and her desolation pierced him in its turn.

As the blurred apparition of Julian disappearing from the cavern caught her eye, Rebekah dropped her chin and followed him out, but not before Connor caught sight of the flash of despair on her face.

"Hey, Thomas, how'd you like to look after Annabelle for a while?" asked Connor. His mind focused on Rebekah. Even though her footsteps were fading and the distance between them grew, he honed in on the clamoring beats of her heart, and the burned-toffee aroma to her scent that he'd not experienced before.

The girl looked crestfallen. "I'd feel... safer with you."

Connor's amusement at Thomas' bashful agitation was forgotten. A worm of concern stirred in his mind at the girl's attention, and the coyness as she searched his face registered at last. *I'm not sure Thomas can handle this.* Rebekah's growing distress twisted inside him. *But, I have to go.*

"You'll be fine with Thomas." Connor nodded at the boy and left them alone together.

"Hey, Annabelle, I can show you around, and where you're gonna sleep, if you'd like." Thomas' voice rose with enthusiasm.

At Connor's closed expression, Emily admitted defeat. "Thanks, Thomas." She sighed, turning to him and smiling.

She was twenty years old with the guile of a woman twice her age. She had grown up fast when she found herself alone at five years old. After her parents died in the influenza pandemic, the social workers had swooped in. Unfortunately, being a 'Good Samaritan' did not guarantee immunity to the disease, and Emily was moved on more times than she cared to remember. She stopped hoping for love when her third surrogate mother died.

Getting love and attention became harder still, when she was swallowed up in a hostel where children were looked upon as mouths to feed and an obligation to be cared for by those who felt fortunate to have survived. At twelve years of age, she discovered there were different types of love. She did not trust, but she craved the words of kindness she got if she let the older men touch her.

I was easy prey for Jonathan. When he caught her out foraging in a darkened department store, her sixteen-year-old heart had almost stopped. He was like nothing she had ever seen. *Vampire was only a word, an invisible threat.* His smile transformed his fierce face into captivating beauty, and he seemed to know her thoughts and how to ease her pain. When he laid his cold grip on her hand, he promised her an existence without fear, but his words "I will protect you" turned out to be a devastating lie. 'Never trust' was tattooed into her soul… but Doctor Connor had punched a hole in her armor, and hope trickled into her bloodstream.

Thomas swallowed loudly at the rush of having her complete attention. "C'mon, I'll show you the well-room where you can bathe. Oscar will be in the kitchen, and I'm sure he'll have some food for us if we swing by afterwards."

Emily's stomach rumbled as a reminder that Julian's tin of peaches was many hours ago, but that was not the sensation she clung to. The adrenalin of the motorcycle ride was far more potent.

She pushed aside the reason she had pretended to feel sick. She deliberately used up all the poppy seeds a long way out, and switching places to ride with Doctor Connor was a bittersweet reward when she was stabbing him in the back. *Perhaps the general won't find us.*

When she had hugged Connor's body and rested her cheek on his shoulder blade, every muscle moving under his skin sent a tremor of excitement through her. *This Rebekah is nothing special.* When they first met, she had looked at the textured honey-blonde hair and brown eyes, and decided that her long, curtain of pale silk and cobalt blue eyes were far more arresting. *Not at the moment, clearly.* Absentmindedly, she wound the greasy strands around her fingertips, reliving a moment when Connor's hand had settled on her thigh as the motorcycle banked. Was he just reassuring her... or? Hope blossomed. *Maybe, just maybe.*

◇◇◇

The moment Connor left the cavern and hit his stride, Thomas and the girl were forgotten. He powered his way through the tunnels, dragged along by Rebekah's scent. It was still tainted with an ionized odor which bit into his sinuses. He moved slowly for a vampire, already rehearsing the control he would need. His urge to look into her face was compelling. *But this is about her safety.* So, he focused on summoning the balance of revival sleep and awareness, with which he could ease her pain.

He caught sight of her up ahead, running her fingers along the left wall of the eight feet wide tunnel. *She looks so vulnerable, like Jonah in the mouth of a whale. No, a pearl in the mouth of an oyster.* Connor pulled in a deep breath, knowing he was going into battle. *I will slay her fears over Annabelle.*

As the tunnel curved to the right he closed the space between them. Skimming past, he rotated on his heel and blocked her path. She stopped with a gasp, and as adrenalin pumped through her, she froze. He had startled her. *But, this time I wanted to.*

Connor stepped forward as she stepped back, and without touching, he moved her into the tunnel wall. Towering over her, he placed his hands on either side of her head. Molding his fingers to the contours of the earthen wall, he was pleased when no telltale shower of earth fell. *Okay, that was gentle.* The gulp in her throat echoed through him as he looked down at her lowered lashes. Watching the shadows moving over her face as she chewed her lip, he waited.

When she finally looked up, he examined every expression. Her chin trembled, her spiked lashes betrayed the tears she had swiped away, and her eyes were black pools of sadness.

Her anguish gripped his heart as though her trembling fist closed around it. *How could I have done this?* Annabelle's interest had caught him by surprise. *What do I know of love?* His lips twitched in self derision. *I have no experience of romance. As a surgeon, I looked into eyes to diagnose disease, searching them for emotion never came into it. A hundred years on, and I'm a bit rusty. I just know my own heart. Surely, she knows it too?*

Connor groaned gently. Revival sleep flooded his mind in time to stop him snapping her neck as he laced his fingers into the hair at her nape and rested his forehead gently against hers. "Hey. Tell me," he said, dragging the burnt toffee aroma into his lungs.

"I can't explain," she said huskily. "Annabelle. She... likes you."

"She's just glad to be safe." Stroking his thumb along her jaw, he gently lifted her chin. "She thinks I saved her. She'll get over it."

"She likes you. She's stronger than you think." Rebekah frowned. "Call it intuition, but she scares me." The cold touch of foreboding skittered along Rebekah's spine, and Connor felt the tremor beneath his fingertips when she shivered. "She wants you…"

She lowered her lashes, and his gray eyes darkened to lead as he sighed heavily.

"Look at me, Rebekah," he said gently, tracing a finger over her furrowed brow.

"No…" Her stubborn streak gripped her heart. "She *wants* you," she insisted. The silence stretched and she finally had no choice, her eyes were drawn back to his face.

He met her desolate gaze, and her pain felt like a blow to his chest.

"And I want you. Only you." His mouth hovered over hers, his cold breath feathering over her skin. The shiver down her spine warmed her this time as she moved her hands to his chest, grazing her thumbs over hard muscle. His breath mimicked her sighs, whispering in and out as her touch held him frozen.

"I love you." His eyes glinted in the dim light. "Just say the word and I'll turn you and take you away from... this." He grazed his thumb over the pulse thundering in her throat. "Say the words and I can love you forever."

He did not need an answer. As his lips brushed over hers, he felt her come back to him. The burnt toffee stinging his throat cooled to the honey scented cocktail he was addicted to. It filled his chest and stole his panting breath.

Rebekah sighed against his mouth and dipped the tip of her tongue inside his parted lips.

"Hold tight," he growled gently as, holding her to his chest, he accelerated effortlessly along the tunnel. The air rushing over her cheeks chilled her face as she clung to his neck and pushed her face into his shoulder. The tunnel whisked into the distance, and, before she could catch a breath, the small cavern of her new den filled her vision.

His words were still reverberating in her ears as she lay back on her bed. Connor stretched out on his side next to her, the fingers of the hand supporting his head spiked through his thick hair, and the expression on his face, as always, made her breath falter. He smiled as he plucked at the buttons of her shirt, and a shaky chuckle died in her throat when he focused his attention on her face.

"Human quick or vampire slow?" Connor growled playfully, arching his eyebrows as his cool fingertips traced distracting patterns over her skin. He finished with the buttons and lost himself in the tempo of her galloping heartbeat, almost like a thrum of panic. The rhythm of it excited him. He ran his finger around the waistband of her jeans, her heart rate hitched up another notch, and Connor suffered an incendiary burn of hunger like a stake through his chest. He watched in fascination as her cheeks flushed, and his hunger burned brighter. Swallowing down a groan, he waited for her words to release him.

"Human quick?" she whispered, her lashes drifting closed, veiling her brown eyes as Connor peeled away her blouse. His own eyes melted to black pools as his fingers stroked over her breast, and the rush of pleasure which moved her body into his was almost his undoing. Connor's jaw tightened as he walked the tightrope of his control. *I can do this.*

He would suffer this a hundred times over to feel this alive.

Tugging her lips gently with his own, he breathed, "Not today, honey." He worked to suppress the sneer pulling at his mouth, wanting to bite, to taste, but he was determined to resist the thickened pulse that tortured him. As he pushed the jeans down, he returned up the inside of her thighs, teasing her damp heated flesh. He grinned as she wriggled her hips.

Rebekah sighed, lifting her knee to invite him in. "Vampire slow is feeling pretty good," she breathed.

"Oh, it gets better."

His gaze sharpened to predatory as it skimmed her body, his vampire vision chasing the blushing tide as the rose bud tip of her breast hardened between his fingertips and with a sigh, he leaned forward and flicked his tongue over it.

As the tide of warm nectar throbbed beneath his lips, flooding her senses with anticipation, he rolled his solid body over hers. Entering her in a slow sensual movement and chasing pinpricks of light through her nerve endings, he melted her doubts away. He locked his pleasure inside his chest and forced himself deeper into revival sleep, tempering every movement with achingly painful care. *Maybe today, I won't bruise her.* But he knew he would.

Rebekah held her breath, savoring the tension shuddering through his frame with each undulating movement. He smiled into her neck. He knew she was waiting for the moment when he would move away, and, take her over the edge with his cool touch. *But not today.*

He found the sweet spot deep inside her, his body trembling as he matched her desperate need.

Fire and Ice: Survival

Staring into her wide pupils, his heart ached when he saw her confusion shatter and her climax shook her. She dug her nails into his shoulders, and, when he could hold back no longer, Connor's desire flooded her body in a delicious cool tide.

"Hey." He touched his forehead to hers. "I said it gets better."

"You stayed," she breathed, her delight illuminating a stunned smile.

"I found out that it's safe." His face was serious, and his eyes glinted with male satisfaction. "I can love you as I've always wanted to. You *do* know I would stay here and never leave your side if I could?" He frowned as she went to speak. "No. Not because I think you need reassurance, but because my heart is tied to yours." His fingers traced her features from eyelids to cheekbones, pausing over her lips before finally he settled his thumb onto the pulse in her throat. "I could fill my vision, my heart, with this image every day, and still, it would never be enough."

He frowned fiercely as he dragged his lips over hers, making himself stop at just one taste.

Much later, they lay still entwined as Rebekah fought the clouds of slumber trying to steal the precious moments she still had left in his arms. Stirring, she mumbled, "Connor? Doing the hot thing... how does it feel to you?" She rested her cheek on his chest and traced her fingers over his stomach, drawing circles in the downy hair which marched down to his groin.

Connor was in hell. He hated this part as much as he loved it. *Vampires never linger, they take physical satisfaction and were gone.* He loved her. His arm cradled her to him, and as her heart beat a tattoo against his ribs, he had every muscle clamped down. He fought the violent need to take her again in every sense, to embed himself inside her softness, and in the same moment finally surrender to his compulsion for her intoxicating cocktail, and drink his fill. An act that if unleashed would crush her fragile frame to dust.

He wrestled his thoughts back into order. Focusing on her words, he raised his head to look at her face. "Well, bathing in boiling water and lying on a bed of hot coals were both painful experiences I'd rather not repeat."

"Oh, I hadn't thought," she whispered.

"Although, losing control when I did not know we were safe was *more* painful. Risking your life." His low laughter lightened the mood. "Remember, we said we'd save the hot sex for anniversaries."

Drowsily, she mumbled, "Only three of those, if we count my final birthday. We'll be the same, once I am twenty-four and you turn me."

Connor said nothing. He was placing his fingertips over the faint bruises he had made on her body. *Vampires and gentleness are uneasy bedfellows.* Her words reminded him that at twenty-one, their pact gave her only three more human years. He never intended to renege on that, but as Julian was quick to point out, vampires were doomed if humans did not breed. *I will not turn her only to watch her die twice. While there is a chance she will live longer as a human, I will wait.*

Chapter 7

Sebastian squatted down and brushed his fingertips over the road. Lowering a knee onto the wet ground, he inspected tracks where tires had pressed onto the tarmac and the moisture moved aside had not yet seeped back. Invisible to the human eye, they were as clear as day to his. Standing up, he grinned. *They left barely an hour ago.*

Emily's scent was delicate. It was a flavor of aniseed which stroked the back of his tongue, rather than an aroma riding the still night air. *A trail bike, so they are off-roading through the fields.* His satisfaction stirred and Sebastian held tightly on to the leash. *Best not count my chickens, but...*

His eye was drawn to the imposing Edwardian house casting shadow over the sidewalk. The impressive gravel driveway glinted with a carpet of amber and golden pebbles. The many stone chimneys transformed the pitched and gabled roof into a confusion of shapes in the darkness. *Definitely a glowering monster.* And a green-eyed monster of his own answered its call.

I bought the crap about Doctor Connor shunning material things. He's taking us all for fools. When Sebastian first arrived in London, hungry to affiliate himself to the force of nature which was Doctor Connor, it appeared that the doctor spent his life at the hospital. And rumor supported that. When vampires shared out the spoils as humans were rounded up and shipped to the farms, Connor turned down a penthouse at the London Hilton Hotel.

That Doctor Connor owned such a prestigious property, and yet kept it hidden, added fuel to Sebastian's pyre of hatred. With every revelation, it burned brighter. For vampires, houses were merely status symbols. *After all, we don't live in them.*

Burying the stone of jealousy inside, Sebastian set off at a lope. He honed in on Emily's scent, but gathered the visual clues as reassurance that he was heading in the right direction. On the road leading out of London, he lost the scent when the riders doubled back over their own trail. Pressing his nose into the square of linen stained with Emily's blood focused his palette, and he recovered the trail quickly, confidently diverting into the sprawling woodlands.

When he found the first clustered patch of poppy seeds on the moss covered ground, his arrogance grew. Not that he needed them, although they would make it easier, but because it let him see through a window into Emily's mind. *She'll be easy to manipulate. Poppy seeds were an inspired choice.* Connor would have no idea Emily, or Annabelle as they knew her, had laid a trail.

By early dawn, Sebastian was keeping vigil in the woods, standing on the spot where Emily's scent left the trees. Looking out over the pasture, he could see a dark scar in the rolling green hillside. *So, this is it.* Weak rays of sunlight slanting across the meadow revealed a tract of flattened grass which, once the dew evaporated, would spring back again.

Beneath the dense canopy of English oak trees, Sebastian took in a deep breath of stagnant moist air which would feel suffocating to humans. He felt relaxed and back in control.

Someone had gone back through the woods, erased the tire tracks, and laid a false trail by lumbering through the undergrowth, creating a swathe of snapped branches, torn and bleeding sap. *But they had not figured on me being here so soon, and the crushed grass was a gift they cannot take back.*

He did not move for fourteen hours, and during that time he constructed a fully formed plan. His contemplations ended abruptly. Reacting like an owl hearing a mouse's step, Sebastian's head jerked around at the delicate whisper of ruffling grass.

He concentrated on the direction of the sound and he was rewarded. *There's Doctor Connor, and his accomplice is here too, although it makes sense.* Sebastian could not ask Serge about the identity of the blond vampire because, as far as the councilor knew, his guardsmen never reached the human nest.

Sebastian's plans moved from a gamble to a certainty when, after pausing to listen and scan the wood, both vampires took off in the direction of London. *Maybe they are both doctors with appearances to keep up. I have no such obligation. I have as long as it takes for Emily's fear of my retribution to overpower her, as it will.* The poppy seeds had told him that.

As a rabbit pokes a twitching nose out of the burrow, lacking the courage to make a run for it, Sebastian caught a glimpse of Emily the following day. Her yellow hair flashed like a beacon in the sunlight. She was with a thin boy, and, although she could not know he was there, her nervous gaze flicked in Sebastian's direction. She doubled over, sinking down to sit on the ground. The thin boy seemed agitated, dancing from one foot to the other with half his body staying inside the tunnel.

They were much closer to the woods than Sebastian expected. The main entrance was disguised by the undulating dips in the landscape, mimicking a natural feature of soil erosion, while this exit emerged where the undergrowth and dappled shadows camouflaged it well.

Clever girl, she has found a back door. It's funny how desperation always finds a way. Sebastian embraced the buzz of triumph as he tuned into their conversation.

"Please, Annabelle, we must go back. We'll get into trouble if Connor finds out." The boy's whisper was as thin as his frame.

"Just one more minute. I'll be fine in a minute." Emily's breathing was fast and shallow.

Sebastian was amused. *And she's faking it.*

"We shouldn't be out here. Please, come back inside." The boy was whining now.

Emily staggered convincingly to her feet. "I won't tell anyone you showed me the tunnel, you can trust me."

"Bravo, Emily." Sebastian grinned with malice as he detected regret on her face. *Not much longer now.*

Sebastian was happy to wait. He leaned against his adopted tree, careful not to let his idle fingers scar the bark. *They'll know I was here, but, how long I waited and how determined I am, they will only be able to guess at.* He waited two days, and three endangered gray squirrels who ventured too close, died. He was a hunter and patience was easy for him. *All I have to do is reel Emily in and back her into a corner.*

"Connor's woman," he mused aloud. *I look forward to learning her name.*

Tracking the human lumbering through the trees, he turned and waited. "Emily, you made it at last. Or should I call you Annabelle?" Her flesh crawling at his oozing tone amused him.

The marks on her body had faded since her escape to the human nest. He smiled as he remembered Councilor Serge yanking at her clothes, exposing her flesh and pressing himself against her. Her revulsion had thrilled Sebastian, and as he smelled the bile burning the back of her throat, he knew she was remembering it, too. *She knows that being my pet would be worse than Serge's attentions, worse than death.*

"I saw you with a human boy before. You seemed close?" Sebastian began the game.

"He's nobody. He's young and smitten. A pawn." Emily met his gaze reluctantly.

Sebastian nodded. "You faked a panic attack and tricked him into showing you the back door, but he likes you. So he could be useful?"

Emily looked shocked at Sebastian already knowing her movements. "Thomas doesn't know anything," she said quickly.

"And what do *you* know? How many, and how long are they staying?" Sebastian couldn't care less. *Councilor Serge may want them all, but I want only one.*

"About twenty, I guess. And they are staying a while." Her shoulders sagged in defeat and she broke out in a cold sweat. Sebastian's sharp hazel gaze skewered her as though he could read her mind.

"And Doctor Connor? When will he be back?" *And there it is, the defiant spark, the evidence I need. She likes him.* It should have made him happy, but jealousy flashed a green filter over his thoughts. *God. Does every girl fall at this vamp's feet? No matter, I will come out on top. Now, to reel her in, and when she thinks she has it all, I'll take Connor from her and break him.* Sebastian moved up a gear. He knew how she would react to the idea of destroying Connor, and seeing him on trial. *She will give up the good doctor's woman to avoid that.*

"He must be coming back to see his woman. After all, he loves her." Sebastian buried the knife in her chest and waited.

Emily bristled at his words. "She's nothing special, just a bit of human on tap, I'm guessing." She fought hard to be casual, but her resentment showed.

"Oh, that's a pity." Sebastian enjoyed the smell of her wounded heart. *They all smell so different.* But he liked the spectrum of pain best. Her aroma was bitter. *How fitting.* "I was thinking of taking her for myself, as a punishment for Connor to bear." He shrugged eloquently. "But if she means nothing-"

Sebastian watched the battle inside her. *Will she do it? Sacrifice her? Or will her better nature prevail? It will make no difference, but still.*

"Well, I wouldn't say she means nothing. Rebekah's just his pet, but he'd still be angry." When she darted a glance up into his triumphant muddy-green eyes, fear made her body jolt – she knew Sebastian saw through the lies.

For a moment, he froze, distracted by the dew drop of information that quenched his thirst. *Rebekah. That suits her.*

Sebastian's eyes were hooded. "Well now, I'm feeling generous." He waited until she looked at him. "How about a straight swap, I take-" He inhaled deeply. "Rebekah off his hands. And you get to comfort him."

His gaze glinted with sadistic anticipation, enjoying the picture in his mind of Rebekah contorted in pain. He felt Emily's heart stutter in her chest. "I lied," she said hastily. "She really *is* just blood on tap. He really wouldn't care," she protested in a whisper.

Before she could take a breath, Sebastian's arm closed around her and pulled her up against his chest. He gripped her hair and pulled her head back, exposing her throat. "Too late, Emily, I know he *would* care." He leaned over her, twisting her hair in his fist until her scalp burned. "Now I know where they are, I could drain you and leave you here, and no one would ever know. No one would care. Now... about Rebekah," he breathed. As his grin widened he let his venom flow. Wetting his lips with a lap of his tongue, a deliberate string of saliva dripped down the front of Emily's shirt. "When can I... see her? When will you bring her to me?"

◇◇◇

Three hours after the council hearing adjourned, Principal Julian was still pacing around his house. Entering his study for the umpteenth time, he glanced at the brown wing-backed reading chair which connected him to his mortal life. Its leather skin was worn and crazed, but the care Julian lavished on it held the fatal cracks at bay. The leather motorcycle jacket hanging on the back of the door would have the same elevated status and care as a souvenir, of sorts.

His mind and body still simmered with the excitement of racing the motorcycle against the breaking dawn. At least, that was what he told himself. He sat at his desk shuffling papers, and pretending that he was not reliving his latest encounter with Leizle, frame by aching frame.

Well done Julian," he said sarcastically. His instinct was to stay away, but he was discovering that he could not.

He had little sympathy for the addict. Be it the friends of his mortal wife, Eva, who depended upon laudanum and smelling salts to provide color, or relief, to their lives, or the Avant-garde of nineteenth century London, who believed that the oblivion of ingesting opiates held the key to their creativity. *Addiction is a weakness. More fool me.*

His eardrums reverberated as a sudden boost in the air pressure inside the room signaled that a vampire was approaching at speed. *Connor? I thought he had a forty hour shift at the hospital.* Julian, grateful for the distraction, crossed the room to greet him before he materialized.

Connor burst into the confined space – his wake threw the heavy brocade curtains into disarray and the decorative coal scuttle in Julian's fireplace was felled by the shockwave.

Julian's ears were still ringing as he took in Connor's stony expression. "What's happened?"

His friend's urgency suddenly deserted him. His wet greatcoat settled around his thighs and the dusting of raindrops glistened like pearls on a frozen statue.

Julian tried again. "Connor, what is it? Is it the eco-shelter? Rebekah? What?"

Rebekah's name released him. "Damn it. Every time I relax for moment, I'm filled with dread as her heart scrambles in her chest. And then, I live in fear until I have her in my arms again. Why didn't I just turn her, Julian? Why didn't I?"

"Why?" Julian thought of Leizle. "Because you didn't choose this." Julian's hand indicated the length of Connor's awkwardly posed frame. "We know the reality. It is not glamorous, it's a battlefield." Julian's face was serious as his own tortured thoughts colored his expression. "If there was another option, for you to become human again, I think you would choose it. I would, in a heartbeat."

The emotional storm abated and Connor whispered, "I'm losing her again." His gray eyes melted from determination to despair. "I went out to Swanley to check on her, to pick up on the rhythm of her heart, but she wasn't there. Greg was waiting at the meeting point. She's been taken. Shit, Julian."

Julian waited.

"She's scared. It is like that night in the woods all over again. Her heart is tired and sluggish. But the sound of it is echoing inside my head, and I can't get a fix on her." He rubbed his open palm down over his face and a mask of horror emerged. "She's in trouble."

"Connor, go and find her. You know that you can." Julian's voice rang with conviction. He tried, for a second, to put himself in Connor's place, and the pain of it scorched his brain. *If it was Leizle who was missing, I wouldn't give up.*

Certainty stiffening Connor's spine, he said, "I'll pick up her scent at the eco-shelter and track her down." Julian watched his eyes glaze with ice as he shut down his emotions and embraced vampire detachment. It had served them both well for decades, and it would focus his mind now. *There will be time enough for emotion when he finds her. Damn it. I don't trust this Annabelle. I hope I haven't waited too long.* "Connor. You need to begin with Annabelle." At Connor's sharp glance, he added, "Talk to her first."

Connor nodded tersely, his silent accord more eloquent than words. As he whisked around and opened the door, he froze as a trail bike engine screamed in the distance. "Who the hell is that?"

They waited those interminable minutes for the bike to finally skid to a halt outside, scattering a Claymor array of gravel over the stone walls of the house. Both vampires urgently scanned the streets for unwanted attention.

"What is she doing?" barked Connor.

Julian had no need to ask who. The taste of cinnamon burnt his nasal lining and he huffed out the smell in frustration. *Leizle, here to torture me.* He was taking so much rap-sleep lately that *he* felt like an addict. He had never seen her naked, but if his imaginings were correct, then she was glorious. *His* vision of her small compact frame had lithe coltish legs, and the high breasts of a girl waiting to become a woman. *A virgin. Another reason to stay away.*

And there she was. "Rebekah's been abducted," she gasped. Her chilled cheeks glowed like coals in a brazier. The rain had plastered her denim pants to her thighs, and her teeth clattered as the cold began to bite.

"I know, Leizle, Greg already found me," frowned Connor.

Her shoulders sagged in relief. "He's not back yet. I'm sorry, I couldn't wait. I thought Julian would know where you'd be."

"Do you know who took her?" said Connor bluntly.

"No, but Thomas won't talk, but I think he knows something." Her frown etched hard lines into her forehead. "I asked him about Annabelle. He went red and ran away." Her face crumpled as fierce concentration became anguish. "You don't think she's on the farm?" Her own experience made that the worse scenario she could come up with.

Connor arranged a reassuring expression on his stiff face. "No Leizle, I don't think she's on the farm."

As Leizle's fragrant sigh of relief tortured him, Julian thought, Rebekah is somewhere far worse. Annabelle's miserable existence, her half-eaten state as a vampire's pet, would be nothing compared to what she would suffer at Connor's hands if Rebekah got hurt. Julian almost felt sorry for her, but then he glanced at Leizle's white face, pinched with concern, and could not.

For Julian's ears alone, Connor said, "I'll begin with Annabelle." His cold face set with rage, and before Julian drew breath, he was gone in a blur of anger-charged agitation.

I would not want to be in Annabelle's shoes. Leizle's alluring scent filled Julian's sinuses, her body heat and the rain percolated to accentuate it, and he acknowledged his own fate. *I can't avoid her any longer.*

He turned to face the bedraggled figure. Her wet hair had darkened to caramel, a brushstroke of dark rose accented her cheekbones and her green eyes gleamed like moonlit algae, almost florescent in the ambient light. Suddenly Julian found his own shoes were not that comfortable.

A few minutes later, a towel dried Leizle, wearing a ridiculously long sweatshirt of Julian's, was sitting on his couch as they waited for vampire dawn. Her wet jeans hanging on the door had no hope of drying. Vampires had no need of heating, and a tumble dryer would be ridiculous when wet clothes went unnoticed.

She put a brave face on it, but Julian felt every shiver as it rippled through her.

He stood in front of the fireplace with his hand resting on the mantelpiece, wishing the logs in the fire were not mil-dewed and damp. "I guess resurrecting the fire is my next task," muttered Julian.

His pose suggested a gentleman at ease, but human mannerisms deserted him. He became as still as an alabaster statue.

Her warm-blooded beauty deserves the heady heights of red-hot passion, not the ice-cold touch of a man who can't even find the words to tell her how he aches to be with her. Her chattering teeth vibrated through his head like a chainsaw, and Julian sighed at the grim reminder.

He could feel her gaze on his skin, and his peripheral vision tantalized him with the delicate beauty of her face. He couldn't help but notice how the borrowed clothes hugged her frame, and he smiled wryly. *She looks better in my sweatshirt than I ever could.* He averted his gaze when glimpses of Leizle's slender naked thighs, which the sweatshirt could not entirely conceal, tormented him.

Steeling himself for closer contact, Julian strode across the room and opened a cupboard door. Pushing tins of food aside, he took out a bottle of water – another concession to his newly acquired association with humans. His lips compressed in a determined smile as he approached her. Leizle's eyes were still glued to where he had stood only nano-seconds before, and he was reminded, yet again, of human frailty. *They have no idea how slow they are.*

Julian rubbed his hands together until friction made his stone palms glow, and then he wrapped his hands around the bottle and warmed the water. Leizle started, and Julian guessed she had just registered that he had moved. He lowered himself carefully onto the couch beside her, unable to resist the impulse to extend his arm along the back of the seat and make contact with her shoulders. He gladly absorbed her jolt of surprise when he pressed the warm bottle of water into her hands.

He raised his brows. "Better?"

"Sorry," Leizle muttered, as she hugged the water bottle to her chest.

"For what? For being cold? Or stupid?" His voice was so low she could barely hear it.

"Both, I guess."

"Don't be." His fingers moved over the copper tips of her hair as he turned to look down into her face. He tried not to focus on how the soft sweatshirt material molded to her breasts. Her legs tucked up beneath her, bared her knees, and his eyes were drawn to the dark shadow where the sweatshirt ended. He swallowed hard as Leizle's breathing faltered. If he ran his hand up beneath the soft fabric, he knew her body would welcome him. The scent of her skin, and the siren call of the damp heat between her thighs, almost overwhelmed him, and he gripped his knee, hard. *Luckily, I don't bruise.*

"I have a council meeting tonight, so, you'll be here alone for a while. I would stay, but my absence would cause comment. After all, we don't get sick, unless we neglect revival sleep or get into a fight. And the council knows that neither of those would apply to me," he said, when at last he dared to speak.

Leizle looked up at him. "No, of course not. It's all a matter of control."

"Control you should be grateful for," he murmured, clenching a harder grip on his knee. The urge to tumble her over and push up inside the sweatshirt was compelling.

"Maybe." She met his green gaze with her own flash of emerald. "Maybe not."

Julian stared at her and said, "I'm not Connor." His lip curled. "It will take more than a pretty face to turn me into a fool." It took every grain of willpower to pull the performance off. Her heart had been racing since she entered the house. The chambers of it cantered with the nervous tension of the motorcycle ride, but when she looked at him, it had hitched up to a gallop. The pull *he* felt echoed inside her, too, and she could not protect herself from him. *So, I'll do it for her.*

Liar, a little voice whispered. *You're running scared.* Even as the harsh words left his lips, each one dropping like a stone, he thought, it's not Connor who is the fool. *True, I have seen him suffer around Rebekah, but I've also never seen him happier.*

He searched her eyes and watched the glow of hope cool to green ice. Her confused desperation played out across her expressive face, and he felt sure he could hear the questions tumbling over inside her head – 'Had she misread every situation? She had thought he was fighting an attraction, but was she wrong?'

The denial nudged at his clamped lips but he turned his face away.

"No, I'm the fool," she mouthed silently, but Julian heard every word as a shout.

He had hurt her again, but as much as his cold chest ached with regret, he told himself it was for the best. His two-hundred-years of stone cold existence left him terrified that he could never make her feel loved. *And I want that for her.*

"I have to go," he said.

Leizle shivered when his abrupt movement gusted a breeze over her bare skin and her next sight of Julian was of him standing at the door, ready to leave.

He had already changed into formal clothes and was buttoning his coat. "Please, keep quiet," he said as he pulled gloves onto stiff fingers. He had not worn gloves at night for decades, but it gave him something to do. "I'll be as quick as I can. Certainly before vampire dawn, and I'll take you home then." He stared until she nodded her understanding, and then she found herself alone.

Chapter 8

Rebekah awoke in darkness. She opened her eyes and it made no difference. The blackness was almost a solid. There was a moment when she thought, 'maybe I'm dead', and then the pain kicked in.

Just as she accepted that the dull ache in her neck was not imagined, a cold clasp on her wrist came into sharp focus and instantly, she panicked, until she realized it was a metal cuff. *Not vampire fingers.* Her body felt sluggish. Even as terror honed her awareness, her heart rate slept. Stirring her leaden limbs required too much effort, and the pain in her head peaked when she rocked it on the thin mattress. *Where am I? What happened?* A rank residue glued her tongue to the roof of her parched mouth, and the smell invading her nostrils triggered a sense of dread in her brain.

She chased a memory in and out of dark corners, catching glimpses of keen eyes, floppy dark hair, and finally, her mind released the terrifying images it had locked inside. Clearly, her subconscious decided she was ready to fully experience immobilizing horror.

Rebekah remembered entering the dining cavern. Seeing Annabelle hunched over at a table, she had an irresistible urge to reverse silently out again. *Would I have?* She would never know, because Annabelle saw her, and the sheer relief which flooded her pale features, with the added plea of an outstretched hand, put paid to Rebekah's retreat.

Annabelle and her labored breathing filled Rebekah's mind. *She was hyperventilating, and needed air.* There was something else, a slicing look and swiftly averted gaze which had made Rebekah's hackles rise. But she chose to blame herself. *What had Harry always said? We all have prejudices, but we mustn't allow them to get in the way of doing the right thing.* Rebekah knew that where Annabelle was concerned, jealousy distorted her judgement. *No, not jealousy, just plain old fashioned hatred.*

Alarmed by Annabelle's frantic gaze, Rebekah shoved her misgiving aside and came to her aid. Annabelle gripped Rebekah's shirt sleeve and clawed at her neck. The sharp gasps tearing at the girl's throat were Rebekah's undoing.

"It's okay. Oscar will know what to do, just hang on to me." Rebekah pulled Annabelle to her feet, put her arm around her, and tried to urge her forward. But she doubled over, too distressed to move.

"I... need... air." The words were a coarse whisper. "Please."

And then Rebekah did the unforgivable. She broke the golden rule; *never go outside without telling the others.* The emergency exit tunnel into the woods was right there. *This is an emergency, right?* "It's okay, I know a way out. Just hold on."

Annabelle braced her hands on her knees, the rippling curtain of blond hair obscuring her face as her head hung down.

The cover on the tunnel mouth worked on a pivot, like a seesaw. Rebekah heaved down on the lever which eased the trapdoor up, and wedging a metal rod into a slot in the frame held it open.

"Okay. C'mon, I've got you." Bearing most of Annabelle's weight, Rebekah started up the gentle slope, relieved when the gray gloom of the night sky came into view. The grass fringed opening of the tunnel looked like an open mouth with vicious teeth. *This is no time for an over-active imagination.*

As they got closer to the exit, a breeze wafted her hair and chilled her damp skin. Annabelle's fingers were ice cold and her breath rattled in her chest. Rebekah hoped they would make it in time. Their boots slipped on the thick mulch packed on the ground at the tunnel entrance, and Rebekah remembered the makeshift barrier of branches which partially obscured their path. *Great for camouflage, not so good for a quick escape.*

"Nearly there," Rebekah whispered, concern etched into her face.

She released Annabelle, who slid down onto the ground. Rebekah hauled aside the gnarled branches and stepped out of the tunnel, giving Annabelle the room she needed to roll onto her hands and knees and crawl out into the moonlight. Lifting her chin, Annabelle gasped.

Hoping she had done enough, Rebekah, too, gulped in the fresh cold air, even though it chilled her brain and stung her throat.

As Rebekah darted forward to help Annabelle to her feet, a band of cold steel snapped around her chest and she gasped.

Annabelle's head jerked up; moonlight bleached her face and fear reflected in her ocean blue eyes as she stared past Rebekah.

The firm grip arched Rebekah back, and her shoulder blades grated over a hard body. Panic jolted through her when cold fingers framed her neck and their unrelenting pressure forced her chin up.

Lifting a foot, she stamped hard. Her boot grated down the iron rod of his shin, and his cold breath when he laughed transformed the sweat on her brow into frost. She closed her eyes. Her breath stayed locked inside her chest, and swallowing became impossible as he pressed her head back into his solid shoulder.

"Open your eyes, Rebekah," he purred, his tone caressing her name.

She squeezed her eyes shut. She didn't want to look. The bony fingers tightened, pressing either side of her jaw until the tendons screamed, and the pain shot her eyes fully open.

"Better," he said, turning her face to his. "Will he miss you, do you think? Doctor Connor? Will he fight for you?" The vampire looked down into her eyes, smiling as his words carved despair into her pinched features.

Her heart clenched as she recognized the face. The riot of black hair casting his features in shadow could not disguise the flash of victory in the mire of his hazel glare.

Sebastian cackled as her body jerked against him and her hands clawed at his arm, her fingernails skidding over the hard shell of his skin.

"No knife with you today, Rebekah? Such a shame."

Tears of anger stung. She kicked backwards and agony shot up her spine as his knee dug into the back of her thigh. She tried to scream, but she had no air left beneath the constricting band of pressure across her body.

A keening whimper filled her ears as his fingers dug in deeper, pinching a nerve in her jaw and forcing her mouth open. She watched him through the array of sparks exploding inside her head as the bow of his lips slackened, and her mouth filled with saliva, his saliva.

She gagged in disgust and, as her world went black, his manic grin faded away.

Lying in the darkness on the thin mattress, the movie reel stalled and burned the image of the vampire's face into her brain. This was more terrifying than her dream, her premonition. *I knew I would see him again.* Revulsion rose inside her, and she tasted bile again. The venom he had fed her sat heavy on her heart. She relived the open mouthed, wet kiss, and her convulsed swallow as his venom filled her mouth. The last noise she remembered, before she blacked out, was Annabelle's scrabbling.

What happened to Annabelle? Is she here too? Did the vampire kill her? Imagining death at this vampire's hands filled her with ice cold fear. *God. I hope not.* "Please, let her be safe," she whispered, and the dank air swallowed her words and tried to crawl into her mouth and fill her lungs.

Connor will be looking for me. She'll have raised the alarm. I just have to hang on. Hope clung on until Rebekah thought of Annabelle... with Connor. "And maybe she didn't," she said.

Dread iced her skin in perspiration. *He almost had me before.* He tracked, hunted and captured her? *But how?* The taunting apparition of an Annabelle who walked through a nightmare, peeled away layers of clothing to reveal purple mottled skin and scabbed over wounds. Her curtain of blond hair swung aside to unveil glacier-blue eyes. The spite behind the glancing look Annabelle had cast her way, the one Rebekah had not been able to decipher when in the dining cavern, was revealed.

She recognized it for what it was. It had been mirrored in her own gaze. *Jealousy.* And she knew. *I have been sacrificed.*

Numbness hung on for a merciful moment, then defeat set in. Tears eased the gritty feeling in her eyes. *How easy will Annabelle find it to comfort Connor, to persuade him to give up hope and let me rot?* "Never," she breathed as anger fought back, incinerating the image of Annabelle and offering her Connor's perfect face to cling to. Her drugged heart tried to race and failed.

The snick of a metal latch resounded in the void, and a gray rectangular hole was punched in the curtain of black when a door opened. *Is it early evening or early dawn?* She was petrified. *The doorway is empty. He's in here already.*

With her eyes stretched wide, she strained to hear as her body burrowed into the thin mattress. Suddenly, his black silhouette obscured her sight.

"Rebekah," he hissed.

The metal cuff gripping her wrist clanged like an alarm bell as she scrabbled up the bed, refusing to let the futility squeezing her chest drag her back down.

He moved silently forward and clasped his cold fingers around her ankles, laying down one finger at a time. His amused chuckle filled her ears. His grasp seared like freezer burn as he slowly, inch by inch, drew her back down the mattress.

The muscles in her neck burned as Rebekah strained to raise her chin and keep her face, her brain, her consciousness, away from him. A whimper vibrated in her throat.

Suddenly, he was on top of her, his weight bearing down and she could barely breathe. Her shoulder blades screamed, and her legs tingled with the splintered glass of pins and needles as her blood flow faltered.

His breath, cold and laced with the stench of rotted meat, filled her lungs and made her retch as he aligned his face with hers. "I saw him with Annabelle."

"Liar," she hissed, and he laughed.

Her teeth clattered as his icy temperature invaded every cell of her body.

His dead weight cut off her circulation, starving her brain of oxygen. Glittering sparks filled the blank canvas of her mind, enticing her to follow them into oblivion.

Sebastian closed his eyes, enjoying the electric charge of her muscles in spasm, the sound of the corded sinews in her neck popping, and the hum of synapses firing in her brain. He savored the journey through her senses as her fear mounted.

Venom oozed from his slack lips and into Rebekah's mouth as he closed the space and smothered her in a wet cold kiss. He swallowed her scream, filling his chest with it, and his cold flesh hardened, pressing into her soft belly.

Careful. He eased his weight. *Don't want to break any bones yet.* He flexed his lungs as her scent scorched his throat. When he sensed her leaving, felt the black fingers of unconsciousness dragging down the blinds, he sucked on her face and sighed, "Nice, very nice, as I knew you would be."

And then, bracing his hands on the bedframe, he leapt to his feet, retreated, and watched her from the doorway. He smiled. He could hear the sudden release of blood rushing into her oxygen-starved tissue. Her consciousness would be returning, and the flood of endorphins would, for a short while, mask the sensation of pain. *She will feel as though she is floating off that mattress.* His grin widened as her body twitched, snapping her limbs into the jerking dance of terror that he so enjoyed. *Such a pity that I have to go.*

I want to take my time, savor her fear, and enjoy bringing her closer to death. Next time he would saturate his sharpened vampire senses in her. His anticipation was a red-hot poker through his center. This visit was quick, but it whet an appetite for her an ocean deep. "I will see you again soon, my Rebekah."

Sebastian closed the door and left the house. He crossed Hyde Park, locking her scent inside, he felt her terror singing through him, and, as he approached the council building his attention turned to Connor. *I'll enjoy making him suffer.*

He arranged his boyish features into the sycophantic smile which Serge had come to expect. *This is a big day.* His expression slipped into a vicious grin before melting back again. *I finally get to see the inside of the council chambers. Next stop, attending a hearing. Reeling Serge in is proving easier than I thought. And, when I get onto the council I can stop pretending.* He paused to take in the marble facade of the council building, an ivory face in the moonlight which seemed to smile down upon him. *Yes, life is good.* He tripped lightly up the steps, and disappeared inside. Once the heavy wooden doors swung closed, only the faint smell of his excitement tainted the air.

◇◇◇

After Julian declared the court session closed, he moved swiftly through the corridors of the council building flanked by his fellow jurors. Alexander and Marius still wore the flowing black robes of their office. Julian had already changed, intent on executing a smooth getaway.

The effort he had called upon to withstand the demands of the hive members in court today left every nerve ending singing with tension.

Matching Julian's pace, Juror Marius said, "It's unbelievable that Serge is pushing for the Hybrid Breeding Project to have a second trial."

The spring in Julian's stride was rooted in satisfaction at successfully opposing every move Serge made, although the repetition was tedious. *Serge is like Doctor Frankenstein, certain that the monster will turn out better the second time around.* "Serge is tenacious, Marius, you know that."

Every argument Serge put forward, Julian dissected and disparaged, more than once, and convincingly.

"I hope we've heard the last of it. We can't risk anymore female humans, and you'd think Serge would realize that by now," Alexander said absently.

Julian agreed with his young companion. "We are one step closer to impressing upon the hive that free range human farming can be a long-term solution. We should be moving forward with that." *Okay, we are a long way off from humans giving their blood freely. But who knows where it could lead?* Leizle's desolate expression when he had left her was another memento of his own agony. He knew how generous the human heart was. *So, who knows?*

"Principal Julian." A wavering voice with strident overtones chased him down the corridor.

Serge. What now? Waving Marius and Alexander onward, Julian fell back and turned around. "Councilor Serge?" He inclined his head in greeting, but his expression was closed.

"I'm disappointed the council are so short-sighted. You're a sensible man. Surely *you* can see our survival depends on hybrid development?" Serge coaxed.

Julian suppressed a smile. *He doesn't like me, but he knows that without me onside he has no hope.*

"You're looking for a permanent solution, surely this one is perfect?"

Leizle and Connor demanded his attention, and he resented wasting his time. As Julian took a breath, ready to fire the words which would cut the councilor short, his hackles rose. An aroma plumed in the air and distaste tainted his palette. The elusive odor played on his mind, and he knew he had smelled it before, and it was important.

He turned to look into the face of a young, boyish vampire with black wavy hair. His courteous smile did not reach his eyes, which glinted in the dimly lit corridor.

"I don't think you've met my protégé, Sebastian? This is Principal Julian." Serge introduced them.

Julian scoured the youthful face. Like a wind chime jangling in the distance, there was something about this Sebastian he found annoying. *I never forget a face. I have not seen this one before, and yet...*

Julian shrugged off the feeling, shelving it for another day. *Right now, I have more important things.* Sebastian's arrogant demeanor almost undid two hundred years of breeding as Julian entertained walking away without a word. The move was almost accomplished as he shifted his weight and prepared to disappear, but the tantalizing trace of that odor held him there.

His attention bored into the hazel eyes, and peeling aside the layers, he identified conceit. The carefully arranged features implied respect. *However, this vampire cannot hide his ego.* Julian almost laughed aloud.

"Principal Julian," said Sebastian. He inclined his head, the untamed hair obscuring his eyes for a moment before his arrogance emerged again as he confidently offered his hand.

Julian mimicked the fake smile. He considered the extended hand as though he had never seen one before. When he looked back at Sebastian, his brows rose in sardonic inquiry. He might as well have slapped the youth across the face.

Sebastian stood his ground, resisting the recoil that Julian detected shuddering through his body. The hazel eyes glinted with calculation.

Should I be impressed? I think not. But I need to know more about this one. Distaste settled as curdled milk in Julian's gut. "I won't shake hands." He paused to recharge his lungs, leaving the insult to hang there like a lightning rod ionizing the atmosphere. "I may hurt you."

It was a deliberate slight. *Let's see how he handles that. How old is this Sebastian? His smell suggests half a decade.* Vampires shook hands to gauge the strength of an adversary, and as a sign of respect to another vampire who they considered to be a worthy opponent. It was presumptive of this one to think a vampire of Julian's standing should oblige. *Arrogant, in fact.*

To refuse a handshake declared the vampire as unimportant. Julian chose to rearrange his shirt cuffs, dismissing Sebastian, although he kept him fixed in his peripheral vision. The moment stretched as Julian waited for the response to come. It would tell him a lot and he wasn't disappointed.

Sebastian's chin rose and confidence puffed out his chest, the smug conceit was no longer veiled as he looked Julian in the eye. "Perhaps, I would surprise you, Principal Julian." He bared his teeth in a manufactured smile, a poor effort at disguising his anger. "I'm stronger than you think."

"Really?" Julian summoned a much more convincing smile of amusement, designed to irritate.

Sebastian's jaw snapped shut as he bit back further comment.

"I suggest you choose your... protégés with more care in future, Councilor Serge," said Julian without releasing Sebastian from his stare. Addressing Sebastian again, Julian added, "As for the rest, we shall see."

He piled another insult onto Sebastian's shoulders by turning his back. He looked at Serge and stated firmly, "You will excuse me."

Julian strode away, ignoring Sebastian's malevolent gaze. The smell still haunted him. He shuffled through his mental filing cabinet, and he could not escape the feeling that, like a blind man sifting through sand, his fingers had grazed upon a familiar object and lost it again. *I'm missing something.*

As Sebastian stared into the space the tall blond vampire had vacated, the missing piece of *hi s* puzzle slipped into place. *It takes a lot to surprise me.* He had recognized Julian as the same vampire who helped kill Councilor Serge's guardsmen, and as the accomplice leaving the human nest with Doctor Connor. *A Principal, no less. I'm impressed that Doctor Connor's co-conspirator is a vampire of such standing.* Sebastian was forced to acknowledge that Julian's powerful aura was even more potent up close. *I can use this, but I'll need to tread carefully.*

Julian's dismissal stirred his contempt. Sebastian tarred him with the same brush as Connor. *They think they are so superior. But I have Rebekah.* He enjoyed the gratification at his victory over them both.

Her milk-white skin had been luminescent in the dim light filtering into his basement. His slackened fingertips feathered together as he remembered her texture. He had not tasted her yet. Councilor Serge's demands delayed that moment. *But thanks to Principal Julian, I will enjoy it all the more.* Sebastian was still infuriated by Julian's rebuff. *He will come to regret that. Rebekah certainly will.*

Sebastian registered Serge's voice as an irritant. The councilor's dry vocal chords made him want to clear his own throat. Reluctantly, he punched a hole through the cloud of his obsession and tuned in to Serge's words.

"Well, have you found her yet?" he asked impatiently, blindsiding Sebastian for a second. Serge's look of inquiry sharpened as he waited.

As Sebastian wondered if Serge somehow knew about Rebekah, comprehension dawned, and he was quickly back on track. "No, I'm afraid Emily has betrayed us. Doctor Connor is apparently irresistible." His lips curved in a convincing smile of regret. "I shall keep looking, of course, but she seems to have covered her tracks well." He met Serge's eye without a flicker.

Chapter 9

Rain beat down upon Connor's shoulders as he made short work of the journey through London. He spared a moment to hope that Julian would be kind to Leizle before every thread of his concentration was braided into one compelling thought. *I must find out what Annabelle knows.* Needle sharp darts of rain bit into Connor's skin, and he increased his speed, reveling in their distraction. They were a physical expression of the dread tingling along his spine.

Leaving London behind, he plowed through woodland, carving a path through the English countryside.

Finally, hurtling down the eco-shelter tunnels, he shed his soaked greatcoat without breaking stride. The flames in the sconces guttered as he whipped past. An avenging angel dressed in steel gray frost, his face was devoid of expression, and rings of cold aluminium barely contained the chasms of his black pupils.

He honed in on the human heartbeats, and headed for those clustered in the meeting cavern. He could smell their agitation. *They don't know I'm here. It will be the panic of the herd when a predator has struck.* His instincts told him Annabelle would be hiding. *If she has any sense.*

Connor filled the doorway, a melting ice sculpture dripping rain onto the floor. His wet hair gleamed as the water ran unheeded down his neck. His clothes were plastered to his bone-white frame, his muscles clearly defined as he considered the scene.

His sudden appearance rattled the group, and they instinctively huddled together. But, as predicted, he did not see Annabelle in the room.

Harry and Oscar stepped forward to greet him but he silenced them with a glare. The first face he sought out was Thomas'.

Connor absorbed the boy's sudden panic as he bore down upon him.

"Tell me what you know." He stopped short of touching the youngster as Thomas fell back.

"N... nothing." Thomas swallowed.

Although Connor's fingers itched to help Thomas find the words, with a monumental effort, he dug up a reassuring smile. "Tell me, Thomas."

The boy's outburst was punctuated by tears. "I showed Annabelle the emergency exit. She had a panic attack."

Connor's jaw twitched as he swallowed his recriminations. His expression fixed as he said, "Go on."

"She had another one, I think. She said Rebekah took her outside. It was not until suppertime that Annabelle told us she had lost her."

"Lost her?" Connor's lip curled.

Oscar stepped up, trying to draw Connor's attention as he said, "She told *me* Rebekah was sleeping off a headache. So, we didn't miss her at first, and when we did, Annabelle said she was hoping Rebekah would come back, and that she couldn't face us."

Without taking his eyes from Thomas' face, Connor said quietly, "So, she lied. Where is Annabelle now?"

"She's in her cavern. Greg's keeping an eye on her."

She's hiding. Let's face it, she has nowhere to go. Another length of tunnel reverberated with his passing as he sought her out.

He found Greg first, standing outside the entrance of her cavern like a bouncer outside a nightclub, his arms folded, and disapproval radiating from every line of his body. A crease which could have been a smile twitched over his face when he saw Connor, and he stepped aside.

Connor swung in through the doorway, scanned the cave, and, in less than a second, he fixed his eyes on her pinched face.

She scrambled off the bed, but before she had gained her feet, Connor lunged forward and backed her into the cavern wall.

"Look at me," he said softly. As she shrank from him, he settled his hand around her throat and lifted her chin. He could smell the nervous perspiration on her skin. He spat his words into her face as he said again, "Look. At. Me."

Her eyes snapped open in a face filled with terror.

Connor was not moved. "Where is Rebekah?"

"I had a panic attack." Her throat worked to swallow against the confinement of Connor's hand.

Rushing footfalls echoed in the tunnel outside, and a cluster of anxious humans poured in through the entrance, stopping short as they absorbed the scene.

Connor cut to the chase. "She went outside with you, and *you* left her there alone?" His cold voice was disbelieving. "Why did you tell Oscar she was sleeping off a headache?"

"I have panic attacks, I just needed air." She gulped, struggling for breath as she frantically searched for Thomas' face. "Thomas will tell you. I only lied because after a while, she didn't come back."

"Thomas *has* told me." Connor eased his grip. His hand shifted on to her shoulder and his eyes traveled down her body before returning to her face. Making an assessment of her stress levels, he leaned in to smell her breath, and the iron-tinged aroma of her blood as it washed over his palette brought him to one conclusion.

"I don't think so. You have never had a panic attack in your life." Connor's pupils contracted to pinpricks of disdain. His lip curled. "Thomas said Rebekah took you outside, and that she did not come back. Now, I want *you* to tell me."

He waited. This was hard, he wanted to sink his fingers into her shoulders and shake her.

"I was scared when we got separated in the dark. I thought she must have come back already."

"Liar," snapped Connor. He could smell her fear, and knew every word was designed to save her skin. *But from who?* What was making her cling to her lies? *She is petrified, but not of me. But I can change that.* He unveiled his thoughts, visualizing shaking her until her neck snapped, and anger shredded the words he snarled. "Annabelle, let me make this easy. Tell me the truth or I will kill you, eventually."

He suddenly realized that his indulgence of humans hinged entirely on his joy at being with Rebekah. *With her gone, I would cull the entire community and not bat an eyelid, if it brought her back.*

"Believe me, I *will* snap your neck and not feel one second of regret." Connor replaced his hand around her throat. "Only Rebekah matters to me. If she dies, *your* death will be a hundred times more painful than your worst imaginings."

His eyes passed over the old bite marks on her shoulders. He tightened his grip, pressing his fingertips into her flesh and marking her with a necklace of bruises. "You have no idea how bad things will get." His deathly calm was more terrifying than his fury as he said quietly, "Now, the truth, please."

"It was a vampire."

Connor sneered. "Tell me something I don't know. Who is he?"

"He appeared from nowhere. He said he was the general, and then he saw Rebekah and-" Emily's mouth twisted in anguish as she said, "he left me, and went after her."

"There is more to it than that, although, given the choice between you and her-" Connor twisted the knife as his eyes raked over her in disgust. "Where did he take her? Which direction?" He ground out the words, his fingers laying a few more bruises into the base of her throat.

The seven other human hearts pounding in the small space of the cavern reverberated inside his head. *I'm scaring them half to death.* After Thomas' display of gullibility, he decided that it was probably a good thing.

"I don't know." Her knees trembled violently.

"So, he said he was the general, and you've no idea where he's taken her, or why he chose her?" A blast of cold air stole her breath as Connor roared with frustration. "You must know something."

Without warning, he clenched a fist and buried it deep inside the wall beside Emily. She flinched as an explosion of grit grazed the side of her face.

He eased his fist out of the crater and said, "Tell me that story, *again.*"

The blood pumping beneath the hand framing her throat ran cold and her face drained of color as he drew his shoulder back, and aimed his fist at her face this time.

"Please, I only know he would have killed me," she sobbed. A bone deep shiver undulated through her body as her knees buckled.

"And you think that I won't?" His snarl sprayed venom over her face. "I *promise* you, if Rebekah dies, you die."

Connor's lunatic rattled at the cell door inside his brain. *I could slip into grave sleep right now and grind her bones to dust.* The act of finding Rebekah was the padlock keeping the door closed as he fought the urge to unleash his fist and obliterate her tight features.

He froze suddenly, then jerked back at a fetid smell filling his nose. With a low growl he pressed his cold face into the girl's neck. Emily finally believed Connor could kill her, too, and she whimpered. Squeezing her eyes shut, she waited for Connor's teeth to tear at her throat and end her life. He pressed his muzzle into her breast, moving up over her skin to just below her collarbone. He pulled in a deep breath.

The stink on her skin was familiar and the information slotted into place. *I know the why now.* The general was the vampire Rebekah had fallen prey to in the woods outside the eco-town that night. Frustration tore a hole in his gut as Connor realized the general's real identity, or what he looked like, still evaded him.

<><><>

Julian shrugged off the nuisance of Serge's protégé, and almost made it back to his house. The leafy suburb of Richmond was a fragrant blur. The tree-lined streets were cool under the canopy of arching branches, and the rain had released the earthy smell that Julian loved. He filled his lungs, anticipating Leizle's scent. *So different from Rebekah's.* As the thought punched a hole into his subconscious, effortless coordination deserted him, memories poured out, and he skidded to an abrupt halt, his coat slapping against his thighs.

Wheeling around, he retraced the journey. He mounted the wide stone stairway and re-entered the council building, scanning the sea of vampire faces as he walked into the council meeting room. Affecting relaxation, he joined in discussions on the day's hearing, hoping to learn something of Sebastian's whereabouts and discovered the arrogant young vampire had already departed.

Julian's memory had kicked in too late. *It was Sebastian I tracked through the woods the night I found Douglas' body.* His thwarted desire for confrontation urged him to give up on this fishing expedition and take a different tack. But, he needed to uncover something which would provide a flash of inspiration. *Until I have a damn clue what the hell to do next, I'm going nowhere.* He was angry at himself. *I should have known.*

A whisper of fabric attracted his attention as Juror Marius appeared at his side. "Marius." Julian inclined his head. "Serge was on form today."

"Indeed." Marius smiled slowly. Everything about him was considered, ponderous even.

"I met his protégé after the hearing," said Julian, casually.

"So, he is not just another guardsman then. Does he have potential?" Marius asked.

"Maybe. However, Sebastian seems to have kept a low profile, until now. No one knows much about him." Just saying the name reminded him of how stupid he had been. "Except that, since he arrived in London, he has been close to Serge."

"Being close to Serge is reason enough for others to distance themselves."

Julian agreed. Aside from his stench, Serge made the beautiful people uncomfortable. His decrepit form offended. Not that all vampires considered themselves beautiful, more that they were not so unsightly that looking at them made skin crawl.

"I think we may be seeing more of him in council. He struck me as ambitious."

"Should we keep an eye on this one?" asked Marius.

"I think Serge is playing a dangerous game. He may discover he's created a monster," said Julian.

The cogs turning inside Julian's mind kept returning to his discovery of Douglas' body in the woods. *Right there, I have him on threatening the food supply. Only Connor and I know where the body is buried, and Sebastian's venom is locked in the tissue. An open and shut case.* Except, condemning him will take time which Rebekah doesn't have. Intuition told him it was Sebastian who was holding her.

"You'll excuse me, Marius." Julian was already heading for the door as he spoke.

His plan taking shape, he passed by the hospital to collect his human blood vials, grateful for the enhanced allocation due to him as principal of the vampire council. With the vials tucked into his pocket, he headed for home. *Collect Leizle, take her back, and find Connor.*

He was later returning home than he intended, and he began to worry about how quiet Leizle had managed to be. Navigating along the hallway on automatic pilot, he stopped in the sitting room and found it empty. The tarpaulin which had covered her motorcycle lay outside on the gravel in a crumpled heap, his sweatshirt was draped over the couch, and her wet clothes were gone.

"Damn it." *I should have known a wounded animal always goes to ground.* "I may kill her myself when I get hold of her, if pneumonia hasn't finished her off first." The other dangers he chose not to think about. Picking up the sweatshirt, he buried his nose in the Leizle-scented fabric and, in that moment, he decided that if she was safe, she was his.

Julian took off along the dark street, glad to be doing something, at last. His powerful run hit the perfect balance which released his mind to choose the words he would need if he was going to convince Leizle to accept him.

Approaching the eco-shelter, he shot across the field, and, arriving in the pitch black tunnel, he was relieved to feel the radiating heat of the motorcycle parked in an alcove. *She made it then.* His pockets weighed heavy with vials of human blood. *It's time to break the news of Sebastian to Connor. I have a plan, but first, I'll find Leizle.* He urgently needed to look into her face.

Chapter 10

Leizle paced her cavern, and the circular route she carved matched her mood. She chased her thoughts, indulging in the he-loves-me, he-loves-me-not game of recrimination. Her dreams lay scattered like discarded petals. She was left holding the bare stem with Julian's words clinging to it, "It takes more than a pretty face to turn me into a fool". *There is no hope, then.*

She had heard the wounded roar of Connor when he arrived back at the eco-shelter a couple of hours ago, and it chilled her to the core. Muted voices told her Rebekah's trail was cold, and Annabelle faced another interrogation. The frenzy of subdued human activity hummed with drama, but Leizle had no appetite for it. The hurried footfalls of Harry and the others barely scratched the surface of her conscious thought. *I've had enough excitement for one night.*

Realizing she could not outrun her pain, she stopped. Her face glowed with perspiration and her teeth chattered as her damp clothes made the chill creep in to her bones. With a ragged sigh, she peeled off her wet denims, unveiling clammy blue-mottled thighs. *Very attractive.* She massaged her cold muscles and wished her heart could feel as numb.

She scrubbed a towel over her damp skin, shoved her legs into sweatpants, struggled her way into a t-shirt, and sank down onto the bed. She ached so much that even her hair follicles seemed to hurt. "Why does it hurt so much?" she whispered, as she keeled over onto the mattress and pulled a blanket up over her.

She lay very still, dry-eyed, and hugging her middle. She tucked her chin underneath the woven covers, feigning sleep. *In case Rebekah comes looking.* Her thoughts stalled at that. *Rebekah is gone.*

In disgust, she flung back the blanket and sat up. "Pull yourself together. Rebekah's in hell, and you're weeping because an iceberg won't hold your hand? Pathetic."

"Iceberg? That's a bit harsh." His whisper swirled around inside her head.

"Great. Now I'm hallucinating," she muttered at the same moment as a cold caress covered the hand on her knee, and the mattress dipped beneath his weight as he settled beside her.

Julian's relief at finding her stung like iodine in an open wound. Her spiced aroma always carried a sharp sting, but now he felt like a burning man and even his revival sleep could barely dull the pain. He drank in the details of her profile, with the dew decorated lashes and the stubborn set of her chin. He savored the surprise vibrating through her body.

She turned to face him after what was, to him, an age of perfect contemplation. Her surprise became confusion as her hand reached out to touch his cheek before she was in control of it. His green eyes deepened to sage as her fingers molded to his chiseled face.

"Julian."

His name on her lips melted the last of his doubts. *She loves me too.* He wanted to turn his face into her palm and bury it in her scent. But, he waited. As he knew it would, the joyful beat of her heart stalled. He watched her face drain of color as his harsh words surfaced in her mind, and her fingers began to fold away.

Covering her hand, he pressed it firmly to his face, and the heat branded him, her scent permeating his skin, feeding his addiction. "I don't have the words," he breathed as his lips brushed hers, and he slipped his free hand tentatively around her waist. He had so much to learn about her softness and his strength. *I'm afraid I'll break her.*

"Do you *need* words?" Her voice broke as she pressed her lips to his.

As he tasted her kiss, his throat aching with greed, he retreated.

Leizle followed him. Resting against his solid chest, she reached up to run her hands through his hair.

His harsh sigh shocked her back to awareness and his urgent departure robbed her of support. She put a hand out in time to stop herself from falling, and her eyes darted around the cavern as she prayed she had not scared him away.

Julian's anguished voice echoed through the cavern as he said, "I'm new to this. You're going to have to be patient."

Her eyes found him standing with his back pressed to the wall in the tunnel outside. His hair was mussed, his cheekbones were blades of white, and his eyes glinted in shadowed sockets. She had never seen him anything less than immaculate and to see him rattled was a glorious revelation.

Shards of jade gleamed in his eyes, and his hands flexed at his sides as he whispered again, "Will you? Be patient and wait for me?"

She nodded slowly and dared to smile.

He pushed away from the wall, and debris rained down onto the floor as he dug out a rock which fitted into his palm and locked his determined gaze to Leizle's. "I could hurt you, so easily," he said. Crumbling the rock to dust took a second, and no effort.

"But you *will* try?" she pleaded softly. "To love me?" There it was, her heart out on the line. She had words enough for both of them.

"I won't try." An expression of fierce concentration bared his white teeth for a fleeting moment. Taking a deep breath and smoothing his features to a gentle smile, he said, "I *will* love you. I can't not."

He crossed the cavern and sat beside her again, with a gap of a foot between them, this time. "How about, you stay still, and I'll try to kiss you?"

Still stunned at his just being there, with a loud swallow, she nodded her head.

He leaned in until he touched his mouth to hers. The tip of his tongue brushed over her lip, and she moaned in frustration. As her heart raced, the cadence of the wet chambers echoed inside him as he relaxed through the desperate need to tear it from her chest.

"Better," he lied as he moved back. The smile on his lips disguised the torture. *Two hundred years of control are barely enough.* Trailing his fingers over her cheek, he said wistfully, "I have to go and find Connor, but I'll be back."

She smiled, but her eyes betrayed her sadness as she fought the feeling that he was slipping away.

He said quietly, "I don't blame you for doubting me. But I *will* be back." He risked leaning forward to bury his nose in her flame-shot hair, taking in a lungful of her scent as a memento, and then he was gone.

Leizle placed a hand to her chilled cheek and closed her eyes. Tumbling over onto the bed and pulling the covers up over her, she ran the scene through her head and dared to hope.

<><><>

As though destiny decreed it, Julian and Connor arrived in the meeting cavern at the same moment. Connor, wired from his fruitless search of the woods, set eyes on Julian's face and absorbed the meaning of his friend's disheveled appearance. Grasping at respite from the hell threatening to bury him, Connor cocked a speculative brow.

Julian groomed his hair self-consciously. "You win," he said.

"I never doubted it," said Connor, soberly.

Julian's happiness dimmed as he murmured, "I'm sorry."

"Don't be."

"What did Annabelle have for you?" Julian asked.

"The vampire in the woods is called 'the general', and he has Rebekah." Connor's voice was tight with desperation. "I've searched the woods for clues, but there's nothing left to track."

"He's called Sebastian," said Julian with quiet conviction.

At Connor's pointed look, Julian told him the rest.

"He's Serge's protégé, and a smart one at that. He's been hiding in plain sight all this time."

"Does Serge know?" Connor growled.

"My gut feeling says Sebastian's acting alone." His matter-of-fact tone crumbled with self-recrimination. "I let him slip through my fingers. I'm sorry, Connor, I have no excuse. I just did not place his smell until it was too late."

Connor's fingernails carved crescent moons into his palms. "Did you smell her blood on him?"

Julian shook his head. "No, only her sweat." *And her fear.* But he kept that nail in the coffin to himself. "I have a plan which will find Sebastian and Rebekah, fast." At Connor's intense look Julian added. "It's at huge personal risk for you, but it's all I've got."

"Tell me the plan. If it saves Rebekah, I will do it."

Clearing his throat, Julian laid out the details he had agonized over. *Every road leads back to this as the fastest solution. How much longer can Rebekah survive Sebastian?* Julian feared it could already be too late.

"Will Anthony cooperate?" asked Julian seriously. "Success depends upon it. I can't do this without him."

"He might need a shove, but for me, yes, he will cooperate." Excitement glittered in Connor's eyes. He had a name to focus his rage on. *Sebastian. I may not survive, but Rebekah will, and that's all that matters.* "Let's go," said Connor.

He left the cavern, knowing Julian would catch up, and every flame in the sconces along the tunnels guttered and died at the shockwave of two vampires hitting top speed as they passed by.

The rain had stopped, and beneath the glowing moon their racing shadows cut through the streets with a knife edge of purpose. They finally stopped on the sidewalk outside the darkened house. Serge was inside, they could smell him.

"Ready?" asked Julian.

Connor's shoulders sagged and the excitement melted from his features as he allowed his desperation to bubble to the surface. His voice rasped as he said, "Ready."

Moments later, with Principal Julian's arrival setting him back on his heels, they were standing inside Serge's study where the councilor had lived out his middle and old-aged human years, and continued to do so during his fifteen years of vampire reincarnation.

Connor guessed it was the only place Serge could find relief from the miserable reality being a vampire had turned out to be. He had bought into the myth that becoming a vampire restored youth and vigor. He had not bargained on remaining old and frail.

"Principal Julian." Serge's wet swallow curdled Connor's stomach. "This is unprecedented."

"These are exceptional circumstances," said Julian with quiet authority. "Doctor Connor has admitted to your charge of 'threatening the food supply'."

Serge's startled gaze darted to Connor. "So, you are here to tell me he's under arrest?"

"He will stand trial." Julian nodded. "But no, I'm here to tell you I want Sebastian's head, too."

"Sebastian? Why? What has he to do with this?"

"I expect you to comply." Julian exposed his teeth in a threatening smile. "Sebastian has abducted Doctor Connor's pet and taken her for himself. That cannot be tolerated." Julian's green eyes bored into Serge, shredding his poorly disguised nerves. "He also has information that the council demands he share. He knows where the human nest is." Julian twisted the knife as he said with contempt, "He's taken you for a fool. Your reputation is at stake, and you will go down with him if you shield him now."

"Let us be clear," Serge said. "Doctor Connor's trial is a formality? He will be found guilty. I have your word on that?"

Julian nodded, and leaning against the wall with casual disregard for the grime of his surroundings, folding his arms across his chest, he waited.

As the smell of stale human sweat and mothballs coated his throat, Connor resisted the urge to cough and shatter the moment.

Tracks in the layer of talcum powder-fine dust revealed Serge's usual routine. The only furniture in the room with a polished surface was his desk, and the display of photos where human faces stared out from behind discolored glass. *His family?*

Connor hoped Serge's hatred would not desert him now. As he fingered the four vials of human blood in his pocket, he decided to give Serge a nudge. "I'm trading myself for Sebastian. You have no choice."

"So, you're telling me Sebastian betrayed me? That he has from the start?" Serge's pleasure at this turn of events glittered in his jaundiced gaze. "He knows where the human nest is, but is keeping

Fire and Ice: Survival

it secret for his own advancement, and he has taken your *human* woman as his pet?" Serge grinned widely, clearly enjoying the illusion of being in control.

Connor buried his satisfying image of Serge's face contorting as he gripped his scrawny throat. "I will admit to 'threatening the food supply', and accept the death sentence. In return, you give up Sebastian's location. My price is Rebekah's safe return."

"And the human nest? Surely you can't think I can let it pass?" Serge sneered at Connor. His bravado slipped away when Julian cleared his throat.

"Oh, come now, we both know this is about Doctor Connor. His woman will be sent to the farm, but she will live. Let us do the trade." Julian pushed away from the wall, demanding Serge's attention. "I respect Doctor Connor, but as principal I cannot condone this, even in him." Julian let his words sink in. "We are men of honor, and a deal *has* been struck." Julian hit his oratory stride. "The vampire community will reel with shock when even a trusted hive member such as Doctor Connor is shown no mercy. They will sit up and show the council renewed respect. We all win," he coaxed, his lowered tone drawing Serge in. "You can choose to take credit for that, or?"

Serge's eyes skittered from one face to the other, finally resting on Connor.

Connor knew they had him. *I just have to close the deal.* "With Principal Julian here to witness it, there is no backing out."

"Very well." Serge made one last demand to satisfy his vanity. "I want your word Sebastian will be taken alive, to answer in court for his part in this plot."

The kill had been firmly fixed in Connor's mind. Sebastian's cold, thick blood filling his throat as it oozed from his mouth. Not feeding – killing. Relinquishing it was hard. "Agreed," he croaked, frustration clutching at his vocal chords.

Serge smiled. "Very well."

Chapter 11

A matter of yards separated Rebekah from Sebastian, with the heavy door to the basement firmly closed between them. Rebekah knew she was alone, because she could not see. The black velvet-thick air grew heavier with every passing moment, and although breathing was difficult, *not* breathing would have been a blessing.

Sebastian's saliva pooled in the contours of her collarbones. She shuddered, and dried tears made her face feel stiff as she finally understood the paralyzing fear of knowing he would return without warning.

She kept her eyes open wide, pinning her blinded gaze on that space in the darkness. The gray rectangle of the door opening would give her barely a second's warning of his arrival, but she clung to that.

This time, Sebastian moved too fast to give her even a second. She felt his body settling on top of hers, and then she saw him. His presence was a vortex which sucked the oxygen from her lungs.

The blackened eye sockets in his pale gray face flashed with chips of ice at every turn of his head. Saliva dripped from the gash of his mouth when it gaped open. Her body trembled as horror immobilized her.

Rebekah's ribcage creaked beneath his weight, and as he shoved his knee between her thighs, bruising the flesh, she screamed. He laughed, expelling rotten breath over her face as his hand covered her mouth. Taking *her* hand, he forced her fingers to caress the bones of his face. Ending with the hideous grin and wet mouth, he buried his teeth in the plump pad at the heel of her palm.

Blood trickled down her forearm and red darts of pain seared through her brain. He ripped her shirt, and the tearing fabric yanked her body violently sideways, and as his lips dragged over the soft swell above her breast, she shriveled inside. Connor's name raced in a litany through her head, a chant which occupied every space inside her, saving her sanity.

"Fight," he breathed. A deep cackle rattled in his throat as he inhaled loudly. "Ah, but your restraint smells delicious. I can see why Connor finds you so exciting." His hand closed on the front of her thigh, and an electric charge of anger galvanized her into action. Connor's name from his mouth disgusted her. If he touched her *there,* she would never feel love again. *I would rather die.* So, she fought him.

Pedalling her knees and flailing her sluggish limbs scattered excruciating pain through tendon and bone, every jarring movement collided with his hard frame, bruising her flesh. His laughter when her burning muscles tired brought fresh tears of desperation to her eyes.

"That's better," he leered, "but I think you have more to give." His muzzle moved to her collarbone and he closed his teeth over it, slowly increasing the pressure, pressing down until the skin broke. She felt the vibration as the bone fiber tried to hold its shape and finally failed with a sickening snap.

Rebekah screamed until the black clouds rolled in and saved her.

Sebastian reined in his disappointment. His fingers grazed tenderly over her still face and he smiled. *Half an hour, I think. And she will be awake again. I can wait.* He left as quickly as he had arrived.

Back in the main reception room of the house, Sebastian stood as a parody of a gentleman lost in thought while the time slipped slowly by. His chin went up and he smirked when he heard the accelerated breath of her consciousness returning. *She is awake, but giving her another hour is of no matter.*

Sebastian straightened his tailored jacket and combed his fingers through his mussed wavy hair as he relished the taste of his moments with Rebekah. *So delectable, she bruises much easier than I imagined.* The musical snap of her bone when it broke had thrilled him, and he shrugged, as if to say, 'it was only a matter of time'. *She is strong and stubborn.* He grinned to reveal teeth still stained pink. *It makes everything so much more enjoyable.*

Reluctantly, Sebastian pulled himself back to the reason he *was* waiting. "I wonder what Serge wants?" The message the guardsmen delivered was annoyingly brief, 'expect a visit from Councilor Serge within the hour'. *And I am expected to wait like a lapdog? The sooner I rid myself of Serge's patronage, the better.*

Checking his watch, Sebastian's fingers stroked over the face of the heavy gold timepiece. *Life is looking up.* He had a nice house in a bowed terrace of Belgravia Square. *Okay, I have ruined the decor by soundproofing a room as Rebekah's cell, but it is a nice house nonetheless.*

Sebastian ran his tongue over his teeth, tasting her blood again. As he closed his mouth, the sound of splintering wood thundered through him and his eyes darted to the doorway. He saw the boulder of black cloth and a distorted white face hurtling towards him at the precise moment he was knocked from his feet and plowed into the wall.

A cold hand gripped his throat as a snarling muzzle shoved under his chin forced it up until he could see only the ceiling. His head dug into the wall, covering his shoulders in powdered plaster. As the cold face moved to breathe into his ear, Sebastian pulled a diamond tipped knife from his pocket, and buried it swiftly, deep into his assailant's side.

Sebastian grunted with pleasure as the grip on his throat clenched tighter with the force of the blow, and then became slack as the needle of pain shocked through his attacker. He pushed against the sagging weight and grabbed the vampire by the neck. Rotating quickly, he, in his turn, rammed his visitor viciously up against the wall. His jaw jutted, he bared his teeth, and growled into Connor's face.

"Ah, the jealous boyfriend. Quicker than I thought, I'm impressed." Sebastian's snarl melted to a sneer.

Connor had expected Sebastian to fight. *Not being allowed to kill him is the problem.* He had *not* expected the burn of a honed blade plunging into his side. *Well Sebastian, you sure as hell aren't ready for what I have planned.*

Connor launched into his performance, responding to the boyfriend jibe as Sebastian would want him to. Disguising his calculating gaze beneath hooded lashes, his icy calm became the grating pants of pretended anguish. The game took three seconds, during which time Connor took every moment to savor the triumphant gloating expression on Sebastian's face.

Connor struggled convincingly, and then let defeat sag his shoulders and leveled his gaze at Sebastian. He cloaked his expression in despair.

"Did you touch her?" His tormented tone was not entirely pretense.

"Oh, I did so much more than that." Sebastian grinned. Tightening his grip on Connor's throat, he spat, "Pathetic. Humans have made you soft, and, to think, I *admired* you." Three inches from Connor's face he leered. "Yes I *touched* her... you'll not be enough for her anymore."

"That's a pity," Connor said on a harsh sigh. "I might have let you keep your eye." His gray gaze became as sharp as a razor and his expression grim while he watched the barb hit home.

Sebastian recoiled, his surprise dissolved to uncertainty as he sucked in air to speak.

With a flick of his wrist, a needle-thin steel spike dropped from Connor's sleeve down into his palm. Before Sebastian could utter a word, Connor rammed the spike up into the soft space framed by his jaw. Sebastian felt the pressure surge into his head and pain lanced through his eyeball before, with a pop, it went dark.

The aphrodisiac of supremacy raced through Connor. He had severed the optic nerve with clinical precision, and the forceful nudge up into the skull caused all three of Sebastian's brain centers to shut down at once. A reboot was a natural consequence, but for now, it was lights out. Sebastian's motor function ceased and as his body folded downward, Connor made no attempt to break his fall.

Sebastian hit the floor with a satisfying thud.

Connor reached around to ease the blade from his side. *Such a shame he's not a doctor. There are many places a well-placed blade can cause damage, and he missed them all.* He grinned at the irony.

Stepping over Sebastian, Connor barked, "He's ready," to an invisible audience.

Dismissing the body, he took a deep lungful of air. *Yes, she's here, but she's hurting.* Easily tracking her scent, he whisked along the hallway until he arrived at an oak door. The muted sounds of Sebastian being removed were of little interest. *Serge can do what he wishes with him.*

Connor reached for the brass doorknob and opened the door as slowly as his wired muscles would allow. When he heard Rebekah whimper, it tore his heart out, and he stopped. *Rushing in will scare her.*

"Rebekah, honey," he whispered coarsely as pushing the door wider revealed what he did not want to see.

Gray light tumbled across the threshold, and her terrified scent stung his nostrils. The stagnant air was ionized with fear as she scrabbled up the thin mattress. Cowering in the darkest corner, her eyes were squeezed tightly shut and she trembled uncontrollably.

Connor deliberately scuffed his feet, letting her hear his approach. He absorbed every vibration rippling through her frame, and listened to the feeble beat of a heart filled with adrenalin, but too lethargic to pump it around her body.

"It's Connor. Rebekah. Honey, I'm here." Connor wished he *had* killed Sebastian as his eyes moved over her body. For once, night vision was a curse. He stretched out his fingertips, and when he finally touched her hand, with a whimper that filled the darkness, she clung convulsively to it. He ached with relief when, instantly, she seemed to know him.

Thank god. The bruising on her tortured body took his euphoric height in finding her and plunged it to ink-stained depths. *I couldn't bear to put her through more pain.*

Connor lowered down onto the stinking mattress. Crumbling the handcuff from Rebekah's wrist in a passing clutch of his hand, he dusted the filings from his palm as he gently curled her into his chest and breathed, "I'm sorry, so sorry, honey."

Listening again to her lethargic heart rate, Connor clenched his jaw in anger as even the relief of him being here barely kicked it into second gear. *To get that much venom into her system he must have bitten her.* Connor's temper flared as he rued the missed opportunity to grind Sebastian to dust.

Following the trail of Sebastian's scent on her skin, Connor cradled her wrist and raised her injured hand to his lips. Closing his mouth over the bite, he sucked gently, tasting the iron-tinged bitterness of Sebastian as he cleaned the wound and stroked his cold tongue firmly over the torn skin to calm the burning. Rebekah lay limply against him, and he was consoled that her trust was so complete. He rubbed his chin gently over her hair in a caress as he murmured again, "I'm sorry, honey."

Connor wanted to take her home to the eco-shelter. *But there is no time, the council are waiting.* Gently shifting Rebekah onto his lap and wrapping her in the thin blanket, he enfolded her in his arms. He felt at peace as his agony began to melt away. *I'm definitely not going to last three years.* In the couple of months since he had met her, he had died a million times. The rollercoaster ride was un-abating.

"Hey, let's get you out of here," Connor said, rising smoothly to his feet. Pulling the blanket higher to protect Rebekah against the rushing wind, he took off for Julian's house.

At Connor's approach, Julian opened the door and stepped aside. "I've got the medical supplies you asked for." He jerked his chin towards the back of the house, and Connor swept down the hallway and into the old kitchen.

Instruments which covered every possible scenario were laid out across the surface of a solid wooden table. Connor settled Rebekah on to it, hitched one hip and rested beside her.

Looking into her face for the first time, Connor buried his emotions deep. Rebekah bore the marks of a prize fighter. Her cheekbone and eye socket had come off worst. *She fought.* His gaze dropped to her collarbone, and he dug a deeper hole to bury his feelings. He knew his anger would not help.

Connor reached out to trace the break. It was a compression fracture, but long shards of the bone were still bonded. "So far, so good," Connor mumbled on a smile. As his cold probing fingers made contact, remorse opened his heart to her pain, and he felt the grinding of the bone more deeply than she seemed to. He slipped into 'doctor' mode and manipulated the loose fragments back into place.

Rebekah winced as the weight of his touch hurt, but she bore it with fierce concentration.

"I'm sorry, nearly there," Connor said. He finally taped a dressing in place, and felt relief when he met her gaze and the haunted look on her face melted away.

Smiling gently, knowing the worst was over, he bound her arm to her side, immobilizing her shoulder. "Just until we get you back home," he said.

The purple lesions on her breast and the bruises inside her thighs were hard for him to witness. He wanted to ask, but he knew she would misunderstand. Sebastian's words haunted him. *If Sebastian has... possessed her, then I will make it better.* He would take her pain, that charred-toffee aroma which washed through her every time she thought of Sebastian, and he would love her until she could no longer think of anyone but him. But he dare not ask.

Julian appeared in the doorway and his eyes strayed over the debris of Connor's ministrations. "You know, you really must get your own place." He raised his hand, forestalling Connor's response. "And no, examination room 2 of the surgical wing does not qualify." He darted a piercing look at Connor, and in a vampire breath, too low and fast for Rebekah to hear, he said, "They're here for you. It is time."

"Look after her. The binding will survive the journey back, but go as slow as you dare."

"That won't be a problem. I think the circus is in town." Julian allowed himself a grim smile. "The word is out, and the courtroom gallery is bursting at the seams. At least Serge is playing into our hands by wanting bragging rights, and taking you in himself. It gives me time."

"True. You can get to the eco-shelter and back before the hearing starts," said Connor.

Julian nodded. "I'll give you a minute." He smiled at Rebekah before he left.

Connor was grateful for Julian's practised, detached facade. It served them well today, but the most dangerous part of the plan was yet to come.

In a gesture that he had used a million times, Connor turned to Rebekah and slipped his hand to the nape of her neck, gently lifting her chin and studying her face. His cold fingertip grazed the bruises on her left cheek, and he sighed as he saw the worry which her veiled lashes could not hide.

"I have been called before the council." He confirmed her fears. "Julian will get you home. But I will be back, I promise." The certainty in his voice resonated. *I will not let her down again.* He stared into her brown eyes until their depths warmed to the chocolate hue which had him addicted. He dropped a kiss onto her upturned mouth and was gone, stirring a breeze which tightened goosebumps over her skin, reminding her that she was still alive.

Left alone, perched on the kitchen table with Connor's promise still ringing in her ears, she closed her eyes, savoring his citrus-fresh scent still hanging in the air, knowing it would be gone all too soon. When she opened them again, Julian was standing there staring at her. She jolted in surprise, and, for a moment, pain shrieked through her collarbone.

"I'm sorry." Julian clearly felt her pain as a vibration, and his imagination provided the rest.

Rebekah smiled. "I'm sorry. You startled me."

"I have something to ask... it's a lot to ask." Julian's eyes skimmed the bruises on her face.

"Ask me. If it has anything to do with helping Connor, I'll do it."

Julian's blank expression focused Rebekah's attention. "I need human blood, a lot of it. I need *your* blood.

Rebekah could imagine he felt like the worst vampire to walk the earth. It *was* a lot to ask, but she had no hesitation. "Take it.' Julian did not need to tell her it was life or death, she already knew that.

Without appearing to move, Julian, his shoulder draped in a catheter lead, was suddenly clutching an empty infusion bag and a tourniquet.

Rebekah blinked in surprise.

Julian was only the second vampire Rebekah had ever spoken to, and as he deftly rigged up a saline drip to help her body replace fluids, she watched him carefully. A million questions filled her head. *But, the only one that matters is, will Connor be okay?* But she felt foolish even thinking it.

"He'll be okay." Julian said with ferocious honesty, "You know him, or you should by now. He's waited a hundred years for you, he's not about to leave you now."

"Thank you, Julian." Rebekah smiled gently. "And you? Two hundred years and still waiting... or have *you* found her?"

"Oh, I think you know the answer to that one." Julian's lips curved in a wry grin. "I'm not there yet, but I'm trying." Animation melted away as he sank into deep thought, and just as Rebekah was wondering if she should fake a cough to bring him back to earth, he breathed fervently, "Tell her to wait for me."

"And, I think *you* know the answer to that one." Rebekah smiled. "But I'll tell her."

The bruising on Rebekah's skin stood out more fiercely against the pallid complexion of blood loss and, as the infusion bag became full, her head began to drop as drowsiness set in.

Julian withdrew the catheter needle, and as she folded her arm over a ball of cotton wadding to stop the bleeding, he held out two painkillers. "Here. Take these, and then I better get you home. Connor will be climbing the walls until I make an appearance."

The journey home was one of lightheaded euphoria for Rebekah. The combination of painkillers and thinned blood worked like a charm.

When Julian left, she lay out on her bed in her cavern, where Connor's scent was strongest. It permeated her sheets and her favorite clothes, and the fabric of her mattress remembered his weight.

She was back in familiar surroundings, but still waiting to feel better. *And I will, once I see him again.*

In that dark basement, the door swinging open had struck terror into her as she braced herself for another assault. But the sound of his voice had punched a hole in her fear, and hope had made her beaten body glow. *He touched me, and everything was all right. I need that now.*

Her bruises throbbed as she supported her arm with a pillow and tried to get comfortable. *He was so gentle, and his face...* Rebekah sighed. His face had all the usual angles and shadows which took her breath away. *But there was more. His face said it all, he's in trouble.*

She couldn't erase the dread that Connor might not return.

He'd be angry if he knew Julian asked for my blood. But Rebekah could not regret finally doing something for Connor that his pride would never have allowed. *He needed me, and Julian had no such qualms.*

Julian had mentioned using dialysis to remove Sebastian's venom from the blood he had taken, but the thing she latched onto was that, it may take a few days, but Connor was coming back.

Fatigue settled an iron grip on her heart as it struggled with the balance of an oxygen deficient bloodstream and the exhaustion of her fear. Slipping beneath a blanket of slumber became an irresistible lure, and her last clear thought was of Connor. *He will keep his promise.*

<><><>

Putting the next step of the plan into action, Julian walked into the blood dispensary at the hospital and sought out the familiar figure of Charles, the blood technician. *If anyone knows where Anthony is right now, he will.* Julian was aware the council was waiting.

"Good evening, Charles. Have you seen Surgical Assistant Anthony?"

"He's waiting for Doctor Connor to start rounds, in the surgical wing, I think."

"Ah." Julian joined Charles behind the dispensary counter and drew him to one side. Dropping his voice, he said, "I'm afraid Doctor Connor will not be returning to the hospital. Can you make sure Assistant Anthony receives extra blood rations, he'll be pulling a double shift."

Charles was stuck on Julian's first announcement. "Not returning to the hospital? But why?"

Julian leveled a steady stare at the small wiry vampire. "You will hear soon enough. Doctor Connor is facing charges of 'threatening the food supply'." Julian shook his head. "And this time, there is no question. He is guilty."

"I don't believe it."

"Right now, I need to talk with Surgical Assistant Anthony, if you'll excuse me."

Leaving a bemused Charles muttering under his breath, Julian exited through the side door and was soon moving through Connor's territory. The I.V. bag of Rebekah's blood was warming his side where it lay secured under the layers of his shirt and coat. *Now, to find Anthony.*

Charles had said the surgical wing. *Examination room 2.* Even Anthony thought of that as Connor's home, so, Julian tried there first.

"Anthony," Julian said, as he entered the examination room, recognized Anthony's hefty bulk resting in the corner, and bore down upon him.

Anthony's body jerked, his revival sleep evaporating instantly. "I'm waiting to begin rounds with Doctor Connor," he mumbled sheepishly. He had literally been caught napping.

Brushing aside Anthony's embarrassment, Julian said bluntly, "Doctor Connor is on trial in an hour, and he will be sentenced to death."

Anthony did a double take. His eyes moved to the empty doorway as though he expected Connor's arrival to prove Principal Julian wrong. "What?"

Julian plowed on. "I will be calling upon you to prepare him for transportation to Storage Facility Eight."

Fire and Ice: Survival

"Doctor Connor?" Anthony's brow creased in confusion.

Julian dropped a hand onto Anthony's bunched shoulder, and looked him in the eye. "Anthony, pay attention, Doctor Connor needs your help."

The younger vampire nodded. Confirming he was up to speed, he said briskly, "What do you need?"

"When you prepare Doctor Connor for transportation, you will substitute the muscle relaxant injection with saline solution. Connor will take care of the rest." Julian paused.

"Okay, and then?"

"When he's admitted to the storage facility, you must find him and rehydrate him with this." Julian held out the bulging infusion bag, and waited.

"But it will be too late. The pronouncement rounds are daily. He could be twenty-four hours into dehydration by then." Anthony was horrified.

Julian was relieved. Anthony hadn't thought to argue. Connor was right that he would help without question. *It saves me threatening him, because in this case, refusal is not an option.* "We have bought him time." As Anthony opened his mouth to speak, Julian held up his hand, demanding that he be allowed to finish. "His rate of dehydration will be slowed by drinking four vials of human blood before he's sent into storage, so, he will have time."

"But his body still has to metabolize an animal blood infusion. Rehydration will be too slow, even if human blood is still present, it will take time he hasn't got." Anthony frowned as if solving a puzzle.

"Unless... the infusion you give him is one hundred percent human blood," Julian breathed quietly.

"But where-?"

Julian drew Anthony's gaze by holding out the bag of blood again.

"You mean? But how? Where?"

"Just take it, Anthony. Explanations can wait. Doctor Connor can't," said Julian. "You have to get it into him in time, or..."

132

Chapter 12

Connor cooperated with his guardsmen escort, matching their pace, even though his natural inclination was for a higher velocity. He obediently followed them in to the council anteroom and sat on a wooden bench to await his summons.

Down the hallway, the vampire community filed into the courtroom.

"Well, Councilor, enjoy your day in court," Connor murmured as Serge entered and took up a position opposite his prisoner. Serge's smile of anticipation stretched his crinkled cheeks tight and satisfaction glittered in his amber gaze.

Connor tapped out a tune on the parquet floor with his boot, just to irritate Serge, and took pleasure watching the guardsman struggle with his own amusement.

A cry echoed down the hall. "Call the prisoner to the dock."

Connor silently entered the courtroom. Six rows of pale faces tracked his progress as he crossed in front of them and stepped up into the dock. Exuding the easy grace of a gladiator, Connor awaited the arrival of his opponent as Marius, Julian, and Alexander took their seats on the dais, behind the jurors' bench.

"You are charged with 'threatening the food supply'. How do you plead, Doctor Connor?" said Julian.

"Guilty." Connor's voice rang out.

In vampire culture, although lying was not expected, they were usually more creative with the truth and tried to wriggle off the hook. *Only a fool welcomes decades in Storage Facility Eight.* To stand before the court and baldly admit to the deception Connor had perpetrated was unheard of.

He almost laughed at the confusion radiating from the gallery. They could see their hopes of entertainment slipping away.

The spark in the eyes of the jurors showed their surprise. Marius shrugged in detached disappointment, and Alexander's gaze lit with keen interest as he clearly wondered why Connor so willingly gave himself up.

"Principal Julian, if I may?" Serge rose to his feet, his parchment dry skin glowing with satisfaction.

"Continue, Councilor," Julian replied.

"Will the court demand that Doctor Connor explain his bizarre behavior?" Serge preened as all eyes reluctantly turned to him.

Connor raised a brow. *I am not sure which part Serge considers to be bizarre. Perpetrating the crime, or admitting to it so bluntly?* He waited with interest as Julian decided which tack to take.

Julian said flatly, "Doctor Connor, please tell the court why you chose to take a human pet."

Connor drew to his full height and looked down at Serge, sensing the thrum of excitement which tinted his jaundiced complexion with a pink glaze. *Serge wants his pound of flesh.*

Arranging an empty smile on his face, Connor said, "No, I will not justify my actions to the court."

Serge spluttered, "The court will compel Doctor Connor to comply."

Julian registered his annoyance by picking up his gavel. Having decided enough was enough, he was about to declare as much, when Connor spoke again.

Connor's smile was genuine this time. "What penalty would you have the court impose for my being in contempt?" His direct gaze made it clear his contempt was for Serge alone. "I am already resigned to the death of locked-in syndrome. Maybe you would add ten more years at stage-two to the sentence?" Connor shook his head. "Don't be ridiculous."

Serge's jaws snapped shut as words deserted him.

Connor grinned openly as Julian called Serge to order.

"Do you have anything further to add, Doctor Connor? Any mitigating circumstances that the court should take into consideration?" asked Julian, his face tight with displeasure.

Connor knew he was backing Julian into a corner, and his sentence would now be harsher to reflect the disrespect of his outburst. "I have nothing further, Principal Julian," he said meekly.

"Very well." Julian sighed. "As decreed by vampire law, I sentence you to the mandatory sentence of locked-in syndrome."

He scanned the faces in the gallery. Connor's performance had stirred their expressions from bored to curious. "With an additional penalty of fifteen years at stage-two for your contempt of this court." Julian's attention zeroed in on Connor with mock severity. "You will be taken from the courtroom to Storage Facility Eight to begin your sentence with immediate effect."

His gavel strike signaled the end of the trial and Julian nodded to the council guards. "Take the prisoner down."

The Principal's disdainful pronouncement conveyed that the trusted doctor had disgraced the entire vampire race. The vampires in the gallery appeared to be carved in stone – shock radiated from them like a heat haze.

Before the vibration of the gavel strike had faded, Connor left the dock. With the manners befitting his station, he paused in front of the bench and inclined his head to the jurors before sweeping from view.

Doctor Connor was being transported to Storage Facility Eight to start a death sentence, and Serge's face glowed with satisfaction.

Connor smiled as fifteen guards jostled for room in the corridor outside the anteroom. "Not taking any chances then," he muttered as the sea of white faces parted to let him through. *Do they seriously think I'll make a run for it?*

Once he was back inside the small anteroom, the door closed with an emphatic click, and a key grated in the lock. Connor's grin widened. *A locked door would not hold me. It's just mind games.*

Connor knew the form, although he was usually on the other side of the fence as the doctor of record at trials where the death penalty was handed out. *The warden will be waiting for me. Anthony will be here within the hour.* No vampire had ever resisted being prepared for transport. *After all, escape would be a hollow victory when it cuts off access to human blood.* Without it, desiccation would be slow and painful as his brain centers surrendered to insomniac dementia.

Connor reached inside his jacket and extracted the four vials of human blood Julian had given him. *As good a time as any.* Connor popped out the stoppers and downed them one by one.

Moments later, the door opened and Anthony entered, accompanied by the warden who would escort Connor into storage. He had the opaque lacklustre complexion of someone who lives almost entirely in the dark.

Connor acknowledged the flash of apology which warmed Anthony's brown gaze. The transportation trolley, upon which rested a lidless steel coffin, became the elephant in the room when the warden dragged it over the threshold.

"Doctor Connor." Anthony's blank expression masked his reluctance as he prepared the syringe of muscle relaxant.

Connor nodded curtly. "Anthony."

A muscle ticked in his assistant's clenched jaw and Connor took pity on him. *Better get this over with.* "Coffin?"

"If you wouldn't mind," said Anthony.

"I have to say, I long for the days of wooden coffins. Still, we have to move with the times, hmm?" Connor climbed into the steel coffin shell, and lay down inside it. He shrugged until he had found a degree of comfort, lifting his chin as he said, "Ready."

Inserting the needle vertically up into Connor's carotid artery, Anthony pushed the plunger home in a quick, practiced movement. Connor's body relaxed, his mouth dropped open as the weight of his jaw sagged, and his eyelids drooped.

Anthony stared into the slackened features and wondered if he should close the eyelids. He dared to drag his fingers down over them, but they drifted open again, hanging there in a hooded gaze. He was uncomfortable knowing that, even in the grip of muscle relaxant, Connor's conscious thought would have remained.

The warden clicked three steel bands into place across Connor's prone form. One secured his chest and biceps, one molded to his pelvis, and the final one fitted over his thighs.

"I will take it from here," said the warden, and, with the assistance of a gray-complexioned colleague, he lifted the coffin and whisked Connor's body out through the door. Anthony remained glued to the spot as if turned to stone, like an actor on the stage no longer part of the plot.

The muffled thud of the main doors of the council building closing acted like the click of a hypnotist's fingers, and Anthony blinked several times. "Julian better know what he's doing."

◇◇◇

The warden and his aide progressed at a brisk run through the night.

Connor's clothes became damp as a drizzle of rain clung to the fibers, but they would dry out in time. *After all, I have fifty five years, Julian is harsh.*

The gray stone walls of Storage Facility Eight loomed in Connor's peripheral vision, and he felt the change in both the temperature and weight of the air when they entered. As the steel door slid back into place, the rubber seal deadened the sound to a dull thump which echoed inside Connor's chest. A yellow glow of a flashlight danced over the walls, and finally, as the base of his coffin grated on stone, he came to rest.

Left alone in the dark, Connor carefully expanded his chest and sucked in the stagnant atmosphere of the stage-one storage chamber. He flexed his fingers, reassuring himself that Anthony was on his side and had substituted the muscle relaxant with a saline shot. Connor was faced with continuing the deception he had started in the council anteroom, and faking it as best he could. The hardest part had been not allowing his thoughts to show on his face, and not allowing his eyes to focus on the passing scenery.

The wardens believed Connor to be awaiting his first pronouncement by a doctor, and that the steel bands were strong enough to restrain him – by the time the muscle relaxant wore off, the dehydration process would have already begun to drain his strength. *No one will check on me, they think I'm paralyzed.*

Even so, with the facility's airtight seals activated, there was no way to walk out of there unnoticed. Everything hinged on Julian's plan.

The high dose of human blood coursing through his system had bought him a few precious hours before graveling would start to set in. The isotopes in the human blood would slow the process, but ultimately, if desiccation exceeded the crucial fifteen percent, he could not be rehydrated and his tissue would petrify. *I need Anthony to perform his rounds before that happens.* Everything could still go wrong.

Connor latched on to his promise to Rebekah. But that led him to visualize the horrors she must have suffered, and he quickly realized that madness lay down that road. Instead, he sought the refuge of revival sleep, and, as Rebekah had done before him, he transformed her name into a litany which would save his sanity.

◇◇◇

Anthony approached the hulking rectangular structure of the storage facility, thankful that an obliging dull blanket of gray cloud covering the sky made an early visit possible. *Good fortune is smiling down upon us.* Striding along at a speed only a notch down from a bull at a gate, with Doctor Connor gone, Anthony adopted the guise of a vampire with a lot on his plate. *With the sudden increase in my workload, my haste will be understandable.*

Rain clung to his damp brown hair, and the tight wet cotton of his soaked shirt brought Connor's restrains to mind. *Faking relaxation must have been almost impossible.*

He remained baffled as to what had happened, and how Doctor Connor ended up in such a dangerous situation. His nerves were raw and the questions were never ending. *But explanations will come later. For now, let's get Connor out of there. It has been twenty hours since transportation. I just hope I'm not too late.*

Anthony adjusted his tweed jacket, and doing up buttons that had never been used before, he concealed the bulk of the infusion bag which was vacuum sealed inside two plastic pouches to contain the odor. Anthony took a deep breath and hammered on the steel door. Waiting for the sigh of the airlock being released before pushing it open, he stepped into the cloying dank atmosphere of the facility.

The chief warden approached when Anthony flicked the switch on his flashlight. The pale yellow beam flitted across unfamiliar features, and Anthony's jaw snapped shut.

Julian had told Anthony not to concern himself about Warden James who had served here for as many years as Anthony could remember. He would recognize Connor in an instant, and would certainly notice if his charge went missing. *Now I know why.*

"I was expecting Warden James?" said Anthony lightly, dropping his light down to spill over the ground and restore shadow to his features. Ignoring James' absence felt wrong, Anthony decided.

The new warden grew by an inch as he stood to attention. "Warden James was given a promotion. I am now the chief warden, Warden Palmer."

"Umm, I'm Doctor Anthony." He also had been promoted, with Connor gone. "I'm here to pronounce deaths. I trust you know the drill?" Anthony pretended to be thinking. "I believe you have a new admission. He may be ready for stage-two." He sought the gray circle of the face turned in his direction. "He was denied blood rations prior to trial. It looks like I will be fast-tracking him."

The warden nodded and whisking efficiently on his heel, he disappeared into the darkness. "This way," his coarse whisper floated back over his shoulder.

Anthony followed the rustle of fabric and kept the thick shadow of Warden Palmer in his sights.

The warden opened the door to the new arrivals chamber, stepped aside and then melted away as he moved back along the corridor.

Anthony listened until he was satisfied he was alone before entering the room. He walked along the row of coffins, flicking his gaze over each expressionless face until he finally met the alert gaze of Connor.

Anthony nodded minutely and Connor smiled.

He carefully withdrew the infusion bag from inside his shirt, and, using a scalpel to slice through the padding of plastic layers, he made a hole through which to connect a catheter tube. He taped

Fire and Ice: Survival

the layers of plastic back into place to contain the smell and settled the infusion bag into Connor's grasp. Working quietly and efficiently, he flicked open the locks on the metal restraints across Connor's body, before inserting the catheter needle into Connor's carotid artery and taping it in place.

Looking into Connor's face, he mimed a squeezing action with his hands and mouthed silently, "Apply constant pressure." Indicating with a tap on his watch that he would return, he nodded abruptly, and left.

Anthony moved silently back along the corridor and sought out the warden. "It is as I expected, he's ready for stage-two."

As the warden made a move to follow the instruction and transfer the offender, Anthony stalled him. "I need to know how many stage-threes are scheduled for skull crushing." He frowned in thought. "Can you report back to me on that? I have others to examine in the stage-two chamber. I will transport the prisoner."

Anthony watched the warden leave. Like all storage facility attendants, he had a very relaxed attitude towards his comatose charges, after all, it was more baby-sitting than guarding. *He would certainly have no reason to distrust a doctor making rounds.*

Making a quick detour, Anthony collected a trolley before he retraced his steps back to Connor. He effortlessly dragged Connor's coffin onto the bed of the trolley and wheeled it at pace along the corridor. He shouldered open the door to the chamber where empty coffins shells were stored. Anthony's torch ranged briefly around the room, and the angular stainless steel containers glinted like teeth in a blackened smile. *All clear. So far, so good.*

"I'll meet you at the main entrance after rounds," Anthony whispered, and he left Connor to continue transfusing the blood. Connor's disappearance would remain undetected. Neither warden of stages one or two would expect him to be in their charge. He had effectively slipped between the cracks, indefinitely.

Connor's hands worked steadily on compressing the bag and maintaining the pressure. Blood shunted up into his neck and he flexed his stiffened muscles tentatively. Feeling the tendons grating, he was glad to have something else to think about. For endless hours he had been mapping the purple bruises on Rebekah's body and trying to keep calm. As the lubrication of blood swelled his tissue and his brain sharpened to crystal clarity, his confidence grew. *It seems to be working out.*

Rolling up to a sitting position, Connor slid out the catheter and massaged the hole in his neck. Satisfied that his vampire speed was fully restored, it took fractions of a second for him to regain his usual confident forceful stride. And, in barely longer than that, he was waiting in the darkened entrance chamber for the weak light of Anthony's flashlight to signal that rounds were finished, and they were getting out of there.

Anthony flicked off the beam in good time, and Connor melted into the darkest corner as he waited. He heard Anthony give the warden his final instruction and dismiss him. Anthony's lone figure approached and Connor fell into step, matching his stride as they both whisked along the exit corridor. Within seconds they were outside, accelerating forward, but keeping their silence. Vampires had acute hearing even when apparently comatose. *Why take chances?* Instead, Connor's hand closed on Anthony's shoulder, conveying a wealth of emotion.

Connor was a fugitive. Anthony, however, needed to return to the hospital and was already late, so, explanations would have to wait. They moved silently through the suburbs of London, and, staying south of the River Thames where vampire clusters were rare, they arrived at the old railway station called Clapham Junction.

Julian said to get a place, and this one is perfect. The large terminal building was like a colossal umbrella below which numerous train tracks converged. Each platform had waiting rooms and ticket offices, and then there were the seized up, rusted trains themselves. *Plenty of places to hide.*

Connor could easily follow the train tracks into many surrounding districts, and, more than that, they provided an express escape route out if trouble came knocking.

The night air was damp, and Connor walked out onto the tracks, balancing on decaying, wooden sleepers which creaked under his weight. He watched Anthony disappear into the gloom, and became still as a stone statue, taking stock. His bulky frame was a blend of jet-black and charcoal, with the moonlight melting his gray eyes to pewter. His bone structure invited moon beams and bent them to his will, dressing his face with intensity. He was a formidable figure which no sensible vampire would consider taking on.

Anthony would return after his shift at the hospital. In the meantime, Connor had begged one last favor of him; to seek out Julian and tell him where Connor had set up residence.

<><><>

Three hours later, Julian and Connor were standing side by side on platform number twelve, congratulating each other on Connor still being alive.

Connor finally opened the topic that had been bothering him since he had set off through the streets after leaving Storage Facility Eight. His lubricated movement was of an engine on high grade oil, and that gave him cause for concern. He asked Julian the question, already knowing the answer.

"The transfusion. It was human blood?"

Julian had the grace to look uncomfortable as he nodded.

A growl rumbled in Connor's throat as he thought of Rebekah's bruised and battered body, finally allowing her face to fill his mind. "Please tell me you didn't?"

"What choice did I have?" asked Julian.

"You could have asked me. It was my choice to make, not yours," Connor replied.

Connor expected an argument and instead he surprised a grin, and in a surge of anger his fist flew out.

Julian's hand closed firmly around it, stopping its forward propulsion three inches from his jaw.

Frozen in the moment of confrontation, his words grating through ground teeth, Connor said, "You could have asked Leizle."

Annoyance flickered for a moment, before Julian said in a reasonable tone, "I'll let you have that one. But there was not time to collect Leizle's blood." He shrugged eloquently. "Rebekah was here in London. Removing Sebastian's venom from her blood remained the fastest solution, and if she had not given it, I doubt you would be here for us to be arguing about it."

Connor's expression relaxed. He withdrew his fist, and a resigned smile tugged at the corners of his mouth.

As the tension drained away, Julian's grin became full blown. "What can I say? I am just glad that you are here to throw that punch. I would do it again."

"I guess you're right, I don't have to like it, though." Connor raised a brow. "I'll feel better once I have checked on Rebekah."

Julian's expression said, 'don't you trust me?'

Connor glanced at his watch. "How much longer is Anthony going to be?"

"Not much longer, but, before he gets here, we need to talk about Sebastian," said Julian. "He's still unconscious."

It was Connor's turn to feel satisfaction. "Good," he said.

"You know this is not over. I hate to state the obvious, but now Serge thinks you're out of the way, he will already be planning his next move."

"You're right, of course. He'll wait for Sebastian to surface, and then he'll know where to look for the eco-shelter. What about you?" Connor asked, "does he suspect your involvement?"

"No, I think not. My condemnation of you at the trial, and the hefty sentence I delivered, has allayed his suspicions." Julian looked at Connor. "In any case, he only understands allegiance as a means to an end. I have nothing to gain in aligning myself with you, and it won't occur to him that two vampires could actually be friends."

"So, your position on the Council is secure?"

"For now, yes," he said.

Connor suddenly turned his head and took a deep breath. "Ah, Anthony's here."

He was some distance away, but his approach was fast. *He's obviously keen to get answers.*

Anthony arrived as a silent apparition, stirring a flurry of autumn leaves. He sought out the sentinel forms of Connor and Julian, and stepped forward to greet them.

"Doctor Connor, Principal Julian." He pushed windswept hair from narrowed eyes. "You look well. That is good to see."

I need to see Rebekah but Anthony deserves an explanation. Connor had involved him twice now in their subterfuge. *The first time, he had no idea he helped save Leizle.* It was a measure of Anthony's faith in Connor that he swallowed the plausible lie without question. *I'll leave that lie intact. He's better kept in the dark for his own protection. But this time there's no getting away from it, he has to know.*

"I am sure you have questions, Anthony, but first, thank you for your help." His fingers stroked over the puncture wound in his neck where the catheter had pierced his skin.

"I was glad to, you know that. But now, I need to know why you were sentenced to death." His attention moved to Julian. "And from where you took the human blood. When the theft is discovered and a storm breaks over my head, what am I to tell the council?"

"There will be no storm." Connor's eyes glittered. "Julian took the blood from a human girl, not from the farm."

Anthony's jaw dropped. "A human girl? But how?"

"She is *my* human girl, and the reason I'm serving a sentence in Storage Facility Eight," Connor said, his low tone rumbling.

As Anthony's shocked eyes searched his face, Connor waited to see which way things would go. As the silence grew, he rocked on the balls of his feet. *Throwing a punch is more Anthony's style.*

Anthony's considerable bulk appeared unhappy being confined by cloth. Every move set his muscles rippling in protest. His mortal frame was thirty years old. He had been the kid in glasses, and being bullied at school had transformed him into a young adult who pumped iron at the gym. His strength, however, had not saved him when he had been drawn into an alley in London's Soho district to break up a fight. He had been a vampire for sixty years.

In vampire terms, he's a juvenile and I can take him. He knew Anthony had no empathy for humans, but he *had* forged a relationship with Connor. *He's not an emotional wasteland, but will it be enough?*

Forty-two seconds later, Anthony had not moved.

That's a good sign. Connor relaxed a little and decided to push him. "I'm a fugitive. I won't ask you to do any more than you have already, but I *am* asking for your silence."

The frown on his face eased. "I can do that."

Connor shot Julian a warning glance. He knew Julian wanted more, and with Connor in hiding it would make life easier. *But it will have to wait.*

"My silence, you can count on." Anthony shot a look at Julian, and, as though he had read his mind, he added, "Nothing more."

Connor shook Anthony's outstretched hand firmly. "Thank you."

Half an hour later, Connor left Julian talking with Anthony, and filling in the gaps. *We are not out of the woods yet. But we have Anthony on our side, for now. I just need to keep an eye on him.*

◇◇◇

The Kent countryside was eerily silent as Connor raced across cool green grass, dyed black by the moonlight. He was used to the silence of creatures shrinking in his presence. Birds swallowed their song. The warm-blooded rabbit, fox and their furry cousins, froze, their wide-eyed stare hoping to catch a glimpse of him as he passed them by. He saw them, of course, but nothing would entice him to bite through their fur or feathers when his Rebekah was waiting.

Connor raced into the mouth of the tunnels, hurtling towards her. It had been almost three days, and he longed to see her face.

He registered Leizle's presence in the dining cavern as he passed by, and with a sigh, he wheeled around and retraced his path.

Appearing back in the doorway, as Connor dug his hand into his pocket, he caught her eye. "Leizle." He opened his palm to reveal a key threaded onto a bronze-colored ribbon. "Julian said to give

Fire and Ice: Survival

you this. His front door is always unlocked, and this is a key to the small sitting room at the back of the house." Connor smiled slowly. "He says if you will dice with death, at least you can hide at his place, even if he's not there. You are to lock yourself in."

A smile lit her features. "So, he thinks of me?"

"Occasionally." Connor grinned.

As he whisked around, blurring Leizle's vision, she blurted urgently, "Annabelle is gone. Oscar and Greg took her across country to join the other eco-group."

"I'm surprised. I know Seth and Greg were comrades, but still-?" Connor's brows climbed to a peak of enquiry.

"They were certainly surprised to have visitors." Leizle's expression was comforting. "They blindfolded her. She won't know her way back."

"I am just glad that Rebekah will never see her again," Connor said. *Neither will I, which is more important to Annabelle's life expectancy.* He remained on the spot long enough to say the words, and then he was gone.

"Later," she called out, laughing, as the breeze of his passing flapped her hair about her face. "I guess you're in a hurry."

Connor was happy to dismiss Annabelle from his mind. *I have other loose ends to consider.* The next few days would be critical and he knew, despite Julian's assurances, Serge would cause problems at every turn. And then there was Anthony. *He will want to feel that he is doing the right thing.* He knew he could convince him to help them. *But to do that, I have to be there to answer his questions, when they start coming, as they surely will.*

Traveling the tunnels down into the bowels of the human eco-shelter, reality struck Connor. To protect the most important thing in his world, he would have to leave her again. He buried the guilt and concentrated on making the most of the time he did have. *For now, I am here and it is enough.*

Guilt was the price of loving, something Connor had never thought possible. But when Rebekah's heart thundered in her chest, holding her close, he could feel it resonating through him and imagine he was alive again. He rounded the last bend, flexing his diaphragm to fill himself with her scent. He smiled as he took in his fix, and locked it inside.

Connor slowed to a walk, and entered Rebekah's cavern, his eyes focusing on the bed hidden in the darkest corner. However, for him, refracted light danced in his vision as she stirred in her sleep. The covers dragged over her skin, and the glittered discharge of static electricity made him falter. If he felt pain in the mortal sense, a migraine would have thundered through his brain.

Sitting down on the side of the bed, he was content to watch her sleep, convinced he could feel the blood in his veins pulsing in time with her heartbeat. *Her blood.* Her lashes fluttered, her eyes opened and focused on his face, and he felt as though the sun warmed his skin.

"Hey," Rebekah croaked, as sleep rolled away.

"Hey, back," he said softly. The subdued lighting cast black hollows below his white cheekbones as he sat motionless. The eerie sense that he could only be seen because he chose it, was etched into every line of his preternatural face. His silver gray eyes found hers, and she smiled.

Connor was at a loss. He had never felt indecisive in his life, alive or dead, but now, looking at her face with the dark circles under her eyes, he had so much emotion that he could not speak. The thought of Sebastian punched a hole in his chest. *What did he do to her?*

Rebekah sat up, reaching out to touch his face. His thoughts were swimming in the turbulent gray of his eyes as she whispered, "Don't talk, Connor."

He overwhelmed her as always. As the words left her mouth, his cool lips sought hers and he kissed her, rolling her down gently and laying out beside her. His fingers traced over the healing indents of Sebastian's teeth on her collarbone, the mark on her breast, and moved to soothe the inside of her thigh, where the bruising stained her with yellowed rainbow hues.

Finally, Connor placed his fingertip over the pinprick wound in her arm where Julian had taken blood. He looked into her face. "You didn't have to." He kissed her lips and breathed, "But thank you." His brow furrowed as, holding onto the pain stabbing through his center at her thick honey scent, he dragged his lips over her mouth and molded his body carefully to hers.

But his closed eyes could not unsee the bruises on her body and the images nibbled away at him like a boiling current in a tranquil sea.

Rebekah gripped his hair with her good hand. "I've missed you, Connor," she whispered desperately. There was something in him that scared her. His pensive expression screamed at her that he was holding back and something was wrong. A tear rolled down her cheek.

Connor moved up onto his elbow and looked down into her face. His gut curled as his demon stirred the acid in his stomach, and Sebastian's face leered at him; 'You'll not be enough for her now'.

He brushed his thumb across the purple bruise under her eye and put the salty tears to his lips. "I don't want to hurt you." His eyes softened as he stroked his hand over her hip.

"Are you leaving me?" Rebekah croaked.

"Am I leaving you? Never," he hissed, pulling back to bore his gaze into hers. "How can you think that?"

"You don't seem happy." Her tone was anguished. "I feel it."

Connor took a deep breath. "I'm scared." His smooth features crumbled for a moment. He moved his hand onto her thigh again. "I don't know what he did. I don't want to hurt you... to remind you of him."

Rebekah put her palm to his firm cheek as she pulled his hand up and moved her thigh, so he could cover her and feel her damp heat burning his palm. "He didn't touch me. I would have died first." She watched his eyes darken as his cool fingertips trembled. "No one, but you, Connor, no one."

His jaw clenched as his fingers stroked and he watched her eyes melt. Relief eased his tight muscles, and, clamoring for the infusion of her heat, he finally moved his body over hers.

As she closed around him, taking him deep into her fiery core, he froze, and with every tremble that swept through her, he felt whole again. The rush of each ruby blood-cell pounding through her heart and flushing her skin played like a symphony inside him. The pleasure swelled to intense pain as his hips twitched and he ached to add to her bruises. He dug deeper into revival sleep as, finally, he moved, and the molten heat of her trailed wild fire through the synapses of his brain.

He drowned in her soft sighs, feeling the ghost of Sebastian being exorcised with every breath she took. Immersing himself as the trembles of release raced through her, and he began to believe. In the delicious afterglow, he took her into his arms and cradled her beside him, and pulling the branding heat of her thigh across his stomach was the sweetest torture he had ever known.

As he lay drawing strength from the after-quakes of desire disturbing the rhythm of her body, he hitched up onto an elbow and stared down at her flushed face.

Resting his hand over her heartbeat, he said, "This is so hard for me. I need you to know that... don't take this for granted." He kissed her surprised, open mouth, dipping his tongue inside to taste. "Your scent claws at my stomach, and my thirst for you is no less now than it has ever been."

Connor sighed, stroking over the puncture wound in her arm as he remembered the feeling of her blood melting through his tissue.

"I wondered if having your blood flowing through me would make it easier." He quirked his lip. "But afraid not, honey, still wanting to tear your throat out." Connor suddenly looked into her eyes. "Sorry, that was blunt."

"No, it is good that I know. So, I've have a tiger by the tail, huh?" Rebekah smiled at him.

"Well, not only his tail." He growled at her and gently rolled over, bracing his body over hers. He rested his forehead on her brow and, feigning a lecherous grin, he proceeded to demonstrate the other parts of him which she could claim as her own.

Finally, as she was drifting off to sleep in his arms, she lifted her head and murmured, "Will you be here when I wakeup?"

He savored the warm breeze her breath fanned over his skin for a moment. Regret laced his tone as he said, "I'm sorry, honey. I've got to go. But I'll be back as soon as I can."

Fire and Ice: Survival

"But you're supposed to be dead, now." Rebekah tried to nudge sleep back to find a clear thought.

"I know, but London is a big place, and I need to know what is going on. I can't leave Julian to face the music alone." Connor smiled into Rebekah's hooded sleepy gaze. "You never know, maybe I can persuade Julian to play 'Little John' to my 'Robin Hood', and we can all leave London for good." His words were flippant but there was a touch of sober consideration. "But don't worry, I'll be back before you know it," he whispered. *If only I could stay... I should stay.* Wisps of Sebastian's ghost unfurled tentacles inside him and tainted his thoughts.

Chapter 13

The wind whistling through the train station whispered of dark thoughts and foreboding. At least, that was Connor's perception from where he stood buried in the darkest shadow, waiting for Julian's daily report. He had been in London too long, and his unease at leaving Rebekah grew stronger with every passing day. *When Sebastian had her, she thought her life was over. She needs me.* "If Julian still has no news on the bastard, I shall bite the bullet and leave London," he muttered. *After all, vampire coma can last anything between days and months.*

Connor held up a hand in salute as he first felt, and then saw Julian arrive. The flash of the gesture in the shadow was enough to draw Julian's gaze.

Julian agreed. "There is nothing you can do in London without being seen," he said. "And as much as I enjoy the sights of Clapham Junction, I can't say I'll miss it if I don't have to visit here for a week or two."

"Anthony seems calmer, now that he knows the whole picture." Connor's raised eyebrow acknowledged the white lie. Anthony knew of Rebekah, and Connor's commitment to her, but Leizle and the rest were complications they decided not to burden him with.

"You saved my bacon there. Serge making inquiries about your dehydration levels was rattling Anthony. You came back just in time. He's had time to get used to the idea now."

"You know, I never meant for you to risk so much." Connor frowned fiercely. "And now, involving Anthony is a situation I feel responsible for."

Julian snorted in annoyance. "*I* involved Anthony. The rescue plan was *all* mine. But trust me, he was glad to do it. Like it or not, vampires are not as callous as we'd like to think." He paused thoughtfully. "Hope is not such a bad thing, Connor. It's eternal boredom which is the real killer."

"And what about Sebastian? When do I get to kill him?"

"I'll know when he surfaces. Serge will act, and I will shut him down in council. That will not be the end of it, but, we'll know he's about to make his next play. And then, Sebastian is all yours."

Connor grunted his satisfaction.

"I'll look out for Anthony. He trusts me now. It's Rebekah who needs you, and you should go."

Connor took one more moment to consider. "You know where I am, and hopefully we won't see Sebastian for a while." With a final nod, he left.

A copse of silver birch trees, their bone-like trunks glowing in the moonlight, marked Connor's progress. Unease crawled through him. They reminded him of bad luck and dark times. *Being further away from this place has to be a good thing.* He gladly left them behind and covered a few more miles until, finally, he picked up speed and made the final approach to the new eco-shelter. As he passed silently through the tunnels, he was surprised by a feeling that he was 'home'. So, I already have 'a place', he thought as he paused on the threshold of Rebekah's cavern.

His skin was chilled by the cold night air, and Connor warmed it with the friction of his palms. Pushing his hair back from his brow, he paused with his fingers interlaced over his head as he absorbed the details of her face. Her sleeping figure was a familiar sight which ignited a glow inside his dead chest, and he put aside the regret that he had not come back sooner.

Connor eased into her bed and took her into his arms. He kissed her shoulder, and when her sleeping breath faltered, he smiled against her skin. His smile faded as he breathed her in. Her aroma, the pheromone-blend which, like a perfumier, he could list the ingredients of, had an accent he did not recognize. He frowned as his palm drifted down over the contour of her hip, and then he felt her heart jolt, fear spiked inside her, and she jerked away from his embrace.

He let her go, partly because restraining her would add to her bruises, and partly because his mind was battling with the altered composition of her scent. *Sebastian's venom? That surely would have dissipated by now?*

He expected her to see it was him, and return to his arms, and when she didn't, his mind reeled.

Connor sat up, a crooked grin tugging at his lips. He held up his hands as if she pointed a gun at his chest, and said, "Hey, I'm sorry, honey. I should have let you sleep." His gray eyes darkened, confusion moving in their depths. "I guess I couldn't wait." He smiled apologetically. "It's been a while. But I'll be good, I promise." Remorse flooded him as he looked at her tired face and noticed that the circles beneath her eyes were dark purple, now. "You're exhausted."

But she didn't relax. His expression shifted to concern as he took a deep breath, and froze. His nostrils flared, and for a heart-stopping moment, Rebekah thought he suspected. S*melled it, tasted it, or whatever the hell he does.* She hoped she would not have to tell him.

"What is it?" he whispered.

Her brain screamed, 'say something'. "Nothing, you just scared me." Her mind skittered around, looking for the words to make this come out right.

Connor reached out to touch her, to bring her back to him, and instinctively she folded her body away. *If he touches me, he'll sense it, and he'll hate himself.*

Everything he thought he knew crumbled. Shock bleached his face, and his voice was harsh as he said, "What did I do, what has changed?"

His thoughts moved into territory which terrified him. And then, the last thing he ever expected was the only thing he could think of.

"Sebastian." The devastating conclusion burst from him as a ricochet.

The horror in Rebekah's eyes made his nightmare a reality.

His face twisted in torment and, in the seconds their gazes met, his distress swelled to ferocity. He reared up from the bed and slammed his fist down onto the bedside cabinet, showering them both in splintered wood.

Rebekah cowered as the storm of his fracturing control broke over her head.

Connor shot to his feet, putting the yards between them which kept her safe. He reeled around, exiting the cavern and staggering away. In the silence of the tunnel, he leaned against the wall and hung his head. His tormented mind chased the images of the horror on her face until anguish overwhelmed him. His snarling roar echoed through the caverns.

"I stayed away too long."

He took off along the eco-town corridors, his demons snapping at his heels.

Rebekah's bruises had faded to a dull blush while he had been gone. He thought Anthony's support and safeguarding Julian's standing on the council was important. *I should have listened to my gut. I should have stayed.* She's strong and she'll be my Rebekah again, thought Connor with determination. As much as he loved her heat, he was relishing doing battle with her for all eternity. But before he turned her, he would lay the ghost of Sebastian. *I'm not about to spend an eternity with* him *inside her head.*

But, at this moment, Connor felt powerless. Spiraling out of control, he charged out into the night and took in a lungful of woodland scented air. He inhaled until he thought he would burst but, for once, he needed to cleanse every cell of Rebekah's scent.

Her addictive odor was driving him insane, and a vampire without sanity was worse than one in grave sleep. He embraced the red wave of bloodlust which eroded conscious thought, chasing away his futility.

I reminded her of Sebastian. Blood didn't scare him, but that thought did.

Connor's civilized facade fractured, stripping him of the veneer of humanity as he wrenched his shirt from his shoulders. He needed to hunt, not *dine*, but to stalk prey that could end him. He needed to go where the hunt filled so much of his mind that thinking of this, of her, was no longer possible.

He disappeared into the distance.

◇◇◇

Rebekah shivered uncontrollably. *I hurt him.* Her thundering heart ached as she pressed her palms over it. She knew now what true terror felt like. There was a moment, before he fled the cavern, when she thought he would lose control. *He said I had a tiger by the tail, and I almost experienced the Connor who would tear my throat out.*

"You could never hurt me," she whispered vehemently into the empty space where moments ago his face had been. But in that split second, she was truly terrified of him, and the guilt of that stunned her.

Connor's gray eyes had glowed with the dull ash of anguish. His ferocious white face had looked truly preternatural when he towered over her and battled to hold himself in check. *Yes, he had been terrifying.*

Rebekah knew that every moment they spent together balanced precariously on Connor's control. When his desire peaked, and his hands could not bear to leave her skin, his ability to not break her human bones was a measure of his restraint. *I know every moment we have is only possible because he loves me.* Tears filled her eyes and she slapped them away.

"Oh God, he thinks he reminded me of Sebastian," she whispered, as the tunnels still echoed with his ferocity. "And, I let him." Sinking back onto her pillow, she covered her face with her hands. She knew this moment changed everything. She wanted to call him back, but the distance between them would already be miles.

She hugged her body. *How could I have let him think something so terrible? But how could I tell him the truth?* It was a truth she didn't know for certain, just a small spark of light which she nurtured. It was a daunting concept that she couldn't find the words to acknowledge, even to herself.

But, damn it, I didn't mean to hurt him. The bloody man moves quicker than I can think.

Connor always surprised her when she was sleeping. The safest time for him to travel was in the dead of night, and it was a talisman she held on to, a little like her own Christmas Eve. Every night she climbed into her bed wondering, *will it be tonight?* Waking to find his body curled into her back, and feeling his fingers restlessly stroking her thigh or cupping her breast was part of the fabric of their dream. It was another facet of his adoration that he could not bear not to touch her. It was not always about physical release, often, holding her close and absorbing her heartbeat was what he hungered for. Loving and being loved was the bedrock of everything he suffered.

It always sent a frisson of alarm through her at first, to find him there, as consciousness struggled to push back the blanket of sleep. And she knew that thrilled him. The satisfied growl rumbling in his chest was evidence of it. But when his hand splayed over her belly, and he stroked the heat between her thighs, trembling of a different kind would flood through her.

And so it had been this time. And that was the problem, they had only that one night together since Connor rescued her from Sebastian. As her need for his reassurance grew, so had her fears. *His hand moved over my hip and I freaked out.*

Rebekah could still see his stunned confusion. "How can I get him to come back? Make him listen?"

If she had the time all over again she would just do it. *How hard is it to just say the words. Connor, I'm pregnant?* Very hard, when she knew he would bury himself in self-loathing. *Damn it!*

She had been sure the fatigue was the effect of Sebastian's venom. But exhaustion transformed into tranquillity somewhere along the line. She was so relaxed lately that sleep was a constant lure.

And then she realized she couldn't remember when she last had a period.

That made her sit up and take notice. *If he had been here I would have blurted it out.* But he was away, and her fears grew like a malignant fist of tension inside her until the knot was so tight it strangled her thoughts.

"God, what a mess," Rebekah sighed. *I've never rejected him, so, of course he thinks it's down to Sebastian.* Even if the truth shocked him, it would have been a relief.

"Where does that leave me?" she whispered.

Rebekah rolled over and swung her feet onto the floor, but as she tried to stand, it took more strength than she had. The lethargy weighing her down since Sebastian's venom had tainted her bloodstream washed over her like waves crashing onto a rocky beach. In the end, she turned onto her back and stared at the domed ceiling until her eyes closed and sleep solved her problems. *When I wake up, he'll be here.*

<><><>

The puma froze midstep, nostrils quivering as he scented the night air. Fear burned as an ignited fuse wire through his brain. Sides bellowing in agitation, he chose survival and his haunches bunched, ready to propel him to safety. The dark foliage beside him erupted with movement as the cat leapt.

The puma's front paws lifted from the ground, and a crunching blow to his side broke three ribs, rushed the breath from his body, and rolled him onto his back. The animal grunted as his diaphragm ruptured and he was pressed into the dirt.

Connor hugged the cat's ribcage tightly in one arm as he pinned the flailing back legs with his knees. He pressed his forearm down onto the cat's throat and the animal yelped as his hyoid bone crumbled. Satisfaction purred in Connor's throat as his naked chest flexed and he pulled in the iron rich fumes of the terrified puma's blood.

Going in for the kill, Connor pushed the cat's head up sharply, shoved his own muzzle into the damp fur, and bit down hard, flooding his mouth with heat. He swallowed greedily in time with the fading heartbeat, filling his stomach and staining his chest with blood.

The puma's body lay slack and the gray clouds of the night sky reflected in the glassy stare of the dead eyes when Connor finally released his grip and roared in frustration. He was left still feeling ravenous.

"Fight me," Connor growled. The fierce expression on his face clung to his skull like a mask. In exorcising a demon, he wanted to feel close to the death he missed out on a hundred years ago. But no prey matched his speed and cunning, and the kill lacked danger.

Connor wanted to fear something solid. He wanted something that could wrestle him to the ground and make him terrified that he would not survive it. He wanted a threat he could understand, not the fear which compressed his chest with dread, the fear that he had lost her, his Rebekah, the fear that nothing he could do would put things right, and that Sebastian had won.

In grave sleep he was a ruthless, efficient predator. The cell door of the killing center inside Connor's head had been thrown open, and his hungry tissue gloried in the gluttony of bloodlust. The synapses of his brain glittered with the emotions thundering through his temporal lobe. His vampire sight was honed to terrifying sharpness as he reacted to the slightest rustle in the foliage with lightning-quick reflexes. His brain was more than rehydrated, it was saturated. And still his feral instincts raged out of control. Insatiable thirst filled every space inside his mind, becoming his refuge.

Connor raised his chin, every corded tendon of his throat bulging as though an invisible leash tightened a collar around his neck. Sanity was calling, but he resisted. *I don't want to come back.* As he stared out over the black horizon, the whites of his eyes tinged pink with the blood of his kill, billowing red clouds dulled his vision and his pewter-rimmed pupils had the thousand-mile stare of a tortured soul.

Surviving one hundred years had been a physical challenge Connor had come to enjoy. Supremacy had been addictive. *But how do I fight ghosts?* Rebekah recoiling from his touch had torn a hole in his heart, and he slammed the door shut on the memory. His eyes grew cold, his stare as glassy as that of the puma lying dead in the undergrowth. With his bare torso stained the greasy brown of blood diluted with sweat, he balanced on his haunches, loose wrists resting on knees, for once, unaware of the satisfaction which accompanied the effortless, lubricated movement of being fully fed.

He surged to his feet and broke into an effortless, easy Kenyan run. The muscles of his large frame bunched and relaxed in concert as he accelerated swiftly, increasing to the velocity of desperation. The windchill, had he been human, would have stiffened his face with freezer burn. He honed in on hunting out his next challenge with grim determination as the need to drive Rebekah from his mind threatened to crush him.

Chapter 14

Julian projected calm as he made his way to the jurors' bench and took his seat between Marius and Alexander.

"Court is in session," he announced with quiet authority. A procession of misdemeanors passed before the austere panel of three, and the session had all the indicators of being predictable. Julian was more than content with 'predictable', however, he had his eye on the last listing of the day.

"The last case on the list is the council verses Guardsman Nicholas."

As Julian sought out Councilor Serge, for the first time since he could remember, he did not object to the aged vampire's peculiar odor. In a disconcerting way, he looked forward to it.

"Councilor Serge, I believe the defendant is under your tutelage?" Julian assessed Serge's appearance with a deadpan expression.

"Principal Julian." Serge rose to his feet. The brown cloth of his jacket hung from bony shoulders which lacked the bulk to give it form. "Guardsman Nicholas is under my guidance, yes."

Julian turned toward the tall vampire in the dock. "You are here to answer charges of 'critical harm'. Have you an explanation for the court to consider?"

"I failed to seek confinement when in grave sleep," the young guardsman said. His face, with its deeply carved expression lines, suggested forty human years of experience. By his smell, Julian estimated that he had the same again in vampire years, although he could not be certain.

"Booking your place in the morgue is basic procedure for grave sleep. What were the consequences?" asked Julian, coldly.

"Guardsman Nicholas injured another guardsman, it was nothing serious," Serge jumped in.

Julian arched a brow at Nicholas. "Injured?" Flicking an icy glare Serge's way, Julian continued, "I take issue with your assessment Councilor. Injury is rarely insignificant. How bad was the injury?"

"I broke his left arm." Nicholas' tone was colorless.

"I know," said Julian, and switching his focus, he pinned Serge with his disapproval. "Surgical Assistant Anthony could not repair the damage and the arm was amputated. It's a pity. If we had Doctor Connor's skill at our disposal, the outcome would have been different." Julian turned back to Nicholas and said sharply, "How could you have failed to confine yourself for grave sleep?"

"I thought I had more time," said Nicholas.

The glacial expression in Julian's eyes stripped him of hope.

"Then you were mistaken. You will spend a month where you should have been in the first place, in the morgue. Present yourself for confinement immediately." Julian's anger flashed. "If you cannot master the idiot's guide to being a vampire, why should the rest of us suffer you? Count yourself lucky it is not the Storage Facility I am sending you to."

Nicholas nodded, and without comment, left the courtroom.

Once the door closed behind the condemned vampire, Julian spoke again. "Before we adjourn..." Julian's raised hand captured Serge's attention. "Councilor, can you provide us with an update on Sebastian's condition?" *What I really want to know is, where the hell is he?*

Councilor Serge's sun-starved decrepit appearance perfectly suited the vampire myth of one who dwells in a crypt and hides in the shadows. In contrast, Julian's appearance would never pass as unremarkable. At over six feet tall, he could hammer home an advantage with one glance. He had lived two hundred years ago in an era when being a gentleman signified breeding. This made some think that Julian was not capable of being ruthless. They were wrong.

Julian emanated the authority of a keen intellect. "Well, Serge?" He dropped the councilor title, rudeness rare in him.

"Thank you for your concern." Serge dipped his chin. "He's progressing, but the rehydration of three brain centers is taking

Fire and Ice: Survival

longer than expected." Serge smiled, and, in an unguarded moment, his pale eyes glittered.

He thinks he has the upper hand, thought Julian. "I would like to satisfy myself that he is comfortable. Where would I find him?"

They both knew Sebastian was not a vampire worthy of a visit from a principal, and certainly not from Julian. The attack on Sebastian had been devastating because Connor knew where to hit, where to drive the spike home to shut down the brain and induce vampire coma. *How long that lasts will depend upon the individual, so, is he awake, I wonder?*

Coma vampires were fed intravenously, and kept at the hospital until brain reboot occurred, but not Sebastian. Serge had broken with protocol, knowing that Julian's hands were tied.

Both Serge and Julian were withholding information. Sebastian's location was in Serge's hands, and he believed Connor to be well on the way to desiccation in Storage Facility Eight. *And he clearly enjoys that thought.* It amused Julian that Serge's gleam of triumph was empty.

"I'll gladly inform you when Sebastian is able to receive visitors." Serge smiled.

This was an insult, but Julian bore it. Serge would learn the location of the eco-shelter when Sebastian surfaced. *It's no surprise he doesn't intend to honor the gentleman's agreement he thinks cost Connor his life.*

"He has surfaced then? I'm glad to hear it." It was a shot in the dark, and Julian watched Serge closely.

Serge's quickly veiled surprise confirmed it. *Sebastian's awake. Pity, we'd hoped for longer.* "Give him my condolences on losing his eye."

Julian's blank expression suggested the news was of no importance, but in his mind, he was already drawing up evacuation plans for the eco-shelter.

Rising to his feet and bringing the session to a close, Julian hid his impatience and kept pace with Marius and Alexander as they moved along the corridors. At the door to his chambers, he made his farewells and passed through it, only to re-emerge the instant the halls were empty, leave the building, and disappear into the night.

Two days ago I told Connor to go and be with Rebekah. Damn it, thought Julian, accelerating along the tree-lined streets until the foliage resembled a vertical sea of turbulent waves. *And now, I need him here.*

A trip to the eco-shelter had an upside. *I will see Leizle.* The prospect moved his speed up a notch, and the trees became an ebony glacier as the detail blended away. Leizle had harpooned his dead heart and made him feel more alive than he ever remembered being. *I'm new to this, and touching her still scares me, even in revival-sleep.* Connor had told him that Rebekah still tested his control.

"That's comforting to know," he muttered.

Turning into the gravel driveway, he had the eco-shelter evacuation fixed firmly in his mind as he mounted the steps and made his way through the house.

He crossed to the wardrobe as he pulled the cravat of his courtroom garb away from his throat. Reaching into the depths of the hanging space, he found the dark shirt and pants he wanted. Turning back into the room, shoving his arms into the fresh shirt, his gaze swept the space and he froze. A small pebble, just like the ones covering his driveway, was sitting on his mantelpiece.

Leizle. An unguarded smile banished the fierce concentration from Julian's face. Digging into his pants pocket, he extracted a key. *I didn't smell her, so, the padded cell works.*

With meticulous attention to detail, Julian had lined the walls of the small sitting room with soundproof padding and then disguised the fact with new plasterboard, shrinking the dimensions by four inches in all directions. The house dated from the Elizabethan era, and Julian had confidently bricked up the window. It was not an uncommon sight in the London of the early eighteen hundreds. Window taxes had lasted a hundred and fifty years, and many older houses bore the scars where families sacrificed the style and beauty of their home. They bricked up windows in the interest of saving enough shillings to put food on the table.

Fire and Ice: Survival

The decor inside the room featured plush carpet, and upholstered furnishings. All hardwood surfaces were covered with thick fabric, and silence, even for humans, was a reasonable expectation.

Julian walked the length of the hallway to the rear of the house and stopped outside the closed door. *I wonder if she likes it?* His mind was cluttered by her face as he inhaled deeply, satisfied that her cinnamon-tinted fragrance was barely detectable. He unlocked the door and pushed it open.

"Leizle?" As the sound of her cantering heart buffeted his ears, his relaxed smile grew wider, but only until the cutting blade of hunger buried itself in his stomach. His stride faltered on the threshold as he gazed at her face. Even with her hand clamped over her mouth, she was entrancing to him.

"You startled me," she whispered. Her eyes were dark emeralds in the dim light of a 20Watt bulb, an acceptable risk in this room alone. The words 'still-dicing-with-death?' died on his lips when she smiled. She swept her copper-shot hair from her eyes, and the movement enveloped him in her scent, stinging his nostrils, and worse, constricting his chest as desire burned inside him.

"Rap-sleep," he muttered urgently.

Before Leizle's smile of greeting had fully formed, he disappeared again.

"Julian?" she whispered, frowning. As she went to say his name again, his cool breath moved over her hair as he groaned.

He was back, and his lips closed over hers in a fleeting, probing kiss. Pain glittered in his eyes as he whispered, "I've got you a blanket, and I'll be back soon, okay?" He stroked a finger down over her cheek, and then he was gone.

Leizle hugged the blanket to her chest. The last time she was here she'd been wet and cold because vampires had no need of heating. "At least he's trying."

Julian's retreat took him to his study where he locked the door. *I need rap-sleep.*

He whisked around the room, hitting the marks he needed. First, he extracted three vials of blood from a chiller box, two human and one animal, which was more than the daily ten percent of human he needed. *But with Leizle here, I'm not taking any chances.* He stopped at the fireplace, downed the three vials and tossed them into the recycling container. Finally, he picked up the small pebble from the mantelpiece, and took it with him as he reclined into the familiar worn embrace of his brown leather armchair.

Content that Leizle was safe, he closed his eyes. Lucid dreams filled his head as they burned through the synapses, glowing like a red hot migraine which pulled his face into a mask of pain, drawing his lips back into a snarl as he passed through the anguish of hell to where the Leizle of his dreams waited.

Julian imagined her crossing the floor towards him, until, reaching out he molded his hands to the soft swell of her hips and pulled her closer. Tracing his fingertips over the contours of her delicate ribcage, he could feel her heartbeat thundering through his own chest as he teased her flushed skin with his mouth. As his body pooled with desire and a ruby flush tightened his velvet flesh, he dreamed of finally drowning in green eyes which reflected the maelstrom of his own emotions, and of showing her how much he loved her.

As his eyes snapped open, with the gatekeeper refreshed and his equilibrium restored, Julian braced himself to face the challenge of the *reality* of Leizle. Her intoxicating bouquet pulled at the beast inside him, as much as the lover.

Julian sat up, opened his hand and stared at the pile of sand that filled his palm where the pebble had been. His smile was grim. *I could probably make diamonds out of coal.* At that moment, he could fully empathize with King Midas. *I just want to touch her without hurting her, is that too much to ask?* Somewhere deep inside, he feared that it was.

Brushing the ground pebble fragments from his palm, Julian headed back towards Leizle. *I will not give her up.*

She was wrapped in his blanket, and the flush on her warm cheeks told him that it was not because she was cold, but because he had given it to her. It was russet with green threads shot through it and that warmed her more, because they were her colors; her hair and her eyes.

Julian sat down beside her, his cold thigh settling against hers, before she had noticed the door opening.

"Well. You're a nice surprise," he said gently. "Sorry about... leaving."

"Nice blanket." She looked up through her lashes, youth making her foolishly coquettish when her eye was set on seducing a vampire.

A growl rumbled in his throat. "I can manage a kiss, if you don't touch me."

"I'm sorry. I know this is hard for you," she said seriously. "Just one kiss."

He rested his lips against hers. A sneer tried to bare his teeth, but he stopped breathing and, keeping her scent at bay, he relaxed into revival-sleep. As it washed through him, he could trust his hands, and he laced his fingers into her hair. Her tongue stroked over his lips and he let her in, cautiously deepening his kiss.

As he pulled away wearing a tight smile, he cleared his throat, swallowed down his venom, and whispered, "That was easier." He looked into her flushed face and felt tentatively happy.

"Much better," she breathed.

"I'll get there, but, it's going to take a while." Fascination etched into his face as he rubbed his thumb over her bottom lip. "What am I going to do with you? I was on my way to see Connor. If I had gone straight there, I'd be going crazy about now wondering where you were."

Leizle sat back and said, "That's why I'm here. Something is wrong. Rebekah's sleeping all the time, well since she came back from..." She swallowed loudly. "She barely wakes at all now. And Connor has been gone for two days."

"Connor's gone. Gone where?" breathed Julian.

Chapter 15

The knowledge Connor was missing focused Julian's mind as he shadowed Leizle back through the woods. The two stroke engine of her motorcycle whined steadily, and Julian knew where she was at every given moment. He circled like a hawk, ensuring that she was the only thing moving through the undergrowth. *Damn it, Connor.* With Sebastian awake, the storm was gathering. *First, I must get Leizle home.*

He swept into the entrance cavern of the eco-shelter and watched Leizle dismount the motorcycle. Her cheeks were red and apprehension glittered in her eyes, and for a moment his reserve was stripped away. Without speaking, he closed the distance between them and brushed his lips gently over hers.

Her bewildered expression delighted him. "I couldn't resist."

"I'm glad," she said, smiling as she rested her hand on his chest.

Julian cleared his throat, telling himself to concentrate. "Rebekah. She's in the hospital cavern?"

Leizle nodded.

"Okay, follow on, Red." He landed another fleeting kiss, and then his words were left hanging in the empty space as her hair whipped around her cheeks.

"Red." Leizle bristled, but her annoyance melted into joy. *Red.*

Julian's own smile vanished when he ducked behind the blackout curtain and collided with Greg.

"Thank God," Greg muttered as he was bounced off the tunnel wall. Righting himself and folding his thick arms across his chest, he said, "I've checked out Connor's usual haunts. If he's out there, he doesn't want to be found." Greg's dirt streaked face glistened with sweat. "And we need a damn doctor."

Julian nodded grimly. "I'll find him. But let's start with Rebekah."

Greg grunted and set off at a jog which Julian quickly overtook.

Entering the hospital cavern, he registered a sea of anxious faces. He caught Thomas in the act of retreating with a wet flannel hanging from his limp fingers. As it dropped, Julian's lightning reflexes grabbed it before it hit the floor.

"Thomas?" He dredged up the name to fit the face. *It's the boy from the woods a few weeks ago.*

Thomas nodded and scuttled away. Ranging his glance around the room, Julian fitted names to the other faces in the group, ending with Oscar and his grimly set jaw. Uncle Harry looked smaller and frailer than Julian remembered, his fists were buried deep in his pockets and he wore the baffled expression of a man who was out of his depth.

Leizle entered the cavern as he turned his attention to Rebekah, gently taking her wrist to check her pulse. Her skin was cold, and she groaned softly.

"Rebekah?"

She sighed and became still again.

His gut feeling was that her sleep was unnatural. *Although, coma doesn't fit, either.* He lifted an eyelid, and, peering into her glazed eyes, he suddenly realized that he had no clue what he was looking for. "Damn it, I'm not a doctor," Julian muttered. *Where the hell is Connor, and why would he leave Rebekah in this state? After all we've been through, it makes no sense.*

Leizle moved to his side, and Julian drew her close.

"We can't rouse her. You don't think Sebastian's venom has poisoned her?" Leizle's face was pinched and white. "She won't die?"

"No, of course not." Julian's optimistic reassurance faltered as the ambient light accentuated Leizle's pale complexion. The dramatic contrast of her vibrant red hair and green eyes made her look almost vampiric. *If Leizle and Rebekah were vampires, life would be so much simpler.*

Julian had no way of knowing if Rebekah was dying, but he couldn't just wait and see. *Connor is gone, but Anthony might be able to shed some light.* They had promised not to make any demands of him outside of his role at the hospital. *But that was before.*

Julian muttered, "We need help." Turning to face the huddle of fretful humans, he decided to be blunt. "I need to bring another vampire in here."

Greg's guarded relaxation disappeared as he said, "Who?"

"Connor's not here and we need a doctor, or the nearest thing I can find." Julian's expression was stern. "Connor's assistant, Anthony. He trusts him, and we don't have a choice. But..."

"But?" said Greg.

"It would be better if you all stayed out of his way. There's no sense in making things more complicated than they need to be."

"Connor trusts him, you say?"

"He's one of the good guys." Glancing at Rebekah's waxy complexion, Julian added, "And we have to move fast." He handed Leizle the damp flannel and said, "Sit with her, Red. I'll be right back."

Disappearing from the cavern before the humans could draw a breath, Julian raced straight to the hospital and tracked Anthony down. Ushering him into a side ward, Julian gave him no choice. "You are already in too deep, Anthony. This girl saved Connor's life, and I don't fancy our chances if we do nothing to save her. Bottom line, if Rebekah dies, Connor will kill us both." *How can he refuse?*

Unsurprisingly, Anthony folded under pressure, and minutes later, Julian was passing by the same oak trees he had an hour before. Then, he had strained to listen for vampires in pursuit of Leizle, this time he was waiting for a reluctant Anthony to keep up. *No doubt he can feel the waters of commitment closing over his head. There'll be no going back to oblivion for him now.*

As the black maw of the eco-shelter entrance came into sight, Anthony muttered, "Hell, I don't have my plastic mask." He still struggled in resisting human blood, and he would never dream of attending the human farm without taking every precaution vampires had at their disposal.

Julian glared. "You'll just have to stop breathing. Take in a deep lungful of air that you can use to activate your vocal chords and talk. Just don't breathe in again while you are in there."

Anthony grunted. "Okay. But stay close, in case I lose it."

Julian slapped his shoulder hard. "This is too important. You can do this."

"She's not bleeding?"

"No," said Julian, hoping he was telling the truth.

With set expressions which would have terrified the hardest of human hearts, both vampires dived into the stagnant air of the tunnels and, like a diver going underwater, Anthony took a deep breath and held it.

Not allowing himself time to think, moments later, Anthony entered the hospital cavern and stood over Rebekah.

To his credit, he did not bat an eyelid when Leizle appeared, even though she was supposed to have died in the hospital months before. At least, that was the story Connor had told when he testified to an unidentifiable human female body in Julian's court.

Leizle shuffled nervously at Julian's side. The rest of the humans were in Oscar's cavern, down on the kitchen level of the eco-shelter, following Julian's orders and putting as much distance as possible between themselves and the rattled Anthony.

The surroundings, filled with enticing human odors, were challenging for Anthony as he began his examination in profound silence. After a quick assessment of Rebekah's vital signs, his hard stare in Julian's direction confirmed that the news was not good.

Julian stood guard at Anthony's right shoulder, ready to apply a headlock at the slightest sign of his control cracking.

"You were right to worry." Anthony carefully probed under Rebekah's arms. "Her lymph nodes are not swollen, so, it's not infection. Has she banged her head?"

Julian glanced at Leizle for confirmation. "Not that we know of, and the drowsiness has been progressive. For about a week, now."

"It could be viral. Encephalitis, maybe. Inflammation of the brain could cause drowsiness and stupor." Anthony felt around Rebekah's neck. "Her throat and tonsils seem unaffected, so, it's unlikely to be a bacterial infection." The silence stretched until Anthony stepped back.

"Tell me," said Julian.

Anthony took in her pale, waxy face and her blond hair, darkened by sweat and plastered to her forehead. Her skin was cold and clammy to the touch, and her eyes, in the moments they fluttered open, had the muddy quality of delirium.

Anthony knew Connor's wrath would be terrifying, and he fretted over what steps he should take. "We need to take blood. We cannot yet rule out a brain tumor," said Anthony. "If you take the sample, I'll wait outside." He forced a grin. "I'll never make it as a phlebotomist. That is definitely Connor's territory."

"Okay, Harry will take the blood. What then?"

"If the white blood cell count rules out cancer, then we could try dialysis. I ran her blood through a dialyzer before transfusing Connor with it. Maybe Sebastian's venom is more potent than we realized." Anthony knew as well as Julian that even though her erratic heartbeat was sluggish and depressed, they would never be able to hide her in a hospital that served only vampires.

"We can't risk the hospital, not yet. Is there any medication in the farm's clinic we could try? Antibiotics, or an anti-viral?" Julian asked.

Humans on the farm still became ill. They were a precious commodity and medicines were constantly being improved upon, because another pandemic was unthinkable.

"Let's take it one step at a time. Draw the blood, and I'll run the tests at the hospital," said Anthony. "Where is Connor? He should be with her, just in case..."

"We don't know." Julian raised a brow. "But I'm sure he has a good reason."

"He must have."

Anthony met Julian's eyes as they both acknowledged the worst scenario. Turning her would rely on her regaining consciousness. Vampire blood needed to be ingested, absorbed and filtered through the stomach lining so the transformation happened gradually. In other words, the dying human had to *feed*.

"We can try injecting adrenalin to bring her round, if Connor decides..." Anthony's voice trailed off.

Fire and Ice: Survival

They both knew what he meant. They could not take the decision of turning Rebekah to save her in this condition. Her illness made vampire incarnation an unknown quantity that only Connor could choose for her.

With a determined nod, Anthony said, "I'll be outside. Two vials of blood should do it." He handed his medical bag to Julian and left.

<><><>

Finally regretting running away, Connor covered the one hundred and eighty miles from Bodmin Moor back to the rolling green Downs of Kent in forty minutes. Pacing like a caged tiger, he banished the last remnants of unrest, stopped and looked out over the rough fields. As he picked out the escarpment of the eco-shelter entrance, a measure of peace settled over him.

His angry despair had burned itself out, at last. He had wrestled with his demon until he felt battered and bruised, and now the gatekeeper of the killing center inside his brain had regained control.

The three hundred and fifty square miles of Dartmoor's vampire safari park allowed the animals once kept in human zoos the illusion of freedom. The only predators threatening them now were vampires, and three big cats had died at Connor's hand before his thirst abated. *Self-indulgence, when I should have been finding a way back home.* His recriminations were hard to put to rest.

I will banish Sebastian's memory, even if it takes a lifetime. Disregarding the heat signatures of humans scattered throughout the subterranean habitat, Connor effortlessly honed in on Rebekah and absorbed her warm scent as an infusion. Hope dimmed as he detected the alien element to her fragrance still, and he frowned. As he tuned into her sluggish pulse, he strained to identify an elusive note. *The tempo is faster, faint but strong.* And suddenly he knew.

His world flipped on its axis as the realization hit him. *Two heartbeats.*

He broke into a run and powered his way over the potholes in the field. Without breaking stride, he whipped along the tunnels.

His anxiety shifted up a gear as he caught the scent of Anthony. *Julian must have been desperate.*

A hundred yards ahead of Connor's driving path, inside the dining cavern, Julian joined Leizle and Greg, sitting down at their table and watching Greg, at least, eat something.

"I feel like a blind man firing a bow and arrow. I don't even know where the target is, let alone the blasted bulls-eye," muttered Julian.

Leizle stared across the table, and seeing her worried face, he wished he'd kept his mouth shut.

She pushed her meal away, untouched. "What are we going to do?"

"Where the hell is he?" Leizle's plate rattled as Julian slammed his palm down on the table. "I would like to shake him 'til his teeth fall out."

The image made Leizle smile, clearing away her frown for a moment.

Julian's explosive movement jolted the other human's in the dining cavern into shocked awareness and broke the tense silence which Rebekah's illness had cast over them all. The sudden gasps gave way to whispered conversations. Across the aisle, on their own table, Harry, Thomas, and three other middle aged men, began eating again.

Greg's features relaxed as he shook his head and chuckled.

As though Julian's aggravation summoned a genie from a lamp, the abrupt increase of pressure in the room set his ears ringing. Eddying currents of air whipped the dust on the cavern floor into vortices, and Julian smiled. "Maybe, I'll let him talk first."

Connor swung into the cavern and was met by Julian's sardonic welcome. "About time."

His attention swept the dining area, the horror-movie effect of dried blood caked on his skin forgotten as Connor said, "Rebekah's pregnant."

Julian's stunned face might have made Connor smile, but he was already descending to the next level of the eco-shelter. Tracking Rebekah's scent, he raced down the slope. An avalanche of dry

Fire and Ice: Survival

mortar hit the floor as his shoulder collided with the doorway of the hospital cavern.

He materialized at Rebekah's side and looked down into her still face. Her eyelids were motionless. *She's not dreaming. This is not sleep.*

"Rebekah. Honey." Calling her name did not penetrate.

Flipping back the covers, he ran his thumb expertly along the soles of her feet. *No motor response to stimuli.* Although worried, he was happier when, laying his palm on her clammy brow, he detected lazy spiraling thoughts inside her brain as her synapses fired in a meandering pattern. *She's not comatose then, she's thinking, at least.* But, to present as level six on the scale of unconsciousness without an obvious cause was baffling, even to him.

He took her unresponsive hand into his and made a sudden decision. "She doesn't need to be here," he said as he swept back the blankets and lifted her into his chest. He walked through the tunnels to her cavern, where he laid her gently on the bed.

Stroking back her damp hair, he said, "I'll be back in a minute." He left her and returned within seconds with his body cleaned of evidence of the hunt and wearing clean sweatpants. Slipping into her bed, he draped his arm over the covers and settled down to wait.

Rebekah was sleeping.

She dreamed of swimming in warm mud, fighting to keep her face above the surface. The mud weighed heavily on her limbs, but it was warm, comfortable, and she had no other thought than to just keep breathing. *That is enough.*

A chill rippled over her skin and she groaned. Her pounding head ached. Cold fingers took her hand and she tugged in protest. *I want the warmth back.* The numbness slipped away as a cold hand stroked gently over her stomach. The familiarity of it beckoned, the warm fog parted, and crystal clarity crashed in as a waterfall of understanding.

"Hey, honey, come back to me." Connor remained lying curled into her back, having held her for hours as he had once before. Never sleeping, he listened to every murmur of her heart and died every time it faltered. He sensed the delirium releasing its grasp and consciousness returning. When he smoothed his palm over her stomach, his hope became joyful certainty when her heart raced in response.

He felt her body tense, preparing for flight, but this time he was ready. His arms held her safely anchored to his chest as she surfaced, and her eyes opened on a gasp.

"Connor." Her lips silently formed his name.

"I know," he said.

She whispered, "How?"

Disgust at his own reaction burned through his memory. *I should have faced my fears, and stayed to banish Sebastian, and then I would have known how wrong I was.* "You have two heartbeats." He nuzzled her neck and breathed, "I don't know how, but we've made a baby... our baby."

"He has a heartbeat?" she said, and he chuckled.

"A strong one, stronger than his mother's there, for a while." Connor ran a hand over her hip. "I thought I'd lost you."

Turning in his arms, Rebekah took his face in her hands. He was her Connor again. His gray gaze was crystal clear and illuminated by his smile.

"Will sorry, help?" she whispered softly. "I am so sorry."

"I'm just glad I came back." He sighed. "I understand now. This baby thing scared the hell out of you... but, we'll work it out." He spread his hands over her back and smiled as he tried to separate the notes in the symphony playing beneath his fingertips. Her heart was slow and steady, and his child's fluttered like a bird inside a cage. "We will work it out, honey."

Connor folded Rebekah into his arms and felt her sigh as a warm breeze which drove doubt away. He registered every nuance of her altered physiology as the doctor in him gathered information. His touch absorbed his baby's somnolent movement and stored it away for future reference.

The dim light in her cavern cast hypnotic shadows across the curved walls. Her body relaxed into his, and, resting his cheek on the top of her head, he smiled. *She's just sleeping this time.*

Fire and Ice: Survival

Connor turned his head as Julian's shadow stretched across the floor and he leaned in the doorway. "Good to have you, back. What happens now?"

"I don't know."

"But she's out of danger? Just sleeping?"

"She's conscious now, at least." Glancing into her relaxed face, Connor added, "We'll talk in the meeting cavern."

"Okay. Two minutes," Julian replied as he disappeared.

With reluctance, Connor eased himself out of the bed and left her a note. "Sleep honey, I'm only a heartbeat away."

Connor's smile persisted throughout his dash along the passageways as, even with the doubt and fear of the pregnancy looming, being with Rebekah again immersed him in joy.

As he walked into the meeting cavern, Julian's impatience hit him full in the face.

The groove worn in the floor was evidence of how hard Julian had found the waiting. "Just dropping off the radar, with all that's going on, Connor? Really?"

Meeting Julian's frustrated glare, Connor focused on the reason for his anger. "Thank you for looking after her, " he said quietly, "and the baby."

"But, how on earth?" Julian muttered.

"I have no idea." Connor looked at him accusingly. "*You* told me it was safe."

"Well, one hundred unsuccessful hybrid inseminations over the last decade were strong indicators. Everything pointed that way."

"Well, it looks like you were wrong."

"And trust you to achieve the impossible."

"Hell, Julian, we have no idea how this pregnancy will go. The onset has not been easy. We're going to have to be ready for anything."

"We have more to worry about than that," Julian stated flatly. "Sebastian's awake."

"Already? I should have finished him when I had the chance." Connor replayed the moment when he shoved the spike up into Sebastian's jaw, and the satisfying vibration as his eyeball collapsed. *I should've gone for the frontal lobe. At least then, awake or not, it would have made no difference. Perfect outcome.*

"Serge will be coming after the humans." Julian's eyes locked onto Connor. "But he'll have to get creative. The direct approach has lost him too many guardsmen."

"But he has to get through you, Marius, and Alexander in council?"

"The Council won't forgive unsanctioned attacks, so, yes." Julian rubbed his pale fingers over his jaw. "I can buy time, but the outcome is inevitable. We have to move the humans again."

"You've got to hold Serge off until we have an escape plan in place." Connor began circling the cavern. "I think it's time to call on this other eco-town. They took Annabelle in, so-"

"Do they know about us?" asked Julian. "You and I?"

"No. Greg doesn't say much, and he only talks about Seth, the Marine he served with. *All* vampires are the enemy in their minds."

"But we can use them as a safe place? If Serge moves before we are ready, we could hide them there?" Julian's eyes narrowed.

Connor stopped pacing and turned to face him. "I'm not moving Rebekah. I need the hospital and Anthony close at hand." He raised his hand at Julian's protest. "Keep me informed, and if things start to look bad, we move the others out. Harry, Oscar, and the rest. Leizle too, but Rebekah stays here."

"As if Leizle will go anywhere and leave Rebekah behind. And she's not the only one you'll have trouble with. Thomas, Oscar, Harry, Greg, they've all been worried sick." Julian laughed harshly.

"I'll talk to them. I know Harry has the beta-blockers and pheromone spray stockpiled for this kind of emergency. He, more than anyone, knows that survival is about necessity, not choice." Connor resumed his breakneck circuit of the cavern. "I will go with him to the other eco-town, to negotiate."

Julian tried to track Connor's hurtling path. "For God's sake, stand still."

Connor stopped, folded his arms and stared at Julian.

"Okay." Julian nodded. "Negotiation and you. Is that a good idea?"

"I will stay out of sight and listen. But, if Harry's powers of persuasion fail him..." Connor frowned suddenly. "Greg and Oscar should go, too, Seth's group have never met Harry."

"They have no reason to risk their camp for ours, you do realize that, right?" said Julian. "It sounds like Greg knows one guy who stepped up and took in Annabelle. It is a huge leap to what we are asking now. A dozen extra mouths to feed, and a vampire in the wings might be pushing it, Connor."

"We won't know until we ask. And if all else fails, then I'll show myself, and offer them protection."

Julian lifted a brow. "Really?"

"Or scare them a little." Connor's laughter was as tense as Julian's frown. "You just have to keep Serge in your sights and give me as much breathing space as you can, and leave the rest up to me. Are you up to it?"

Julian nodded seriously.

"Great. Just Rebekah, my baby, Anthony's cooperation, and Leizle to worry about. Easy." Connor grinned. "You're right about Leizle, she won't leave Rebekah. Although, you've got to take some of the blame there." He laughed at Julian's resigned expression and clapped him on the back.

Rubbing a hand over his face, Julian looked at the domed ceiling for inspiration. "She's too young, and I shouldn't be stopping her from living." He locked eyes with Connor. "I'll be away for a while. I'll do my best to stall the council for as long as possible. Try and persuade her to go if you can."

"I understand." Connor knew how hard it was for Julian to ask him that. "I guess things get more complicated from here on in, for all of us. Welcome to my world."

Chapter 16

In the dimly lit alcove where the tumbled bed bore witness to Rebekah's restless slumber, Connor smoothed his palm over her warm skin as he reluctantly rolled away. Resembling an apparition swirling around the cavern, his blurred form changed color as white skin was covered by black cloth, until finally, he stopped moving and sat on the side of the bed, fully clothed.

"Sleep, honey, while you can," he said, smiling down into Rebekah's drowsy eyes. Her scent had altered again, and he could feel another storm brewing inside her. *I just don't know what form it will take.* He leaned over to kiss her lips, placing his cool palm over the rounded swell of her stomach. "You too," he muttered. "I'll be back soon."

"Do you think it will work?" Rebekah said, the words muffled by a yawn.

"Greg and Harry should make contact today." Connor's eyes darkened. "It will work. I'll be there to keep watch, don't worry." With a graze of a cold fingertip down her cheek, he was gone.

Running in a circuit which followed a five mile arc around the eco-shelter location, Connor made sure the coast was clear before he left the area. Fine tuning every vampire sense at his disposal, he absorbed the nocturnal symphony of wildlife before it died at his whistling approach.

A fox darted across Connor's path, lost in the chase of a rabbit that scurried on ahead through the undergrowth. With the sound of crunching bone, the fox triumphed, and the scent of blood sailed on a light breeze. Registering Connor's presence, the white blaze on a deer's tail flashed as it dived into the thick foliage. *You would have been too late.* The wind played over his unyielding skin as he smiled. *But today I'm not hunting and you live to fight another.*

Satisfied that it was safe, Connor altered course and headed for the coordinates agreed upon with Oscar, Harry, and Greg. Connor's part had already been completed; he dug the burrows and filled them with food and sleeping bags. The away team had traveled by

Fire and Ice: Survival

day and hit the marks agreed upon to hide at night. Connor was meeting up with them now, before dawn on their second night out. *Greg knows the terrain. I'm sure they'll be there waiting.*

He could disable a man with a grip on the carotid artery, knowing precisely where to dig in his thumb and cut off the blood supply. Connor was happy to have him along on this trip, after all, it may yet turn into the engagement of an enemy. *Who knows what tales Annabelle has told to justify her eviction from the eco-shelter. Greg's combat skills might be useful.*

Three hours remained before Connor need concern himself with dawn's fingers tearing holes in the black velvet night sky. As he skirted the trunks of towering beech trees on the final approach, he smiled. The odor of sweat laced with the hint of dopamine drifting in the air confirmed that Greg was true to his word. *They're here.*

Connor reduced his speed as though he collided with an invisible wall, then stepped forward.

"Hello Harry." The man's heart leapt in his chest at the sudden arrival and Connor grinned. "Sorry, I didn't mean to startle you."

Greg glanced over his shoulder but his movements did not falter in the act of refolding the sleeping bags. Tugging the drawstring bags closed, he forced them back into the space under the tree roots. Standing and nodding in greeting, he said, "Connor."

Oscar appeared holding a clutch of sticks in a closed fist, all cut to the same length. "I've left the signal." Pointing through the trees, he said, "One stick per person, left inside a hole in a tree on the edge of the glade."

Connor raised a brow. "How do they know when to look. Looking every day lays them open to discovery. Repeating a pattern of behavior is never a great idea."

"Owl call." Greg laughed quietly at Connor's expression.

"Hey, don't knock it." Oscar chipped in. "The old ways are always the best, lad. There are no barn owls in these parts."

Connor cocked his head, about to say 'fair enough', when his chin went up and he said, "Four men. One is young, lighter than the others. About half an hour out." He looked at Oscar. "How do they know where to meet?"

Oscar held up the sticks again. "Grooves carved into the sticks. Coordinates, if you know what you're looking at." He rubbed a hand over the back of his head. "Our last meeting was a little less... controlled. I couldn't think straight for a week after delivering Annabelle. I'm not going through that again."

"And they are coming here?"

Greg gave Connor a 'what do you take me for' look. "No, we've got a trek of about fifteen minutes. The meet is at oh-five-hundred."

"Better get moving then," said Connor, "I'll hang back."

The three men moved quietly through the wood. Greg checked his compass at intervals until he stopped as though 'X' marked the spot. "This is it." He nodded at Harry and Oscar, and they settled down to wait.

Within a few minutes, four men stepped out from between the trees. The tallest man carried a staff, but his grip on the shaft made it clear it was a weapon, not a walking aid. The other two heavyset men wore frowns, and a thin boy, maybe nineteen, also seemed to glower but his complexion was waxy and his respiration sounded shallow.

The tall man smiled, and all hell broke loose.

The boy collapsed. His legs folded beneath him and his breathing began to rasp. He tumbled forward and his companions froze.

A white, long-fingered hand appeared from nowhere, supporting the boy's head and guiding it to a soft landing. The moonlight revealed a wraithlike, rigid white face, with eye sockets cast in cavernous shadow. The black clad figure knelt beside the boy's prone body. Curling pale fingers beneath his knee to bend the youth's leg, the vampire pushed up the fabric of his pants and sank his teeth into the boy's calf muscle.

The man with the staff burst into action first, bellowing as he lifted the stick and rushed forward. Connor, continuing to bite into the boy's soft flesh, shot out a hand, and the clutch of his palm filled with sawdust as the stick disintegrated in his grasp.

Fire and Ice: Survival

Greg moved in fast, coming up behind, he shoved his arms underneath the tall man's armpits and locked his hands behind his friend's head as the man grunted.

"He's with us, Seth." Greg hissed into his ear, "I'm saving your bacon. You really don't want to pick a fight with Connor."

Oscar faced the remaining two men with his palms upraised in surrender.

"Just wait," muttered Harry.

As the rattled older man fumbled for words to explain the unexplainable, Connor surged to his feet and spat out a mouthful of blood. Wiping the back of his hand across his mouth, he faced the man who still held a broken piece of his staff. "Let him go, Greg."

The man yanked his arms from Greg's slackened grasp, saw Connor's blood spattered face and bellowed, "Traitor." He roared, as he swung around and launched a well-aimed punch at Greg's face.

His fist was swallowed by Connor's grip as he absorbed the impact but resisted crumbling the human hand to dust. Keeping his hand folded around the clenched fist, Connor grabbed a handful of Seth's shirt and finally got his full attention.

"Snakebite," Connor said.

"You can trust him, Seth. He's one of the good guys," said Greg.

The boy groaned and clutched at his leg. Black cloth torn from Connor's shirt was already tied tightly above the bite mark as a tourniquet. Commonsense dawned in the tall man's eyes, and Connor released Seth's fist.

Connor submitted to Seth's probing gaze and said, "I think you owe us a favor. Adder venom won't kill a healthy human. But this boy is far too thin, and fighting a chest infection. You could have lost him."

One of the men helped the boy to sit up.

Maintaining his grip on the man's shirt, Connor continued, "So, you are Seth? Good to meet you at last."

Seth slumped as the realization hit that his boy could have died were it not for this fierce looking vampire.

"Funny," said Seth, "Greg never once mentioned you."

Connor let him go and shrugged. "He probably thought you wouldn't understand. As you said, you'd think he was selling you out."

Seth shot his comrade a loaded glance and grunted. "Appearances are deceiving. Greg's a solid guy."

It was an apology of sorts, and Greg waved a hand that wiped the slate clean.

Connor turned to Harry. "I guess this is where I leave you to negotiate."

"I think we can take it from here," said Harry.

Connor scanned the stunned faces. "I'll leave Greg and his men to fill you in on why we needed to meet." His eyes moved quickly over the youth. "And I'll get some antibiotics for the boy, I'm a doctor."

As Connor raced the dawn, headed back to see Rebekah, his thoughts turned to Annabelle. *I'm glad she didn't come.* She *has reason to fear me.* Rebekah had suffered in ways that Annabelle could not imagine. *It would've been hard to gain their trust if I had got my hands on her.* Picturing the thin boy and knowing he had tasted clean blood, Connor was satisfied he had sucked out all the venom. *I'm sure Harry can close the deal.*

Chapter 17

Greg entered the dining cavern, rigorously rubbing a towel over dripping hair, and then he gave up. He sat down beside Oscar and Harry, picked up a mug of hot tea and cradled it in his palms. Resting his elbows on the scarred tabletop, he slipped into a weary silence.

The tidemark of dirt around their necks and the sopping wet towels slung around their shoulders were evidence of the gruesome last day of a trek home through a sustained deluge which had battered the tree canopy until the water came pouring through.

Connor sat at their table, too. Hidden beneath the wooden surface, his hands gripped his thighs as he listened to their news. He was painfully aware of their heartbeats. Even the chill on their skin could not detract from the alluring scent of the blood-cells pumping beneath it.

Julian has been away too long, this time. I need human blood. The taste of Seth's boy was still fresh in his mind and the dehydration in Connor's brain distorted his vision.

The warm blood of the three men radiated as heat haze. Connor narrowed his eyes and allowed wish fulfilment a moment of freedom, imagining Greg, as a worthy adversary who would thrill him, draining of color as the hot tide of his blood filled Connor's stomach.

Connor pushed the demon back into the cell and slammed the door shut as he pulled Harry's face into focus. "So, you have their agreement?" he asked.

Greg toweled the nape of his neck as he answered. "Seth has agreed to take all of us." He shot a wry glance at Oscar.

"I'm not going," said Oscar emphatically.

"Then, neither will I," said Harry.

"Whoa, hold on one moment." Connor's granite glare swept over the bedraggled humans. "After all you've been through, you will all go."

"Even Rebekah?" Oscar's square jaw was set.

"No, not Rebekah. You know I need the hospital nearby. This new colony is not the place for her or our baby."

"Exactly," said Oscar. "And, unlike you, she has to eat. I'm staying."

"I see." Connor nodded slowly. "I can see the sense in that, but you, Harry. They will need you there."

"There's a condition to their hospitality," said Harry.

"Go on."

"Seth's son, the snake-bite kid, it's not just him that's ill. Their sleeping burrows are damp and poorly ventilated." Harry pulled a piece of paper out of his pocket with a diagram pencilled on to it. "We need two cubic feet of clean air per person to ensure the oxygen levels stay at twenty one percent. I agreed you would dig out a new sleeping cavern, with better ventilation shafts, after all this is done."

Connor's lips twitched. "Hiring me out, hmmm?" He chuckled. "I never thought you had it in you."

As Harry flushed, Oscar leapt in. "How is Rebekah?"

"The exhaustion has passed. She has trouble sleeping now." Connor frowned.

Since Connor's return from the meeting with Seth, fear cramped his chest every time he held Rebekah. When he kissed her skin and a blush blossomed beneath his lips, the scent of her blood was tainted with a scorched aroma which fed the confusion in his mind.

"She has *trouble* sleeping?" asked Oscar, frowning, as if the shift took away the firm ground from under him. "What happens now?"

"I would say, she has mood swings, but that's only the tip of the iceberg. I'm keeping her under observation. Leizle's with her now."

Oscar drained his mug of tea and banged it decisively down on the table. He stood up. "I'll get cleaned up and cook her something nice."

Connor smiled. Oscar's solution was not far off the mark – a full stomach would solve a lot of Connor's problems, right now. "And I'd better go and check on her. I'll catch you guys, later?" Connor said as he got to his feet and headed for the door.

His rush along the tunnels was eased by revival sleep as instinct told him to prepare for the worst. *Her adrenalin levels are through the roof.* He heard Leizle's yelp of pain and increased his speed.

Rebekah no longer slept, her rioting emotions allowed no such relief. The circles under her eyes were deep violet now. With her anger and frustration only ever a heartbeat away, when it boiled over Connor was the only one who could get close to her. The missiles she launched were well aimed and even Leizle wore three layers of clothing as protection.

The problem, well not a problem under other circumstances, thought Connor with a wry grin. *Is that, if I contain her, to get her to eat or rest, she becomes ravenous... but not for food.* She had torn several of his shirts in her hunger for him. *If making love is the price to get her to sleep, I'll gladly pay it. Except it isn't love, it's lust, pure and simple.*

The thought still excited him. "Win, win," he muttered as he rounded the last corner, appeared at her cavern doorway, and surveyed the scene.

"Get out!" yelled Rebekah. Her face flushed in anger.

Backing up against the wall, Leizle twisted her shoulders to protect her face as she held onto her arm. She felt a nudge to her side and the roughened stone surface snatched at her sweater as she was buffeted sideways. The world literally spun for a few seconds before she found herself standing outside in the tunnels, looking up into Connor's impassive face, and she wished the eyes staring back at her were green, instead of gray.

Connor was already thinking of Rebekah, but he read Leizle's expressive face and in a low voice he said, "If he stayed away, he had no choice, be patient." He, too, was impatient for Julian's return. *I need human blood, and my biggest problem today will be not helping myself to Rebekah's.*

Leizle nodded, rubbing her bruised wrist as she muttered, "Longer sleeves next time."

But he had already gone.

Leizle *had* been patient, and listening to the low seductive murmur of Connor's voice as he closed in on Rebekah, all she felt was jealousy. She was a girl desperate to become a woman. She had promised to wait for Julian. *But waiting hurts.* And a worm of doubt was eating its way through her heart. *Will he ever be brave enough to really love me?*

She inspected the darkening bruise on her wrist. She had asked Rebekah once about the marks on her body, and her joyful smile had stunned Leizle. *I, too, would trade a body full of bruises to feel joy like that.*

<><><>

Inside Rebekah's cavern, Connor advanced slowly. He removed his shirt. *It's coming off, anyway.* He thumbed the top button of his pants open as he walked forward. He was naked by the time he reached for her, but he had no qualms about that. He was here to offer himself to ease her hunger. *And my own.*

Even her agitation was alluring to him. As anger boiled through her, Connor's stride paused. Her aroma invaded his nostrils, and it shot through him as a knife thrust to his groin. His lust was more than equal to hers. Even sinking into revival-sleep could only dull the cutting edge of the compulsion to just close the distance and feel her soft heat close around him.

These last few days had been the Rebekah of his lucid dreams come true. For fear of hurting her and his baby, he played the passive role which most men, vampire or human, had fantasized about for centuries.

Stepping up behind her, Connor took Rebekah into his embrace, trapping her in his caged arms as he had done the night they first met. The frisson of alarm burned like wildfire through her veins, and heated his palms where they clung to her skin. Then, they had both fought the urge to press into each other, not so, now.

As he spread his hands over her swelling stomach, she turned to him. The pinched anger on her face dropped away, and her eyes were drawn to his face. The brittle edge in her gaze dissolved to molten heat. She took his face in her hands and kissed him deeply, dragging her lips insistently over his until his smile let her in.

Fascination overwhelmed her as she cooled her palms on his taut cheeks, feeling his muscles moving beneath the smooth silk of his skin. The hot ashen sparks of anger faded to a lava flow of desire. She kissed him again, slaking her thirst for his cool scent, like iced tea on a hot day.

Rebekah sighed as Connor peeled away her clothing, his fingertips caressing her curves.

"Connor," she breathed, and it was that word which kept him sane. It resonated inside him and held the storm at bay. Restraint burned through his body, hungry for release, but his name on her lips held him still.

As she clung to him, he effortlessly lifted her and wrapped her thighs around his body. Mindful of his child, he supported her as he walked to the bed and lowered himself onto the mattress with her straddling his lap. Every dream of Rebekah he had experienced when in rap-sleep rampaged through his mind as he laid back and his hooded gaze took in the radiance of her enraptured face.

She breathed his name again. Her hot thighs framed his hips as she sank down onto him, taking his aroused body deep inside, her heat pooling as moisture on his thighs. He wanted to touch her rounded stomach and to mold his hands to her heavy breasts, but he took *his* pleasure from watching her take hers.

He locked an iron band of control across his chest. His tight throat trapped his breath inside as he fought the desire which flooded him every time she moved, seeking out the release she needed. As she traced her fingers over his abdomen, stroking the muscles framing his pelvis, his control crumbled. His hips twitched as, unable to rein in his response any longer, his fingers closed over her thighs in a gentle grip and his own climax washed through him.

Rebekah's world was draped in a haze of contentment as she finally relaxed into Connor and passed out. Shifting to fit his body to hers, he pulled her into his chest. At last he got to touch her, and experience the endless movement of his child rolling beneath his palms.

"Go to sleep little one," he murmured as he pulled the blanket over them both.

He molded his hands gently to her swollen belly and immersed himself in the battle of the two heartbeats inside her. In one moment they were in accord, forming part of the same melody, but then one raced on ahead in an impatient scamper, pattering faster every time the tiny unborn body tumbled over beneath Connor's fingertips. *What lies ahead? How long will this volatile coupling of anger and passion, last?*

Touching his nose to her shoulder, he breathed her in, and venom flooded his mouth, pooling in his throat. The urge to bite burned as a cavernous yawn aching for release. Her warm skin was a siren call inviting him to take a deep draft of the warm nectar pulsing underneath.

Connor closed his eyes and embraced the torture. She was too pale. *She needs all the blood she has to get through this. My time's running out, where the hell is Julian?*

His wakeful hours were spent wrestling with the unknown. *The baby is larger than it should be at this stage.* They only had her missed periods to go on. *This should be her third, maybe fourth month, but her size indicates six months, or more. And the rate of growth seems to be accelerating like a runaway train.*

Rebekah stirred in his arms as the baby struggled for comfort, bumping against his palm. Connor thought of the heavy duty cot he had already built and smiled. It had taken him less than an hour to turn branches of oak tree into sturdy bars and to weave rods of metal into a sprung chainmaille base. If nothing else, the baby would have somewhere to sleep, whenever he was born. Connor's gray eyes were bleak. *That is... if the baby sleeps at all.*

The last few weeks had been tough. *She's gone from being almost comatose to this powder keg of emotion which keeps her from sleeping, so, what's next?*

Staring into space illuminated by candlelight, Connor's vision darkened when the fanciful shadows dancing over the walls of the cavern became the angel of death. The enticement of murderous hallucinations stroked over his dehydrating vampire brain. *Where the hell is Julian? I'll have to leave the eco-shelter if he does not turn up soon.*

Fire and Ice: Survival

Sebastian remained a loose cannon which made Julian's visit to the eco-shelter fast and infrequent. Connor felt like a mole living in the dark – not knowing what the hell was going on frayed his nerves. But, more than that, he missed his friend.

Chapter 18

In the jurors' anteroom at the council building, Julian shot a glance at his watch as he crossed to a brass framed mirror and straightened his white cravat. Lifting his chin and studying his reflection, his lowered lashes unveiled a blank stare of indifference.

Councilor Serge had put in an application for an emergency hearing, and everything would unfold in the courtroom in a matter of minutes. *He has the advantage of surprise, although, if I factor in Connor and Sebastian, I will not be far off the mark, I'm sure.*

It had taken longer than first thought for Sebastian's memory to return. Being awake was only step one in the road to recovery, it seemed. *It allowed Connor to focus on the pregnancy, for a while, at least.* Julian admitted to harboring a slim hope that Connor's spike had caused permanent amnesia, but no such luck.

Now, it was showtime.

Julian had a reputation of shunning Serge to uphold. This was the performance he prepared for as, satisfied with his appearance, he turned back into the room.

"Well, gentlemen, Councilor Serge demands our attention, again." Julian cast an eye over Marius and Alexander. They both stood like statues, their heavy silence more fitting to a graveyard.

Marius stirred. "It is our function."

"True, but let's hope this latest application is worthy of our attention," said Julian. He knew them both well. *Boredom and eternity make for a dangerous cocktail. I have a bad feeling about this.* Serge's involvement in exposing Connor had given him a louder voice, and the jurors were, for now at least, inclined to hear him out.

As though he read Julian's mind, with resignation, Alexander said, "Julian, we are obliged to listen. He is a councilor." The newest juror had served four decades, and he felt as Julian did, that far too many hearings revolved around Councilor Serge. "Unless he has something new to say, we will dispatch him quickly and move on."

"Well, let us proceed." Julian shrugged into his principal's robe and walked to the door. *And therein lies the problem, I'm certain he* will *have something new to say.*

He walked along the corridor towing Marius and Alexander in his wake, feeling their presence like a hand resting on each of his shoulders. They were a daunting sight in their juror's garb.

They entered the courtroom, and within three strides, Julian reached his chair and inspected the assembled vampires lining the gallery. They rose at his entrance with barely a rustle of disturbed cloth. *A full house, Serge has been lobbying, it would seem.*

Julian took his seat and struck the bench with his gavel. "Court is in session." He latched onto Serge's tight smile. "Councilor, you have the floor."

"Principal Julian. Jurors." Serge bobbed his head. "I have come to report the discovery of a nest of humans."

"Nest?" Julian asked. *The shadow boxing is over, then, but is Connor ready?* "Exactly how many is a nest?"

"My information puts the number at forty humans."

"I find it hard to believe that we could have overlooked a nest of *forty.*" Julian raised a brow in genuine surprise. *Who is lying, I wonder?* Julian was intrigued. *Has Sebastian exaggerated his hand? Or is Serge trying to make his case more compelling? No matter.* "Information, you say. So, you have not seen the nest first hand. Who supplied this information?"

"My protégé, Sebastian."

"And he is here to explain himself?" said Julian. At Serge's nod, Julian raised his voice. "I call Sebastian to bear witness."

Clearly waiting in the wings, Sebastian materialized at Serge's side. Assessing the jurors with his one good eye, he dipped his chin. "Principal Julian. Jurors." He reached up to push back the hair falling onto his brow, and then abandoned the gesture, letting it hang to partly obscure the view of the milk-colored pupil of his dead eye.

The prominent reminder of Sebastian's failure brought Julian pleasure. *It will give Connor some satisfaction, at least.* "Sebastian.

If we accept that you know the location of this nest, why then, did you not come forward earlier?" Julian enjoyed twisting the knife.

Sebastian's good eye sharpened with annoyance.

"And the numbers." Julian glanced at Marius and Alexander as he said, "Are you sure you are thinking straight?" *The claim of forty humans is ridiculous.*

When Sebastian bristled, Julian suppressed a smile. *Will he crack, I wonder?*

"Sebastian located the nest before his... accident." Serge met Julian's eye, defying him to comment. They both knew Serge was breaking their agreement. He believed Connor to be in the late stages of locked-in syndrome, and that Julian could not argue against his proposal without revealing his own collusion to release a human pet.

Serge thinks my hands are tied, and he's right. Julian waited.

"I will vouch for Sebastian." Serge added quietly, "My word as a councilor holds weight here, surely?"

Marius raised a hand, requesting Julian's permission to comment. "You are proposing we mobilize the council guardsmen to capture the nest as farm stock, correct?"

Serge nodded.

"If there are forty humans, Principal Julian, then I consider it worthwhile," Marius said thoughtfully. "Let us allow Councilor Serge a little latitude. I am sure he would not support an application he knew to be false. He's aware the court would not countenance such deception." The threat was clear. Serge could make history as the first councilor to be stripped of his title.

"Very well, we will mobilize the guardsmen." Julian uttered the words knowing, that he would have to move fast and warn Connor. *I have lost this argument. Further objection will raise suspicion.*

"While I have the council's ear, may I propose Sebastian as a hive councilor?" Serge's eyes skittered to Sebastian as he spoke.

Julian's jaw dropped open in disbelief, and he snapped it audibly shut, drawing Sebastian's narrowed gaze. *He has cards that I don't know about. But I'm sure he will show his hand soon enough.* "We will take it under consideration," Julian replied. "I'm not sure Sebastian's commitment to the hive is proven, he has only been with us a few months, after all."

"Surely, contributing forty humans shows commitment," smiled Serge.

Touché. Julian inclined his head. "If indeed, that proves to be the case."

Sebastian's innocent expression irritated Julian. They both knew this was about Rebekah and revenge.

"You must be relieved, Serge. The council guardsmen are of a better caliber than your own." Julian's smile was condescending, driving the jibe home. "Is there anything further?"

Serge shook his head.

"Sebastian, you will give the council a written account that substantiates your claims here today, and then the council will plan the strategy. We will convene in one week. At which time the date will be set for the gathering of the *forty* humans." A raised brow gave the court the message that Julian considered it a waste of time.

"Court adjourned." Julian rose as the gavel dropped from his hand, and headed out of the door.

In the jurors' anteroom, Julian changed into street clothes with disguised urgency, and like a flow of quicksilver, each action led effortlessly onto the next.

Marius appeared, interrupting the flow and demanding Julian's full attention as he said, "Principal Julian, if there is a nest of forty humans I see no reason to wait a week before we move."

"Go on." Julian clenched a fist behind his back.

"The guardsmen should be despatched as soon as Sebastian gives us the coordinates. It makes no sense to delay." Marius frowned.

"Four days then," Julian said decisively as he pushed his arms into his jacket.

Alexander raised a brow in silent inquiry.

"Cerebral reboot causes temporary psychosis. I will not waste time chasing down Sebastian's distorted perceptions of reality. We will wait four days." *I have no idea if that is true, and neither do they.* Julian consulted his watch and said, "Now, if you'll excuse me, I'm expected at the blood dispensary." He exited the room at a sedate pace which surged to breakneck speed as soon as the door closed behind him.

◇◇◇

Outside the council building, Julian paused on the wet sidewalk. The downpour of cold rain soaked his hair and flowed along the grooves bracketing his tight mouth. *Four days is enough time.* He set off for the hospital. His reassurance faded as he calculated that keeping Connor *fed* for four days could be a big problem.

Julian shouldered aside the thick glass door at the main entrance of the hospital, intent on collecting his vials of human blood, the higher allocation due to him as principal. The first time he took advantage of it was when hatching the plan to have Connor condemned to Storage Facility Eight. It had literally been a lifesaver.

Now I have Connor to feed, I use my full quota as a matter of course. On each visit, he took and signed for the same number of vials. Julian smiled. Of course, it meant regular trips to the eco-shelter, and the chance to see Leizle was a lure he indulged, despite the guilt he felt.

Pushing through the jellied-plastic sheets of the dispensary doors, the sound of them slapping closed made him focus and drove Leizle from his mind.

Connor hunts for animal blood, but the vital ten percent of human... Rebekah would offer it in a heartbeat, but he would die rather than feed from her, right now.

As a doctor, Connor knew the early symptoms of human blood deficiency in vampires, altered consciousness preceded by blurring vision. But once delirium set in, he would be past self-diagnosis. The state of altered consciousness would make the thought process needed to unlock the individual brain centers impossible. *Connor's living on the edge.*

Fire and Ice: Survival

Julian's expression lightened as he remembered the levity Connor brought to his predicament. *How did he put it? 'I won't feed from Rebekah. Harry's neck looks about as appetizing as a dry twig, and I'd rather not wrestle Oscar or Greg into submission, so, if you could bring me enough to keep the hallucinations at bay, then life's looking up'.* A full blown smile flickered over Julian's face for a moment.

He had been away from the eco-shelter longer than he planned. *And now, a visit is urgent.* The silent throng of vampires queuing for blood stepped aside at Principal Julian's approach.

He stopped opposite the young vampire at the dispensary desk. "Charles."

Charles looked up from his modest height. "Sorry to keep you waiting, Principal." He darted around to pull a tray out of the refrigerator behind him, clearly trying to impress with his efficiency.

Julian smiled, genuine amusement in his eyes. "Take it easy, Charles. It's busy. Are you on your own today?" He jerked his head at the growing number of vampires filtering into the dispensary reception area.

"The super-tanker noma... um mariners caused a hold-up. I'll be back on track in no time," said Charles.

Julian scooped up the vials of blood offered, placed six of them in his pocket and drank the remaining two.

Indicating the growing throng, Julian said, "They have nothing better to do, right now, just remember that. However, I do." With a half salute, he turned and left the dispensary. As he headed toward the exit, an agitated voice cut through the air.

"Julian!"

He whipped around, and seeing Anthony's worried face, he retraced his steps.

"Sorry. *Principal* Julian." Anthony corrected hastily.

"I think Julian is fine, under the circumstances."

He dropped a hand onto Anthony's shoulder. His face was whiter than Julian had ever seen it.

Anthony jerked his head towards the door of an examination room, and Julian followed him inside.

"The blood tests are back." Anthony's brows rose pointedly. Even in privacy he was not going to say her name.

"Ah, good, but she's somewhat recovered. Dialysis will not be necessary, it's not the venom in her system," Julian responded. *I had forgotten Anthony took her blood.*

"There's an anomaly."

"Yes, we discovered that for ourselves. Well, our friend did. He's back with us now." Julian's direct stare filled in the gaps as he waited for realization to hit.

"I'm glad to hear that." Anthony chose his words carefully. "The blood test showed inhibitory neurotransmitter levels consistent with a vampire in revival sleep. I wondered if her fatigue could be the result of... relaxation. A fetus hydrating a developing brain center." Anthony glanced around and snapped his jaw shut. He had said enough.

"Thank you, Anthony, that's useful to know. We're in the dark here." Julian's lips quirked wryly. "Our mutual friend will be grateful that you're on the team."

"Err, can I ask to be kept informed, from a research point of view." Anthony's curiosity burst from him. "But how?"

"At this point, no one knows." Julian made no attempt to hide his disquiet. "There's a dangerous road ahead for all of us. I'm going to check on the patient now, and I'll pass on your concerns."

Anthony opened the door again. "If there is anything I can do-"

"I'll let you know," Julian said as he took his departure.

The streets of London were a shimmering tapestry of gray slabs racing beneath his feet as at last, he set out for the eco-shelter. Passing through the woods, Julian shuffled everything he needed to do into an order. *Feed Connor. Check on Rebekah. Get the plans to move the humans out underway, piece of cake! But will Leizle cooperate? I think not.*

Chapter 19

Connor listened to Rebekah's stuttering breathing and frowned. Even while she slept, each time the baby kicked, she held her breath. His fear of hurting her grew more urgent with each passing day. Her ravenous hunger for his body was finally fading. He grinned. He must be the first man on the planet who felt relief when his lover's appetite waned.

Being with her, feeling her body respond to his, continued to fascinate and excite him, but the specter of hurting her was growing into a larger monster. He had used all the vials Julian had left, and now, the darkness in the cavern shimmered as he lay on his back with Rebekah resting on his chest.

It was not only the baby who craved her blood. Connor ran through the exchange where he said to Greg, Oscar, or even Leizle, 'Hey, after you've had lunch, do you fancy letting me take a bite out of you?' *Where the hell are you, Julian?*

As if his thoughts conjured his presence, Connor heard the wraithlike whisper of Julian calling his name in a drifting echo meant for his ears only. *Thank god.*

Relief drove Connor from Rebekah's side, although he still took time to replace his solid bulk with a bolster cushion of support. In a hurricane of activity, he raced his own shadow along the tunnels and into the dining cavern, coming to a stop with a flourish which sprayed fragments of dried earth into the air.

"Julian." Connor strode forward, frowning as he finished buttoning his shirt.

"Enjoying becoming a father, then?" Julian quipped, but, remembering Anthony's words, his expression became serious.

"I've left Rebekah sleeping, but for how long, who knows?" Connor's stiff features barely moved as he said, "Sorry to be blunt, but have you brought human blood?"

Julian's sharp look took in the clay-colored undertone to his friend's white complexion, the skin stretched tight across his cheekbones, and the dull glaze of his eyes. Connor's fingers trembled as he buttoned his shirt collar. In vampire terms, that Julian even had time to see the button in Connor's fingertips meant he was running in slow motion.

"Of course." He took two vials from his pocket and tossed them into the air.

Connor caught them, drained both and tossed back the empties.

"Are you okay?" asked Julian.

Connor crossed the cavern and sank down on to a wooden bench.

"Early signs of human blood starvation. Disturbed vision, inner ear coagulation, tendon tremor." A clinical diagnosis tripped from Connor's lips as he flexed his diaphragm, inflating and compressing his thorax, effectively massaging his heart to simulate circulation. "I'll be okay, now."

"But for how long?" This conversation had no high points. *I have only bad news.* "It looks like you needed that just to return you to ground zero. I have two more day's supply. But, what if I don't get back in time?"

"If I become unstable, I'll leave."

"Can't you feed?" Julian already knew the answer.

"From Rebekah? No, she's having trouble making enough blood to feed the baby. I think he has thirsty vampire tissue. She looks drained all the time." Connor slanted a cunning glance at Julian. "There's always Leizle." He laughed as a warning flashed in Julian's eyes. "I thought not," he chuckled. "She asks after you, by the way. She worries that you seem busy."

"It's probably best that I am busy." Julian's eyes were cold. *It'll be safer for her if she moves out with the others, and easier for me.*

Julian touched the remaining four vials of blood still in his pocket. It meant four days of survival to Connor, but two were his own. "I don't know when I can come again."

"Why? What has happened?"

"The council guardsmen are mobilizing. They are coming here to capture the humans. Sebastian and Serge have made their move."

"They can't mobilize without your order," said Connor, understanding dawning as he shot a searching glance at Julian. "You've given the order. How long?"

Fire and Ice: Survival

"I delayed them as long as I could, but, only four days. Marius pushed me."

"Thank you, every day of warning is a gift."

"Connor, you need to move them out."

"They are ready. I even got through to Harry." Connor grimaced. "There's no persuading Leizle and Oscar, and of course Rebekah stays with me."

"I wish I could say I'm surprised. I know it's no consolation, but at least I'm in control of the attack."

"I hope I won't have to kill you." Connor laughed, but they both knew it was a warning.

"I will declare myself if it comes to that. It's Sebastian you must look out for, he thinks you are dead and he's after Rebekah." Julian growled gently. "There's no other reason he would risk the Council's wrath when forty humans proves to be a lie."

"Forty?" Connor laughed, harshly.

Julian drew another two vials of human blood from his pocket. "This will see you through for a couple of days. If you can sleep, three, maybe." Julian handed them over. "You may have to ask... someone."

"They know what we are, sure. But knowing it, and being bitten by it, are not the same thing." Connor mulled over the candidates. "I'll consider it."

"Good, but perhaps it's better if you don't tell me, hmm?" Julian rested his hand on Connor's shoulder.

Connor laughed. They both knew that if he fed from Leizle, Julian would smell his venom.

"I better get going."

Julian exited the dining cavern and turned left instead of right, taking the tunnel which led deeper into the eco-shelter. His skin glowed as the dim bulbs in the bulkhead lights flickered with each pulse of the generator. The constant humming was loud to his ears, but not as loud as Leizle's breathing. He focused on her voice as she began to hum nervously, and he smiled.

Does she know I'm here? The smile dissolved as he realized why he was.

If he had a beating heart it would have been pounding. *I have no idea where to start.* He paused outside, absorbing the sounds and scent of her and locking them inside. *They may have to last awhile... forever, maybe.*

When he reached Leizle's open doorway, Julian retreated into shadow as he gauged her mood, sensing that her emotions were having an epic battle with reason. *Maybe I won't have to hurt her. She's already wrapping her heart in stone.*

He felt like a coward as he hoped she would help him, and that her head would rule her seventeen-year-old heart.

The wall of the cavern blurred as tears filled her eyes and Leizle wiped them away with the back of her hand. *Maybe Julian will never find Connor's strength. Unlike him, I don't have forever.* And the waiting was killing her. "It's for the best." Leizle breathed.

"What's for the best?" Julian hid his face in the shadows.

She jumped, darting a glance over her shoulder. Turning quickly away again, on a deep breath, she said, "I've decided not to wait. I have a life to live. I can't wait for you."

Her racing heart told Julian how hard this was for her. He studied her determined profile and whispered, "You're right not to wait." Her breath hissed quietly, and he chose the refuge of sinking deeper into revival sleep, stamping down the urge to close the space between them and change her mind.

"Goodbye," she said.

It was a brave try, but the tremor in her voice stirred a shower of splintered glass in his chest.

"Goodbye," he whispered and vanished.

The night air dragged over his set expression as he crossed the meadow. Accelerating as he entered the woodland, he skimmed the tree trunks, leaving scraps of dark cloth behind as they shredded his coat.

She's stronger than I thought. But she was wrong if she thought he had failed her. *I want it too much to fail.*

He had lived in a vacuum for two hundred years. No one chose immortality, but he had done more than that. *Eva's death stole my appetite for life and I chose death.* Julian smiled grimly. Only when he became a vampire did he realize that the scoundrels and thieves of London were a good food source. Their smoky unwashed stench was repulsive, but they were never missed. And with every heart he drained, his own became colder and harder.

This year would be his two hundredth anniversary of emptiness.

He had put ten miles between him and Leizle before he realized he wasn't empty now, and that she fulfilled him. He turned around and shed his tattered coat without breaking his stride. Minutes later, he was standing, as before, in the shadowed tunnel outside Leizle's den, working out what to say.

Six yards away, sitting hunched over and hugging her middle, Leizle was lost in a world where all the men she knew were old enough to be her father, and she had just made the biggest mistake of her life by lying to Julian.

She leapt to her feet and sprinted for the doorway.

He'll be angry. She could hear him lecturing her now. The battle of words played out in her head. *'How many times have I told you, Leizle?'.* "Yes, Julian, I do know..." she muttered. *Vampires don't need headlamps, and wrapping the motorcycle around a tree will seriously damage my health.* "So? I don't care."

She left her cavern, entered the dark tunnel, and barreled forward into a fast run.

She appeared like a beautiful apparition sprinting towards him. Bending his knees to absorb the impact, Julian waited to catch her.

The collision with a cold smooth wall winded Leizle, and she struggled to regain her balance. Julian slipped his hands around her waist and hitched her up his body, closing his mouth over hers and stealing what little oxygen she had left. He inhaled her essence and yearning flowed like hot lava through him, pooling in his stomach and warming his groin. The growl in his throat rumbled inside his chest.

Leizle's head reeled, but instinctively, she recognized him and kissed him back.

He began walking, feathering his lips over hers as he returned to her cavern.

The light in her den laced gold through his hair as she buried her hands in it. She pulled him closer as he lowered her down onto the mattress and settled his body next to hers. With a whisper of space between them, he deepened the kiss, molding his lips urgently to hers.

"You don't have to wait." He moved her hair back from her face, lacing his fingers into it, and his thumb traced down to rest on the pulse thudding in her throat. "You don't have to wait."

His tangled hair framed his face and he had never looked fiercer than he did at that moment. Intensity hollowed his cheeks, and a battle raged in his eyes. "I can do this, Red," he whispered, as his hand skimmed down her body.

"You came back."

"I never really left, not in here." He took her hand and held it to his silent chest. "If I had one, it would be yours," he said.

"You have a heart, Julian. I see it every time I look in your eyes."

"I waited two hundred years to feel like this." Julian's smile was apologetic. "I'm not going anywhere, even if it would be better if I did."

"I don't want you to go." Leizle ran her fingertips along his jawline, still checking that he was really there.

Reading her mind, he said, "I'm here."

As he kissed her again, he closed the space between them and her heartbeat echoed in his chest. His hands tingled as they spanned her back and slipped inside her sweatshirt. Pushing it up, he felt the turbulent current of her rushing blood vibrate through him. Venom flooded his mouth and his shoulders knotted with need as she trembled in his arms. The heat of her thighs branded his skin as Leizle groaned and pressed closer, her questing hands tugging open his shirt.

Burying his face in her shoulder, Julian mumbled, "Not today."

Her breath caught in her throat as he smiled against her skin. "Just not today, Leizle. You've never been with a man." Julian raised his face to look at her. "I'm still a man. I want to, you know that. But I want it to be right."

He welcomed her penetrating look, waiting until her smile chased the clouds of doubt in her troubled gaze away. He leant in to kiss her shoulder, finding restraint he never knew he had. The pulse beating in her neck drew his mouth. He laid his lips on her carotid artery, and they stung as if blistering with sunburn. He thought of Connor being here, needing her blood, and doing this.

His voice grated as he said, "Can I bite?"

Excitement coursed through Leizle at his words. Her pulse quickened and he could hear the turbulence of it as a hypnotizing whisper. He lifted her shoulders from the bed and his breath fanned her neck in chilled expectation.

"Can I bite?" he whispered again, and as she took a breath to answer, he closed his jaws firmly. Anticipation of biting into her fragrant flesh tightened his body, and before he filled his mouth with her blood, his throat vibrated with a guttural sigh of ecstasy.

Julian's vision blurred to red. Pleasure shot through every nerve ending and his thirsty tissue ached. His jaws clamped down hard, and like dry earth waiting for rain, he drowned in the cocktail of her moisture. Leizle clung to him, gripping his shoulders, and his restraint faltered. *I have to stop.* He drew in a final deep draft of her blood and froze. Settling his thigh in between hers, he pulled her closer, moving in a gentle rhythm which dragged his hunger from his throat down into his groin. On a deep sigh he relaxed his jaw, and stroking his lips over her skin, he found the will to pull away.

Julian clawed his way back from the edge. He gathered his senses and the bloodlust dispersed like the hot pinprick sparks of a fading firework. He traced a soothing tongue over the wound in Leizle's neck and sighed.

Holding her, Julian fitted her body into his, her soft breasts and stomach brushing the hard planes of his chest. She played her fingers over his collarbone and shoulder as though she couldn't bear to not touch him. *Still making sure I'm here,* Julian guessed.

Her vibrant features relaxed as lethargy crept through her and she rested her head against him. When her breathing became slow and heavy, he knew she was fighting sleep.

He had never enjoyed 'hugging', but her cheek warmed his chest, his arms folded around her, and, with her satin skin touching his from chin to thigh, he discovered a kaleidoscope of emotions.

Reluctantly, he whispered, "Hey, I have to go, Red."

She mumbled in protest, and he rubbed his chin over her hair as he said, "No, you must sleep. You know there are things I have to do. Connor has his hands full with Rebekah and the baby, and moving the others out." A frown flitted across his face. "I want you to go with them."

She shook her head. "Not a chance."

"If you won't go, then do as Connor says, and stay safe." His hands stroked a persuasive rhythm over her back. The top of her head grazed his jaw as she nodded her agreement, and he was satisfied.

"Sorry, Red. I do have to go." He eased her from his embrace, smiling as she groaned half-heartedly. He held her hand as he stood up and dropped a kiss onto the corner of her sleepy smile.

At the doorway, he raised a hand in farewell, but she was already sleeping. As he turned away he was glad he had at least one piece of good news for Connor. *Small comfort, but at least he will be fully fed.*

Julian tracked Connor down, sitting in deep shadow in the tunnel outside Rebekah's cavern. He slowed abruptly at the anguish radiating from every line of his friend's body.

Connor had stiffened into a hunched posture, one hand near his chin and a clenched fist resting on his knee, like a cinder-gray statue of Pompeii captured in a moment of despair. His sight remained locked on Rebekah's sleeping form and without turning his head, he took in a deep breath. "How could I have done this to her?" His features were a blank slate. "I've been working it out. She must have been pregnant before we believed it to be safe. But I was always careful, so, how?"

Julian's silence weighed thickly in the air.

Connor finally turned his head. "What do you know?"

Relaxation followed by a rapacious appetite for physical release. Not hard to guess. "Anthony said the blood tests showed elevated chemical levels commonly found in vampires in revival sleep." Connor's calm acceptance was reassuring. *This is not a new thought for him.* "Anthony thinks the fatigue could be the side effect of the baby's brain developing our stress reduction center."

Connor's suspended hand finally dragged down over his cheek. "That's what I feared."

He focused again on Rebekah's face. In the dim light, the purple circles staining her closed eyes enlarged the sockets to the proportions of a skull.

"That would mean her violent mood swings are a side effect of the baby's brain developing the appetites controlled by rap-sleep." Connor paused.

Julian knew where the conversation was going. *But Connor has to say it.*

"So, that leaves us with the baby developing a killing instinct and the bloodlust which guarantees our survival." Connor's frost-clouded eyes focused on Julian. "What happens next? Will Rebekah be flooded with murderous thoughts of grave sleep? And will there also be a feeding frenzy inside her fighting its way out?"

Julian remained silent. There was nothing he could say.

"Whatever it takes, I'm not losing her." Connor stood up. "I'll need Anthony and the hospital. We are not going anywhere."

Removing the two remaining vials of human blood from his pocket, Julian pressed them into Connor's hand. "It is not much. But this will guarantee you four days. I'll be back by then, on my own or..."

Connor looked into Julian's saddened face, registering for the first time the flush staining his cheekbones. He knew Julian had risked a lot to give him the extra time; he knew how hard it was to stop when the scent which clawed at you finally flooded your throat.

"Thank you, Julian. Four days will be enough." Connor inclined his head and returned to studying Rebekah's sleeping form. "I'll move the others out."

Julian gripped Connor's shoulder. "Good luck, I'll do what I can."

Twenty minutes later, Julian crossed the River Thames and exchanging the fragrant memories of Leizle for the anticipated stench of exchanges with Serge revolted him.

Arriving in his neighborhood of Richmond, he entered the house. Stripping his torn shirt and muddy pants from his body as he walked, he headed for the bathroom. He took his time returning his outward appearance to the usual façade, and a smile lit his green gaze as he relived the stolen moment with Leizle. Like Connor before him, Julian felt changed by the blood coursing through his veins – her blood brought with it the thrill of awareness.

Dressing once more, he tidied his appearance, running his fingers through his hair until the mask of complacency was complete. *Looking the part is half the battle.*

His focus for the next few days would be persuading Marius and Alexander to break with protocol. He needed them to accompany the council guardsmen and attend the capture of the human nest in person. *The claim of forty humans is nonsense. The jurors will come down hard on Serge and Sebastian if they see that firsthand.*

Chapter 20

A pair of grazing roe deer bounded urgently through the woodland undergrowth. Their short barks of alarm punctured the damp air in an echo of warning, and Connor enjoyed the explosive movement of their chaotic flight as he hunted them down.

One animal died as Connor snatched it out of the air and buried his teeth in its neck in one powerful move. He rose smoothly to his feet, wiping blood from his face as he watched the female disappear. *She'll live to see another day.* Connor hunted males in the interest of survival of the species; females would always be more valuable.

Returning home, Connor paused on the edge of the pasture, his torso draped in the weak shadow cast by a clouded sky already streaked with pale lemon icing as the sun slipped towards the horizon. *It's almost time to leave.* He raised his chin and closed his eyes as the warm breeze stroked over his bare copper-streaked chest. The hunt had been short, but satisfying.

With a deep cleansing breath, Connor loped across the meadow into the eco-shelter tunnel. Making his way to the laundry cavern, he filled a bucket with water and emptied it over his head. He repeated the process, sluicing the water down his body until his chest was clean and the blood had lifted from around his fingernails. *They know I'm a killer, but they don't need to see it.*

As Connor pulled a clean black shirt over his damp body, he embraced the buzz of nervous energy which accompanied being well fed. He mentally thanked Julian for his sacrifice. He had three days left. *It took Oscar, Harry, and Greg two days to make it cross country to the other camp with Seth. This group is larger, but three days should do it.*

All Connor had to do was get them to the rendezvous point. He could trust the men to get the group the rest of the way.

He walked down the dimly lit tunnel until he reached the meeting cavern. Stopping on the threshold, he watched the group of humans moving purposefully around the space, loading up backpacks and tightening ropes. Their nervous excitement for tonight's expedition wafted enticingly over his palette, even through the layers of cotton, wool, and oilskin, but the blade of hunger inside him was blunt. *The hunt was well timed.*

Content that the preparations would be completed in time, and thoughts of Rebekah luring him away, Connor turned on his heel and went to find her. He had satisfied her appetite for him again and left her sleeping. The heartbeats of her and his child were always there on the edge of his consciousness. *The baby never seems to sleep.* The rounded swell of her stomach rolled restlessly in perpetual movement, and even when she slept, she groaned as the baby fought for room inside her.

Sensing a human presence in the dining cavern, his speed slowed, and stepping over the threshold, he found himself alone with Leizle for the first time since Julian had left. She was deep in thought, her chin resting on her hand, and she jumped when he appeared.

"Sorry, didn't mean to startle you."

"That's okay." Her smile lit up her face, and he could not help but smile in response.

His expression softened as he registered the pallor of her cheeks and the raised bite mark on her neck. *I wasn't sure how Julian's attentions would leave her.* He had expected her to feel melancholy because Julian had left again.

"You seem happy." Connor lowered himself onto the seat opposite. "I told you he would come."

"You did, and I'm glad I waited." She swallowed loudly. "Connor, will Julian ever find it easy to be with me?"

"Honestly? Not a chance." Connor's laughter warmed his expression as he placed his cold hand over hers. "But don't you see? There's the proof. He would suffer anything to be with you."

"Is that how it is for you?"

"Yes, but so much worse now. Part of me wants to turn back the clock." His eyes closed for a moment. "If I had let her go that day, outside the hospital, would we be here now with her life in danger?"

Fire and Ice: Survival

"How *did* it happen? The baby?" A tight grin of embarrassment flitted across Leizle's face and, as the wound on her neck throbbed, the scent of her blood wafted to fill the space between them.

Connor appreciated her aroma, and easily resisted the twist of hunger in his gut. He covered his enjoyment with a raised brow of sardonic amusement.

"Well not *how*... you know what I mean."

"I really don't know." Connor looked her in the eye. "So, don't expect too much from Julian until we figure it out. He won't want to see you in the same place."

Leizle nodded. "At least he's agreed I can stay." She smiled as she remembered how, holding her as if she was made of glass, he had asked her to leave with the others. She refused. When he had said "I want you to go", his every touch on her skin made his words a lie.

"I see everyone is getting ready," said Connor with satisfaction.

"Yes. Have you decided on the time?"

"We will leave at sunset. Seth and his scouting party will meet us four miles into the wood. I'll escort the group that far." Connor inhaled deeply. "If you need me, Leizle, just shout. I will be no more than twenty seconds from her."

The silence stretched as the uncomfortable thought of being away from Rebekah drained his vitality. *Is the grave sleep stage of pregnancy far away? Will it be quick, or a slow burning hunger?* Connor's features were pinched tight.

Leizle cleared her throat, calling his attention back.

Suddenly intense, he met her gaze. "It's not too late, you know. Julian will find you when this is over."

"I will stay," she said. "For Rebekah. But honestly? For me too."

Connor nodded as he rose to his feet. "Anyhow, if you change your mind... But for now, I have to go." With a brief wave, he left.

"Never going to get used to that," Leizle muttered as she stared at the suddenly empty space, resisting the urge to look behind her in case he was kidding around.

◇◇◇

Connor left the communal areas behind, taking his time to walk along the narrower passageways leading down into the living caverns.

With the vampire community fifteen years out of hiding, Connor was out of practise at *pretending* to be human. Unchecked, his explosive preternatural force was alarming, and if he was going to escort the humans through the woods tonight, they could do without that kind of excitement.

His eyes swept the profile of the tunnels, which provided the constant of an easily regulated, sheltered existence. Connor wondered how the eco-shelter humans would take to the harsher alfresco existence of Seth's group of survivors.

They had an Anderson shelter approach to underground living; sleeping in camouflaged bunkers buried in the woodland floor, when in hiding from vampires and the elements. But, in essence, they were tree dwellers. Mature trees of immense girth grew to over twenty meters high, and their broad leaved foliage provided concealment for the wooden hideouts constructed within the span of their branches. From what Greg had said, they scaled the trees using wooden pegs, and footholds gouged into the tree bark.

Of course their survival owed itself, almost entirely, to blind luck. Situated half way between Maidstone and London, the camp location of Seth's tree dwellers fell into an area outside the hunting ranges of the surrounding vampire hives.

As Connor drew nearer to her cavern, he tuned into Rebekah's vital signs. *She has company. Uncle Harry.* Connor enjoyed the buzz of pleasure he detected running through her, and as much as he feared for her, he would watch from a distance. Her serotonin levels were normal, and happiness, sleep, and appetite were once again in harmony. *But for how long?*

Stepping silently over the threshold, he melted into the shadows and leaned back against the wall. Rebekah's pulse raced and he smiled. Her pleasure at his arrival radiated the warmth of happiness through him, too.

Fire and Ice: Survival

She was sitting on a chair, and to him she was perfect, even though her tousled blond hair was a tumbled mess of golden strands, and the purple smudges around her eyes sockets persisted.

She had worn the masks of anger and desire every waking moment for so long that, seeing her now, with her features relaxed made him smile. He contented himself with watching her hands stroking perpetually over her stomach, and breathing in the warmed honey accent of her scent. *She's glowing today.*

Catching sight of Harry, Connor did not need his preternatural senses to see the sadness on the old man's face. *He doesn't want to leave Rebekah. I can understand that.*

"I should have visited more often, Rebekah. I do know that." Harry flushed with embarrassment. "I blame myself."

For Harry, his guilt over his part in Douglas' treatment of Rebekah made burying himself in his work an easy option, and Lord knows, he had plenty to do. Anthony had taken over the task of providing Harry with all the chemicals and pills needed. Ensuring the eco-shelter community had a stock pile of beta-blockers and pheromone suppressants was a very convincing way for Harry to keep his mind busy, and to avoid thinking about what had gone before. That he had sold Rebekah out.

"It's all right, Harry." Rebekah smoothed her palm over the tumbling movement of her child as she looked into his sad face. Just the thought of Douglas still chilled her to the bone, and forgiving Harry should be hard, but Connor and the baby made it easy. *Douglas making me his wife compelled Connor to act. Without one, there would not have been the other, so, yes, I can forgive him.* "I'm happier than I ever thought possible," said Rebekah quietly.

"I'll always be sorry. But, if you are happy now, then I am glad." Harry's anxious gaze moved to Rebekah's stomach and it was clear he couldn't understand her happiness. Connor may be honorable, but he was still a vampire.

"I wish you could come with us. Will you be okay?" Harry nodded self-consciously at the baby. "Will you let me know?"

"Of course." Rebekah's eyes wandered over the cavern walls until she found Connor's face. Her breath caught, as always, at the sight of his raven black hair and intense pewter gaze. Until recently, she had seen him through desire hazed eyes and committed every nuance of his expressive face to memory, but now, with crystal clear vision restored, he was more beautiful than she remembered. "Of course we will," she whispered.

Connor appeared suddenly beside them as his need to be with her overwhelmed him.

Startled, Harry said, "I love you, Rebekah." Jumping awkwardly to his feet, he flicked a glance up at Connor as he moved to go.

"Harry," said Connor, quietly.

Harry stopped moving, riveted by Connor's stare.

"Make sure everyone takes beta blockers and uses the suppressant spray before we leave." Without looking away, Connor reached for Rebekah's hand, circling his thumb over the inside of her wrist. "Julian gave us four days, but it's better to be prepared, in case the group need to hide."

Harry's preoccupation clouded his rheumy eyes. "I'll go back to the meeting cavern and make sure they are all ready."

"It will be tough for a while. But if you listen to Seth, it will work out."

"About Seth and the others, how many are there?" asked Harry.

"Seth will have three scouts with him." Connor stood very still, sensing that Harry wanted to bolt. "I dropped off pills and spray when I delivered the antibiotics for his boy. They are coming a lot closer than last time, so will be dosed up too." Connor had also told Seth to leave his boy at home. He had been clear on that. *Able bodies only on this trip, it's too important.*

Harry began muttering to himself as he moved quickly across the cavern and out of the door.

Connor turned to Rebekah. "We're leaving in the morning, but I'll be only seconds away, I promise." He dropped to his knees in front of her, spreading his hands over her stomach as he looked up into her face. "Nice to have you back, my Rebekah, not that I didn't enjoy your... appetites." His brow lifted suggestively.

Fire and Ice: Survival

Rebekah smiled at him. "Can't stand the pace, huh?" she murmured. She may have had no control, but she remembered every moment, and a flush stained her cheeks red.

Her love filled Connor's chest with warmth, and, as his hunger washed over his palette, he smiled back. "Oh I could go a few more rounds, but honey, I missed you." Rising to his feet again, his fingers drifted over her cheek as he settled a gentle kiss on her lips.

◇◇◇

Julian moved through the wet streets of London on his way to the council buildings, happy, for once, that he would be presiding in council for the usual mundane range of offences. Sebastian had yet to provide the coordinates the court waited for. He glanced at his watch, as he always did whenever the sands of time streamed through his thoughts. *I still have time to stir Marius and Alexander into action.* Because Serge had made the court application, *he* would be the council representative out in the field during the humans' capture. *And that will not do.*

A stench of rotting meat assailed Julian's nostrils as he passed along the eastern boundaries of Hyde Park and, ironically, he knew the odor instantly, this time. *Sebastian. Lying in wait.*

Julian carried on walking, and as Sebastian stepped out of the trees on his left, Julian shot out his arm and closed his fingers around the young vampire's windpipe. "You've picked the wrong day to cross me, Sebastian," Julian spat, glaring into the muddy hazel eye that widened in surprise, and ignoring the milk-white dead pool of the other.

Sebastian froze for a moment before he grinned.

Julian eased his grip enough to allow speech. "Well, talk, that *is* why you're here."

"You know there aren't forty humans because you're protecting them," Sebastian croaked, his eye glinting. "Guilty of 'threatening the food supply', Principal?"

"That's a very bold accusation, Sebastian." The urge to snap his neck twitched through Julian's fingertips. *How much rope shall I give him?*

"I *saw* you." Sebastian's throat gurgled with the venom which could not drain past Julian's fist. "You, Doctor Connor, and eight guardsmen. Does that ring a bell?"

Julian's eyes glazed with manufactured boredom. "Go on."

"No one else needs to know." Sebastian's lowered tone shared his confidence. "I have yet to give the council the information they need to despatch the guardsmen. At the moment." He tapped his temple. "It's still locked in here."

"That is gratifying," said Julian with a smile.

Julian lifted Sebastian until his toes barely brushed the ground. The silence was broken only by Sebastian's efforts to swallow. He waited. *I'm not going to make this easy. Let's see how far he will go.*

"How gratifying?" croaked Sebastian.

Julian resisted a bark of laughter at Sebastian's nerve. *Or stupidity?* "No doubt you have a price for this convenient attack of amnesia?"

"The council..."

"Councilor Sebastian?" Julian asked. "And what guarantee do I have that your memory will not suddenly return?"

Sebastian tugged at Julian's arm until he relented and allowed his feet to touch down on the sidewalk once more.

"You'll have to take my word. I believe that with Doctor Connor gone the fate of the humans no longer matters to you. So-" Sebastian paused for effect. "To coin a phrase, your secret is safe with me."

"You've given this some thought, I see." Julian appeared to consider Sebastian's words. "But I'm intrigued." Tilting his head, with a half-smile, he mused quietly, "You say I have 'threatened the food supply'? Where is your *proof*? Why would anyone take your word over mine?"

"You made a deal with Serge. I'm sure the council could be persuaded to take a closer look at your involvement with Doctor

Connor. How much digging would be needed, do you think, before they find evidence of your partnership?" Calculation roiled in the depths of Sebastian's good eye.

Julian's expression filled with mock regret as he said, "So, I'm guilty of allowing my respect for Doctor Connor's surgical expertise to cloud my judgement, nothing more." Julian's hooded eyelids concealed his realization. *Unless a closer look uncovers that Connor has escaped from the storage facility. Then the evidence would be compelling.* Julian tightened his grip on Sebastian's neck. "Now, here's the thing. I see a flaw in your plan."

Julian watched with amusement as Sebastian's mobile grin became fixed. His hazel eye glazed over while Sebastian ran back over their conversation and failed to find the flaw.

"I think not," he said.

"Do you want to know where you made your mistake?" Julian asked, his face expressionless. "*You* have no proof. All you have is *circumstantial* evidence." Sebastian's windpipe creaked beneath Julian's fingertips. "It's tempting to end this now, and kill you, but that will send the wrong message."

Serge would never buy Sebastian's accidental death. *Better to let the human nest be found empty.* Julian had to have faith that Connor had a plan to safeguard Rebekah. *He'll hide her until after the attack.* A prickle of unease ran along Julian's spine. *How far will Connor go to save her? If it were Leizle, I'd sacrifice myself.*

Sebastian wriggled in Julian's clawed grip, his fingers digging into his tormentor's arm.

"*Knowing* is not enough, Sebastian. Now, *I* have an insurance policy. A human body you left drained in the woods, riddled with your venom." Sebastian rocked back on his heels when Julian released him suddenly. "Now, *that's* what I call proof." Julian's eyes narrowed and he allowed harsh laughter low rumbling expression. "How much of an irritation would you be, I wonder, interred in Storage Facility Eight alongside Doctor Connor?"

Sebastian shook with frustration. His face tightened as he gritted his teeth, and a clotted blood aroma filled the air. The spark of anger in the hazel eye cooled to calculating rage and Sebastian tensed, preparing to attack.

"How good *is* depth perception with just the one eye?" Julian breathed conversationally, his powerful air unassailable. "How old are you? Sixty years turned?" He shook his head, glaring into Sebastian's face as he snapped, "Don't insult me, boy." Julian stepped back. "Go, before I change my mind and break your neck."

Sebastian fell back to a safe distance and said, "I guess I'll see you in court, *Principal* Julian."

"I look forward to it. You've got a couple of days left to be smart or stupid. Your call." Julian stared him down before, turning, he strode away.

Julian was almost disappointed that Sebastian was not stupid enough to try and take him out. *Now I know the worst.* His gut told him Rebekah was still the prize, but he had the measure of Sebastian's ambition. *He wants the power of being on the council, and thought he could blackmail me into giving it to him.* He continued on his way along the exposed side of Hyde Park with a grimace frozen on his face. *Of course Sebastian won't stop there. He'll stab me in the back if he gets the chance, but Connor will finish him, and I'll enjoy seeing it.*

Chapter 21

As he entered the dining cavern, Connor took a deep breath, sampled the air, and smiled. His arrival galvanized movement in the assembled humans who hitched backpacks up onto their shoulders and shifted from perching on the wooden tables to standing.

With a nod, Connor acknowledged the thumbs-up from Harry confirming they were all dosed up for the escape.

"They have enough food and water for four days," said Oscar, resting a hand on Harry's shoulder as though their fifteen years of alliance could be committed to memory through the skin of his palm. "You go careful, Harry."

"I scouted the area, and we're good to go," said Connor, "Greg, you bring up the rear, I'll be waiting in the woods." Connor turned to leave, but then swung back into the room, calling, "Thomas?"

The company parted and Thomas scuttled into view.

"You've stayed out of trouble for a while. Good lad, keep it up," said Connor and he was rewarded with Thomas' smile.

"Okay, Greg, let's move them out."

Connor's sudden departure blasted chilled air over their tense faces as the group shifted forward.

Harry led the way along the tunnels until they regrouped in the entrance cavern, nervously looking out over the rough pasture.

The slim pink crescent of a new moon glowed in a black star littered sky. Over the next two weeks the moon would become the bright disc of a silver dollar, but tonight, the impenetrable darkness provided perfect concealment. They darted out across the meadow in single file, heading for the long grass and crouching low.

At the top of the rise, in the sheltered embrace of the trees, Connor smiled as he watched their beetle-like progress. The darkest night on the lunar cycle was merely a placebo. Their movement was as clear as day to Connor's sensitive retina. *But they feel safer in the dark, thinking they are invisible.* He stood, listening to the sound of the woodlands nocturnal mutterings, taking comfort of the assurance that they were moving out in time.

Still breathing hard from the exertion, the sixteen refugees gathered around Connor in the thick shade inside the woods. Dread bleached their features until they were as white as his own, and fear sent tremors through their bodies. Connor manufactured a smile of reassurance. His pale chiseled expression hardened as he listened, redirecting his focus to make one last check on Rebekah before they left. *She's anxious, but not for herself.* Connor sighed. *The sooner I return with good news, the better.*

Satisfied the group was ready, Connor laid his hand on Greg's shoulder, passing over control as he stepped back and melted into the undergrowth. With Greg on point, they moved through the woods at a steady pace, following the compass setting previously traveled with Oscar and Harry.

Out of human sight, Connor brought up the rear, acting as the perfect deterrent to those who might otherwise fall behind. Some in the group still didn't know what to make of him. *Sheepdog or wolf?* After fifteen years in hiding, trusting a vampire proved difficult.

Three hours later, when Greg gave the command to fall-out, sixteen weary bodies sank gratefully down onto the soft moss-covered earth. Slumping against tree trunks and using their backpacks as makeshift cushions, they smothered groans of relief. The cool dark air soothed their glowing cheeks and the water they drank down had never tasted better. Waiting in silence was difficult, but for some, staying awake was harder.

Finally, Seth stepped into view with his staff clenched in his hand and every angle of his tall frame awkward with tension.

"Seth," said Connor, inclining his head.

The tall man swallowed loudly, not meeting Connor's eye.

Connor's head jerked round. Directing a penetrating gaze into the darkest shadows of the undergrowth, he vibrated with anger.

"What's wrong?" whispered Greg.

"Why did you let her come?" Connor growled.

Seth shrugged, grimacing as the cramped muscles in his neck burned. "I couldn't stop her, she followed us."

"Do you know what she did?" Before Seth could answer, Connor added, "It doesn't matter."

He closed his eyes, flexed his ribcage and filled his lungs with the damp night air. Her aniseed scent scorched his nostrils, and now, saturated in her aroma, his fingertips tingled in anticipation.

"Annabelle." His voice was low and persuasive.

Greg stiffened at the sound of the name and hissed, "Seth. No."

He, at least, knows there is reason to fear. Connor tapped out the compelling rhythm of the girl's rattling heartbeat on his thigh until his patience wore thin. "Annabelle, come out." His harsh whisper wafted through the leaves of the trees, and then his silence held everyone still.

The woods echoed and creaked as she made her way over roots and mulch, and finally, she emerged. Focused on her feet, she concentrated on avoiding ground elder and nettles. The curtain of blond hair hid her face. *But she cannot hide the sweat of fear on her skin.* Connor's smiled viciously as he recognized the jerky movement of muscles which fought to drive her forward when all she wanted to do was run away.

Licking dry lips, she rolled away one small pebble of deceit. "My name isn't Annabelle, it's Emily, I lied."

Her blond hair was shorter and darker, and without the luster he remembered. Her apprehensive blue eyes, which could not quite look at him, were the color of turbulent white water.

Connor's fingers flexed as he imagined seeing those eyes darken. The desire to drag clouds of pain across their surface became an overwhelming urge and he moved fast. His black garb blurred into a thunder cloud of movement, and the bark of a tree bit into her shoulder blades when Emily leapt backward in fear.

"Do you think I care what you are calling yourself today?" Connor stood barely six inches away with his hands braced on the tree trunk either side of her head. "Why are you here?" He snarled and the rush of his breath over her skin closed her eyes.

Keeping her eyes squeezed shut, she swallowed. "I wanted to come."

"Why?" The tree trunk vibrated painfully beneath her shoulder blades as Connor slammed his hand down and made a palm sized dent in the bark.

"To get it over with... this." Her face crumpled into a pinched fist of terror. Forcing her eyes open, she whispered, "To say, I know what I did, and I'm sorry."

Connor smiled, allowing venom to drip from his teeth. Chips of ice glinted in the coal-black shadow of his eye sockets. "Sorry?"

He retrieved a hand from the crater in the bark and dragged his fingertips along her collarbone. As they reached the graceful bow in the middle, closing his thumb and finger over it, he squeezed slowly. Adrenalin rushed through Emily's brain at the searing pain of his touch, and, the sensation of holding a hot poker in his hand as her skin flushed, exhilarated him. Connor leaned in close, whispering, "This is a bare fraction of what she suffered." He pinched harder and purple bruises blossomed beneath his fingertips as the capillaries collapsed and the bone fibers began to creak.

"Please." Her blue eyes darkened with pain, and a dry gasp burned her lungs.

Connor's eyes gleamed as Emily's knees buckled, but the downward slide made the pain bite harder, forcing her to brace back against the tree and bear it.

Every pair of eyes remained glued to Connor's face in horrified fascination. His anger was a tangible force which made breathing difficult. For Connor, their thundering hearts were a prelude to the keening cry building in Emily's throat.

Suddenly, the spell shattered as a tall sandy-haired man barreled his way through the bushes. He burst into the clearing, his face contorted in anger. "Take your hands off her."

Metal flashed dull gray in the dim light as the young man raised a fist holding a knife and rushed at Connor.

Connor sighed at the interruption, irritated that he would lose sight of Emily's terrified expression for even the half second it would take to disable the man. His fingers twitched as he considered darting out a hand, twisting the man's grip and slicing the blade across his own jugular. Instead, Connor grunted in satisfaction as Greg tackled the rushing figure from behind and wrestled him into an arm lock.

"Don't be a bloody fool," Greg snapped.

Adrenaline tainted testosterone flooded Connor's nostrils as the young man struggled. Greg's hold tightened and his mouth dropped open in strangled protest.

"Ah, the boyfriend," said Connor, glancing at the cramped features and shrugging. "We all deserve a fighting chance." Reaching out, Connor plucked the blade from the man's slack fist and ran his thumb over the jagged edge, scoring a line into his hard tissue. Like dragging a nail down a blackboard, the blade screeched, setting human teeth on edge as Connor stared into the young man's face.

Releasing Emily, Connor whipped around, threw the knife, and buried the blade and half the hilt in an adjacent tree trunk. Connor said quietly, "I'll make you a deal. You pull that out and she gets to walk away without the broken bones I have planned."

Connor smiled and his loosened grip rested like a necklace around Emily's throat. Waving a hand in an 'after you' gesture, he invited the youngster to approach.

The metal end-stop of the knife handle glinted like a malevolent eye, daring him to touch it.

Greg withdrew, and the only sound was the young man grunting as he tugged his clothes straight. Clearly wondering what the hell he had gotten himself into, he stepped forward.

Keeping a wary eye on the vampire's menacing presence, the youth recoiled when the brittle smile abruptly disappeared from Connor's tight white features, and his dark head whipped around as a sound pitched for vampire ears alone riveted his attention.

Leizle's screaming. Connor's anger evaporated. His narrowed gaze stared back through the wood as though his sight could burn through the obstacles hiding the scene from his view.

"Rebekah." Her name drifted through the trees as Connor vanished.

Emily cried out in pain as Connor's fingers dragged away.

As he accelerated rapidly, Connor locked the pleasure deep inside his chest as a consolation prize. His diamond-hard nails had dug deep, scratching across Emily's throat. *If Serge created a monster, then I have branded her.* Like a carved scarlet letter, his jagged tear in her flesh labeled her a 'liar'. His satisfied roar echoed through the woodlands.

Connor crashed through the woods, oblivious of the splintered tree branches shredding his clothes and scoring lines in the velvet sheen of his granite hard tissue. He ricocheted from tree trunks as he leapt clear of the ground and, grinding his footprint into bark, launched himself dozens of feet over densely packed brambles.

She's shouting for Oscar, now. Connor heard it as an echo which the leaves on the trees tried to swallow, but each syllable seared a hole in his brain.

The path he cut across the meadow tore grass out by the roots, and churned up the ground.

Leizle's scream still hung in the air as the twenty seconds he promised elapsed. Connor's shoulders collided with the tunnel walls, showering dirt onto the floor as he shaved seconds of the time by taking the shortest path.

Drawn like iron filings to a magnet, he hurtled into the empty dining cavern and was bombarded by a metallic cacophony of pots and pans crashing to the ground.

The smell of iron rich blood flooded his brain, and instinctively he salivated before the kick of hunger registered.

The first thing he saw was Leizle with her hands clamped over her mouth, her bulging eyes transfixed with horror. He swung into the kitchen and stopped, taking in the sluggish tide of blood flowing across the floor, transforming the cracks in the tiles into a crimson spider's web, with Rebekah at its center, sitting in a pool of sated hunger.

Remnants of raw liver clung to Rebekah's face. Connor slammed his vocal chords shut as his ravenous gaze grazed over the curves of her blood-soaked frame. Blood oozed from her mouth, and every rapturous bite she took laid a river of red down over the swell of her stomach and pooled in her lap.

Fire and Ice: Survival

Leizle's hyperventilating breath and the blood dripping through Rebekah's cotton skirt onto the tiled floor were the only sounds Connor could hear.

Shedding his muddy greatcoat and dropping it at his feet, Connor pushed into revival sleep, clamping down on the feeding frenzy flooding his brain in the euphoria of anticipated pleasure. He surged forward and scooped Rebekah up from the floor.

"Hey, honey, let's get you cleaned up," he whispered as the urge to kiss her, to dip in and taste the blood, molded a snarl to his lip.

His appearance unleashed a litany of words from Leizle as she finally took a gasp of air and muttered, "Thank God, thank God, thank God."

Connor settled Rebekah into his body, uncaring that the pool of blood in her lap saturated his shirt and flowed freely down the front of his pants. Rebekah clasped her hands around his neck, and, resting her cheek onto his chest, she relaxed into him.

"I was so hungry," she murmured.

Connor smiled, his voice tight with relief as he replied, "It's the baby, honey." A lucid sentence, even one four words long, was a good sign. *It's not yet the feral hunger of grave-sleep, but...*

Connor stopped in front of Leizle. "She'll sleep, now. Try not to worry. She'll be okay." His gray eyes were sincere. *But for how long, I'm not so certain. How long before this hunger becomes grave-sleep?*

He adjusted Rebekah's weight, and his baby kicked him in the ribs, hard, as it shifted inside the ever restricting space of her abdomen. *The baby's big.* Connor spanned his palm over the saturated fabric of her dress and calculated the size of the bump stretching her skin tight. *Six pounds and growing fast.* "I don't know how long we have left, buddy, before you break a few ribs," Connor murmured in a low vibration for his ears only. *Staying close to the hospital is the right decision.*

As Oscar's footsteps thundered along the tunnel and across the dining cavern, Connor lifted an eyebrow at Leizle. "Uh-oh, we're in trouble, now," he said in a theatrical whisper with 'yikes' written on his face.

Leizle looked around at the devastation, some of which had been her doing when she panicked and hurtled around the kitchen. She laughed ruefully, "You're not kidding, *big* trouble."

Oscar stepped over the threshold and skidded to a halt like a train hitting the end-stop on the siding. He was sweating and his chest heaved from the exertion of running. His wet shirt sleeves were dripping, and he automatically resumed wiping the soap bubbles from his big hands. A frown disguised his concern as he took in Rebekah's blood soaked appearance and Connor's calm control.

"Cut yourself shaving, lad?" His eyes skirted his domain and his mouth sucked lemons as he added, "Guess we're having liver and onions, without the liver then?"

Connor grinned sheepishly.

Oscar mopped his face with the damp towel and stepped aside. "The bath tub is filled and ready to go. I guess the laundry will wait." He looked at Rebekah's blood streaked skin and jerked his head. "Off you go. Me and Leizle will clean this lot up."

Connor's eyes were drawn to Rebekah's blood smeared face as her head dropped back onto his shoulder. Absorbed in her rapt expression, searching her hooded gaze, he penetrated the fathom deep pools, and the molten currents of her contentment warmed him. Her intoxication was tangible, settling a somnolent mood of relaxation over her.

But not so, for the baby. The vibration of tiny teeth grinding together resonated through Connor's chest like the arcing of electricity. *The drip feeding of the umbilical cord is whetting its appetite. How long have I got?* Connor's grim thoughts painted pain across his face as his lips tightened and his nostrils flared.

Attracting Leizle's attention, Oscar raised a skeptical brow. "Well, lassie?"

She blushed at the mess scattered at her feet. "I'll help clean up," she muttered, and moved away, reaching down to pick a pan up from the floor.

Oscar waited until she was making her way across the tiles, concentrating on gathering the utensils scattered far and wide, before turning his attention to Connor.

He inspected the grim stone-hard features and asked, "So, tell me. First, raw liver, what's next?"

The mask cracked, and for a moment Connor's uncertainty broke through. "I don't know. We've never been here before."

"But you have a plan, right?" Oscar's voice was the low breath of a prayer.

Connor's gaze sharpened as he said, "This is the final stage, and she cannot be on her own. I may need to act fast. If things go bad, can I rely on you to get yourself and Leizle to the safety of the other eco-town?"

"Go bad? What the hell does that mean?" Oscar stared Connor down. "She's not going to die?"

"Trust me, Oscar. I may need to take drastic measures, but I won't let her die." Connor's eyes drifted to Rebekah's relaxed features. "You have my word." Suddenly the smell of the blood caked over his body, dragging talons of thirst through his dry throat, became the nightmare of *her* blood. Connor's muscles jerked as the thought tore through him, and only movement could relieve the pain inside.

Oscar grunted. "Go and get her cleaned up. We're all in the dark, but, I have your word?"

Connor nodded and left the kitchen. Walking quickly down the tunnel to the laundry cavern, his preternatural stride absorbed the rocking motion of his movement.

A spring water well served the cavern. A generator heated the water which ran through the network of copper pipes, and as Connor walked past, he pulled two towels from the folded pile and draped them over a heated water pipe running along the wall. They heated the room efficiently, which made sense of giving it the dual purpose of a bathing area as well as a laundry.

The still surface of the water in the Jacuzzi-sized tub reflected their image like a mirror. As Connor moved to the edge his thigh brushed over Rebekah's blood soaked dress, and the water stirred as scattered droplets floated like red rose petals for a moment, before melting away into the crystal depths.

Lowering them both into the pool, he uncoiled the movement in a silky smooth descent. The water saturated his pants and snatched at the cotton of Rebekah's dress. The blood swirled in crimson-colored strands before billowing in pink clouds as the warm current stroked over his skin.

The water lapped at Connor's chest as he subsided into a sitting position and held Rebekah close. The rising tide made her shiver. Lifting her blood-soaked dress away, he gently turned her to face him and settled her onto his lap. Peeling off his shirt, he tore away a square of wet fabric and immersed himself in the task of stroking it over her somnolent features.

As the streaks of dried blood melted from the ivory skin of her shoulders, he dipped his chin to kiss them. Wrapping her in his arms, he cradled her to him, and, resting her head upon his shoulder. He was content to stay.

He detected the moment when the electrical activity in her brain subsided into a hum. He knew she was asleep and could not hear him. *But still, saying the words out loud will be a relief.* "I don't know where this will end, honey, I just know that this blood thirst is only the beginning, and we should be worried." *I can't do this alone.*

He savored the feeling of his skin on hers. The caressing current of water cooled her fevered flesh and warmed his, but the bath was cooling fast. Reluctantly, he rose, and, with easy grace, stepped up out of the pool. Tugging the warmed towels from the pipe, he swaddled one around her and fashioned a turban for her wet hair with the other.

Back in her cavern, he sat her on the edge of the bed, drowsy and compliant, as he dressed her in cotton pyjamas. While his body still retained heat, he laid out and held her against his chest until the feathered strands of her hair dried.

She was deeply asleep when he took up his vigil. *The bath calmed the baby, which is good.* Connor lay on his side with her body tucked into his. Hitching up onto his elbow, he could watch every nuance of her face. His fingers spanned her swollen stomach as he gauged the mood of his child.

His thoughts turned to Julian and the descending guardsmen. *The next few days are crucial. If I have to get her into theater, I'll do whatever I have to do.*

Chapter 22

The silence in the full gallery of the courtroom was charged with anticipation. Julian called the court into session, and Sebastian entered the dock to enjoy his fifteen minutes of fame. Julian took one look at the glint in the vampire's good eye and knew which side the tossed coin of fortune had landed.

Make the most of it, Sebastian. It will be all you'll ever have. Julian opened the proceedings. "You have remembered the location of the nest? I understand from Councilor Serge that you were confused for a while." Julian's intent bored into Sebastian, the message clear; your life hangs on this moment, think carefully.

Sebastian closed his eyes and massaged his eye sockets.

Julian could imagine the rainbow-colored explosion inside his head as the optic nerve compressed. *Although, I guess half of the light show is missing for him.*

"Are you ready?" Alexander broke the silence, the rustle of fidgeting fabric welcoming his words, a sure sign the rows of vampires in the gallery grew tired of waiting.

Sebastian eyes snapped open and his hazel-tinted spite strobed into Julian's mind. "Yes, I am ready. The nest is thirty five miles from this spot." Sebastian pointed in a southeasterly direction off to his right, although his eye remained locked on Julian.

Julian's lips compressed at the carelessly pointed finger. Sebastian gave it no thought, but Julian, even after two hundred years found moments to marvel at it. *Vampire sense of direction is unerring.* The low body temperature congealed blood, and the accumulation of iron deposits in their sinuses intensified the earth's magnetic field. They were homing pigeons in human form, and Sebastian's finger was as accurate as a compass needle. *One hundred and twenty four degrees, four minutes, twelve seconds South East. Spot on.*

"Head out through Swanley and follow the old M20 for ten miles. Turn east through the woodlands for two point seven miles, until you reach a glade of silver birch trees..."

Julian silenced him with an upheld hand. "Sebastian, remember where you are. The location is to be divulged only to the guardsmen." Julian bared his teeth. "You know that."

"I am happy to lead the guardsmen there myself." Sebastian smiled.

"That will not be necessary. You lack the status with this court to lead the guardsmen." Julian twisted the knife.

Fearing he was losing control, Serge got quickly to his feet. "I presented this petition. It is *my* place to lead the guard. Protocol demands it."

Serge is right, protocol allows him to take command. Julian smiled. "And are you willing to die if Sebastian is wrong? Fall on your sword, so to speak?"

Serge's body jittered. "The council can't demand that of me, Principal Julian."

"*I* can, Councilor Serge, and, in this case, I will." *My one consolation to this performance is that glory has a flip side.* Serge could be sentenced to locked-in syndrome for wasting the guardsmen's time. *And Sebastian, of course, will follow him.*

Ignoring his stunned expression as Serge sank back into his seat, Julian's attention shifted to Sebastian. "You will go with Captain Laurence to the guardroom, and to him alone, you will reveal the whereabouts of the human nest." Julian's tone warned Sebastian that there was no coming back from this.

Serge stood up again.

"Councilor Serge?" said Julian.

"I should be there with Sebastian, Principal Julian."

Julian's jaw ticked. He could not think of a reason to deny Serge's request. "Very well."

Sebastian left the dock to follow the captain of the guard out of the courtroom, and Julian caught the gloating glance from Sebastian's jaundiced eye in his peripheral vision. *Connor will need me there to deflect summary execution. He has broken out of a storage facility. The guardsmen will deliver the death penalty, there and then. No hearing, required. Although I'd like to see them try.*

As the door swung closed behind Sebastian, Julian intoned, "Court adjourned."

Twenty seconds later, he stood at the mantelpiece in the jurors' anteroom staring into space. Waiting for the Captain's report was a low point for Julian. He couldn't show his hand and make a case to the juror's until the coordinates were known, and so, he adopted a pose as outwardly lifeless as those of Marius and Alexander, despite his churning gut.

The knock upon the door reanimated the gathering, and Julian said, "Come."

A tall vampire entered and inclined his head. "Principal Julian."

"Captain Laurence." Julian's brow raised in invitation.

"We have the coordinates." The captain strode across the room and handed over a folded piece of paper. "They have been memorized by the platoon."

He wore the olive-green greatcoat of the council guardsmen uniform, and his jet-black hair and strong jaw put Julian in mind of Connor. He had been captain of the guard for almost three decades, and a moment of regret crossed Julian's thoughts. *If Connor has confrontation in mind, I hope Captain Laurence is not the heroic type.*

Julian took the piece of paper. "I see no reason to delay further. If Councilor Serge is ready?"

The captain's lip curled in distaste, and Julian smothered his amusement by checking his watch. "If you deploy at oh-two-hundred, we'll have six hours before daylight."

"Yes, sir." The captain executed a precise turn, glided swiftly out of the room, and closed the door behind him.

Julian waited out the fifteen minutes until two o'clock in silence. He felt the eddying currents whisking through the space beneath the closed door as the twelve guardsmen 'fell in' and began their whispered flight along the corridor. The subtle drop in room temperature signaled the opening of the front doors of the building which would precede the platoon filing out over the threshold.

Each of the guardsmen had been turned at aged twenty six, when at the physical peak of human fitness. They were vampire shells who enjoyed the physicality of the fight. Their free will had been scooped out and replaced with an illusion of status. *They do as they are told. Nothing more, nothing less.*

Serge's shuffling footfall was a long way back, and Julian grinned as he imagined the feeble form chasing along behind. The guardsmen were impressive when in full flight. The fortunate thing about allowing only Serge to accompany them was that they would be cooling their heels while waiting for his arrival. *It will give Connor a warning.*

It also gives me time to catch up with them. "Marius, Alexander, there is more to this." Julian looked from one impassive face to the other. "I think we should be there."

"Even if that is true, why would a capture detail need our presence, Julian?" Marius' expression was bored.

Julian disguised his frustration. The guard would be hurtling through the night in formation, effortlessly eating up the distance. *Connor will be expecting me there at the start.* Urgency tugged at his muscles, and staying still required all his willpower.

"Precisely, who is Sebastian? Does it not seem strange that he should find this nest so conveniently?" Julian glanced at Alexander. "If there is a nest, then they have remained hidden for fifteen years, surely they warrant our attention?"

"I must admit to being intrigued." Alexander finally roused himself. "To avoid detection for so long requires skill."

"You both know better than to trust Councilor Serge. I wish to see this 'capture' for myself." Julian sensed he had their attention at last. "There is more to this, and I will be there to witness it."

He removed his principal's cape and cravat and pulled on a long tailored coat. *If Connor cannot move Rebekah, then discovery is inevitable. With the jurors present, I can negotiate a compromise. Surely, a hybrid pregnancy is a compelling reason for restraint.*

Julian's resolve penetrated and Alexander said, "Very well, I will bear witness."

When Marius nodded in agreement, Julian contained his sigh of relief; showing emotion was not expected.

He straightened his coat and crossed to the door. "Shall we, gentlemen? I'm keen to see Serge's expression if Sebastian has played him false." Julian stepped out into the corridor, and in a formation as tightly woven as the guardsmen, the three vampires headed out into the night.

Julian enjoyed the liberty of movement, and easing his stride to full speed, his chest filled with exhilaration. He brushed away the discomfort at the thought of Leizle. *Connor will make sure they are safe.*

<><><>

Rebekah paced the floor of her cavern, and Connor, sitting on her bed, delivered a superb performance of relaxed contemplation. His hooded gray gaze trailed every step she took. *Her heartbeat is strong and her sweat has her usual pheromone balance.* After his charge through the woods, his relief at finding her safe, even though he hadn't expected to find her drenched in blood, had long since worn off. Since she had woken up from her blood-lust stupor, she could not stop moving.

Rebekah reached the cavern wall and huffed in irritation as she turned on her heel. She teetered for a moment before regaining her balance, and then walking forward again.

Every muscle in Connor's body remained primed and ready to catch her if she fell. He flexed his ribcage, flaring his nostrils and drawing in the breath she had released as he checked for the pear drop odor of high blood sugar. *Okay, her pancreas is working fine and insulin levels are good.*

Reclining on the bed, Connor reached out a hand as a wince of pain tightened her face. "Hey, honey. Come sit with me." He waggled his eyebrows in suggestive enticement. "Just think of it. These ice cold fingers smoothing over your sweaty skin will cool you down in no time." Connor wriggled the fingers in question in time with the eyebrows.

"Sweaty? Gee thanks. You sweet-talker, you." Rebekah smiled, but her eyes remained dull; the purple circles outlining her eye sockets were the color of coal dust.

Connor rolled off the bed, circled the room to collect the arnica ointment and appeared behind Rebekah. Revival sleep flooded into his brain center, unwinding the tension in his muscles before, reaching out, he laid a gentle hand on her bump. He closed his eyes and tuned into the glittering array of the sparks of the baby's nervous system. *The baby's agitated.* His jaw clenched when Rebekah winced, and tension jerked through her as the baby jabbed an elbow into her kidney.

"It's a bit like having a prize-fighter in there, hmm? C'mon honey, lie down and I'll massage some arnica ointment into those bruises."

"Okay. You win," said Rebekah, glancing over her shoulder.

Connor's ready smile disguised his worries. The doctor inside him shuffled endlessly through the medical and surgical options which lay at his disposal. *Pathetically few.*

Persuading Rebekah over to the bed, Connor made her comfortable with cushions at her back and exposed the taut skin of her stomach. His fingertips slipped over the purple patches mottling the satin of her skin, and the baby's movement beneath his palms settled to a coiled stillness which made him frown. The wave of electrical activity in the small brain delivered a jolt of static through his palms as suddenly, with an audible slap, an explosion of movement inside her belly knocked his hand away. A bruise blossomed where the crushed capillaries bled out and resolved into a tiny footprint. Connor calculated the force needed to do that, and he stepped back with his hands in the air.

"I think Leizle had better take over." He looked into Rebekah's pain pinched face. "Sorry honey. My touch completes a circuit. His vampire senses are picking up on mine." Connor inspected the new bruising, and pinning a reassuring smile in place hid the guilt swilling in his stomach. *This is all my fault.*

"How about a bath? That always calms him," said Connor.

"You do know the prize-fighter could be a girl? Right?"

Connor grinned. "I know that. I just can't bring myself to call our baby 'it'. A 'she' is just fine, honey."

"Okay. 'He' is fine too, for now."

Fifteen minutes later Rebekah was languishing in a warm bath which featured high on the list of baby-calming techniques.

"I've had so many baths this week, I feel as though I'm water logged." Rebekah held her pruned fingers up for inspection, and closed her eyes to enjoy the rumble of Connor's laughter rippling down her back.

He could not deny that laying back in a bath with her resting against his chest swelled his dead heart with joy. As his hands traced the curve of her heavy breasts, his fingers absorbed the creaking in her ribs every time the baby struggled for comfort. *She can't go on like this.*

The persistent grinding of the baby's teeth was a constant hum inside Connor's head now. *How long before he takes a bite out of his mother? I need Anthony and the hospital.*

"Honey, you know, I won't lose you?" Connor's cool breath on her wet shoulder rippled a shiver down her spine.

"Lose me?" Rebekah's voice was heavy with sadness. "And the baby?"

"If I have a choice to make, I will choose you. I have to tell you that." The tension in his face folded a sneer over his lip. "The baby's developing the brain center which ensures a vampire's survival, the bloodlust of grave sleep." Connor allowed his words to settle.

Rebekah sighed. "I know. But he wouldn't hurt me."

"He might." Connor tuned into her cantering heartbeat. "If he gets a taste for blood, eats through the umbilical cord. Who knows what the baby will do in grave sleep?" Connor pushed her hair back from her face, lifted her chin gently and kissed the corner of her lips. Her head fell back against his shoulder and resting his cheek on hers, he said, "Today, when Julian gets here, I will declare myself and get you to the hospital."

"But you are sentenced to death." She turned her head, trying to see his face.

Fire and Ice: Survival

"Julian will be there. It will work out." Connor dropped a kiss onto her nose. "I promise." *I have no idea if Julian can pull it off, but we have no choice.*

"Are they on their way? The guardsmen?" Rebekah whispered.

"They will be here, tonight, yes." Connor's eyes glinted with silvered determination. "They will listen. They won't launch an attack upon me lightly. They know the consequences."

As Rebekah took in another breath to interrogate him, Connor surged up from the water, lifting her with him as he stepped out onto the tiled floor. "Enough about that. While he's quiet, let's get you fed."

Rebekah recognized an evasive manouver when she saw one, but right now, trusting Connor was all she had. The thought of food flooded her mouth with saliva and she was suddenly ravenous.

Connor towel dried her skin and helped her into a sweatshirt and pants, detaching the plastic tether of the price tag with a pinch of his fingers.

"More new clothes? Have you cleaned out every Mothercare outlet in London?"

"Probably." Connor grinned as he took her hand, and they headed towards the kitchen and food.

Oscar and Leizle stopped talking as Rebekah appeared. Getting up from the table, Oscar went over to the range and with a smile of his lips and clouds of worry in his eyes, he said, "What would madam like today? I'm an expert at flash-frying, braising, and sautéing. So, what's it to be? Lamb, pork, or chicken?"

"Pork chops?"

With the decision made and a heavy skillet in his hand, Oscar threw himself into the task with brittle enthusiasm.

"Oscar?" Connor's concentration centered on his back until he turned around with an inquiring glance.

"You know what to do?" Connor said, glancing at Leizle's white face, too.

"Yep. The panic room is well stocked. We can hide there for days if we need to. Don't worry about us, lad." Oscar jerked his head in Rebekah's direction. "Just look out for her."

"Hey, Rebekah, come sit with me." Leizle's calming air was like oil on water.

While Oscar cooked – if heating pork chops for a few seconds on each side could be called cooking – Connor tuned out the staccato of worried heartbeats playing as a symphony through his senses, and found comfort in the two that mattered. His child slept at last.

He scanned Rebekah's exhausted features and realized that the endorphins flooding her bloodstream were barely taking the edge off the ache in her bones. As her ribcage came under more pressure, she would not cope. *Getting her through this will need help I can't give her here.* His hand clenched in frustration. *I'm looking at a C-section, I know that.*

Connor detached himself, drifting away to stand at the cavern entrance.

Oscar brought food to the table which tasted as good as it looked. Although no one managed more than a mouthful, apart from Rebekah, who wolfed her's down without pausing, finally looking up as she wiped the back of her hand across her chin.

"What?" she muttered at being the center of attention for three sets of eyes.

Leizle laughed.

"Nothing wrong with seeing a girl enjoying her food," said Oscar as he got to his feet and removed the plates.

"*I* enjoy my food," Leizle teased, "I just let it touch the sides on the way down."

"You eat like a bird, young lady. There's nothing of you," Oscar quipped with a big smile.

Rebekah listened to Oscar and Leizle bouncing words off each other. Their voices became the soothing ebb and flow of ocean waves breaking on the shore. Tiredness crept over her again and her body felt heavy.

Her eyes wandered over to Connor, and she was mesmerized by his frozen features and trancelike state as he stood like a sentinel at the entrance of the dining cavern.

Fire and Ice: Survival

Connor listened to the shift in the breeze, the movement of leaves, and the rumble of excitement inside the approaching guardsmen. *They're almost here.*

Rebekah studied his strong profile one moment, and in the next, he vanished. Her brain registered the blur, but her eyes were too slow to track the path of his departure. She took a deep breath, and regretted it instantly as the needle jab of a stitch pierced her side. *I'm a vital part of this. If he cannot hold them off, Connor will come for me.*

Leizle squeezed her hand and concern furrowed her brow. "You okay?"

"Serves me right for eating too much," she said weakly.

Rebekah stared at the space Connor last occupied, and then the ground overhead began to shake.

"It will be okay," she muttered, looking at Leizle and Oscar. "He'll be okay, I know he will."

Rebekah remembered watching wartime documentaries as a child, where the grimy-faced population of a beleaguered London took refuge in the subterranean tube train network. Black and white footage panned row upon row of sleeping bags, bodies cocooned like exhausted caterpillars. It seemed more like a breathing morgue where they lay ramrod straight in huddled masses, each taking up as little space as possible. Perpetually locked muscles made relaxation a forgotten art as terror and apprehension were a constant rolling current of emotions.

Rebekah felt like that now. The baby kicked, making it hard to stay silent.

She locked her eyes onto Leizle's face and gripped her hand tightly, comfort and reassurance flowing between the two girls until Rebekah's bloodless fingertips lost all sensation.

Their eyes darted around the cavern. Fear took hold of them as the earth above shook in short explosive tremors. Mortar crumbled from the height of the domed ceiling, raining down upon the hardened grit floor, and Rebekah understood the horror of actually hearing wartime bombs landing, and never knowing if a direct hit would start an avalanche of rubble.

Rebekah's insides churned with every blow landing above their heads. *Is Connor fighting for our survival, or his?* Her heart clenched in fear, and she fought her own battle inside as the baby kicked hard and she doubled over in pain.

"Maybe we should go to the panic room, make you comfortable. Just in case-" Leizle scanned Rebekah's pinched features. "It would be safer, Rebekah." Leizle tried to laugh, clearing her throat, as she said, "I know we were told never to play inside refrigerators, but hey, this one is the size of my bedroom back home, and it's kitted out with everything we need."

"I know all that." Rebekah rushed on as Leizle tugged persuasively on her fingers. "But, no," she whispered, "he needs me, and he will come. But you and Oscar should go."

Oscar snorted loudly and sat beside Rebekah, hugging her fragile shoulders carefully and oozing confidence as he said, "He'll be fine, lass. He'll be back before you know it."

"Yes." The sound echoed around her head, but stayed trapped in her throat. *He'll win, I know he will.*

With every earthquake tremor rumbling through her bones, the baby kicked, like he, too, was fighting alongside his father. Her face drained of color, leaving her exhausted features resembling a death mask of purple-stained eye sockets and waxy pallid skin. The pain in her chest begged her to breathe, but the baby twisting inside forced her breath out.

The cavern walls began to swim before her eyes. Dropping her chin down onto her chest, she groaned, "Connor."

Leizle fell to her knees in front of Rebekah, looking up into her face. "Hang on," she said, gripping her pale fingers. "Is it the baby?"

Chapter 23

Connor traveled the tunnels like a silent wraith until he reached the sackcloth curtain marking the threshold where the human and vampire worlds collided. He moved the draped cloth aside and flexed his diaphragm, tasting the atmosphere beyond it and quantifying the sense of excitement thrumming on the breeze. *There are twelve all told, and they are waiting. For Julian? Surely not.*

He did not want to leave Rebekah behind in the dining cavern, but if he revealed her presence, it *had* to be when he could protect her.

He stepped forward into the moonlit clearing and searched the row of faces for Julian. His quiet tone finally sliced through the night air as he asked, "Who is in command here?"

A shockwave of surprise rippled through the ranks of the guardsmen. Captain Laurence stepped forward, his astonishment obvious. "Until Councilor Serge arrives, *I* am in charge." The captain's eyes glistened with polished jet. "And *you*, Doctor Connor, should prepare to die."

"You have the authority to order that, Captain Laurence." Connor inclined his head, spreading the relaxed fingers hanging loosely at his sides. "However, I'm here to negotiate."

The captain's lip curled. "You lost your right to negotiate the day you stood up in court and betrayed your own kind by keeping a human."

"My own kind?" Connor's eyes narrowed. "Every butterfly was a caterpillar, once. Think man, they *are* us. We were them. How can you have forgotten that?"

Contempt glittered in Captain Laurence's stare, and Connor knew he would have to fight. *The man respected me. Finding I have feet of clay must make his own footing seem precarious.*

The captain's tone stripped the regret from his words. "I'm sorry. I deal in black and white. The law is clear. You escaped from Storage Facility Eight and the punishment is summary execution."

"I think Principal Julian would hear me plead my case first."

"Perhaps. However, Principal Julian is not in command. Councilor Serge will be here momentarily."

"In that case, how many guardsmen are you willing to lose?" Connor smiled.

The moonlight transformed his sarcasm into a macabre mask, and every vampire knew they could forget the Queensbury rules of engagement. Doctor Connor's human society may date from 1910, but, this would be bare knuckle fighting, guerrilla warfare, and not the ridiculous discipline of an English regiment.

Captain Laurence raised a clenched fist, extending an index finger skyward. At the signal of three clockwise rotations, two guardsmen moved into action.

Connor scanned the faces. As with all trained fighters, they had orchestrated plans of attack. The vampires, moving to take up their set-piece positions, screamed their intentions. Being an instinctive combatant, Connor's face relaxed as he visualized the encounter.

Clutching at the element of surprise, the vampires flew at him.

Staring at a midpoint, Connor let the rest blur out of focus as he calculated their speed. He tingled in anticipation. The vampire on the right would hit first. Even though he lagged behind, the intent etched on his face radiated the steely resolve of being the first over the top.

When the lead vampire lunged, Connor took two steps forward, swinging the blade of his hand in a devastating arc which crushed the vampire's oesophagus. Number one clutched his throat, surprise radiating across shocked white features as an inhaled gasp whistled through snapped vocal chords.

Guardsman number two swung in from the left, as the second prong of the attack. Already committed, there was no going back, even though he was the central focus of a six foot three, cold, hard, calculating warrior.

Connor made eye contact, his sneer baring teeth as a low growl rumbled in his throat. The guardsman set a course two feet wide of Connor's left shoulder. Digging his heels in, he stopped abruptly, leaned away, and unleashed a roundhouse kick at Connor's outthrust chin.

I'm impressed, thought Connor. The force of it would have broken his jaw and shattered the vertebrae of his neck, had it landed.

As appreciation rattled through his mind, Connor whipped up an arm, blocking the move as the weight of the vampire's boot accelerated his leg forward. The iron hard muscle in Connor's forearm held firm, and the guardsman's shin fractured, a moment before a seismic tremor tore through the cartilage in his knee.

Barging forward until the hamstrung vampire hit the ground, Connor smiled as the shockwave rattled through his own chest, stirring exhilaration. He planted his boot on the vampire's neck, his steely regard coated with hard frost as he said, "You're lucky. I feel generous, today. You get to live and learn."

Glaring from the edge of the battlefield, the captain ground his teeth when the crack of the splintering shin bone signaled the fall of the second guardsman.

At that moment, Serge sprawled into the clearing like a parachutist overrunning his landing, and drew the captain's irritated gaze. Pulling himself together, Serge joined Laurence at the head of the platoon. The range of impassive guardsmen stood like a row of olive green-clad chess pieces, equally spaced and waiting to be directed to move.

"Councilor Serge," said Captain Laurence grimly, his attention boring into the distance.

Serge followed the direction of the captain's stare, and all expression melted from his features as his jaw fell open. "Doctor Connor."

Only Connor's deliberate footfall disturbed the stunned silence, reverberating through the ground as he advanced and stopped ten yards away.

Serge took a deep rattling breath.

"Well, *Councilor,* can you smell *forty* humans?" Connor shook his head. "You've been played, yet again." His scorn unveiled a gunmetal gray gaze. "As for 'summary execution', would you like to see how that will play out?"

Connor felt the current of nervous excitement rippling through the line of motionless guardsmen.

Serge bellowed, his voice crackling like a spitting oil fat fire, "Arrest him."

Captain Laurence jerked around to look at Serge's contorted face. "Arrest?"

"I want the hive to witness the execution of Doctor Connor. Arrest him."

At a signal from Captain Laurence, four guardsmen moved forward, their teeth grinding in locked jaws. Their eyes were alight with bravado. Connor knew that whatever gambit they ran through their minds, they could find only the promise of broken bones.

They fell into paired sets, and Connor shook his head in disbelief. *Really?*

Primed and ready to attack, two stepped closer. They had the scent of the hunt, but Connor stole their thunder. *This should be fun.* He rocked on the balls of his feet and extended both arms in surrender, allowing them the satisfaction of grabbing hold of him and feeling in control. Their confusion at his compliance made their clawed fingers dig in harder.

"I came to talk."

"Talk? You took out two of Principal Julian's guard, and you want to talk?" Serge's saliva rattled in his throat. "Such arrogance."

Connor's still expression was carved in alabaster, the moonlight picking out the crystalline shards glowing beneath his skin. Fully fed capillaries glinted; the tough pale red threads bore evidence of the one hundred years which had forged his tissue into velvet draped rock.

He raised his brows in inquiry. "Arrogance? Arrogance is when you can't deliver."

As the words floated on the evening breeze, Connor released the coiled tension he held in check. Twisting his hips, he kicked backwards and shattered the knee-cap of the vampire on his right, who fell away, tearing the sleeve from Connor's shirt as he tried to save himself but lost his grip.

As the second pair rushed in, Connor gripped the bicep of the vampire still clutching his right arm, and launched both his feet forward, cracking the ribs of the leading guardsman. As the stunned opponent flew backward, the back of his skull shattered the cheekbones of his partner coming up behind.

Connor's feet were back on the ground before the guardsman beside him reacted. He swung around and grabbed Connor by the throat.

"Do you want to try it?" Connor's grin was maniacal as though the mercury gray of his eyes poisoned his brain.

The vampire's own eyes glowed with excitement as he increased the pressure.

Connor's clenched jaw pulled the tendons in his neck into cables of steel, denying the vampire's probing fingers purchase.

As bewilderment glazed his attacker's face, Connor stabbed an index finger hard into the notch at the base of his throat and crushed the vampire's windpipe. His eyes widened in shock, and Connor said, "And there is your second mistake."

His fingers remained rammed into the vampire's neck, who's puffing breath splattered Connor in cold congealed blood. Waving the fingers of this free hand in front of the vampire's face, Connor said, "Never release one restraining hold to gain another. You see, now, I can do this."

The conversational tone was psychosis in action as movement illustrated the words. He drove his fist up in a blow which detached the vampire's jaw. The shocked white face disappeared from sight as his head rolled backwards.

The vampire had an upside down view of Councilor Serge's creaking form rushing forward, until the grass rushed up to fill his vision. His face was crushed into the field by his own shoulder blades pressed into the back of his head when his body hit the ground.

A shift in air pressure indicated the distant approach of vampires hurtling through the forest at speed, and Serge's frustrated anger galvanized his wasted limbs into agitated movement. His tumbling gait stumbled over every pothole in the ground, his arms waving like a crow in its death throes. Closing in on the focus of his overwhelming jealousy, Serge launched himself at Connor's throat.

You've gotta be kidding me. Connor cocked his head and decided it was payback time.

He drew to his full height and waited until Serge's clawed hands clambered up his body. He enjoyed the full visual impact of the tantrum as Serge's nails skidded over the tight skin of his chest and his shirt shredded under the attack.

With a deadpan expression, Connor locked eyes with Serge, clamped his hand over one withered wrist, dragged the tobacco yellow fingers away from his face, and extended the thin arm upward.

Serge's anger collapsed into panic as his stretched tendons creaked.

Connor suffered the stench of Serge's breath as he smiled into his face. "Game over, Councilor."

The bones in Serge's wrist crumbled as, with a sharp twist, Connor whipped the old vampire's arm down at a sickening angle, dislocating the joint and snapping the shoulder blade like a twig. It was a symphony of delightful sensation for Connor as he focused on the vibration of crackling bone.

Serge's features folded into a hideous grimace.

"Now, *you* were arrogant." Connor released his hold, letting the dead weight of the arm drop.

It swung, bumping against Serge's thigh, hanging on by slack skin and stretching tendons. The fabric of his coat sleeve was all that prevented it dropping to the floor as the brittle capillaries in Serge's skin snapped like strands of uncooked spaghetti.

Clutching the limb to his side, Serge fell back, his mouth gaping in disbelief.

Connor switched focus as a spike in the air current whooshed in his ears. Turning, he braced for impact as Captain Laurence appeared from the darkest shadow like a bolt shot from a crossbow. He hit Connor in the center of his chest. He was too late to save Serge's arm, and Connor grinned as he realized the delay was driven by his reluctance to help the councilor at all.

Connor's ribcage shuddered beneath the force of the captain's shoulder charge and his voice whistled through grinding teeth. "You don't want to do this."

Thrown through the air, Connor landed on his back. He plowed a path through the grass and soft mud, coming to rest like a half-buried corpse with his head resting on a dune of earth.

As Captain Laurence bore down upon him, Connor surged to his feet and feinted left.

Overrunning his mark, the captain pivoted on the spot and, crouching low, the two vampires circled each other.

To flee would concede power, and neither would do that. They lunged and dived in explosions of blurred movement, looking for weakness and applying pressure which could force a mistake. Blocking and parrying, neither vampire gave an inch.

"I was not always captain of the guard, you know." Captain Laurence's fierce countenance gathered shadows as he rocked in a hypnotic rhythm. "Special Air Services, 'Operation Nimrod'. Ring any bells, Doctor?" he sneered.

"And yet, arresting me is not as simple as it seems. It must be frustrating for you. How is life without an MP5 sub machine gun on your hip? Hmm?" Connor taunted. "1980's London and the Iranian Embassy are a long time ago."

"You know what you are dealing with then."

"You must have hung back, or they would have known you were a vampire. Such a shame." Connor's sympathetic shake of the head was designed to irritate.

The captain's white face tightened in response. "On the contrary. I spiced things up." Laurence grinned. "Putting my foot through that window was not an accident. It forced the commander to give us the go, and I was first one in. I enjoyed killing." He cocked his head to one side, and the blackened coal of his eye sockets homed in on Connor's face. "We've passed the point of arrest, wouldn't you say? Attacking Councilor Serge changed that."

"Ah, so we are back to summary execution?" Connor laughed. "Have you got time to carry out that threat?"

Certainty settled in Connor's chest. *Julian and the jurors are almost here.* A pulse of compressed air rushed ahead of their hurtling mass and Connor picked up their approach in the way a bat collects sonar waves. The trees made it impossible to get a clear signal, so timing was not precise. *But they are coming.*

A sneer drifted across the captain's face as he, too, heard the commotion in the woods.

Connor grinned. *The clock's ticking, he'll make a mistake, and I'll be ready.*

"Principal Julian won't allow it," said Connor. "I calculate you have thirty seconds." He straightened to his full height and extended his arms in a deceptively casual invitation. "Do you still think you can take me?"

"I lived by the creed 'Who Dares Wins'." The captain laughed. "I'll take you, or die in the attempt."

Laurence disappeared suddenly, and Connor rotated fast. Predicting the move, Connor tracked the trajectory as the captain hurtled out in an arc around behind, and then closed the distance again with devastating speed.

Connor did not quite complete the turn, and the force of the captain's skull ramming into his side exploded a kidney. A pulse of pressure punched into his diaphragm as the captain's iron grip closed around his middle, and the unfamiliar sensation of being winded whooshed the breath from between Connor's teeth.

Grabbing the back of the captain's coat, Connor rode the wave of momentum which spun him around. The death-grip tightened around his waist and his lower ribs creaked under the vise-like pressure.

As Laurence's head burrowed under his arm, Connor slammed an elbow down on an exposed shoulder blade. Connor felt it crack. Twisting sharply, he punched the tensed blade of his knuckles into the base of the skull which was grinding into his hip. Connor's feet left the ground when the captain reared, and the crushing bear hug hoisted him upward.

Kicking out hard, Connor crunched his boots into the captain's knees. Laurence hissed when a second blow took his feet out from under him.

As Laurence fell, Connor's feet hit the ground. The captain's clawed grip dragged away and the pressure tore the intercostal-muscles between his lower ribs, and Connor felt the blades of bone crack and collapse inward.

The captain dropped to his knees, and his dead weight buried him thigh high in dirt. Connor planted a boot between his shoulder blades and delivered an explosive kick. Laurence's bulk shunted forward, excavating a crater when he fell face first into the soft ground. His head snapped back when his chin hit a rock, and the crack in his shoulder blade opened into a crevice.

Regret crossed Connor's mind, and in that moment, his respect for the captain grew. *I'm amazed he's still fighting.*

The crater of earth cradling Laurence's body abruptly spat dirt into the air as the captain flipped over onto his back.

Too late to retreat, Connor jerked his chin down hard, protecting his throat. The captain lunged, going for a stranglehold but settling for a tight grip below Connor's cheekbones. Forced onto his knees into the tumbled earth beside the captain's prone body, Connor stiffened and resisted being pulled down to share his grave. He stared down into eyes, hard with steely determination. Dirt sat in clumps on the face looking back, and fell into his mouth when he grinned.

The pressure of the Captain's thumbs crushed Connor's bottom lip and his teeth began to creak.

Gripping the captain's wrist, Connor dug his own thumb into the soft tissue of the joint until bone crumbled. He clenched his jaw tightly shut because if he relaxed, it would be torn away. The glint of ice in the captain's eyes told Connor there would be no mercy.

"I can take you, and a broken wrist won't stop me," said the Captain. His fingertips hooked into the base of Connor's skull until the vertebrae screeched, cartilage rubbing on bone.

Connor drew back a fist and drove a punch down into the captain's belly. The first blow separated the muscle wall. Laurence automatically raised his knees in protection, tightening the oblique muscles and opening them up. Connor's second blow, with fingers pointed in a blade, sliced through the transverse abdominals and entered the abdominal cavity. One shove, driven by the force of Connor's braced shoulder, pierced a hole in the diaphragm.

The captain's clawed grip slackened in shock.

Connor pulled away and, resting back on his heels, he stared into the smooth expressionless face of the defeated vampire.

"Finish me."

As the moon came out from behind a cloud, Connor looked down into eyes the same steel gray as his own. He spanned his hand over the smooth forehead and applied the pressure needed to crumble his cranium and stirred his fingers through the blancmange-like texture of his brain.

Connor rose to his feet at the same moment Julian stalked into the clearing.

Julian registered the depleted row of stunned guardsmen before seeking out the figure of Connor standing amidst a field of fallen opponents. As he absorbed the scene, Serge hobbled over.

"Principal Julian." Serge's anger tightened face unfolded to speak.

Julian silenced him with quiet authority. "Stand down, Councilor Serge."

As Connor walked forward, wiping Laurence's congealed blood from his hands on the tattered cloth of his shirt, the councilor scuttled away.

Julian raised a brow and said, "You *have* been busy."

Connor's fingers probed the bottom edge of his ribcage through his shirt and pulled it back into alignment. "Not entirely unscathed. It's a shame he had to die."

"Laurence? Damn. I'm sorry, Connor. I hoped to get here in time." Julian's head jerked round at rustling in the woodlands behind him. "Fall back, Connor. It's show-time."

Connor backed into the shadows, smiling at the withering glance Julian shot in Serge's direction.

Marius and Alexander entered the clearing in unison, the biting autumn breeze whipping their robes into frenzy. Marius' black hair glistened like the pelt of a sea lion as he put his hands to it and scraped it back into a slick skull cap. He surveyed the scene with black eyes, his blown pupils swallowing their usual lively spark, expanding them to dead pools of censure.

Arriving on Julian's left shoulder, his glance sharp, he said, "A battle? The forty humans had a champion?" Disapproval compressed his lips. "Who would be foolish enough to fight the decree of the council?"

Alexander's stride was more deliberate. The moonlight burnished his hair to the color of wet sand, and the spark of interest in his eye was like the sun's rays breaking through early morning mist. Everything about him spoke of rain soaked splendor. He put the puzzle pieces together as he breathed in the stench of battle, tasting fine particles of dirt emulsified in the air and smelling decaying congealed blood as spice in the cocktail.

While Marius waited for an answer, Alexander's brows climbed in shocked surprise as he recognized the distinctive silhouette of Doctor Connor.

The jurors' arrival prompted Serge to rush forward again. Spraying saliva, he stated the obvious. "Doctor Connor is alive." Serge turned, tried to indicate with a wave, and abandoned the move when releasing the hold on his wrenched arm let it slip further from his sleeve towards the ground.

Marius' gaze doused the guardsmen in disgust. "What's going on here?"

Julian silenced them all as he called softly, "Doctor Connor."

Connor stepped forward. His face wore gray smudges where the captain's fingertips had dug into flesh and compacted the tissue fibers. A row of scythe shaped cuts ran down his nape from hairline to collar like a tattooed line of stitching, evidence of where his spine had been compressed.

He pulled the shredded shirt from his shoulders, making a final effort to clean his hands before scrubbing the cotton fabric over his features. The movement wiped all expression from his face. *This is it. Rebekah's life hangs on the next few moments.* Connor closed his eyes for a second, and a fleeting frown tightened his muscles. *She's in pain.* The pinched expression biting into her features was as clear to him as if she was standing right beside him.

"Jurors Marius, and Alexander." Connor inclined his head respectfully, flint-gray determination glittering in his eyes as impatience knotted his stomach. *I'm not sure how much time I have left.*

The breath hissed from between Marius' teeth as a flood of moonlight brought the carnage strewn across the field into sharp relief. "This is a surprise." Marius' glance bored into Julian's profile. "What are we really here to witness? Right now, I favor arresting Doctor Connor and sweeping this nest for the forty humans." He glanced at the guardsman to his right. "I see nothing here to change my mind."

Without taking his eyes from Connor, Alexander said, "I agree. We are on thin ice. I vote for Doctor Connor's summary execution, and sweeping the nest. Anything less leaves us open to charges of perverting the course of justice for our own ends. Unless you have any objection, Principal Julian?" Stirring the currents of contention in the clearing, Alexander's tone invited his leader's confidence.

Marius took in a deep breath, and with flared nostrils and slackened jaw, he washed the night air over his palette. "We are wasting time. Let's first determine the size of the capture, because one thing is certain," He glared at Serge as he continued, "there are far less than forty humans here." Marius waved the nearest guardsman forward. "Sweep the tunnels for... "

Julian raised his hand and Marius' order was left hanging. "Let us hear what Doctor Connor has to say first."

"He escaped from storage, and killed and maimed council guardsmen. We do not negotiate, Julian, you know that." Emotion colored Marius' voice for the first time in the hundred and twenty years since Julian had known him. Julian smiled. *It seems we all crack eventually.*

"Even if he holds the key to our survival?" asked Julian.

"What performance is this?" Marius was irritated. "What exactly have you brought us here to witness?"

"You would not believe me if I told you," he muttered. "Connor?"

"I've been accused and convicted of 'threatening the food supply'." Vehemence resonated in Connor's chest. "Councilor Serge leveled the accusation at me on many occasions without proof."

Connor waited for the jurors to accept this as a truth.

Marius inclined his head. "Until, as I recall, you admitted to it." His tone was cold and closed.

Connor ignored him, knowing that what happened in council that day no longer mattered. "The failure of our breeding program means we are immortals faced with certain death. We need solutions, not empty rivalry." His voice dropped to a whisper. "While I can't pretend to know how at the moment, we *do* have the capability to breed."

An exasperated breath interrupted him. "A very nice tap dance, Doctor Connor, but theories are not enough to save you now." Marius looked at Alexander. "Surely you have heard enough?"

Connor's calm tone cut through the air like a knife. "And what if the theory is proven?"

"Proven?" Marius expelled a derisive laugh.

"You will see," said Connor, and, in a whisking tornado which made Serge cling on tighter to his useless arm, he disappeared back into the tunnel mouth.

The guardsmen twitched, reluctant to see their quarry disappear. They looked at Julian. "Let him go. He will be back."

As the seconds ticked away to minutes, the assembled vampires forming an arc of standing stones, Alexander said, "How can you be so sure?"

Julian met the young juror's eyes, raising a brow. "You are about to discover that Doctor Connor has more to lose than his life."

Chapter 24

The lynching party waiting outside in the meadow was of no consequence. With every step Connor took along the tunnels, he felt Rebekah's pain more acutely. *Shit! Time is running out.*

Her ribcage creaked and Rebekah scrunched her eyes closed. Gripping the edge of the wooden bench, she doubled over, groaning. Without warning, cold sure hands covered hers and, when Connor's distinctive aroma rode the cool breeze moving her hair, she opened her eyes.

He looked up from where he knelt on the floor in front of her, and she knew she was hallucinating.

"It's time, honey." His slate gray gaze was gentle. "Let's get you to the hospital."

He scooped her up and with an easy gliding gait, he powered towards the doorway.

"What about Oscar and Leizle?"

Connor chuckled, and the rumble through his chest made her breath hiss when the baby kicked. "Sorry, honey. They are safe. They know what to do."

Holding on tightly to his shoulders, she welcomed the chilled breeze on her hot skin as Connor moved swiftly through the tunnels. He finally stopped, lowered her gently to her feet and held out his hand, smiling as he said, "It will be okay. They are not going to hurt you. I won't allow it, and Julian is there." Connor cocked a comedic brow. "He knows I'll have his 'guts for garters' if he lets me down now."

Pulling her close and fitting her in to his side, he squared his shoulders. Stepping out of the reception cavern and into full view of the clearing, he announced, "This is my Rebekah."

A hiss filled the air as Rebekah's pale face caught the moonlight. Her heartbeat thundered in her own ears and through the chest of each of the assembled vampires. Her rounded stomach was obvious, and every vampire ear heard the whisper of the child's heartbeat as an alluring echo.

"We have our first hybrid pregnancy." Julian took up the argument. "We can't ignore what this means."

Faced with a sea of shocked ambivalence, a wave of cold apprehension gripped Rebekah, building to a slicing pain as the baby felt it too. Black clouds rolled in to obscure her vision, and she whispered Connor's name as her knees folded and consciousness left her.

Connor swooped, effortlessly gathering her up into his arms. Straightening again, holding the precious burden to his chest, he turned and met Julian's eyes. They both feared this declaration had come too late.

"She needs a blood transfusion, right now," barked Connor. Rebekah's waxy complexion told the tale. Her bone marrow was not making enough blood to feed this hungry baby. "If she is to survive, if this baby is to survive, I need to get her to the hospital, now."

Connor glared at Marius and Alexander, and each shocked white face thawed enough to give a sharp nod. Without a second's pause, Connor crossed to a guardsman, demanded his greatcoat as a blanket for Rebekah and, as fast as he dared, he set off towards London.

He hurtled through the woodlands holding Rebekah close, cradling her head into the hollow of his shoulder.

He assessed her trembling frame, and her honeyed scent dragged hunger through him. When he pressed his lips to her forehead, the languid scattering of plump blood cells tingled as a caress, stroking an invitation over his lips. But the sluggishness of the enticing flow tortured him more. *Her temperature is dropping.* His urge to bite was strangled by the concern twisting his gut when he realized that her blood capillaries were collapsing. *She's going into shock, starving her brain of oxygen.*

The synapses firing inside her head were the firework display of a migraine thundering through her skull. They vibrated through his jaw, littering his own vision with the sparkling dust storm of her pain.

He accelerated, daring to unleash a little more speed as he surged forward. He was not yet certain the guardsmen would not give chase.

Marius and Alexander's stunned disbelief had given way to curiosity, of that he was certain. Their questions would come thick and fast. He was confident Julian would talk them round, but the unsettling feeling of staring eyes haunted him, making the hair on the back of his neck stand up. *No one is giving chase, so why?*

He scanned the woods urgently, unable to shake the feeling of being followed.

When Rebekah shuddered in his arms, he shoved paranoia aside and quickened his stride, bursting from the cool green shadows and darting across the gray gloom of a small glade. Slipping between the ghostly white tree trunks of a row of silver birch trees, he changed direction and dived into the darkness, instinctively choosing the protection of the dense canopy.

Fierce concentration buried his gray eyes in shadow as he dipped his chin and found equal space for the twin tasks of moving fast and monitoring Rebekah's condition. *She's holding her own, but if the balance tips, I'll just go for it.*

He would risk death-defying speed to save her life by any means left to him.

Sebastian pressed back into the girth of a massive tree trunk. His palms caressed the warm wood and his cheek scraped over the rough surface as he turned his face away from the gusting draft of Connor's flight. He anchored his fingers into the bark as he resisted the compulsion to hurtle forward in pursuit.

As the wake of Connor's passing settled, Sebastian's good eye squinted after him, tracking his nemesis with accuracy honed by loathing. The sight of Connor holding Rebekah in his arms knotted Sebastian's features with fury.

He revealed the location of the nest, and meekly agreed when Captain Laurence instructed him to wait in the guardroom until they returned. But, it had not been difficult to stay downwind of the jurors as he followed on behind, although, his slower, deathly silent progress meant he only heard the battle.

Fire and Ice: Survival

When, finally, he caught sight of the nest and saw the littering of bodies, the walking wounded, and the jurors standing and waiting in the meadow, he could not work out what was happening. *The humans could not have fought the vampire guard.*

He had come to watch the scene unfold, to fill his fibers with the scent of Rebekah again, and to see her captured and plan his possession. *With the boyfriend gone, I could almost taste her flesh.*

Unease had rattled through Sebastian as he watched Councilor Serge gripping an arm below a shattered shoulder.

Principal Julian and both jurors radiated expectation. Following the direction of Serge's glare, he, too, focused on the coal black gash in the hillside. Sebastian watched with disbelief when Connor walked out into the moon light, and to make matters worse, he had *more* power than before. *Rebekah carried his child.*

Sebastian had sank back into the thick, broad-leafed foliage before he joined the rank of the toppled vampires the doctor had fought. When Connor appeared, scything a path through the woodlands, Sebastian buried the heat of anger beneath cold calculation. *He has bought freedom, not only for himself, but for Rebekah and his brat.*

His eyes bored into Connor's back as he whisked by, and his plans for the doctor's death took shape. *But not before he has seen Rebekah and his child die.*

Chapter 25

The terrain became more challenging, and Connor swung through the dense undergrowth oblivious of the brambles snatching at his clothes and dragging barbs across his cheeks. Tucking her head into his shoulder, Connor covered Rebekah's face with his hand, protecting her from the thorns and keeping the chill of the rushing air at bay.

Without warning, the feeling of being watched, again bit into Connor's skin, and he lost his focus for a nanosecond. An impenetrable thicket of ground elder interrupted his flow, its clustered mass reaching up from the charcoal depths. The soft boggy ground sucked at his feet and, instinctively, he launched into a forceful leap, crouching low to absorb the impact of landing.

The jarring motion rattled through Rebekah, her gasping breath scalding his neck as she groaned loudly. The baby wrestled in protest, his tumbling weight bouncing off the hard wall of Connor's stomach, and bruising the fragile canvas of Rebekah's stretched skin.

Connor felt one of Rebekah's ribs crack – sounding like a gunshot to his keen ear – and guilt punched through his center. His gaze stabbed through the trees, calculating time and distance, and the clouded ice of bleak determination lit his eyes. *Almost there.*

He left the soft ground of the woodlands in favor of a gray ribbon of asphalt and moved through the outskirts of London, his effortless coordination smoothing out the bumps along the miles of uneven sidewalk.

Becoming aware of a vampire bearing down upon him, this time, he knew it was real. *Julian has caught me up.* He heard the whisper of Julian's long stride, with his gait, speed, and rhythm playing like a familiar tune through Connor's chest.

"About time," Connor threw over his shoulder.

"I'll have to get you to carry a pregnant woman more often," Julian quipped. "It slows you down some."

"Her rib has cracked. I need to get her to the theater suite in case..." Connor cut off the words. His thoughts hit a brick wall that he did not want to see past.

Julian's frown reflected Connor's concern. "I'll go on ahead and warn Anthony to get things ready."

As he accelerated away, Connor shouted, "Tell him we will come in through the side entrance. Through the morgue."

'Through the morgue' was a torturous string of words and, as he flicked his glance down at Rebekah's face, the mud brown delirium in her gaze was not reassuring. Shadowing Julian's path, Connor calculated his arrival in microns and milliseconds.

Connor visualized the environs of his theater, recounting and discarding the surgical tools laid out in drawers and on trolleys, before swearing under his breath. "Damn it. I can't even scare up the basics. A gynaecology kit and some sutures left over from the last human examination in the hospital, maybe..." He knew without doubt that he did not have anesthetic, sedatives, or even an analgesic.

She'll need all those. He had no control over the sharp jabs of movement deep inside her. He felt powerless when the cracked rib moved in an unexpected vertical direction, tearing the intercostal muscle, and she groaned.

Connor glued an assessing gaze onto Rebekah's face and forged ahead to maximum speed without missing a beat. Each vibration through her bones caused her to frown and her lashes to flicker. He gauged the coma scale as eight. *A midpoint reading is reassuring. But it mustn't drop below six.*

The medulla controlled respiration, heartbeat, and vascular reflexes. Connor inhaled deeply, and mapped the electrical activity which flared as hot spots inside her brain. *Only brainstem damage will interrupt those reflexes.* Her reduced blood supply and oxygen levels could lead to precisely that. *She needs a blood transfusion, now!*

The wind tunnel effect when he hugged the hospital wall snatched at Connor's coat-tails as he took the shortest route around the building. The polished marble reflected their image and, in

Connor's tainted imagination, he saw a carrion crow carrying a corpse.

Here we go. He reeled around and, at full tilt, barged his way backwards through the door and into the morgue, his broad shoulders absorbing the impact of the collision.

His movement through the familiar space inside was a blur. He dodged smoothly around the linen hampers, and pounding on each pair of sheet-metal doors with a swift double jab of a clenched fist cleared them out of his way; he left a five knuckled imprint in each.

He was out of sight before the doors ricocheted from the walls and showered crushed plaster onto the waxed linoleum floor.

Inside the operating suite, he zeroed in on Anthony's serious face and delivered a barrage of information, a forceful measured stride across the room punctuating each item on the list.

"Anthony, get to the human farm. I need a gynie kit. I need scalpels: sharp-edged blades for muscle, blunt-edged blades for the uterine wall. Sutures. Anesthetic. Sedatives. Epidural block kit. Amniotic needle and muscle relaxant." Connor looked down into Rebekah's face as he forced the words out. "But first, we need type matched blood, and lots of it."

Julian frowned. "I hadn't thought of that. So, not just a case of dropping by the dispensary and commandeering blood then?" The naiveté of his thoughts brought a grim smile to the principal's face.

Connor shook his head. "If Rebekah was AB positive, we'd be home free, universal recipient. Fortunately for us, the four blood groups taste different."

Julian's raised brows said 'really?'. "I can't say that I've noticed. Each human tastes different, sure. But blood groups?"

Connor laughed. "It's only important when doing surgery on humans. It's part of the job, like being a wine connoisseur, the protein molecules in each blood group are different. They stick to blood cells as antigens, or are in suspension as antibodies, according to the blood type. Type 'O' blood cells are smooth like tapioca. The antigens coating A, B and AB blood cells gives them a textured surface. It's just a matter of knowing the subtle differences."

Fire and Ice: Survival

There was more to it, involving the parietal lobe of the vampire brain, but, looking at Julian, Connor decided to stop there. 'Awestruck' was the word that came to mind.

"If you sampled the recipient, it's easier to match it. The problem is shock has reduced Rebekah's blood flow, and her capillaries are collapsing."

Connor refocused his attention on Anthony who was clearly memorizing his list of instructions. "Anthony?"

"Yes, Doctor Connor."

"Rebekah's blood type is B-positive, so the donor has to be blood groups B or O, positive or negative." Connor's eyes narrowed. "Before the pandemic the chances were sixty percent, but now, who knows. Anthony, without taking a sample from her..." Connor's chin dipped, indicating Rebekah's slackened body. "Can you cross match blood by taste with one hundred percent accuracy? Because if you make a mistake the haemoglobin rush will kill her."

Anthony shook his head. "I can't guarantee it, no."

Connor was torn by relief. He knew he would not have trusted this to Anthony's palette in any case. As the flow of conversation stalled, Connor laid Rebekah gently down onto a padded emergency-room trolley, perfectly placed for the dash to theater which he dreaded would come.

"I don't want to leave her, Julian."

He placed a cushion under Rebekah's knees, easing the tension of the taut skin over her distended stomach. Connor's grip closed around her wrist. "Her pulse is thready." Smoothing his hand over the baby he could feel the undulating edge of the fetus' spine, and moving to the left he found the heartbeat. "One hundred and ninety five beats a minute, so the baby is struggling, too."

Connor hissed as a surge of electricity stung his hand and shot up his arm. The nerve endings in the baby's body lit up, releasing a storm of static energy as the small body jerked and tiny muscles went into spasm.

Rebekah's eyes snapped open and she screamed. The shrieking note rose to the screeching pitch of a diamond cutting glass. A sickening crack rent the air, and her body folded around the baby as if she had been kicked in the stomach.

"Anthony!" Connor's voice spliced fear and confidence into a command that galvanized action. "Here, brace your hands either side of her chest, support it. Now."

Standing at Rebekah's head, Anthony slipped his hands in under her arms and held her ribcage still.

"Revival sleep, Anthony. Don't crack anymore ribs." Connor's warning was directed at Julian, too, as he jerked his head, calling him forward.

"What should I do?" said Julian.

"Support her pelvis and keep her spine straight."

Rebekah's scream still bounced from the walls as Connor pressed his lips to her forehead, and they stung as though her gray skin was made of hot ash. "Stay with me, honey."

Connor vanished, and as the shoved door banged closed and followed a pendulum swing back into the room, he returned, shouldering his way back in again. He carried a syringe filled with amber fluid, fitted with an amniotic needle, in one hand, and was dragging a trolley holding an ultra sound machine behind him. Swishing the trolley around into the room, he tossed a tube of conductive gel at Julian's head. "Cover her stomach with that, and Anthony, don't let go."

Julian smeared the gel over the swell of the baby, and Rebekah moaned as his fingers streaked bruises over her skin and the baby fought inside her.

"Okay," said Connor.

He nudged Julian aside to run the ultra sound sensor over her abdomen, and his eyes were drawn to the monitor. Seconds later, he lined up the syringe and pushed the needle through her belly and into the baby. Watching the image on the screen, Connor advanced the needle through the ghosting grays and whites of the image, and into the tiny chest cavity. He depressed the plunger and a spider web of black ink lines spread in a filigreed network throughout the baby until the tiny body stopped moving.

"You've killed it," Julian whispered.

"No." Anthony looked at Connor's severe expression. "It's muscle relaxant."

Connor was intent on running the probe over Rebekah's skin and frowning at the monitor. "The dose was thirty millilitres. The heartbeat is slow, but at least the baby can no longer bite."

"Bite?" said Julian.

Connor nodded. "Rebekah needs blood, the umbilical cord is dehydrating and the baby's starving. This is the final stage, and I think he's in grave sleep now." Connor's finger outlined a plumed cloud on the monitor screen. "He has bitten the uterine wall. That's a bleed. He's feeding."

The needle was still in place, with the syringe barrel rocking gently in time with the panting breaths racking Rebekah's body. "Julian, do what you can. Try ten millilitres at a time. Keep her alive." Connor's gray eyes were calm. "If the baby dies..."

Julian stared at Rebekah, and said, "She won't die. I won't let that happen."

"I'll be gone less than half an hour. The siphoning sheds should be full, and I just have to cross match the blood. Anthony, the medical center is well stocked with antiseptic, iodine and SteriPacks. I'll leave that to you. We'll meet back here when you're done."

Connor was already moving towards the door, drawing Anthony along behind him. Finally committed to leaving her, he launched himself forward in a desperate effort to outrun the demons of time and uncertainty.

Focusing on what he had to do now, Connor tried not to think further than that. He tried not to let the doubts crowd in, and to think of Rebekah's life as sand in an hour glass slipping through his fingers. *How much time is left?*

Anthony took up a flanking position on Connor's shoulder as they left London and headed west, out to the farm.

Without looking around, Connor issued his final instructions. "Stay with me until we are inside, and then get the job done and get back to Julian as fast as you can."

They skimmed effortlessly across the moonlit expanse of meadowland, the grass rippling beneath their feet like waves on an oil black sea. The mammoth siphoning sheds skulking in the distance dominated the scene as they bore down upon the run of meshed-wire fencing blocking their path, and both vampires reluctantly reined in their speed.

No matter how many times he visited the human farm, the air of despair and desolation always hit Connor in the gut. The immaculate vista of lawns beyond the first perimeter was interrupted by two other fences. The sturdy metal fabric marched across the landscape, secured to tall metal posts which reached up into the starlit sky. It marked the end of a carefree existence, and the beginning of having every movement logged and questioned, in both vampires and humans.

The human farm was the vampire equivalent of Fort Knox. The most precious commodity to vampire survival was protected within these walls. Connor hoped other hives were as careful with their humans. If vampire hives became adversaries, hell bent on poaching the stock of others, the chaos did not bear thinking about.

Right now, the fences would be enough to contend with. Connor's appraising glance took in the twelve foot height of the barrier as he rubbed his fingertips over his bicep where a deep groove carved into it still glittered like newly quarried quartz. *Even I get it wrong sometimes*. The razor wire which meandered along the top edge of the fence glinted in mocking invitation.

"Three fences. Crap. C'mon Anthony," Connor muttered.

Scaling the woven metal, he jammed his boots in, stretching the holes, and deformed squares to starbursts with his hands. Adrenaline drove Connor effortlessly over the top. Dropping to the ground, he jogged towards the next barrier, shouting, "Guard! Guard!" He barked the word.

Connor scoured the boundary, looking for the vampire warden. He checked his watch. "It's three a.m. The siphoning sheds will be full. Where the hell is the guard? They can't all be in there."

"I think I see him," said Anthony, arriving at Connor's shoulder and pointing into the mid distance.

Fire and Ice: Survival

Beyond the second fence, which marked the middle of no man's land, a coal-black shadow moved.

Connor stepped forward and shook the chainmaille barrier until it rattled and his grip compressed the tidy squares into nuggets of metal. "Guard."

Seconds later, a stern-faced vampire materialized before them.

"LH5839204. Doctor Connor on council business. Open up," said Connor shortly.

Anthony provided his own personal identity number as the vampire opened the man-sized gate and stepped back.

The gatekeeper glowered. "Supervisor Matthew is not expecting you."

"I'm not here to see the supervisor," muttered Connor.

"State your business," the vampire said flatly.

With one look at the tight smile on Connor's face, Anthony said quickly, "This is *Doctor* Connor. Have you taken leave of your senses?"

The vampire fell back as Connor's fierce expression cleared a path as easily as a snow plow. His muttered apologies were brushed aside as Connor set off at a run, following the scent of blood.

Anthony peeled away and disappeared from view, headed for the more immediate location of the medical center.

The siphoning annexes loomed as vast silver-gray rectangular constructions, their brushed-steel exteriors burnishing in the glare of the compound floodlights. Connor set his sights on the nearest set of loading bay doors.

Pushing briskly through them, he made a quick detour into the scrub room. He plunged his ice cold hands into a container of boiling water, dried them on a sterile cloth, and then yanked on his white coat. Automatically, he pressed a soft plastic mask into place, which fit the lower half of his face like a second skin.

Striding to the end of the short hallway, he barged the swing door aside and stopped short when Supervisor Matthew materialized in front of him.

"Doctor Connor." Matthew's neutral tone and blank expression could not hide the resentment glinting in his eyes.

Connor had not seen him since their last run in, when he tore a strip off the supervisor for allowing blood tainted with clots to enter the vampire food chain.

"Good evening, Supervisor Matthew." Connor's grin was empty. "I'm looking for B-positive compatible blood. Fourteen pints should do it, and I'll need more on standby. Think you can manage that?"

"Is this for the hybrid birth?"

"I see good news travels fast." Connor scowled lightly.

Matthew nodded. "Juror Marius alerted us. I expected you to bring her here, to the medical center."

"You and I know better. Your track record for human childbirth is not encouraging." A hard glare added contempt to words softened by the plastic mask hugging his face. "Come with me." Connor led the way into the siphoning hall.

Entering the cavernous space, the labored breathing of dozens of rows of reclined humans swelled the air with dread and fear. The restraints pulled tightly across each donor's chest and pelvis did not cause them pain, not unless you considered the reeling sensation of plummeting blood pressure which played havoc with their state of consciousness, to be pain.

Connor clenched his jaw. Even the scene of suffering could not prevent his mouth flooding with saliva, and the hot tide of hunger rose in his throat as the full bodied aroma of blood wafted into his brain. Tamping down the jarring blend of distaste and excitement, Connor moved forward.

Closing in on the first procession of bodies lying on the stainless steel beds, Connor's keen gaze assessed the pallor of each face, inspected hands for evidence of good circulation, and finally, he lifted half-filled bags of blood to check the color of each sample.

Behind his own plastic face shield Matthew's features were tight as he followed along the row.

"It has to be type B or O," murmured Connor urgently.

"It should be simple enough to test it." Matthew nodded briskly and moved off down the line, headed for the blood storage facility until Connor called him back.

"It has to be fresh. The blood in storage, with the way we keep it, will have begun to decay. It doesn't matter to us, but humans need the antibodies and antigens to be intact. We're against the clock here."

"I'll collect some fresh bags from today's harvest, then, and take them to the clinic for cross matching."

"There's no time."

Supervisor Matthew looked irritatingly smug. "Well, unless you have a better idea."

Connor pulled away his mask and drew in a deep breath, tensing as the salty aroma of human skin filling his nose enticed him to feed.

Setting off in a grid-like search, Connor paused for a nanosecond at each bedside, analyzing the smell from the site where a siphoning tube snaked from the vein and down into the transfusion bag. Frustration curled his lip as he wasted precious time detaching each tube from the catheter, collecting a droplet on his finger and tasting it.

A vampire intern, with a mask firmly in place, scuttled along behind him repairing the damage and restoring the connection.

Finally, Connor found a faster way. Gripping the patient's wrist and pressing it to his nose, if the blend of iron and amino acids stroking over his sinuses seemed promising, Connor dug the blade of his thumb nail into the patient's wrist, tasted the blood and then nodded sharply to Matthew.

A blend of bloodlust and amazement smeared across Supervisor Matthew's features as he pressed his plastic mask closer.

"B positive, tag him," Connor barked and moved on.

"What do you want me to do?" His strangled speech was easily understood by Connor.

Grab a crate, I have less than half an hour to get the blood back to my operating theater, and tag that man. I may need more."

Matthew galvanized into action. Whisking away to collect a deep stainless steel cart, by the time he returned, Connor had gathered four transfusion bags. He let them slip from his grasp into the crate and continued on down the row.

Pressing his nose to a further fifty wrists, Connor cut into another half a dozen arms, and repeated his harvesting of the almost-full bags of O-positive blood. Connor's smile was grim as the infusion bags in the stainless steel container formed a satisfying pile, their oily plastic skins glistening in the ambient light.

He felt a pang of regret as human terror registered in his mind. He knew they did not see him coming, they just felt the unexpected chill of his touch on their sweating flesh. The echoes of their panicked cries were still reverberating around the cavernous space when Connor decided it was time to go.

He tipped the crate of I.V. pouches into a linen laundry bag, guiding the flow like a fisherman with a slippery catch, before tugging it from its metal frame.

"Supervisor Matthew, tag the donors and find me some more. I may be back." Twisting the neck of the linen sack around his fist, Connor slipped out through the doorway. He left the human farm complex and headed out at speed. The heavy fabric of his dark coat flapped wildly as he took the direct flight of the crow he resembled.

Chapter 26

The hospital came in to sight and, like a man coming in on a zip wire, Connor hit the sidewalk running. He changed direction abruptly and barely avoided a collision with the wall when he skimmed through the doorway, tearing his coat on the wooden frame as he held the linen bag safely out in front.

Back inside the operating suite, his eyes darted to Rebekah, and relief cramped his chest.

Anthony was there already, wearing a half smile of triumph. Connor nodded his approval at the sensor pads scattered over Rebekah's torso and the steady beep of a heart rate monitor.

The items on Connor's list were laid out on surgical trolleys in an orderly fashion, and he itched to just tear open the C-section kit and deliver the baby, but common sense prevailed.

"Julian?"

"I have given the baby three more doses of muscle relaxant, but, it's still feeding.

Connor crossed to Rebekah's side and wrapped his hand around her upper arm. "Her blood pressure is ninety over fifty. We've got to get the transfusion up and running."

Pulling the laundry bag open, he fished out a bag of blood and hooked it up to an I.V. drip stand.

He probed the flesh of her arm, growling gently because finding a vein proved as difficult as he feared. It was like looking for a needle in the haystack of her collapsed circulation. Connor quickly placed a tourniquet around Rebekah's arm, closed his eyes, and ran his fingertips across her skin. Before he could second guess his 'find', he opened his eyes and gently inserted the needle. Finally, the cannula he pushed beneath her skin darkened to burgundy. He sighed with relief. "Thank God, I found a vein," he muttered, and, with a deft stroke, taped the cannula in place.

He opened the valve on the I.V. bag, and, watching the plastic coils of the hose twitch like a disturbed snake, he made sure the blood flooding in had no air bubbles before hooking it up to the catheter.

"We can't speed this part up. It's a waiting game, now." Connor laid his hand over Rebekah's and her fingers jerked. "I can't use an epidural for a C-section, she's dehydrated and the epidural space will have shrunk. And I don't want to anesthetize her. If I can't monitor her responses to pain she could slip into coma. I need her to be able to drink blood, if it comes to that."

"Do we have any idea how long it's going to take?" said Julian.

"Honestly? With the baby still draining her, we're looking at a few hours. Normal rate is an hour and a half per unit, but with a 23-gauge needle, and the risk of cardiac arrest if we rush this..." Connor clenched his jaw. "I'll find a way to turn her if I have to, I won't let her go."

Julian pressed for a solution, "Surely there's some way we can inject her with your blood?"

"Into her stomach, maybe." Connor was non-committal. "Nothing else but 'drinking' is guaranteed to work. Only the act of feeding would release enzymes into her mouth and stomach, and lining of the gut has to filter the vampire blood for the transformation to work. If I infuse her into a vein, without the filtering process, anaphylactic shock will kill her anyway."

"Rebekah has to be conscious then? To turn her? Able to drink from you?" asked Julian.

Connor nodded as he stroked his fingers across the radial pulse on Rebekah's wrist. "Getting as much human blood into her as we can, and keeping the baby relaxed, is our only option, for now."

The resounding ping of the heart rate monitor marked out the seconds as they stretched to fill minutes and then hours, and there was no room left for words.

Julian stood back and watched Connor. Breathing in deeply, he said, "Marius came by earlier."

Connor's head jerked around.

Julian deflected the irritation clouding Connor's glare with an upheld hand. "They need to know, to field the questions. A lot of vampires died today."

"What do they need to know?" Connor pushed his hand angrily through his hair, transforming sleek, black satin strands into a clutch of charcoal fragments.

"That there is hope." Julian paced the room at speed. "Think of it as damage limitation. Alexander and Marius will watch your back more eagerly if they believe a solution to vampire survival could come out of this."

Julian stopped talking abruptly and focused on the theater door.

The metal groaned as the door whipped aside and Marius materialized as if their words had conjured him. His eyes settled on Rebekah's rounded stomach and moved over her pale face. "Any change?"

"Juror Marius. I see the vultures are gathering. I hear you wanted the baby born on the farm." Connor's eyes darkened to flint.

Marius inclined his head. "I meant nothing by it. We want the pregnancy to succeed."

Connor released Rebekah's hand and reared to his feet. Whipping across the room, he backed Marius into a corner.

"The pregnancy? This is *my* baby..." Connor's grinding teeth forged his words into bullets. "And *she* is my destiny. I will kill more vampires than I killed today to save her."

Marius' oil-black eyes absorbed Connor's anger. "Talking of deaths, Doctor Connor. Serge has called for your arrest, again."

"The council can go to hell," spat Connor.

"Just so," Marius said calmly. "The council will wait. I did not think you would leave her." The obsidian glaze of his eyes caught the light as he raised his chin.

Without releasing Marius from the traction of his glare, Connor barked, "Another dose of muscle relaxant, Anthony. The baby is stirring."

Rebekah sighed harshly as Connor's words moved Anthony into action. Pressing the plunger of the amniotic syringe, he delivered another ten-millilitre dose.

The beeps of Rebekah's heart rate monitor tap danced with arrhythmia for a moment, before the sinus node fought for control of her heartbeat and won. Connor frowned. "Councilor Serge can go to hell. Until my baby is born, everything will wait. Tell him if he comes inside my hospital, he will lose the other arm."

"Even with one arm, he's more trouble than he's worth." Marius' marble complexion folded into a rare grin. "I came to assure you that, when the time comes, we will give Serge enough rope to hang himself, and earn a sentence of locked-in syndrome. In which case, you will have the pleasure of moving him to the stage-three of skull crushing." He tilted his head as he added, "I still wonder at your own escape. Maybe one day I will ask the question."

Connor matched Marius' idle tone. "And, maybe one day, I will tell you."

"Juror Marius, what's the news on Sebastian?" Julian asked.

Marius stood to attention as he replied, "No one has seen him since the guardsmen were deployed, Principal Julian."

"He's more dangerous than Serge. He *believes* his delusions." At Connor's piercing glance, Julian bared his teeth. "He took me on. He thought he could blackmail me."

Marius bowed his sleek head as he buried his own speculations. "I could set up a hunt? Although..." Looking at Connor, he added, "I mean no offence, Doctor, but you took out the best captain we've had in thirty years. It's a pity."

"I regret it, too," Connor said simply. "He fought well, and came close to beating me."

"The last vampire we hunted down was Jack of London." Julian's low tone drew Marius into the confidence. "It was my first collaboration with Connor, on council business. Sebastian may not kill and disembowel women, but he's worse than that, he's the insidious killer who goes unnoticed."

Disgust tightened Julian's face as Connor agreed with his assessment.

"Deploy the guardsmen. Find him. Sweep the hospital, Marius. Every linen hamper and cadaver drawer. I don't want any stone left unturned," said Julian.

Connor nodded decisively. "Things could happen fast here, Anthony. Go to the dispensary, feed, and bring blood back for me and Julian."

With each vampire bent on his own task, Marius disappeared as quickly as he arrived, closely followed by Anthony.

Facing Connor, Julian measured his words in case they were overheard. "There are others to protect."

"And Sebastian knows their whereabouts." Connor was grim. "You'll need to protect her."

"If Marius fails to find him." Julian conceded. "And as soon as the birth is over." Julian paused in his latest circuit of the room to look down at Rebekah. "She looks... pinker."

"I'm still hoping to talk to her before I operate." Connor framed her face and trailed a finger over an ivory-tinted cheekbone. "You can do this, honey," he whispered.

Julian stood on Rebekah's other side. "At least, hypothermia did not set in."

"Although, the drastic measures I took then were effective-" Connor's smile froze into a grimace as he turned a stunned expression to Julian. "It was then."

"What was then?" Julian's brows drew together.

"The conception." Connor breathed. "The timing is about right. We know the gestation period of the baby is accelerated. It was about the right time... it was then."

"When? What?" Julian's tone was exasperated.

In an awed tone, Connor said, "When she had hypothermia. I took a bath in boiling water so I could warm her, and I lost control." His regret weighted his words with lead. "It was a freak occurrence. It makes sense. Our core temperatures must have been the same at the moment of conception. it adds up."

Julian's brows climbed as he considered the chances that the mystery had been solved. "Are you sure?"

"Yes, I'm sure. But the council must not be told yet."

"Okay." Julian waited for more.

"If this is blurted out, there will be a frenzied epidemic of oven-baked vampires and freezers bursting with blue humans. No, we have to think about this."

Julian nodded slowly.

"Let's get Rebekah through this first." Connor took her hand, moving his thumb over the back of it as he tested for dehydration. Inhaling her scent like a smoker taking a hit of nicotine, he snapped his jaw shut and expelled her cocktail of hormones, pheromones, and the bouquet of her blood gently through his nose. His sensitive sinuses shot the information to his brain. "If we can keep her stable for another three hours, and run through two more units of blood, I might be able to go with an epidural." He looked into her face. "Her brain activity is encouraging." Connor smiled lightly as he said, "She may well come round before then. Things are looking up, Julian."

A cautious feeling of euphoria filled the room as the theater door whipped open.

Anthony's red lips and the flush over his cheekbones told Connor he had fed. *Not just fed... feasted.* Connor nodded his approval, and stretched out his hand for the blood vials, which he needed too.

When Anthony approached, Connor's face compressed into a mask of rage. An odor clinging to Anthony's clothes assailed Connor's nostrils and, reeling around, he shot out through the door. A vortex of low air pressure whisked through the room, and the word 'Sebastian' hung in the air.

Without stopping to think, Julian took off after him.

His confusion solidifying on his face, Anthony froze, still holding out Connor's vials of blood as if an invisible hand still waited to take them.

Rebekah stirred, and her groan reanimated the stunned vampire. Anthony crossed to her side and laid his palm over her forehead. Hope swelled inside him. *The activity in her brain has moved up a level, maybe she's waking up.* "Connor better get back here soon," he muttered.

The operating theater door banged shut behind Connor as he flew along the wide hospital corridor. Ricocheting from side to side, with the purpose of a heat-seeking missile, he beat his fists on the closed doors lining the walls. Their metal hinges creaked in protest when each one flung open, and Connor barely paused as he sampled the air just inside each room.

He didn't make it this far. Sebastian's scent had wicked into the fabric of Anthony's shirt. *Did he brush past him? Or did Anthony walk through a suspended cloud of his stench?* Connor knew how scents could stain the air, like those in the ladies' powder room of cheap hotels. Not the perfume on their bodies, but the musk of cheap sex they tried to disguise. Some odors were thicker than others.

"He was definitely here," Connor muttered darkly.

His fist was followed by a shoulder charge through a doorway when Connor caught the scent. The room was empty but the stench was stronger. "He passed through here." Connor looked around the deserted area. The mattress on the metal bedframe was covered in plastic and the pillow was pitted as though it had been shaken out. Connor crossed the room and took a deeper breath. *He took rap sleep.*

With the puzzle piece slotting into place, Connor moved back out into the corridor and stepped straight into Julian's barreling path.

"He was here, lying in wait, maybe, long enough to take rap-sleep, certainly." Connor frowned.

"I know him better than you do. He has a plan. He's waiting for the birth." Julian scanned the corridor in both directions.

Connor's eyes darkened as he visualized Rebekah after her last encounter with Sebastian. Her bruised body and shattered collarbone were the sick bastard's idea of foreplay. "Julian, stand guard. You can see the morgue door and the entrance to the surgical wing from here. I'm going after him."

"You had better come back fast. You might've drummed the resuscitation procedures of a newborn into me, but you're going to have to do the hard bit." said Julian.

"I'll be right back," said Connor as he shouldered the exit doors aside.

Picking up the scent again, he raced along in the slipstream of Sebastian's flight path. The pungent particles clustered in satisfying plumes. *He was hesitating. He's near, I know it.* Focusing his gray gaze front and center, Connor pushed the pace to the limit of control, his shoulder crumbling plaster when he cut the corners in the corridor.

Connor's chest cramped tight and he stopped breathing when he caught a glimpse of a snarling face with one hazel and one cataract-frosted eye. He launched towards it with rage-driven determination. Closing him down, Connor could almost taste Sebastian's desperation as his outstretched fingers clutched at the fabric of his quarry's flapping coat.

At that moment, three sensations fractured Connor's concentration: Sebastian's huff of anxiety flooded Connor's mouth with venom, Anthony bellowing his name scraped alarm down his spine, and Rebekah's bloodcurdling scream crushed his heart with fear.

"Damn it." The woolen fabric teased his fingertips for fractions of a second before Connor applied the brakes and wiped the wasted opportunity from his mind. He was already halfway back to the operating theater when Julian added his shout to the layers of anxiety.

Chapter 27

Rebekah's last clear memory was of being tucked into the side of Connor's hard chilled body and walking out into the moonlight outside the eco-shelter. The row of vampire faces terrified her. Their frowns framed darkened eye sockets and, as Rebekah held her breath, a tourniquet tightening around her chest prevented her breathing and then everything went black.

Her consciousness meandered like a shoal of silver fish undulating beneath rolling ocean waves. The blackout curtains of her eyelids danced with pinpricks of light as the fish scales glinted like scraps of aluminium foil twirling in dazzling sunlight. And then, they darted in a new direction and were draped in dark shadow.

Confusion folded her brow and her face ached. She heard Connor's voice, arguing, it seemed. The problem of lifting her eyelids became too difficult to contemplate, so she stopped thinking, and the void of unconsciousness claimed her again.

The relaxing rocking movement made her feel safe – she was in Connor's arms. But lilting momentum, like riding an ocean swell, ran aground with a jolt, and a blow to her chest doubled her over and her bones creaked. Pain took a bite from her stomach and the bone suddenly snapped.

Her throat burned as a rasping breath screamed inside her head.

The world seemed to stop moving, and her body felt heavy. She wanted to stay there in the world where she couldn't feel her limbs. But then, pain flooded in as a metal grip of cold hands framed her ribcage and another spanned her hips. Her brain yelled at her to do something to make it stop. Panic clawed inside when her body lay like a heavy corpse, and a deathly chill spread over her stomach. Relentless pressure cutting through her skin like a skewer, pushed the pain through to her spine.

Her mind ran screaming along a jagged path before dreams crowded her head again and darkness welcomed her with open arms.

There was a moment when nothing hurt.

The relief of ice cold fingers stroked her temples, and the name Connor was written in script across her brain.

Her lashes blurred her sight when she struggled to raise heavy eyelids, and she abandoned the swallow which caught in her throat.

Rebekah," a tentative voice said, as though trying the word out for size.

The voice was low, and it was not the familiar warm resonance she expected. Her heart picked up a notch as she shrank from his touch. Forcing her eyes open, she saw a stranger's face. His white skin glowed with pearl fragments. The eyes, shadowed by frowning brows, were brown, but flecks of bronze foil gave them a preternatural metallic sheen.

It's not Connor. Rebekah's body bypassed the sluggish responses of her brain as fear jolted up her spine, her abdomen tingled as the skin stretched tight, and her heart rate pumped adrenalin at breakneck speed. The keening scream tearing its way out of her throat vibrated the air particles in the room.

Anthony snatched his hand away and backed up. "Connor!" For the first time since he had died, Anthony was scared.

As Rebekah's scream died away, the silence was filled by the rush of Connor bursting into the room.

It took fractions of a second for him to understand the situation. *Shit, she's never met Anthony.* "Rebekah, this is Anthony. It's alright. He's on our side. Honey, it's alright." Connor closed the distance and framed her face with his hands. The whites of her eyes flashed as they remained glued to Anthony like a mongoose's to a snake.

"Rebekah, honey. It's okay, trust me."

Finally, peeling her gaze from Anthony's nervous grin, she found Connor's face, and for the first time in what seemed like eons, she smiled.

Gently touching his forehead to hers, his breath fanned her lips as he said, "Welcome back."

Her lips reached for his, returning his kiss as her dry throat tried to say his name.

Fire and Ice: Survival

"I'll get you some ice chips," he said, holding onto her fingertips until the last possible moment as he moved away to reach for the icebox.

Just as the scream of the heart rate monitor slowed, and the tension drained from the room, Rebekah hissed and clutched her side. She suddenly arched and threw her head back on an agonized groan as the baby distorted her stomach in a jerking spasm.

"Anthony. Scan. Quick."

Connor collected a syringe of anesthetic from the surgical tray and stabbed it into the I.V. line near the catheter, depressing the plunger slowly until Rebekah's body went slack. Working as one, Anthony passed the ultrasound probe over her abdomen. Connor checked her pupils were equal and reactive, and that her pulse rate was regular, at least.

Anthony stopped the sweeping movement of the probe, abruptly. "We have an internal bleed."

The black inkblot stain on the monitor screen said it all. The amniotic sack was swelling with Rebekah's blood.

Connor introduced another ten millilitre dose of muscle relaxant into the baby as he swore loudly, "Damn. The adrenalin in her bloodstream stimulated the baby and diluted the effect of the muscle relaxant." Connor closed his hand around Rebekah's upper arm, and stared helplessly at the monitor, watching the shadowy image of the bleed grow. "Blood pressure is dropping. We are delivering this baby, now." Connor glowered at Anthony. "There's going to be a lot of blood. Go pack your sinuses before you put your mask on. Don't let me down in there. If she dies, you die."

Connor was not joking.

Anthony dived out of the operating suite and rushed into the suture room. Frowning fiercely, he tried to banish his doubts. *I can do this. I CAN do this.* He had knocked grown men senseless in the boxing ring when human, and being splattered in blood had never bothered him. He would kill for some of that immunity now. It was only his tenacity that kept him in Connor's favor. *Doctor Connor believes in me.*

He scanned the rows of shelves piled up with back-up supplies of the dressings, I.V. catheters, and sterilizing alcohol he had collected from the clinic at the farm. He was quite tempted to find a new use for the alchohol. *Maybe it will deaden my sinuses if I snort it.*

Picking out half-a-dozen tubes of fibrous cotton padding, he inserted three into each nostril, facing the possibility that Connor might need to operate and remove the ones which became lodged in his sinus cavity. *But better safe than sorry.* He rolled cotton gauze into tightly packed wads and put them into his mouth. There was no gag reflex to bother him, so he pushed them down into his throat as far as his oesophagus.

He pressed his transparent plastic mask firmly into place and stepped back into the operating suite, feeling tentatively confident. *I will not breathe during the operation.*

The scrub room was deserted, but low scuffing sounds came from operating theater two. Anthony paused, uncertain what to do for a moment, until his decision was made by Julian walking in.

Julian cocked his head and said, "Don't just stand there, scrub in." His serious expression was distracted as he moved around the room loading up a trolley with bags of blood, saline I.V. pouches dosed with antibiotic steroid combinations, sutures, clamps, and anything else he could lay his hands on. Tossing the words over his shoulder while he moved around, he said, "I'm the dirty nurse."

Interesting title. Unable to speak, Anthony grinned at the thought, giving Julian an ironic thumbs-up. Thinking of Julian as a 'dirty' anything, was a stretch.

Julian shrugged, humor was lurking behind his expression, but there was no time to indulge it. "Connor said something about 'circulating the sterile field'. When I asked him, 'what the hell does that mean?', he gave me that flattering label." He recounted his instructions. "I touch all the things that you both can't because you are sterile." Jerking his head towards the door through which he had appeared, he said, "Getting Rebekah in there and keeping everything germ-free has been interesting. I've scrubbed in three times, and I'm not even operating."

Anthony grinned in his turn as he scoured his hands beneath boiling water pouring from a swan's neck faucet. He nudged the paddle lever with his elbow, turning off the water, pushed his arms into the gown Julian held up, and shouldered his way through into the operating room.

Rebekah had been intubated to protect her airway and the bellows of the respirator sighed. Not breathing for her, but oxygenating her blood. Her body was draped in sterile green linen and, through a square hole cut in the fabric, Connor was staining the tight skin of her abdomen a greasy brown with an iodine swab.

"Her low blood pressure and body temperature should help us now," said Connor. "It will slow the bleeding when I make the incision."

But, increase the risk of the heart stopping. Anthony's throat worked as the frustration of not being able to talk kicked in.

Connor did not need the monitoring equipment common to human surgeons. His hand took accurate temperature readings as though his palms were filled with mercury. His fingers recorded her blood pressure and pulse rate with a fleeting touch. Pressing a thumb gently onto the tissue over her cheekbones told him she was still too dehydrated for an epidural block. *So, I have to take the anesthesia option. As long as she does not bleed out on the table.* Connor sought refuge in action, and pulling a tray of sharp- and blunt-edged scalpels forward, he squared his shoulders.

"Julian, go and prepare the resuscitation cradle for the baby." Connor leveled a serious look at both vampires. "Bring it in here, turn on the heating lamps and prepare the finest gauge suction tube we have. I'll tell you what temperature we need the lamps adjusted to when I discover if the baby has warm or cold blood."

Julian's brows climbed as it dawned on him, "We have no idea what to expect, do we?"

"No idea..." Connor's words faded as he gently squeezed Rebekah's thumbnail for pain response. *That's good.* He absorbed the wave-form of electrical impulses inside her brain. *She is definitely under, the anesthetic is working... maybe too well.* Connor was silent as he made his final preparations.

Julian disappeared through the doors to complete his mission.

"Ready?" Watching Anthony's fists clench and release, Connor added in a conversational tone, "You let me down, Anthony, and I will kill you." Connor was satisfied when he met Anthony's earnest brown regard. "I'll be walking out into the sun, and I'll be taking you with me."

Anthony stepped purposefully forward, and Connor said grimly, "Swabs."

He picked up the scalpel, spread his palm over Rebekah's relaxed stomach muscles, and took in a deep breath. Closing his eyes for a moment, he prayed. Pressing the blade to her skin, he made a six-inch incision in the lower part of her belly.

Anthony quickly swabbed away the oozing blood and stepped back.

Changing scalpel, Connor cut through the muscle wall. *Next, the blunt scalpel blade, which will wear through the uterine wall.* He mentally rehearsed the sawing action which would protect the baby from injury. *It's been a long time since I did this.* Connor's concentration faltered. His hackles rose as he sensed danger thickening the atmosphere.

Connor heard the muffled, ferocious growl and glanced up in time to see Anthony tearing his mask away as though he was suffocating, and his mouth frothing with white fragments of shredded gauze. The blood soaked swab in his hand shook violently and his brown eyes were drowned with sorrow. Anthony backed away, even as his muzzle folded with a vicious snarl and his fingers stiffened into a clawed grip.

Damn it. All he had to do was swab, pass the forceps, and hand the baby over to Julian. That was it! Connor tensed, ready to fight.

As the cotton gauze spilled out of his mouth, and his gaze crazed with bloodlust, Anthony lunged forward. Connor pressed one cold hand firmly over the incision in Rebekah's stomach, stemming the bleeding with his ice-cold touch as he swung around. With his other hand, he buried the scalpel blade squarely into Anthony's chest, at the base of his sternum. As human instinct took over and Anthony's shocked fingertips closed over the hilt, Connor gripped him by the

Fire and Ice: Survival

throat, compressing the carotid artery on both sides of his neck at once.

"Julian," Connor bellowed as he felt Rebekah's blood filling his palm.

Shock released Anthony from its stupefying hold and he pressed mindlessly into Connor's grip, his jaws grinding as he lashed out, clawing at Connor's chest. "Julian," Connor bellowed again. The tendons in Anthony's neck creaked. *I don't* want *to break his neck.*

Anthony's eyes closed as Connor's fingernails cut into the softer tissue under his jaw, stretching the ligaments to tearing point.

Rebekah's congealing blood oozed out from between Connor's tight fingers and he was a heartbeat away from ending the stalemate – applying the pressure which would rupture Anthony's oesophagus and snap his neck.

Julian burst into the room, and Anthony's snarl reverberated the air in the nanosecond he had to absorb the scenario.

Swallowing convulsively, Julian averted his gaze from Rebekah's blood-draped form. He coughed to expel the warm, nectar-laden scent of blood which rushed into his brain like a hit of heroin.

"Get him out of here," Connor grunted harshly.

Anthony was no longer putting up a fight. He hung limply in Connor's grasp cooperating as much as he could, with his eyes begging forgiveness.

Connor's voice galvanized Julian into action. His hands replaced Connor's around Anthony's neck, and he lifted him bodily, whipped around, and removed him from the room.

The moment Julian's hands touched his, Connor dismissed Anthony. The shutters came down, and all that existed in his mind, filling his heart with dread, was Rebekah. As he turned back, he did not look into her face, he couldn't bear it.

He opened the tap on the I.V. drip to increase the transfusion rate as he moved his hand and swabbed the incision. He shifted rapidly into vampire-overdrive. If nothing else, he would know fetal distress instantly, he had the echo of both their heartbeats pounding in his chest every moment.

Connor's hands were a blur of purposeful agitation. The blunt scalpel incised the uterine wall and his bone white fingers became stained red as he gently eased the baby's head down, turned the shoulders, and, cradling the tiny haunches, lifted his daughter to rest against his chest for a fleeting moment. He gently laid the baby down on Rebekah's belly, her softened abdomen dipping under the weight and molding to the infant's folded form.

A bubble of joy forced its way into his throat, even in the midst of the blood-soaked horror. *Our daughter is 'alive', or half-alive?* Uncovering the mysteries contained within her tiny frame would wait.

Moving swiftly around the operating room, Connor gathered all he would need. He opted for active management of the third-stage of labor. Speed was all he could cling to. It was saving his sanity... *and Rebekah's life.* He injected Rebekah with Syntometrine, inducing a strong uterine contraction to stem the bleeding.

He did not clamp the umbilical cord before administering the injection. He was not above taking a calculated risk with his daughter's life, the shunt of oxygen-rich blood would cause 'overtransfusion' in a human baby, but Connor decided that with her appetite for blood already raging, the rush would be a good thing, and provide her with nourishment while he saved Rebekah.

Connor held the cord, feeling the current of blood dragging across his palm, and when the surging tide faded, it was time. He clamped the cord, cut it, and lifted the baby from her nesting place high on Rebekah's stomach. Gathering the tiny limbs in his splayed fingers, he tucked the fragile curled ball into his body, ready to hand her over to Julian who arrived at that very moment and stopped dead on the threshold.

The sea of red flooded Julian's sight and raked talons of thirst down his windpipe as he croaked, "Connor."

Clutching the baby to his chest, he inspected Julian closely.

His daughter had already taken a piece of his heart in her tiny fists and refused to release it. Connor's eyes narrowed over the surgical mask which clung to his face as he inhaled sharply, assessing Julian's agitated scent. Gray eyes stared into steady green ones as, satisfied his friend was safe, Connor barked, "Take the baby, she has a temperature of around thirty-five degrees. Don't let her overheat."

Julian clamped his jaws shut as he scooped the baby from Connor's embrace and raced through the theater door, letting it bang shut behind him.

Connor moved fast; fear clawed at him, but he didn't let it in. He switched from general to local anesthetic, injected directly into the wound. *She should surface quickly, respond to pain stimuli at least.* He had three distinct incisions to close, all of which he could have done in his sleep, if anguish were not tearing him up inside.

Rebekah's flesh felt cold to his touch as he closed the final layers of tissue, and his fingers, usually so swift and sure, trembled as he prepared to tie off the final suture. He allowed relief a space inside him. *Thank goodness even vampire slow is still faster than a human surgeon could have operated.* Rebekah had no time to bleed out, even though Connor had two lives to contend with.

He searched her face, knowing he would be reassured by even the smallest flicker of an eyelash. *But, nothing.* His eyes stung without the lubrication of tears. Vampires can't cry.

"Please, honey, stay with me. Stay with me, baby," Connor muttered as he finally laid the needle down. He raised her chin, eased the intubation tube out, and he did not move until he heard Rebekah's breathing take up its own rhythm, becoming slow and regular. His fingers found a pulse, strong and steady, and he tuned into her body, straining every fiber to listen.

And there she was, only a soft murmur that hummed a low note through him. *But she's still here.* He renewed the transfusion bag and sank onto a stool to sit beside her. Her head dropped to one side, her relaxed expression soft. He scanned the fine bone structure, absorbing the details he had grown to love – the full bottom lip, the delicate nose, and arched brows – willing them to tighten with emotion. *I'd settle for a frown of pain right now.*

He pulled his mask and cap away and pressed her cold hand to his cheek; the surgeon had left, and he sat as a devastated lover, willing each heartbeat to be followed by another.

Connor could do nothing but wait. *I can't even turn her.* He could smell the sedative saturating her system. *Even if I thought she was strong enough and I used adrenalin to bring her round, it would cause internal bleeding so soon after the operation.* He had nothing left but waiting.

A few yards away in the recovery room, Julian was summoning calm. *I know what to do.* Connor had been the best and worst of tutors in the few weeks they had available. He had imparted his knowledge on infant resuscitation in succinct, precise lessons, quizzing Julian endlessly until he felt as though his brain was overheating.

Though Julian had tried not to see it, smell it – *there was so much blood.* Even with Connor's hand pressed to the incision, holding back the tide, it seemed that Rebekah's life was draining away between his fingers.

His mind locked onto the procedures Connor had drilled into his head, and Julian wiped the vivid red image away. He concentrated on massaging the tiny chest. But, all the theory in the world had not prepared him for the dread that his touch would crush the fragile, bird-like bones. The tiny honeycombed structure Mother Nature had painstakingly formed could shatter like spun glass.

The baby's skin was waxy and lucent-white, and, as the delicate ribcage creaked under his fingertips, Julian hoped he was not causing internal damage. He took comfort in the fluttering heartbeat that tugged at his throat. *Should she be breathing?* Every time Julian thought he caught a whispered inhalation, it stopped. He marveled at each breath that caught him unawares. *I have no idea what 'normal' is for her, but she's stable.*

Needing Connor's reassurance, he re-entered the operating theater and the atmosphere overpowered him, as if the room had filled with water. The air was charged with the conflict of tenacity and resignation. It coated his mouth and dripped down inside his lungs, until a fist of pressure ground into the hammock of his diaphragm. The silence was broken only by the shallow whisper of Rebekah's breathing.

Julian felt he was looking in on the mausoleum of Miss Havisham's wedding breakfast. The spine-chilling eeriness of Great Expectations, a compelling tale he had read, had seemingly leapt from the page and found a three dimensional existence here in this room. *There are no cobwebs, yet,* but Julian had the feeling that if Rebekah died, Connor would be found sitting there holding her hand, decades later. He would, of course, have starved and hardened to granite by then, and she would be the waxwork skeleton that Charles Dickens had so vividly described.

He cleared his throat. "Connor, the baby is okay, I think, at the moment. What should I do?"

Connor's pale gray gaze drifted to Julian's face, grief dressing his eyes in cloudy condensation only one step away from cataracts.

"Keep her temperature constant and syringe water into her mouth." A frown cast the frosted gaze in shadow. The bone-white mask which his dehydrated face would become was revealed for a moment when Connor compressed his lips and swallowed hard.

"Other than that-" Connor shrugged, feeling the added weight of responsibility, but unable to move. "Try syringing blood. Types B and O should be safe. She'll be okay if you keep her hydrated." His voice dropped to a whisper, "She just needs her mother..."

Connor turned back, settling back into his vigil as though he had not stirred.

Julian tore himself away. The tenderness that clothed Connor was hard to bear. The devastating image of Dickens' Miss Havisham, wearing only one shoe, with her bridal gown hanging in tatters as grief put an end to every thought and action, shouldered its way into his mind again. He turned on his heel and departed. *Connor has to get through this. Rebekah has to.*

Connor could hear the baby. He struggled to find comfort in that, but for now, he could think only of Rebekah. She was still hanging on, still there with him. He changed the transfusion bag twice more. Dawn arrived and then faded to dusk again. The smell of congealed blood was thick in the air, but he had no will to move. Hardening was setting in, and, at this moment, he didn't care.

He sensed Julian's occasional intrusion and instant withdrawal, and was glad. *I don't want to let my fears breathe... say them out loud.*

Connor's dry eyes remained locked to her face. He burned his will into her, until finally, he felt it, a glow as her brain synapses arced. A thought had moved through the cerebral cortex. As the glittering array of signals hummed through Connor, a tentative smile tugged at stiff cheeks which had not moved for so many hours.

Each one of her thoughts sparked another, and at last he believed. A rumbling growl escaped, expelling the toxic dread saturating him, and bringing a concerned Julian instantly to his side.

Julian silently held out a vial of blood; he was still struggling with the overpowering cocktail of aromas in the enclosed space.

But, when Connor reached out to take it, he realized his ligament sheaths were fused, and would not release. He had allowed dehydration to creep up on him.

"For God's sake, Connor," Julian muttered as he yanked roughly on Connor's hair and poured the blood into his mouth. "You're surrounded by the damn stuff," he said gruffly, hiding the relief that filled him, too.

Connor kept his chin raised as he waited for the reservoir of blood swilling in the back of his throat to seep through the tight space between his cramped vocal chords and finally lubricate his windpipe and oesophagus.

"Thank you," he croaked.

Connor continued to stare at the ceiling as though he was praying to unseen forces until, taking another vial of blood from Julian's waiting hand, he drank it himself. Dropping his chin at last, Connor reached across the blood-stiffened linen and folded his fingers around Rebekah's relaxed hand.

"Thank you."

Julian was not sure if Connor's thanks were for him or if, indeed, there was a deity who cared. *Have we finally found a patron saint of vampires?'* His smile at the prospect faltered when Rebekah's fingers twitched inside Connor's cold clasp.

Fire and Ice: Survival

Her eyelids fluttered open, and a groan grated in her throat.

Connor rose quickly to fill her vision as he said gently, "Hi, honey. You had me worried there for a while."

Rebekah focused on his beautiful face. The gray tint to his skin was not something she had seen before, and her fingers itched to push back the blue-black hanks of hair falling over his brow.

His cool palm framed her cheek, and he smiled. Joy stirred in the depths of his gray eyes. "We did it, honey." Connor's lowered tone resonated inside his chest as he said, "We have a baby girl, you did it."

His smile widened as her eyes filled with tears.

"Hey, how're you feeling?" Connor held her hand, which was warmer now, and he thrilled at the smile blossoming on her face.

"Can I hold her?"

"Sure," Connor's eyes found Julian's across the room, and questions crowded the space between them as he realized he was not sure how his daughter fared.

"I'll go and get her," said Julian with a reassuring nod.

The color drained from Rebekah's face as she struggled to lift her shoulders, and Connor clucked his disapproval. "Careful, honey," he said, and three pillows materialized from nowhere to support her in a more upright position.

Julian wheeled the perspex cradle into the room, and a ball of white swaddling moved as the baby girl fought to uncover kicking legs and flailing arms.

"Can I hold her?" Desperation roughened Rebekah's voice, and the baby was settled into her arms before the words had died from her lips. Connor was already there, too, hitching up beside her to gaze into the baby's small, delicate features. They were entranced by the tiny little girl, her ivory-toned complexion and steady heart at odds with the strong jaw which clamped onto Connor's experimental finger, causing him to grimace in pretended pain.

In answer to Rebekah's inquiring glance, Connor said on a laugh, "You won't be breastfeeding. She does not have teeth, but her gums have edges like razor blades, and her bite... well, ouch!"

Rebekah looked down at the miniature perfection of her face. "So, how...?"

"She'll take your milk from a syringe until we find an alternative. I am sure we can adapt a bottle. We'll think of something." He met Rebekah's eyes and lifted a speculative brow. Stroking a thumb across her cheek and collecting a tear, one of happiness, he hoped, as he said, "More importantly, what are we going to call her?"

"Seren," breathed Rebekah as a tiny fist gripped the end of her finger and it turned an angry red color, throbbing painfully until Connor carefully prised the baby's fingers open. "Got her dad's strength, by the looks of things." Rebekah grinned.

She glanced up at him, and the sigh of his cool citrus scent filled her with happiness as he brushed a gentle kiss over her lips.

"Perfect, like her mother," Connor husked, "Seren." Her name meant 'star', a pinprick of light in the black shadows, and it was what she was to them.

Connor laid his palm over the tiny abdomen and absorbed the vibrations of her body, losing himself in the hum of her tiny muscles flexing and the sluggish flow of blood moving like a lazy river under her skin. His hopes were high.

"With a human circulatory system, there is a good chance she has bone marrow capable of renewing blood cells." Connor glanced at Julian. "If that proves to be the case, she will always have the essential human isotopes flowing through her. Maybe not at a rate that will satisfy her thirsty vampire tissue, but it could mean that she can top up with animal blood alone."

Julian said slowly, "The council can wait until we are sure."

"So, here she is. Seren, the perfect blend of vampire and human, a hybrid," whispered Connor in distracted contemplation, losing himself in the perfect picture of his beloved and his child.

Julian sank back in to a shaded corner, digesting the scene and wondering what the future held for all of them. All he knew for certain was that things would never be the same.

A while later, Connor asked, "Where is Anthony?"

His world was turning again. Rebekah and his baby slept, and, even though the horror of the last three days was etched into his soul, he felt in control and his world expanded to take in others.

"In the morgue." Julian laughed. "He's in a cadaver drawer. I put him there for his own, and everyone else's, protection."

"Really? Still?" Connor found it in himself to grin. "Go and let him out."

"Sure?" Julian quirked a brow. "I think he considers it penance. I've been down there to make sure he doesn't starve, but he told me to leave him there until you said he could come back."

"And if I said the word, he'd dehydrate and die?" Connor met Julian's eyes. "I guess he would, he must feel like hell."

Connor decided Anthony's good points outweighed the bad. "Go and let him out. After all, he went to the eco-town when Rebekah fell ill and I was away letting my inner-beast get the better of me. I owe him for that, alone."

Connor's head jerked around as Rebekah stirred, and Anthony was forgotten.

◇◇◇

Like the evil presence in the fairy tale, Sebastian heard of the birth and made his plans. He considered himself the most cunning character in the story.

Serge has to demand justice for his injuries, and the council will want news of the baby. Doctor Connor has some explaining to do, he'll have no choice but to leave her. Sebastian sat on the parapet of the hospital building, looking out over a black skyline where the silvered slice of the moon picked out the spires and chimneys of London. *Will Connor's sidekick be left in charge when the council calls? Will he remember me from our fleeting acquaintance?*

Sebastian lay back, as he forgot the city. His eyes scanned the glittering dusting of stars and allowed them to melt into a haze as he indulged in a little wish fulfilment. *What will the baby taste like?* Saliva flooded his mouth as he considered the tender, marshmallow-like texture of muscles that had yet to be torn in exertion. *Nectar.*

Chapter 28

Leizle walked the circumference of the meeting cavern for the fourth time before admitting defeat. *I need to sleep.* Being underground, time crawled by, and, since Rebekah had been whisked away by Connor, tension was like a pneumatic drill etching scenarios into her brain, giving her a permanent headache. She had worn a track into the hardened earthen floor. *Another day, and no more news.*

Oscar had kept her company for a while, but she knew her perpetual movement was driving him insane. His presence was still reassuring. The sound of pots and pans crashing together in the kitchen cavern echoed through the tunnels, and she would have smiled had her head not been pounding.

The clanging reached a crescendo and then suddenly ceased. Leizle waited for the agonized oath which would let her know it was Oscar being clumsy and nothing more sinister, but there was only silence. *It's too quiet.* Oscar's large, hearty frame was never this quiet. Visions of a vampire invasion, so swift that it had silenced his gasp of fear before he could shout out, drenched her in sweat.

She rushed forward on legs which were suddenly stiff with reluctance.

The naked flames which lit the tunnels danced her shadow mockingly over the walls. Images of the talon-fingered 'Nosferatu', the first vampire captured on celluloid in 1922, dragged his claws through her imagination. The aged poster she had seen as a child had printed its own copy into her young mind; it had gloweringly declared the character as a 'symphony of horror'.

Leizle's legs moved faster as she shook off the crippling fear and outran her demons. She needed to see Oscar's ruddy complexion and know that he was there to protect her. *Of course he's alright. Buried under half a ton of kitchenware maybe, but he's fine.*

Running flat out, she executed a ragged turn into the dining cavern, and entered the kitchen, where she stopped dead.

"You thought I'd forgotten, eh?" said Oscar.

Leizle's pounding heartbeat distorted Oscar's words as she bent double trying to catch her breath. "What?" she wheezed.

"Happy birthday?" said Oscar, suddenly wondering if he had taken the concept of 'surprise' too far when Leizle looked about to keel over.

Her frown evaporated as she finally found enough air to say, "My birthday. How did you know?" She placed her hands on her hips. "And, what on earth was all the noise about? You scared me half to death."

"Well, let me see. Your eighteenth. Rebekah told me. And, I wanted to surprise you, and I couldn't think of a subtle way to get you here." Oscar frowned. "I think that was all the questions. So, Mademoiselle, let's eat."

"Can I go and change, first?" Leizle glanced down at her grubby jeans and sneakers.

"Sure," beamed Oscar.

An hour later, Leizle and Oscar were relaxing at a table with empty plates and full stomachs.

"How did you get ingredients for a cake?" Leizle put her elbow on the table and rested her chin in her hand as tiredness made her head feel heavy and filled it with shifting sand.

"Ah, that would be the wonders of powdered egg. I'm afraid even Connor could not find any fresh ones."

"He was in on it, too?" Leizle's green eyes glowed in the lamplight. The sand in her head shifted and made room for Julian's chiseled features, as she asked, "Will we see them soon, do you think?"

"Rebekah? Connor? Or Anthony... ouch!" Oscar's pained expression was real, even though Leizle's kick in the shin was playful. "Sorry, lass. There's no telling when they'll come. But, at least we know Rebekah and the baby are okay."

"Yes, we know that much, I guess. But, nothing else, and I'm going nuts." Leizle's smile was tight with disappointment.

"It was good of Connor to send Anthony to tell us." Oscar reached out to cover her hand, putting a stop to her restless tapping on the table top. "They will come."

"I'm sure they will," she said. Exhaustion made sleep an enticing form of amnesia, and Leizle finally gave in. "If feeding me was a ploy to get me to sleep?" Leizle smirked. "You've done a grand job."

"I couldn't let your eighteenth go by without a celebration," Oscar said.

"Thank you. G'night Oscar." Getting up, she dropped a kiss onto his cheek, and set off on the walk back to her cavern. She kept her eyes front and forward when passing Rebekah's doorway. *I've spent too much time in there.*

As birthdays go, she'd had better. *And I've never had one without Rebekah.* Yawning widely, she lay down to sleep. Her head was filled with past birthdays, Rebekah, and Julian. As her eyes drifted closed she hoped she would dream about him. A half smile bowed her lips as goosebumps sweeping over her skin rekindled the sensation of Julian's caress.

Too cold to touch her yet, Julian sat and watched her sleep. His face was chiseled in ice. His dense tissue had forged a path through the bitter-cold night and he still wore the frost of its touch. Plumes of refrigerated night air cloaking him condensed as moisture on the polished stones of her cavern walls.

The heat haze of her slumber was a brazier of hot coals to his senses. Everything about her burned him, even her titian hair; every time she moved and the light caught it, its fiery strands licked flames across his retina.

Julian sighed, he'd come to find her. He wanted her with him, even though it would mean hiding her in the soundproofed room inside his house for the time being. He had been unable to concentrate not knowing what she was up to. *She has a reckless streak that tears me open whenever I think of it.* Julian's smile was rueful as he admired the stubborn chin in evidence even while she slept.

Tendrils of Leizle-laden hormones tortured him, drifting across the cavern to bind him, tighten his chest, and tempt him to taste her... to bite.

Retreating urgently, he retraced his steps to the laundry room where he turned on the faucet and poured hot water into the large Jacuzzi-like pool.

Shedding his clothes, Julian lowered himself into the water until he disappeared below the glassy surface. His dense tissue settled him on the bottom, and he eased into the meditative state of revival sleep. In a moment of crystal clarity, Julian knew he could command the pain and suffering of loving Leizle. *She makes me feel alive.*

Unable to resist her call, he surged up and emerged from the water. Dressing quickly, he shrugged into his shirt and, with the damp towel slung around his neck and his jacket dangling from his fingertips, he left the cavern. The naked flames of the torches sizzled and spat at the spray of moisture as he shook his wet mane to clear his vision, and rubbed the towel over the saturated strands.

The sudden draft of his arrival in her cavern drew a soft moan of protest from Leizle. Standing with the towel hanging from distracted fingertips, he ran his hand through barely damp, blonde-bronzed hair and focused on her sleeping form.

He allowed her scent to infuse him slowly, panting gently. He filled his lungs little by little, until he felt her in every fiber, and the searing hunger to touch her had been eaten away to merely a ravenous burn. His cheeks were flushed from the vials of human blood he drank at the dispensary and the animal blood he had hunted down on the way. *I haven't seen her for days, so I'm taking no chances.* Languishing deep in revival sleep, he felt almost human. His desire was earthy and physical and, drawn by her alluring scent, he laid out on the bed beside her.

Propped up on his side, he settled his palm at her waist, and his cool, minted breath feathered her neck. He smiled as a frisson of exhilaration darted through her soft center, and the kiss he pressed to her shoulder dusted her skin in a shiver.

A glorious flush of heat flooded her breasts and tingled through her belly and thighs as a feline stretch arched her body, releasing the tightly wound spring of tension. Closing his eyes, Julian rode the warm wave of her scattered blood cells, and the curves of her body were a model of the perfection he had constructed in his mind.

She rolled towards him. He ran his hand over her contours, moving carefully over her thigh, hip, and ribcage, and pulled in a deep breath as he warmed his palm on her breast. Stroking his thumb over burning skin to tease, she was the perfect fit as he knew she would be.

When he closed his lips over her soft mouth, he felt the relaxation of slumber slip away and confusion spark through her brain in an electrical storm of activity. The disorientation of delicious excitement suddenly dissolved into panic and her pulse rate peaked as she pulled away.

"Don't go," he muttered, his thumb continuing to caress in languorous circles until his fingers at last closed over her nipple and, lifting his head, he locked his darkened sage eyes to hers.

"You're really here. It's my birthday." Her sleep-scrambled words tumbled as the distracting tug of his fingertips thickened her thoughts.

"Happy birthday," Julian purred as he hovered over her lips again.

Leizle's eyes glazed with pleasure and her fingertips played with the edges of his open shirt. Never taking her eyes from his, she peeled the fabric away, spreading her palms over his taut muscles. With every stroke of her hands, her expression of wonder gave way to longing, touched with uncertainty.

A half-smile softened the chiseled planes of Julian's face as he allowed her to explore. Motionless, he veiled the intensity in his gaze as she stroked the muscles of his chest and down over his braced abdomen. When her fingers pulled at his pants, his hand closed over hers, holding her still.

Her agitation sang of a girl on a voyage of discovery, her intoxicating scent was spiced with nerves, and as Julian breathed it

Fire and Ice: Survival

in, raw satisfaction settled in the pit of his stomach. *She has never been here before.*

He moved to kiss her again with a growl rumbling in his throat. "I want to, you know I do," he breathed as his hand covered her buttock and he pulled her into his groin, demonstrating his frustration. "But, I want it to be right, and there are other things."

Julian ached with restraint as he took his time, exciting her skin with his caress.

Leizle was lost as the surge of longing gathered her thoughts and whisked them along, tugging them beneath the boiling surface of desire. Every vision of Julian was an explosion of light, and every touch of his cool skin grazing over hers was a sensation she could hardly bear. Anticipation came up for breath, when finally, his hand covered her stomach, his fingertips stroked down and dipped between her thighs. Her gasp delighted as much as the damp heat of her arousal tortured him.

"There are so many other things." His chest rumbled with satisfaction. "You won't be disappointed, I promise."

Trailing his lips down over her body, he followed the flush his fingers laid over her skin, pausing to dip his tongue into her tummy button. Her shudders vibrating beneath his lips were entrancing. Anticipation flooded his mouth as he dared to taste her. Dipping his head between her thighs, his cool mouth savored her excitement.

His demonstration left Leizle breathless as, holding her carefully, but not letting her escape, his tongue played over her sweet scent until the shivers racking her body almost drove him crazy.

He smiled against her trembling stomach, trailed kisses up over her breasts, and kissed her lips just as her bones turned to jelly. He molded her soft curves to his, tucking her gently into his side.

Julian almost appeared human, lying out on his back with a hand supporting his head and a slumbering Leizle nestled in to his chest. Except that his face was bone-white with tension, his eyes blackened pools of hunger, and his harsh panting breaths barely eased the pain.

He promised himself he would make her first awakening perfect, and it had almost killed him. The knife blade in his throat he could manage, but the surge in his groin which pulled at his velvet heat when the thigh she draped over his pants brushed his naked stomach, he could not. He was a hunter, and the perfect texture of her skin was a blank canvas he ached to mark as his, to brand her. His compelling desire to possess her and emblazon her flesh with his ownership gnawed away at his restraint.

"Don't leave," her sleep-laden voice begged.

Julian was stunned. His vampire speed would have whisked him away before she could register it, but she already knew. *Almost before I did, she knew.* He thought about telling her he needed to feed, but distaste clenched his throat. He had a vial of blood in the jacket he'd discarded. *It will take but a moment.*

"I'll be back before you can miss me," he said, and he went.

Leizle's body rocked when his sudden departure released the mattress springs and rolled her onto her back. As her shoulder blades settled onto the cotton sheet, and she began to feel lonely, he was back.

"You see, vampire quick can be a good thing," he laughed down into her upturned face.

"It has its uses." Leizle flushed beneath his scrutiny as the morning-after feeling of embarrassment clutched at her heart. She had never experienced it before, but her instincts were undeniable. She steeled herself for Julian's regrets.

His amusement melted as his gaze swept her body, dark patches clustered as rouged paint daubs on her skin. "Got a *few* battle scars, I see," he whispered. Even though Connor had told him it would happen, the reddening marks gave him pause. His eyes wandered back to her anxious face, and his smile dissolved her doubts. "I'll have to try harder next time, hmm?"

His hands stroked over her thigh, and the languorously happy expression which blossomed on her face moved him quickly back to satisfaction. He nuzzled her shoulder as he murmured, "We should be getting back."

"I am coming with you?" Leizle asked. She didn't want him to leave her again, and hope flushed her cheeks.

"You read my mind, how could I leave you now?" Julian let a feral grin spread across his face, inhaling the scent of her quickening pulse, an instant response as he moved over her.

An hour later, Julian helped Leizle to pack the bare essentials. Like a satellite drawn to a planet, his movements mirrored hers, their silence filled with contentment as his touch flirted with her skin at every opportunity.

"I can't think straight." Leizle smiled.

"I can come back," he said, winding a copper strand of her hair around his finger and looking at it as though it held the secrets of the universe. "I want to check on Oscar, in any case."

"Is he leaving tonight, too?"

Julian found focus with difficulty and nodded. "Seth and Greg are meeting him in the woods. They'll be fine, and I'm sure Harry will be pleased to hear the news." He glanced into her face and smiled. "The worst is over, Red." He laced his fingers through hers and said gently, "Let's go say goodbye to Oscar, okay?"

"Okay," she said firmly, and felt the bones in her fingers creak before Julian released his grip with an apologetic glance.

"Sorry, I forget. You better do the holding bit." He waited as she folded her fingers around his relaxed hand before they moved towards the door to say goodbye to the eco-home... for now.

Chapter 29

The meadow surrounding the eco-shelter bore the scars of battle. The fallen guardsmen, like crumbled statues in an ancient graveyard, had become their own graves and headstones. The night air was heavy with mist, and to say it clustered as if drawn by the magnetic force of evil would sound dramatic, but Sebastian stood in the shadows; his wavy hair weighted with moisture and the frost-colored pearls decorating his dark coat complemented the clouded hue of his unseeing eye.

He had not moved for many hours, his feelings never stirred, even while watching the sun's heated fingertips glowing red as they gripped onto the horizon – as though reluctant to leave – and the rise of the silver moon bleaching the color from his surroundings.

The bitter cold suited his mood. The human nest was empty.

So, this is where Doctor Connor tore off Serge's arm and went head to head with Captain Laurence. A sneer revealed venom-drenched teeth, and as sarcasm struggled with envy, he muttered, "What passion he must have felt, to risk so much." Sebastian sluiced the rain from his hair, letting it run in an icy flow down his neck. He tugged hard at the roots, pulling the flesh on his face tight, and his eyes glazed with hatred. "His pain will be keener for that."

Curiosity rooted him to the spot as he tilted his head, and, playing the moonlight over the glistening dew on the field, he studied the trail of compressed flora. The crushed blades of grass revealed the route where a hefty man had crossed into the wood. *I only missed him by an hour or two.*

Disappointment buried a blade in Sebastian's chest. He took off across the meadow and the blackened maw in the hillside loomed large and swallowed him whole as, for the first time, he set foot inside his nemesis' lair.

Inside the pitch black tunnels, his feet glided soundlessly over the glacially-polished floor. *Polished to minimize noise, I'm sure. A kicked pebble this close to the threshold could bring death down upon them.* His clawed fingers scored deep lines into the tunnel wall, dislodging gravel and pebbles to scatter over the floor and spoil the hard-won meticulously smooth finish. The screeching sound of his nails kept him company as he progressed further, marking the territory as his.

The heavy odors of mud and potatoes coated Sebastian's nasal lining and he guessed it was deliberate. *Another form of camouflage, a prey well-versed in the potency of odors.* Their efforts were impressively effective. He slipped past the heavy curtain of sackcloth, and the atmosphere on the other side was a banquet of human odors.

Absorbing the cocktail of delights, he considered the possible outcomes if *he* had been the vampire who made this discovery. *I would not have let sentiment cloud my judgement. I would have ruled them, and bent them to my will.* The imagined excitement of terror-laden blood pumping through human veins dripped venom down his chin.

With measured curiosity, Sebastian paced the tunnels. *Such a wretched existence.*

The meeting cavern smelled of human tenacity and determination. There were hiking boots lined up along one wall, and wet weather gear of all sizes still hanging on metal nails. Sebastian laughed aloud at the rock climbers' headbands with flashlights attached. *Pathetic creatures, like moles stumbling around in a world where eagles dare.*

The dining cavern and kitchen smelled of carbolic soap and a strange woodland essence, and his fascination waned as the hope that the habitat was not the empty shell it appeared, died.

It makes life simpler, of course. The only human who mattered to him now was Rebekah, and her baby.

Sebastian checked his watch and smiled. It was midnight. *The council favors two a.m. as the perfect time to convene. So, I have two hours to rile up Serge, and have him demand satisfaction in court.*

He grinned as confidence gathered his thoughts and wove them into a plan. *And, Doctor Connor will have two hours of ignorant bliss before the hammer falls. Principal Julian, of course,* is the *council, and he'll have no choice but to attend.* "Council protocol is inescapable," mocked Sebastian, enjoying the irony of 'physician, heal thyself' and a principal hogtied by his own status. *And the boxer? I'm sure I can get past him.*

Turning on his heel, Sebastian beat a path back along the tunnels scattering the cold gray ash of extinguished torches in his wake.

Urgency drove him forward as he plowed through the woodland, using his fists to splinter dry winter branches, imagining Connor's face as his target.

He crossed over the River Thames and stopped on the sidewalk outside Serge's house. 'Phase one' of his plan tasted sweet. He arranged his features into the suitably shocked expression, ready to open the first scene in his play.

Sebastian took the steps up from the sidewalk four at a time and pounded hard on the wooden front door. The echo rushed down the hallway. Seconds later, the door eased open, and four bony fingers curled around the edge.

"Councilor Serge." His tone of concern was convincing.

Serge pulled the door open and raised thin brows.

"I just heard. Is it true Doctor Connor attacked you?" asked Sebastian. Indignation started in his voice and filtered through him until it puffed up his chest. "He can't get away with that."

Serge's eyes were needle-sharp in the gloom. A cloud of fine dust stirred when he turned and retreated down the hallway. "Walls have ears, Sebastian, come in," he said tightly, throwing back over his shoulder, "And close the door."

Following Serge inside, the sharp concentration of his one hazel eye pierced the older vampire between the shoulder blades. Like an eagle tracking a mouse, Sebastian kept him in his sights.

The disturbed cobwebs in Serge's study filled Sebastian's mouth with fibrous strands as he stopped on the threshold to look around. Fresh tracks circling the room had forged new paths through the sediment of dirt on the carpet. The councilor's detached desiccated arm lay on a chair, the bony fingers curled into a fist of protest.

The museum which preserved the vestiges of Serge's mortal life had suffered the equivalence of a hurricane. Even the framed photos of his human family had been pushed aside to make room for the leather-tooled tomes of legal reference books that Serge still poured over. He had not been an educated *man*, but he was determined to use the upcoming decades, centuries even, to become an educated vampire. Sadly, a crisis had come before the educating part had progressed very far.

"What are you planning to do?" Sebastian's eye settled on Serge's jaundiced, sun-deprived face. "What does protocol demand?"

Serge shrugged. A hefty volume lay open on his desk. "There seems to be nothing, other than the charges I have already leveled at Doctor Connor."

Sebastian arranged a thoughtful expression on his face. "You know, in the Durham Hive, a wronged councilor had the right to challenge the offender to a duel."

"A duel? A ridiculous notion." Serge stretched out his one good hand and spat, "Do we tie one of Doctor Connor's arms behind his back? Ridiculous."

"There were witnesses, correct?"

Serge's rheumy eyes narrowed. "The council guardsmen, and the jurors."

"So, the circumstances are not in dispute. Go and petition the jurors. They cannot refuse you if they witnessed the crime." Sebastian's voice dropped to a persuasive whisper. "This is your chance. Throw down the gauntlet, and Doctor Connor will have no choice but to accept. Vampire law demands it, no matter how uneven the opponents may appear."

Serge drew in a wet breath, and cackled. "A duel to the death? *My* death." Humor melted, and malice glinted in his eye. "Are you trying to get rid of me?"

"*You* would not have to fight. The council would appoint a proxy combatant. They saw the man tear off your arm. They have no choice." Sebastian's barrage of words had a hypnotic rhythm.

"Someone of my choosing?" Serge smiled, and his tongue slipped along his lips as though revenge was a sugar coating he could taste. "My general, perhaps?"

Sebastian bowed in implied complicity. "Of course. But-" Sebastian shot his cuff and looked at his watch. *Half an hour gone.* "You have to strike while the iron is hot. Go now, and demand that the council convene tonight, before Doctor Connor can take his brat and disappear."

Serge crossed the room, and, using a hideous handshake, picked up the arm lying on the chair. He swung the appendage up and cradled it across his chest. Looking at Sebastian, he asked, "Shall we?"

"I think it best if I hang back and act as your insurance. If you agree, I thought I'd go to the hospital and make sure Doctor Connor obeys the summons. And then, I'll come in behind him."

The prospect of satisfaction renewed Serge's fervor – his neck creaked as he nodded so hard Sebastian felt like he should be ready to catch the councilor's head, in case it, too, fell off. "Good idea," Serge muttered and headed quickly for the door.

The old vampire disappeared along the hallway and, as the front door closed behind him, Sebastian smiled. *Of course, Julian could nominate Serge a proxy, but why would he pass up the opportunity to rid himself of the councilor, once and for all? And, while Connor is faced with the ludicrous prospect of fighting Serge, I'll take the good doctor's reason for living and suck the lifeblood from it.*

"Phase two," muttered Sebastian as he whisked the cobwebs into a storm of dust devils and slipped soundlessly from the house. Skimming down the steps, he turned towards the hospital and picked up speed.

Serge's labored flight was slow as juggling the granite weight of his detached arm put a strain on his wasted legs.

Sebastian easily caught up, but hung back. *I don't have to suffer his company.* Like a predator flanking his prey, he made sure Serge entered the council building. As the door swung shut, Sebastian peeled off on a new course, devouring the last mile to the hospital.

Approaching the main entrance, he leapt up, clinging to the masonry. Hooking his fingers into the cracks between the marble slabs, he scaled the slick surface of the wall as though gravity

Fire and Ice: Survival

worked in his favor. Swinging up onto the stone parapet, he settled on the roof, crouched on the corner of the building.

If he glanced left he could see the gray ribbon of sidewalk outside the morgue exit, and, to the right, the main doors. *From which one will they emerge?*

When the waiting stretched to half an hour, Sebastian checked his watch and frowned. *Pity, I couldn't have gone in with Serge.* But then, they'd expect him to stay until the time of the duel, and that would ruin everything he had planned. *Serge's passion is real, and he thinks I will fight for him. He will demand satisfaction.*

To gain a better view, Sebastian lowered his knees onto the slate-tiled roof and eased forward. With his chest brushing the masonry, he leaned out over the edge. Hugging the contours of the stone, he hung there, unmoving.

At last, Juror Alexander arrived. He carved a direct path across the park, and the lines of his body transmitted urgency as he disappeared into the main entrance of the hospital.

Ah, here we go. Excitement dragged a sneer across Sebastian's lips.

Will Doctor Connor and Principal Julian refuse to attend the council? Can they? Sebastian found it intriguing that the London Hive had been brought to the brink of anarchy by a small bundle of skin and bone which amounted to an abomination. *A third species.* Sebastian scoffed at the notion, but his gut knotted. *At best, an immortal food supply, tainted by human weakness.*

Two figures streaked away from the building, kicking up moisture from the damp sidewalk. The blond hair of the leading vampire glinted like fool's gold in the moonlight. *Julian leaving with Alexander.* Sebastian tuned into the fast-moving conversation.

"How did Serge come up with this?" Julian's voice drifted on the breeze as an ambient whisper which filtered into Sebastian's mind.

"I have no idea, but, he's correct. Doctor Connor maimed him deliberately. Not as part of a fight gone awry." Alexander's heavy tone vibrated through the air.

They are worried. That's good.

"So, he is demanding satisfaction under the 'impairment of hunting' clause?" Julian's laughter was tight. "Serge hasn't hunted a darn thing in all the years I've known him."

Alexander nodded. "Nonetheless, he is now unable. Marius is looking into the precedent in the Durham Hive, although it seems to be an open and shut case."

The words drained away to a babbling brook of musical tones, but Sebastian could imagine the rest. *'Will the charges stick?'* Yes. *'Is the only resolution a duel?'* Yes. Sebastian settled back on his haunches. *Not long now.*

Like a gothic gargoyle with a demonic aura, he grinned with unconscious relish when Julian returned alone, disappeared into the hospital, and, after some minutes, emerged with Connor at his side.

Impressive. Sebastian compressed his lips in reluctant respect. *They do not hang around, that's for sure. Seeking a quick resolution, perhaps?* Sebastian strained his ears to hear.

"Why do I need to be there? Surely, Marius and Alexander can deal with this." Frustration fired Connor's words like bullets.

"We have not been here before. You may *have* to fight him." Julian's tone was colored by disbelief.

Connor's harsh laughter rode the air as they ramped up their speed and the darkness of night swallowed them.

Sebastian honed in on the twin tailed comet of their racing shadows until they faded from his sight, and then, he made his move.

Chapter 30

Sebastian launched himself fearlessly over the edge of the hospital parapet. His chest collided with the wall as he swung around to face the smooth marble. He hung from the lead gutter for a moment before descending fast and hitting the sidewalk with a crunch which cracked a paving stone.

Pushing aside the heavy glass doors leading into the emergency room, Sebastian took his bearings, and indulged in a mental run through of the next few minutes. *The last few minutes for Rebekah and the doctor's baby.* An acid pool of resentment settled in his stomach as he remembered the feeling of Connor chasing him down, breathing down his neck and forcing him to flee the hospital. Was it only two days ago? *Not this time.*

Taking a shortcut through the morgue, he slipped through the door marked 'authorised personnel only', and closed it silently. The eerie quiet of the surgical wing wrapped itself around him. *This is it. No turning back.* He leaned against the polished steel door and scanned the corridor for vampires.

Faint sounds echoing through the chambers of the hospital made it hard to know if it was safe to make a move. He finally decided he could not wait. *It's better to take a risk.*

First things first. Phase three, I need a syringe.

He whipped along the corridor. He could smell Rebekah. S*he's here in the surgical wing, but the boxer is here too.* That was not a surprise.

He scanned the row of closed doors and ducked inside a treatment room. The floor felt gritty underfoot. Looking down, Sebastian noticed the residue of white quarry dust at the same moment as its calcium-enriched odor coated his nasal lining. *Bone dust. Did the last patient lying on this treatment table walk out without losing a limb? Were they luckier than Serge?*

A tray of instruments rested on a wheeled trolley in the corner of the room, and on it was a syringe filled with an amber liquid. It was a veterinarian bovine-grade syringe with a tempered-steel needle, because anything less would bend if pushed into vampire skin of more than thirty years of age.

Sebastian picked up the syringe, depressed the plunger, and emptied the dose of muscle relaxant into a basin. Flipping open his coat, he tucked it inside his shirt.

Back outside the room, Sebastian focused on the double doors at the end of the corridor with the word 'exit' written above them. Each yard he covered tightened his gut with grim pleasure, until the doors abruptly disappeared from view, eclipsed by Anthony's stern face.

The surgical assistant sidestepped to block Sebastian's path when he tried to dodge around him.

The armful of dressings, surgical tape, and analgesic tablets he had cradled to his chest tumbled to the floor. Anthony clenched his fists and said, "What the hell are you doing here?"

Sebastian met Anthony's glare head on. He waited for the attack, and felt a moment of confusion when it never came. But then he realized that Anthony expected an answer. *He doesn't recognize me.* It was on the tip of his tongue to say he was lost, but he had used that excuse last time their paths had crossed. *Of course, I had two good eyes then.*

Sebastian looked for any glimmer of recognition and settled for something closer to the truth. "I have been sent by the council. They want Doctor Connor to attend, urgently."

Anthony bristled, stepping in close to drive home his animosity. "You will leave, now." Crossing a line which vampires rarely dared to, reaching out, he gathered a fistful of Sebastian's shirt. His lip curled and the tendons in his neck stood out like cords as he yanked Sebastian up until their faces were level. "If I see you here again, I will kill you."

Sebastian's hackles rose, but he swallowed his own anger and eased on a mask of contrition. Dropping his gaze, he let his body go slack and dipped his head, acknowledging Anthony's alpha status.

He shrank further when Anthony's grip relaxed and his heels touched down onto the floor. *All brawn, then.*

Fire and Ice: Survival

Releasing the fistful of fabric, Anthony stepped back, still watching closely as Sebastian turned away.

With his back to Anthony, Sebastian slipped the syringe out from inside his shirt, pulled out the plunger, and filled it with air. Feinting away, he increased his rate of turn and dived forward again.

Anthony's instinctive left jab shot out and lined up his target. He followed it up with a devastating right cross and satisfaction registered on his face at the juddering vibration which raced up his forearm.

Sebastian's cheekbone creaked and then crumbled. He rocked back on his heels, and a clattering sound tumbling down the corridor took Anthony's attention with it.

He knew that noise. He had heard it more times than he'd like to admit – something metallic and surgical hitting the deck and skidding along the shiny floor.

Both vampires took off in pursuit.

Anthony was running and scanning, but could see nothing to give meaning to the sound he heard.

But Sebastian knew what he was looking for. He brought his body into jarring contact with Anthony every few feet, keeping his opponent off balance, and then Sebastian's eagle eye found his target.

He fought to judge the distance with monoscopic vision and, at the crucial moment, he scooped up the syringe. Changing trajectory and closing him down, Sebastian wedged Anthony's broad frame up against the wall.

He shoved the needle in an unrelenting upward stabbing action into the side of Anthony's neck, depressing the plunger fast and shunting the air in the glass chamber into the carotid artery.

Anthony's shocked features folded in pain when the air bubble rode the tide of propulsion and entered his cerebral cortex.

His pupils opened to black chasms as Anthony descended into vampire coma. He dragged clawed fingers over his face, burrowing them into his features as if he could release the pressure inside his brain. He staggered until his shoulder blades hit the wall and he slid down it, his heels scrambling as a seizure gripped him.

Sebastian's apologetic mask fell away and the muddy-green hazel eye glinted with malice. He leaned over the prostrate Anthony and breathed into his face, "Maybe Doctor Connor can siphon the air pocket out." He shrugged. "That's if he can diagnose the problem. That's the beauty of *not* using the muscle relaxant." Sebastian added carelessly, "There may be brain damage, but you weren't using much of yours, in any case."

As though chatting with a good friend, Sebastian sat back on his haunches and continued, "I wondered if Connor's arrogance would run to openly keeping her in the hospital. He is so cocksure of his own authority." Patting Anthony's chest, Sebastian shook his head. "So much more pain for Connor, to have sacrificed his faithful boxer to a lobotomized existence." He registered the uneven dilation of Anthony's oil-black pupils and satisfaction rattled in his chest.

With a final slap on Anthony's slack shoulder, Sebastian rose to his feet, and the silence draped him in calm. Surgical wards were usually deserted. Vampires were treated here and walked out. *Unless they had lost a leg, of course.* He set off along the hospital corridor with open confidence, knowing two things – first, the council was in session, and second, there was no one left to challenge him.

The hot coil of anticipation drove him forward. *This is my moment.* Sebastian could barely contain the venom flooding into his mouth. He had yet to decide if he would kill the baby first, or save it for after, and take the time to savor the taste.

Sebastian had drank the blood of the urchin brats of the coal miners in Durham. One lad had come running into their hovel to find Sebastian pretending his satisfaction came from being buried between his mother's thighs. The child's eyes widened, and its mouth gaped at seeing the torn flesh of its mother's throat, and the river of blood staining the coupled bodies red. The scream which had gathered in the young chest as a mewling sound was never released. Sebastian had swooped in to swallow it as he bit into the pasta-soft windpipe, still too young for gristle to spoil the pleasure.

The vampire hybrid phenomenon disgusted Sebastian, although knowing Connor was the father made objectivity impossible.

He could almost taste Rebekah's blood pumping into his gullet. Her scent pulled him forward as he took in a deep draft of it and hunger heightened the ecstasy of the hunt. Turning the corner and scanning the row of closed doors, his acute senses latched onto her smell, and that of the baby. The aromatic tendrils clustered around the fourth door on the left were tinted a cool yellow by his heat sensitive vampire retina.

Taking pleasure in the game, Sebastian paused at each door, with his muzzle almost touching it, to breathe in the smell of dried paint and dust, before moving on to the next. The alluring scent beckoned him on, until finally, he rested his forehead against the fourth door and filled himself to saturation point with her fragrance.

Sebastian grinned and his cheekbone collapsed, dragging down to expose the ice cold glare of his milk-white eyeball. He relived the moment when Rebekah's collarbone had snapped between his clenched teeth and a shudder of eagerness racked his body. This time, grinding her frame to dust and feeling her skeleton crumble beneath his weight was the climactic feeling he sought.

He turned the handle and pushed the door open.

The aromatic plume of warm-blood hit him as he slipped into the room, drowning his mouth in a saliva and venom cocktail. *She won't know I'm here until she's dying.* He anticipated the open-mouthed kiss which would smother Rebekah's scream and fill her throat with venom, and hunger jerked him into the first step towards her bedside.

He barely registered the tight grip clamp onto his shoulders until his feet had already left the floor, and, launched into the air, his coat tore as it dragged across the ceiling. He hurtled across the room and slammed upside down into the opposite wall. His dense body folded into the deep crater it punched into the plasterboard before he began to slide downward.

When his feet hit the floor, Sebastian sprang into a half-somersault, and, twisting in mid-air, swung out a vicious kick, aimed at his unknown foe.

He was rewarded with a grunt when his boot made contact, and a satisfying crunch of impact shuddered through his femur and into his braced knee. Using the whipping momentum to swing upright, Sebastian drove the heel of his hand towards the jaw of his assailant.

He grunted when his flexed wrist creaked within a crushing grip. A sharp twisting action wrenched his shoulder, forcing Sebastian into a forward somersault to save it from dislocation, and he landed heavily on his back.

A boot compressed his throat, and he stared up into the amused face of Julian. A gray stain on his jaw bore Sebastian's heel print.

"It's like fighting a box of frogs," Julian said with a grim smile. "All that leaping about is very theatrical, don't you think? We were going to kill you quickly, but, honestly?" Julian looked down into Sebastian's nervously twitching eye. "We decided to have some fun. After all, you are into playing games, hmmm?"

Connor strolled into view. "Really, Sebastian, did you think we would leave Rebekah and my daughter unprotected?" He shook his head, his hardened steel gaze locked on to Sebastian's face. "Tut, tut, tut," he enunciated.

Sebastian's fixed grimace collapsed on one side, and a sound like a hacksaw blade grating over granite filled vampire ears as his detached cheekbone tore through muscle fibers.

Julian cocked his head. "I see Anthony got one in before he let you pass."

The hideous mask shifted again to bare teeth. "He may regret being part of your game this time."

Connor jerked his head towards the door and tapped Julian fleetingly on the shoulder. "Go, check on Anthony."

Julian's boot was replaced by Connor's fist as he gripped Sebastian's neck in a vise, burrowed the tips of his finger into the firm column of flesh, and yanked him to his feet.

Julian disappeared into the corridor, and silence flowed like lava to fill the space with hatred.

Sebastian strained to turn his head, his eye skittering around the room, hunting down the information he wanted. "So, she's not here?"

Connor laughed as Sebastian's good eye clouded with confusion. "Oh, you can smell her, alright." He jerked Sebastian a foot to the right, allowing him sight of the hospital bed where a cluster of heated terracotta stones cradled a stainless-steel bowl filled with a rust brown liquid.

"A bowl of warmed blood and some of her sweat-soaked linen. You were so easy."

The door-catch clicked as it swung closed, and Julian materialized inside the room with Anthony hanging over his shoulders – the muscles in his broad frame shuddering with convulsions.

Julian crossed quickly to a gurney pushed back against a wall, and lowered Anthony onto the thin mattress.

"What the hell-?" Connor cut himself short at Sebastian's gloating sigh.

Julian shook his head, and the sound of Anthony's grinding teeth vibrated through Connor.

"There's no obvious cause, but, he's in a bad way. His pupils are blown. You may have to pronounce him."

The tubular-steel frame of the gurney took up the rhythm of Anthony's convulsions, clattering as his shoulder banged against the plasterboard of the wall.

"Crush his skull?" Connor glowered.

Anger arced between the two friends like a static charge.

Connor's head whipped back around, his features hard as granite. "What did you do?"

Sebastian stared him down.

Connor's free hand grabbed a handful of hair, pulling some out by the roots as he yanked Sebastian's head back. He tightened the stranglehold until the tendons in Sebastian's neck vibrated in protest. "Killing you here without an audience is easy. And if you don't tell me what you did to Anthony, then you have two minutes left." Connor leaned in and hissed, "You want a chance to fight me, prove what a warrior you are? You got it. Marius is granting Serge's demand for a duel. If you want the glory of taking me down in the arena, tell me what you did to Anthony."

Sebastian snorted through gritted teeth. "I'm not stupid. You'll kill me anyway."

"Oh no, you have my word." Connor's cold rage coated his skin in a glacial sheen. "Dying here is too good for you, Sebastian. I *want* the hive to witness your humiliation. I will take you apart, all legal and above board. With permission granted to tear you limb from limb."

Sebastian's eye glinted with fervor as, mockingly, he extended his hand.

His lip curling in disgust, Connor gripped the hand and shook it once.

"He's full of air, like you."

"What the hell does that mean?" Connor spat as he absorbed Sebastian's closed expression. "Julian, check the corridors for the weapon." Connor adjusted his grip, burying his fingertips into Sebastian's cheeks. "You know, if I put a hole in your face, you'll find feeding extremely challenging."

Moving fast, Julian spun out of the room and back in again as though the door was a turnstile. Holding out the empty syringe, he said, "A full-body dose of muscle relaxant."

Shaking his head, Connor replied, "No, you heard the sick bastard. 'He's full of air'." He mimicked the malicious tone as his needle-gray gaze pierced Sebastian's. "How much air?" he demanded, and the blast of his cold breath crackled.

"A full barrel," Sebastian replied with a deliberate indifferent shrug.

Sebastian's grin gave Connor the purchase needed to prise his teeth apart. He dug his nails into his cheeks, and, for a moment, every particle in the room hung suspended. Connor's features became a mask of manic satisfaction as Sebastian's panicked hiss sliced through the air and the molars on both sides of his jaw dissolved into rubble.

The sound of crumbling teeth was overlaid by the explosive crack of splintering glass. Julian crushed the syringe in his hand when the gurney screeched, taking up the pounding rhythm of Anthony's cantering bodyweight, and the tubular framework buckled.

"Where did you inject him?" Connor glared into Sebastian's contorted face.

Sebastian's throat worked as fragments of teeth scraped down his gullet in a noisy swallow, clearing the way for his words. "Use your imagination, Doctor."

"I'm guessing you're a jugular kind of guy."

Sebastian's grating laugh sprayed a shower of tooth enamel, but Connor grinned as a shadow of irritation darkened Sebastian's eye before he looked away.

"So predictable."

Connor's bitter amusement died as Anthony's convulsions reached a sudden crescendo. Powdered debris rained onto the linoleum floor as his jerking elbow punched a hole in the wall.

"Let's get him into theater," Connor barked as he threw Sebastian at Julian.

Connor whisked the gurney from the room, using all his strength to hold it still as Anthony's shoulders rocked alarmingly.

The flailing Sebastian ricocheted off Julian's chest as he brushed the glass fibers from his hands and prepared to touch something disgusting in the same moment. Grabbing Sebastian by the scruff of the neck, from his superior height, Julian yanked hard until Sebastian's feet barely grazed the floor.

"I have to say Sebastian, you're definitely not looking your best at the moment," Julian whispered, before driving him forward. He used Sebastian's face as a battering ram to bounce open the door which was swinging back in Connor's wake.

Inside the theater, Connor hoisted Anthony onto the operating table and fastened restraining straps across his body.

Anthony's skin had a slate-gray cast and his eyes were open, but dull black pupils had swallowed all but a circular thread of his bronze irises.

"I don't know if you can hear me, but you're going to be fine."

The theater door banged open to announce Julian's arrival, and Connor pulled the mantle of surgeon firmly into place.

Moving Anthony's head as quickly as the jerking tendons in his neck allowed, Connor located the wound in the carotid artery where an ice-white pockmark punctured his flesh. He picked up a syringe of muscle relaxant, diluted it with saline and inserted it into the soft space under the tight jaw and injected a small amount until the sinews in Anthony's neck slackened.

"Here, Julian." Connor tossed the remainder of the dose across the room to where Julian held Sebastian. "If he twitches, jab him with that."

Connor turned back and took a quick inventory of the tray of surgical instruments.

He inserted a catheter into the pockmark, and fed the transparent thread of plastic tubing into the carotid artery until three inches had disappeared. His commentary was for Julian's benefit, and he hoped, for Anthony's, too. "I'm just going to try and draw off some blood." Connor attached a syringe barrel and eased the plunger back until he felt the resistance as he created a vacuum. "There is no blood yet. That's good, Anthony. This is the air I'm pulling out."

Julian grunted his approval as he asked, "He's going to be okay?"

"Maybe," Connor said carefully. "Okay, we have blood."

The thick, brown paste of dead, congealed blood snaked into the catheter tube. Connor paused, and checked Anthony's pupils. "Damn, one is still dilated. There's an air pocket in there." Connor muttered, "I need you here, Julian. Knock the bastard out."

Sebastian hit the floor face first as Julian buried the needle in the base of his neck and shot the plunger home. "Thought you'd never ask," he said as, stepping over the sprawled vampire, he arrived at Connor's side.

Connor spanned his hands over Anthony's cranium, sliding his fingers slowly across his forehead and around the skull until he cradled the back of his neck. Closing his eyes, he absorbed the sluggish electrical activity. He pressed his fingertips into the area behind the ears and grunted. "The air pocket is compressing the cerebellum. That explains the seizures."

Julian's brow rose in inquiry.

"It's the area of the hindbrain which controls coordination, balance, and muscle tone." Connor frowned. "I don't want to drill into his skull, old bone is brittle and it might crumble, so we'll go in through the ear canal."

Connor crossed to the blood storage cabinet and pulled out an I.V. bag left over from the preparations for Rebekah's operation. Stabbing a needle into it, he filled a syringe and injected fresh blood into the flesh around Anthony's ear, like a surgeon performing a Botox treatment.

"What are you doing?" asked Julian.

"Hydrating the tissue, so I can reattach the ear."

"Reattach the what? No, don't tell me." Julian snapped his jaw shut.

Connor laughed. "I'm getting soft in my old age. Usually, the ear would end up in the garbage." Massaging the site with his thumb, he laid the needle down and looked into Julian's reluctant face. "Here we go. All you need to do is hold his head over to the side. Are you ready?"

"As I'll ever be," grumbled Julian as he placed his hands where Connor indicated and locked his muscles in place. His smoothed features smothered his expression of dread.

Connor worked fast, slicing a scalpel blade around the back of the ear. He pulled the stiff cartilage forward and rested it on Anthony's cheek. Lifting the tacky edge of the small disc of the eardrum with surgical tweezers, he exposed the chambers of the inner ear. He fed a small-gauge catheter tube into the space and, with a gentle screwing motion, advanced it through the tissue of the ear canal. Connor wore a path through the fragile bones and into

Anthony's skull until he could feed the catheter into the space where the temporal lobe rested above the cerebellum.

"Okay, here we go." Connor grunted with satisfaction as the tube again filled with air before the greasy, brown stain of blood extruded in. He moved to look into Anthony's eye, watching as the pupil shrunk and readjusted to match the other.

"Hello, Anthony. Back in the room, hmm?" Connor grinned when Anthony reached out a hand and tugged on his coat. "Hold still, buddy. I have to put you back together. Don't want to spoil those boyish good looks."

Reversing the process, Connor used tweezers to reassemble the puzzle pieces of bone and replaced the eardrum. He finally turned the cartilage of the ear over, pressed it back into place, and manipulated the surrounding skin until the edges of the incision aligned. Stitching porcelain was not going to work, so he applied a line of glue.

Nodding to Julian, Connor stepped back and dropped the glue tube onto the tray.

Anthony swung his legs over the side of the bed and sat up. Cradling his neck where the tendons remained half asleep, he smiled sheepishly. "Please, tell me you got the bastard." Anthony's slack vocal chords slurred the words, but concern was written clearly on his face.

Connor jerked his head to indicate the pile of dishevelled fabric and tumble of limbs in the corner of the room. "Yes, we got him. And, better yet, you get to watch him die in the arena, in-?"

"One hour, at the Royal Albert Hall," said Julian.

"The duel is to take place at the Royal Albert?" Connor's brows climbed in surprise. "You're not afraid we'll trash the place? This is a fight to the death, Julian."

Julian jerked his head towards where Sebastian lay. "But the acoustics are so good, and I want to hear every breath of his pain when he dies."

Connor thought of the impressively large acoustic discs which hung from the concertina-styled steel ceiling of the Hall. Viewed from below, they reminded him of haemoglobin cells floating in suspension. He grinned. *Funny, how we are all obsessed with blood.*

"But, you're right. The Hall has always held a special place in my heart," said Julian thoughtfully.

Queen Victoria had declared it open in 1871, and, okay, Julian was long dead by then, but being able to witness her reign in its entirety, and the abiding love she had for her prince, Albert, had given him some hope for mankind. "It seems fitting. The place commemorates one of the greatest loves in British history. This duel is about nothing, if not love."

"I think Wembley Arena would fit the bill better," said Anthony. "I fought there many times in my boxing career. Though, I can't vouch for the acoustics." His brown gaze filled with the gold-tinted glitter of nostalgia. "My ears were ringing most of the time. You know, becoming a vampire turned out to be the best cure there is for tinnitus." Anthony's face softened in a wistful smile.

Laying a hand on Anthony's shoulder, Connor said, "I don't know if you'll have perfect hearing in that ear, but you should get some of it back. I did as little damage as I could."

"I'm alive," Anthony slurred, "I'll settle for that."

Looking as if he was giving it serious thought, Connor said, "So, you'd recommend Wembley Arena?" His eyes were alight with amusement when he heard an irritated cough and turned to meet Julian's 'for goodness' sake' expression.

Suppressing a grin, Connor said, "The Royal Albert Hall it is then."

He moved swiftly across the room to nudge Sebastian with his boot. Rolling him onto his back, Connor scanned the relaxed features. Sinking to his haunches, resting his loose wrists on his knees, he said in a conversational tone, "Hello, Sebastian, I know you can hear me. One hour from now, you will regain your body function in the Albert Hall, dressed for the duel." Connor flicked the flap of Sebastian's tattered coat collar. "Or should I say 'undressed' for the duel." The taste of anticipation vibrated his vocal chords and lowered his voice to a feral growl. "May the best man, win."

"Will he be ready in an hour?" Anthony speculated.

"The relaxant was diluted. He'll be ready," grinned Julian.

Connor sprang back to his feet as the sound of fabric brushing over fast-moving hard, smooth bodies filled his ears with a cluster of wraithlike whispers. He pinpointed the sound, staring at the precise spot on the wall as if his gaze penetrated bricks and plaster. Without turning his head, he said, "The guardsmen are here."

The door rattled in its frame, and Julian turned to face it as a tall vampire burst into the room.

"Captain Gerrard." Julian nodded briskly.

Gerrard quickly masked his surprise at the prone figure of Sebastian, and settled startling blue eyes on Julian. "Principal Julian." He bowed at the waist and snapped back to straight. "Juror Marius ordered us to escort the combatants to the arena."

"Efficient, as always." Julian inclined his head. "Has Juror Marius also selected the guardsmen from Captain Laurence's elite squad? The four marksmen required on point during the duel?"

"Yes, sir. They are already in place."

Julian waved an arm to indicate Sebastian. "The challenger will need transporting. I will accompany Doctor Connor myself."

Captain Gerrard's deadpan expression was commendable. Connor liked the man instantly as the twitch of his lip was ironed out with a dose of starch and the quicksilver glint of amusement in his eyes was immediately doused by shadow. *This is Captain Laurence's successor? Let's hope the hatchet has been buried.*

As the small company of guardsmen moved around the room and bore Sebastian away, Connor said, "Marksmen? I'm getting the impression you have done this before, Julian."

"What are the marksmen for?" slurred Anthony, still having trouble forming his tongue into shapes needed for speech.

"They will have tungsten carbide tipped cartridges in high-powered rifles. Armor-piercing rounds. If either combatant descends into grave sleep, they will go for a headshot." Julian's tone was brisk.

"Nice," muttered Connor. "And how will they know?"

Fire and Ice: Survival

"A probe in the base of your skull – into the brainstem – will read the brain activity."

"Ah. Any other little gems I should know about?" joked Connor.

"Apart from the fact that you will be wearing very few clothes and have your skin oiled to deflect the blade strikes, no."

Connor circled the room in a tornado-burst of energy, arriving in front of Julian and standing toe-to-toe, an ironic smile whitened his cheekbones. "Thanks, friend."

Julian's hand shot out to grip Connor's arm. "All joking aside. Don't underestimate Sebastian. He's as slippery as an eel."

"I know." Connor's eyes narrowed as he manipulated the chunk of granite buried beneath the skin of his side, residing there like a golf ball-sized tumor – a momento of Sebastian's blade strike in their last conflict. "He is like a cancer, mutating and infecting everything he touches. I'm ready for him."

Julian nodded, satisfied.

Connor turned to Sebastian's latest casualty. "Anthony, are you up for being my second?" He searched the brown eyes for the familiar cast of an iron will. "I need someone who can throw me a knife without taking my eye out, and…" Connor raised his eyebrows in a mocking expression of shocked revelation. "Julian throws like a girl."

They all knew Julian would be presiding over the duel, but he still swallowed a wave of indignation, masking his moment of gullibility with a grin. "Marius will send out another escort if we don't get moving."

It was Connor's turn to grin and bear it when Julian landed a playful blow on the back of his head before the three vampires moved as one towards the door.

Chapter 31

Julian took the lead and, flanked by Connor and Anthony, headed quickly across London through Hyde Park, finally pausing at the bottom of the steps at the Prince Consort Road entrance to the Royal Albert Hall. The stairway glistened as the night air laid a carpet of dewdrops over the cold granite. The broad sweep of stone steps was punctuated by flat elevations, until, at the top, the eagle eye of a towering charcoal-black statue of Prince Albert looked into your very soul.

As Julian said, this is about love, thought Connor. Albert had died of typhoid fever at the age of forty-two, and been forced to abandon his beloved Victoria to a gray existence. *I have no intention of dying again, here today, and leaving my Rebekah to that fate.*

Standing at the feet of the cast-iron likeness of Albert, Connor swept his eyes over the night sky. The enchanting effect of the Northern Lights which caused gasps of pleasure in humans were seen every night by vampire eyes. Dawn's fingers laid a determined pink haze across the canvas, like an artist rubbing away at a blackened window pane to let the light struggle through; nothing would deny it passage, and darkness would be eroded by that invisible hand, until sunshine yellow and bright blue filled the sky. *The inevitability of dawn.*

"They are safe?" Connor's deep voice rumbled like an earthquake inside his chest. Even with the jurors onside, speaking of Rebekah and Leizle felt like a risk.

Julian listened to the whispered anticipation of the assembled vampires seeping out through the stone facade of the hall, before responding in a low whisper. "Yes. They are safe."

"And they know they must wait until we come for them?"

Julian put his hand on his friend's shoulder. "Connor, they are safe." Julian grinned. "Even Seren seems to know to stay quiet. Although, it appears she doesn't feel pain and she does not cry. Which is just as well, because she doesn't sleep much, either."

"I know. She's a law unto herself," Connor said in an awed tone, his gray eyes alight with pride.

Anthony shuffled his feet impatiently and coughed.

"They are waiting, Connor," said Julian.

Looking towards the magnificently appointed double front doors, Connor absorbed the atmosphere. He took in every detail, fully appreciating the gravitas of the moment. He was about to step over the threshold into this impressive oval-shaped edifice and fight for his life, and his love.

The Hall was constructed in terracotta-red brickwork. Like an American wedding cake, it ascended in tiers of arched windows framed with cream colored stone, each one narrower than the one below. The dramatic facade drew the eye upwards, to finally rest upon the pièce de résistance, the huge 135 foot glass dome. It glittered in the moonlight as though it was sculpted in ice. The littering of stars thrown into the night sky looked like diamond-hued chips which had sprayed from the chisel blade that carved it.

"Let's get this over with," Connor said.

"Connor, when we get inside, the guardsmen will detain you as the 'accused' and escort you to your chamber to prepare for the contest."

Julian waited for his friend's curt nod before he stepped forward and pounded three times on the solid wood paneled door.

"Who calls upon the council to answer?" An officious voice gusted through the cracks and crevices of the portal.

"Someone enjoys pomp and ceremony," Connor muttered.

Julian spared a glowering look before he joined the performance. "Principal Julian commands entry." As his words faded, the imposing doors silently drifted open.

The vampire doorman stepped back and Captain Gerrard took charge. His blue eyes lasered into Connor's as he said, "If Doctor Connor will come this way."

Anticipation of the battle hit home like a clenched fist in Connor's gut. He could no longer stand still and, hurtling forward, his sudden acceleration scattered his escort of guardsmen like pins in an alley.

Captain Gerrard peeled away from the group and instinctively fell in beside Connor. *A guardian with a charge to deliver? Or a hunter glued to his prey?* The wrong-footed guardsmen circled back into the appropriate formation and raced to catch up.

Connor swallowed a bark of laughter as Julian's words echoed through the hallway. "Fall in and do your job, you numbskulls."

"Did you know Captain Laurence?" While they were alone, Connor decided to lay the ghost.

Captain Gerrard nodded curtly. "I did."

"I did not want to kill him..." Connor's glance unveiled genuine regret. "In other circumstances, I would not have needed to."

"I was apprised of the situation. Jurors Marius and Alexander made it clear the battle was ill conceived by Councilor Serge."

Connor hung onto an impassive expression, suppressing a wave of distaste which rose at the mention of the councilor.

Captain Gerrard paused, before adding, "I agree with the jurors."

Grimacing wryly, Connor asked, "And the marksmen?" He stopped moving and turned to face the captain. "Captain Laurence's elite squad?"

Gerrard cut to the chase, his tone crisp as he said, "All Special Air Services trained. All turned by Captain Laurence, himself." He compressed his lips in an ironic smile. "They earned 'elite squad' by the number of 'impossible' missions they came through unscathed when pretending to be human. Each man was handpicked by Captain Laurence, and was loyal to him."

"Note to self," Connor wore his best poker face as he added, "watch my back." *Does Julian know, I wonder? I will bet on 'not'.* "And, how does this work? Why four marksmen?"

"One for each compass point, to cover all the angles. The target zones are eye sockets, face, or ear canal. Base of skull at a push." Captain Gerrard shrugged. "There is no hiding place out there. But, above all else, Doctor Connor, they are professionals. You will have only one enemy in the arena today, you can rest easy on that."

"You'll forgive me if I remain skeptical," Connor replied as he burst into action again.

Fire and Ice: Survival

Captain Gerrard kept pace and then overtook him, cutting across Connor's stride and herding him down another corridor where a row of cream-colored doors punctuated the wall. Stopping outside the last door, the captain said, "You will find everything you need inside. Please do not leave the room."

Connor paused with his hand on the door handle. "Where is Sebastian now?" he asked.

"This is 'stage left' of the orchestra pit. Challenger Sebastian is 'stage right'. You will not meet until you enter the arena." Captain Gerrard dipped into his breast pocket and pulled out a gold watch. "You have eight minutes."

The metal inside the door-catch shrieked with disuse when Connor turned the handle. "Nice watch," he tossed over his shoulder, as he pushed the door open.

"My grandfather's," replied the captain as it dropped out of sight back into the pocket. Turning on his heel, he disappeared from view.

"Some hope, then," muttered Connor. *Sentimentality is good.*

He stepped into the room and surveyed the preparations laid out before him.

A dead expression settled on his face as he moved quickly. *Eight minutes.* He stripped, and, standing naked, liberally applied oil over every inch of his solid frame. Sinews stretched as he contorted his body into extreme poses, limbering up and reacquainting his psyche with how each tendon behaved under duress. He massaged every muscle, working the pewter-colored flecks of the gray oil into his skin until he resembled a life-sized soldier, cast in lead.

He wiped his hands on a chamois leather cloth before delving into a jar of grease. Distributing it evenly over his palms, he ran his fingers through his hair, combing it back from his strong brow and pushing through to his nape until he had tamed the thick black filaments into a slick skullcap. The chill of his scalp thickened the grease to a hard gel which held his hair firmly in place.

Finally, he stepped into the black leather loincloth which molded to his hips and supported his groin. The modesty flap of soft pigskin clung to his contours, slipping like satin over steel, and allowing his thick thighs to move freely.

Stretching out his triceps and deltoids, Connor twisted, enjoying the cracking of the cartilage in each of his joints, and relishing the explosive release of tension. He frowned as he manipulated his side, again investigating the dehydrated knot of heavy tissue he carried as a grim reminder of Sebastian's blade. *My hands were tied on that occasion, I wasn't* allowed *to kill him.*

A feral grin clung to his silver-tinted face and his eyes darkened. As pleasure rippled through his honed musculature, he sprang into a series of six feet high tuck jumps, landing each one silently. *The eight minutes are up.*

"Showtime," breathed Connor. He swung open the door, confronting Captain Gerrard, who froze with his hand raised, about to rap his knuckles on it.

Connor cocked a brow and prompted, "Eight minutes, Captain. Let's go."

The corridors whipped into a time warp tunnel as Connor's fluid gait devoured the distance. The black curtains which hung from the platform of the stage, hiding the inner workings of the theatrical process from the view of the audience, parted at his approach by invisible hands, as though his forceful presence repelled them, and he stepped out into the arena.

He advanced with a long, relaxed stride, his fingertips brushing his thighs and his core muscles braced. His chest and abdomen appeared cast in metal as a deep inhalation swelled his girth and he raised his chin in an attitude of confrontation.

Connor stopped one quarter of the distance towards the center of the oval polished-wood floor which lined the belly of the Royal Albert Hall. It measured eighty-six yards in length, from the facade of the upper circle to the huge pipe organ which dwarfed the staging area.

As he stared along the longest axis, Connor's acute vision made out the misshapen contours of Sebastian's shattered cheekbone and the hollows where his teeth no longer supported his face.

His situation mirrored Sebastian's, who was similarly attired. Although he was shorter than Connor by three inches, and his build was more wiry than muscular, he too, exuded dangerous intent. *His skin was stained with a copper dye and he resembled a statue cast in bronze.*

The dramatic figures suited the surroundings, but, there was a more serious purpose to their appearances. *The colors are by design. The marksmen need to know which head they are aiming at, and the 'seconds' need to know whose hand they are tossing the weapons to.*

The gallery bordering the arena extended at a thirty-degree angle, and in a seemingly endless number of occupied seats, rows of pale faces lined the circumference. The boxes of the dress circle, with their heavy brocade curtains in cream and gold, lined the vertical facades on three sides. Inside each one, ashen gray features were buried in shadow, their keen eyes glinting with the reflective hunger of predators. *A full house. But, I don't know if the acoustics are great... there's nothing to hear.*

The silence oozed to occupy the spaces inside the hall. As dead air, devoid of currents, filtered into Connor's head and settled against his eardrums, his skin cried out for sensation.

Connor rolled the balls of his bare feet over the polished oak floor and the soft crunching sound of cartilage concentrated his mind.

He scanned the arena, familiarizing himself with the battle zone. As his 'second', Anthony's position was ten yards back, on Connor's right shoulder. He stood behind a chest high toughened steel screen which shielded the combat tools he would deliver into Connor's hand when it was time.

A youthful-looking vampire played the same role for Sebastian. *I guess, Serge is of no use, having only one arm.* Connor stared at the youngster, and the focused intensity in the eyes gave him pause. He honed in on the vampire's odor; the combination of parchment and granite dust, like carbon dating, was the measure of aging in vampire skin. *Older than Sebastian, then, maybe sixty-five years. His sixteen human years mean nothing.*

He picked out each of the four marksmen. The one positioned behind him, and the other behind Sebastian, were elevated in the sixth row of the gallery, with an area of dead space around them as though the seriousness etched into their faces created a force-field. The remaining pair were at battlefield level, to his left and right, behind the boards marking the boundary of the combat space.

Three of the faces were familiar. Two of the marksmen had laid their hands on him that night in the meadow. *And now, one has a shattered kneecap, and the other has broken ribs. Great!*

Marius and Alexander flanked the marksman's position halfway along the curved edge of the arena on Connor's right side. Julian and Captain Gerrard stood beside the marksman at the midpoint on his left. A radio antenna extended from a console beside Julian, with standing space behind for the operator. *Presumably the receiver for the transmitted signal from the brainstem probes.*

Finally, there was movement.

A vampire approached from behind, but Connor's gut reaction was that there was no threat, and Charles, the small vampire from the blood dispensary, who Connor always thought of as a terrier, appeared at his side.

Julian's voice whispered inside Connor's head as he announced the tasks which Charles was about to perform.

Ah, the famous acoustics. Connor quirked an appreciative eyebrow in Julian's direction, knowing that even at thirty yards, Julian would see it.

"Blood technician Charles will insert a probe into the base of each combatant's skull." He looked from Connor to Sebastian, and back again. "If either combatant descends into grave sleep, the duel is over. The marksmen will end it with a shot to the target areas on the head." Julian stared hard at Sebastian's bronzed, oiled form burnishing in the light. "Sebastian, as 'the challenger', your code-color is 'red'."

Sebastian nodded his understanding.

Julian's eyes drew a line across the thirty yards of polished wooden floor to alight on Connor. The silver accents in the gray paint picked out his muscle definition as he stood still as a statue. "Your code color, Doctor Connor, is black."

Connor jerked his chin in acknowledgement, glad that Julian had not called him by the correct title, 'the accused'. *He knows how much that would rankle.*

Julian checked the marksmen were paying attention before issuing the directive, "Charles, you may proceed."

Connor smiled reassuringly.

Charles picked out a black metal disc with a needle protruding from the center. "The needle will be inserted below the brainstem, into the spinal cord. It will not hurt, but you may hear the cartilage grinding when I push it home."

It looked like steel, but Connor knew better, his tissue would not succumb to something so soft. *Depleted uranium, maybe.*

Directing his narrowed gaze over Charles' head, assessing Sebastian's smile. Connor said quietly, "I'm not turning my back." His ribcage rattled with the low frequency of the growl punctuating his words.

Charles nodded and moved around Connor's considerable bulk. "Code 'black'. This eliminates the chances of mistaken identity," he murmured.

With a grunt, Connor dropped to one knee, lowering his chin to his chest to make a space between the base of his skull and the first vertebrae. Charles pushed the needle home, and Connor opened and closed his jaw to ease the pressure inside his head.

Handing Connor three glass tubes filled with blood, Charles said, "One human, and two animal. It will take a few minutes before rehydration kicks in." His face folded into a lopsided grin. "But, you know that, of course."

As the small vampire moved to the other end of the arena and repeated the procedure on Sebastian, Connor watched. *It's a big responsibility for the young man. Duels are a once-in-a-century occurrence.*

A slight smile creased his gray-tinted skin as he listened idly to the same instructions being issued, but in a colder tone.

Connor downed the vials of blood in quick succession, veiling his surprise as the contents of the last one lined his gullet. *All three were human.*

Charles' face remained carefully blank as the young vampire returned to collect the empties. Connor dropped them into the cloth bag Charles held out, and hooking his finger over the edge, he anchored the vampire to the spot for a fleeting moment.

Looking up, Charles cleared his throat.

'Thank you,' was implicit in the look Connor gave, ever mindful of the gallery filled with vampires who had nothing better to do than listen in.

Charles disappeared as quickly as he had arrived.

Julian stepped out into the arena, and stood at the epicenter of the gathering storm. "This is a fight to the death." His voice resonated around the hall. In a theatrical homage to the days when the death sentence was still on the statute books in England, he wore a square of black linen on his head.

"There will be two bouts of ninety seconds," Julian continued. "The third has no time limit. No quarter shall be given, or asked. Only one vampire will be left standing. Is that understood?" He stared at Sebastian, his look of disdain penetrating the distance of twenty yards and causing the bronze-stained jaw muscle to twitch.

Sebastian masked his annoyance with a slow blink.

Connor nodded sharply.

Julian clicked his fingers in the sharp crack of a starting pistol as he commanded, "Begin." In an instant, he vanished from the battlefield.

Anthony stepped out and tossed the first weapon into the arena – the 'otta' was an 'S' shaped stick made of wood from the tamarind tree, with a heavy knot on one end.

Rotating on one foot in a forceful arc, and reaching overhead, Connor closed his hand around the thick hardwood girth of the otta as it somersaulted through the air.

Charles' surprised whisper rang through the arena. "Not a blade?"

"Think of it as tenderizing the meat, tearing the fibers to prepare it for slicing," was Julian's grim reply.

Connor lowered his arm, letting the weighted end drag the shaft through his palm. Gripping the smooth hilt, he faced Sebastian, and, swinging the otta head in front of his chest, he drew figures of eight in the air.

Sebastian mirrored his movements; the combatants' eyes locked as they swayed from side to side.

Drawing Sebastian into the dance, Connor swung the otta overhead, lunged in, and landed a two-handed axe blow, cracking into the shaft of Sebastian's weapon and sending the swinging weight careering off course. When Sebastian stumbled, Connor jabbed the knot of hardwood into his stomach, and heard the bottom rib crack.

Connor bared his teeth in a taunting grin.

Sebastian launched a swinging blow. Twisting away, Connor dropped to one knee, and a jarring vibration shook him as Sebastian's counter strike slammed into the fleshy part of his shoulder.

Shifting his grip to mid-shaft, still kneeling, Connor's stabbing blow crunched the otta head into Sebastian's sternum.

Connor surged to his feet.

A hyena badgering a lion, Sebastian crouched and lunged, dodging back when Connor swung the otta above his head. His silver skin glistening as his torso flexed, building a smooth hypnotic rhythm, and offering his chest as a target.

He could feel the human blood rushing into his nervous system, sharpening his senses and Connor's concentration hit the sweet spot. His muscle fibers began to hum with the exhilaration of full hydration. Sebastian moved in slow motion by comparison, his calculation written clearly on his face.

Swaying in time with Connor's fluid movement, Sebastian rocked back and forth as he doubted his accuracy in judging distance with one eye. As the ninety seconds ticked away, desperation flooded in, and Sebastian dived forward.

Like a matador, Connor danced away, guided Sebastian's barreling weight under his arm and slammed his otta down on Sebastian's back. The crackling sound of compressed bone filled Connor's ears, and he grinned. *His shoulder blade will crumble with the next hit.*

"Bout two," Julian called out, as once again, he snapped his fingers.

The sound vibrated inside Connor's head like the crack of a dry twig. Both vampires backed away, each hurling the ottas in the tumbling spin of a boomerang back toward their corners.

Connor shrugged off the disappointment and jogged toward Anthony, massaging his shoulder and reforming the contours of the muscle. *That, and a stiff thigh... not bad.*

Anthony launched a 'modi', and Connor leapt in the air to receive it, pushing his hand into the dagger's D-shaped grip, and fitting it snugly over his clenched hand. The three-inch blade, with undulating edges resembling a gazelle horn, protruded in an extension of his fist.

He spared a nanosecond to reflect on using weapons of the ancient martial arts discipline from which all others were thought to have been born. *Kalari. Level playing field – few vampires can be old enough to have used them before.*

Rubbing his thumb over the leather grip of the modi, Connor waited the fraction of a second it took Anthony to throw a compact circular shield along the same trajectory. It whistled through the air as Connor broke into a run. Keeping pace with the whirling, silver disc, he reached out and anchored his grip onto the shield's leather handhold.

Sebastian darted into Connor's peripheral vision, the light refracting from his bronzed, oiled frame.

Connor charged forward in a circular path, and, leaping ten-feet into the air, descended upon Sebastian like an eagle falling out of the sun.

Ducking to one side, Sebastian swung his shield up and covered his face. His foe's slicing blade bit into Sebastian's shoulder.

A juddering sensation shot up Connor's arm as the serrated edge chiseled its way into the firm flesh, and tore a fillet of tissue away. The wooden floor splintered when Connor landed, and he sprang back when Sebastian lashed out and scraped his shield across Connor's chest.

The crouched metallic figures circled the arena. Julian's "box of frogs" joke settled in Connor's head as he tracked the weaving and bobbing of Sebastian's misshapen face. *A slimy customer.*

Connor moved suddenly, slamming his hefty shield into Sebastian's blocking forearm and forcing him back. He pounded the side of his clenched fist into Sebastian's shield, protecting the blade edge as he dented the metal.

Repeating the twin strikes of shield and fist in fast succession, his rotating shoulders took up the rhythm as he pummeled first on bone and then on steel.

Sebastian fell back in jerking strides. He flung his body from side to side, dropping lower and lower, until he was forced to roll away. Regaining his feet, he unleashed a roundhouse kick towards Connor's chin.

Connor dodged to one side and used his shield to drive Sebastian's leg back down. Using that momentum, Sebastian swung back up and jabbed his blade at Connor's throat.

Connor threw his shield to the floor. The clatter resolved into the hum of a weaving gyroscope, as he folded his fist around Sebastian's and stopped the blade's forward propulsion dead.

A shroud of silence settled as Sebastian's roar of satisfaction faded.

Connor tightened his grip around the bronze stained fist, and, digging the needle-sharp point of the modi into his own skin, he dragged the tip of the blade down his chest, scoring a line through the lead-tinted dye on his pectoral muscle. He settled the point at his heart, his derision boring into Sebastian's brain. Rotating his wrist, tightening the screw, Connor forced Sebastian to bow down as the tendons in his shoulder grated.

"So close, Sebastian," he said, staring down at Sebastian's contorted body.

Sebastian's drooping eyelids veiled his gaze. He folded further forward, relaxing in defeat. "So close," he muttered.

I'll play his game. "No quarter given, are you ready to die?" Connor waited for the counter attack.

Sebastian dropped his head and accelerated his shield forward in a horizontal arc. The polished steel glinted as the metal edge gouged a groove into Connor's hip.

Connor did not flinch, his tensed muscles as hard as the metallic color staining his skin suggested.

"Muscle fibers in the gluteus medius run *vertically*." Connor clucked his tongue. "Anatomy one-oh-one, Sebastian."

In a single sharp movement, Connor yanked Sebastian's knife hand down, and flipped him over onto his back. He hit the wooden floor and the thump rang around the hall.

Planting his foot on the battered shield lying across Sebastian's greasy chest, Connor pressed down until his ribcage creaked.

"C'mon, Sebastian," Connor gloated, "is this all you've got?"

Hatred filled Sebastian's eyes as he refused to speak.

"Bout three." Julian's strident announcement fractured the tension.

Connor leapt back as though the shield delivered an electric shock through the sole of his foot. His gaze sliced across the tight features of the closest marksman. *I'm not giving them an excuse.*

"Saved by the bell, this time." Connor stared down at Sebastian's prone figure and inhaled deeply, expanding his chest. "But, can you survive more than ninety seconds? I don't think so."

Sebastian rolled to his feet, lowering his shield in a defiant display. His shattered cheekbone grated as he grimaced. "We shall see."

Julian's bark reverberated around the cavernous space. "Combatants, fall back to your corners, now!"

Still clenching the modi, Connor backed away, scooping his shield up from the floor without breaking his stride. A glow of satisfaction settled in his gut when Sebastian reached back to investigate the missing flesh over his shoulder blade.

Sebastian's fingertips dragged over the chalk dust finish where before there had been the slickness of oiled skin. The pupil of Sebastian's good eye contracted to a pinprick of rage.

Connor's enjoyment filtered across the gap. "I wouldn't worry about that." A wheedling tone wafted on a breeze, as he said idly, "Have you looked in the mirror, lately?"

In a gut reaction, Sebastian's body jerked forward, before he reined it in.

Connor's shield fell from relaxed fingers and he spread his arms in invitation. The oiled skin of his torso flowed like mercury over hard pebbles as he beckoned in the timeless 'bring it on' gesture. "We don't need weapons, Sebastian. You think you can take me." His features tightened in a beguiling smile. "We can end this, now," he said. His pupils widened to dark, hypnotic pools. "Just say the word."

Sebastian took a step forward as the magnetic pull of Connor's will reached into his mind and echoed his own desires.

"Combatants!" Captain Gerrard's sharp tone broke the spell.

Sebastian shook his head, dislodging Connor's wraithlike presence, and moved raggedly back to his end of the combat zone.

So close. Connor heaved a sigh, and muttered, "Damned pantomime."

He backed up a few more strides, before turning away and easing the tension from his muscles in an explosive sprint across the arena.

Connor was still a dozen yards from Anthony when a draft of ionized air stung his nostrils. The hairs on his nape stiffened as a wave of static electricity enveloped him. His instincts could not yet make sense of it, but he knew he was about to come under attack.

Anthony stepped out from behind the protective barrier of his weapon station. "Don't touch him, boy," he yelled, "get back to your corner."

Connor read Anthony's fierce expression and executed a turn which carved a trench, and sawdust spat from the polished wooden floor. Following the direction of Anthony's glare, Connor's eyes narrowed as he watched Sebastian staggering, and his childlike 'second' dashing out to steady him.

Events clicked into place as Connor's brain shifted into a faster gear than the vampires around him. He had the advantage of a nervous system running on the highest grade of stimuli – human blood – and everything happened at once.

The youth grabbed Sebastian's arm, resting the other hand on his back, before he leapt back at Anthony's command.

Sebastian's animation suddenly died. His limbs froze in a twisted posture as though he was pushing through pain which tried to double him over. He threw his head back and the gnarled ropes of the sinews in his neck strangled a groan.

A seizure gripped his body and tore at his muscle fibers, pulling the curves in his skeleton to ramrod straight. Sebastian's chin snapped downwards and he concentrated a demonic glare on Connor. His hazel eye glittered with malevolence. His blind eye glistened with an amalgam of silvered fish scales as though his milk-white pupil was determined to see.

Connor called out, "Julian, he's in grave sleep."

At the same moment, Charles' detector stuttered, stringing a series of agitated clicks together until they became a continuous shriek. His hand went up and he shouted, "Code red, code red, code red."

Julian took up the call. "Marksmen, target code red."

Sebastian's features froze in a silent scream, capturing his rage as a festering pool of hatred. He hurtled forward and four red dots tracked him, anchored to his head as though they were buried into his skin.

"Fire at will," Julian's command focused every set of vampire eyes on the blood red threads of light which connected four rifle barrels to their 'mark'.

Facing Sebastian, Connor planted his feet wide, balancing his weight as he watched the crazed figure closing in fast. With another three bounding strides accomplished and still no rifle fire, Sebastian suddenly flung his arm back, and, like drawing an arrow from a quiver, his hand reappeared gripping a bare stiletto blade.

Connor recognized the diamond-tipped stiletto which had gouged a hole in his side the night he had rescued Rebekah. His eyes darted across to Sebastian's diminutive second, and the malignant grin on the boyish face landed a sledgehammer of certainty in Connor's chest. It explained how Sebastian got hold of the blade.

The youth's eyes glittered with the manic intent of an unbalanced mind. *Clever, using the gash I carved in Sebastian's back as a sheath... ironic.*

As the boy's smile widened, Connor dished out his own brand of swift justice. He eased the leather grip of the modi from his knuckles, and with the flick of the wrist, launched it in an arrow's flight across the intervening forty yards. He watched with satisfaction as the three-inch blade shattered the bridge of the young vampire's nose and buried itself in his skull. The force of the blow flung him backwards, and the thud of his body hitting the floor drowned out everything else for a fraction of a second.

Connor's attention snapped back to the bronzed form bearing down upon him. He waited a further nanosecond for the peppering of gunfire, anticipating the screaming flight of four high-powered depleted-uranium bullets which should be ricocheting inside Sebastian's head. *But... nothing. What the hell?*

He started to run. *Sitting duck is not my style.* Zigzagging across the arena, he headed for the ten-foot high hoarding which bordered the fighting space. He knew exactly where Sebastian was by the storm of clashing currents stirred by his bullish approach.

The sound of Sebastian's jaw grinding away the few teeth he had left grew louder as he gained ground, using the slipstream of Connor's barreling bodyweight to find speed born of insanity.

Accelerating, Connor dragged Sebastian along with him. As the stiletto blade jabbed into the broad muscle on Connor's back, he eased into a longer stride. *I need him close, but, not that close.*

He focused on the boards rushing towards him, and targeted the dead center of one panel. He accelerated up the vertical barricade and, when he ran out of wall, launched himself into a somersault. His flight took him overhead, and Sebastian crashed chest first into the hard barrier, and spun around.

Connor landed, regained a firm foothold, and was ready to move again.

Sebastian committed to a vicious shoulder charge, clasping the stiletto blade close to his chest.

Connor risked an angry gaze into the face of the nearest marksman. *They should have taken the shot by now, shit... I should have hung on to that modi.*

Captain Gerrard's sharp tone grated over Connor's nerves. "Fire at will, dammit. Take him down."

Him? Who is him? Connor decided not to wait and find out.

He closed the gap on Sebastian, mirroring his aggressive charge. *A moving target is harder to hit.*

Deathly calm gripped Connor as he honed in on the points of danger with military precision. The four taut, red tethers of light still focused on Sebastian, creating the bizarre illusion of dragging him around the arena like the strings of a puppet. *A breathing space then.* Though, that could change at any second. *A lapse in concentration could be fatal. Are they biding their time?* Calculating his options, he decided the demented, salivating Sebastian remained the most immediate threat.

The twenty seconds of Sebastian's grave sleep yawned as a chasm of chaos to Connor's lightning-fast brain.

Sebastian rushed in and Connor twisted away. Sebastian's shoulder grazed across his chest and the uppercut destined for his gut, accelerated through thin air and buried the diamond-hard stiletto tip in Connor's tricep. He felt the pressure as it skewered his hard tissue, and then sliced it open as Sebastian's momentum carried him forward.

As Sebastian passed beneath his raised arm, Connor delivered a vicious rabbit punch to the back of his neck, digging a blunt blade of knuckles in hard; a matador wearing down a bull. *The blow to the brainstem will scramble a few of his reflexes.*

Connor allowed Sebastian's blade strike to spin him around, and pinned his stare on the crazed vampire's receding back.

Sebastian turned to come at him again, and only three laser beams of light marred his face.

Fire and Ice: Survival

Connor registered the heat of the roving laser beam like a cigarette burn on his skin, and instinctively launched into a somersault. *Target acquired.* He shielded his head with his arms as his body revolved in mid-air, and his thoughts were crystal clear. *Take out the rifleman first* – a grim smile creased his cheeks – *all four, if I have to.*

The marksman had him in his sight. The burning sensation on his flesh told Connor the precise path of the laser beam over his twisting, contorting body.

Controlling his speed, he spotted the ground. As his feet made contact with the floor, the percussive force of a bullet leaving a rifle barrel deadened his eardrums. Connor saw the glint of the tungsten carbide tip closing fast and dived out of the way.

The bullet casing plowed a scorching line across the dense tissue of his thigh. His hydrated flesh oozed a weak plasma and granite dust solution. The tearing sensation over his skin lasted only a fraction of a second, but it filled his mind with anger which stayed.

Julian bellowed, "Disarm those men, now."

Captain Gerrard galvanized into action. Passing along the rows of seating, dragging the council guardsmen in his wake, the captain commanded, "Lay down your weapons. That is a direct order. Do it now. You are relieved of your commissions."

Connor had other things to worry about.

Sebastian bore down on him, slashing out with the blade. The driving force of the manic swipe grated the sharp knife along the lower edge of Connor's rib and sliced into muscle.

Connor was pissed off, now. He whipped out his arm, landed a powerful backfist squarely in Sebastian's face and shattered his other cheekbone.

The mindless anger of a predator rumbled in Sebastian's throat. His collapsed muzzle permanently bared his teeth. Venom dripped freely from his detached jaw as he lunged forward.

Keep moving. Connor broke into a forceful run as another bullet whistled across his heels and thudded into the steel barricade next to Anthony.

"Anthony, my shield, on my mark. Three, two, one, now."

Connor swiveled as he counted, judging the distances of the potential targets around him. Anthony hurled the round plate of metal like a Frisbee, and Connor leapt to catch it. As he landed, he rotated on one foot with the shield tucked in close to his body. He whipped around, winding up speed until he became the blur of a silver-draped tornado. Splinters erupted in a plume of sawdust as another bullet buried itself in the floor behind him, his body stopped moving, his arm swung through, and he released the circle of toughened steel to spin across the arena in a perfect discus throw.

He froze as his eyes tracked the shield through the air.

The crunch of steel demolishing stone vibrated inside the marksman's skull like the bite of a chainsaw blade through bone. The rogue shooter dropped his rifle and grabbed his head, holding it in place for a moment. He looked down at the silver gray plate of the shield slipping down his chest, before his head slid down, and his body folded down into his seat like a headless ghoul.

Instantly dismissing the marksman, Connor looked for Sebastian. The click of a rifle cocking snapped his head around. He sliced a sharp glance over at Captain Gerrard.

"Tell them to stand down, Sebastian is mine!" yelled Connor.

He turned back, his features carved in granite. His eyes glittered as he flirted with grave sleep, letting his mind dance around the edges of it as the human blood inside him banged on the cell door inside his brain. *But I want to see Sebastian die, not just feel it.*

Sebastian stank of ice-cold aggression. He had armed himself with a kopis sword while Connor was dodging bullets. The recurved blade glinted in the dim light, accentuating the sweeping edge from concave at the hilt to convex at the tip which could deliver a blow with the weight of an ax. *Shit.*

"Connor. Here." Anthony's calm tone cut across the arena as he launched a sword with an arcing backward swing.

As Connor's hand closed around the hilt, he swung it over his head. Balancing the weight in his palm, he rotated the grip loosely in agile fingers. The blade gathered momentum, and he danced forward.

Sebastian's rhythm was a relentless thundering drum beat as he swung the kopis in devastating arcs. The force of the clashing blades shuddered up Connor's braced arms. He parried and blocked, swinging up and back, scraping metal over metal until the hilt of his sword locked with Sebastian's and he pushed him back a step.

Connor controlled the pace, taking his time, and could smell the frustration oozing from Sebastian's bronzed skin as venom sprayed from his hanging jaw.

The gaping mouth became the focus of Connor's mind. "You can do better than that, Sebastian." His whisper echoed around the hall, floating up to dally in the space overhead, before falling again in a confetti of irritation.

Sebastian roared, and, as his sword hit the top of an arc, he switched to a double-handed grip. With both hands raised overhead, he grinned into Connor's rock-hard features. His biceps crackled as the muscle fibers tore with the sudden exertion of delivering a cleaving blow destined to slice into Connor's skull.

As the sword whipped down, Sebastian lifted his chin and growled. Connor stepped in close and dropped like a stone onto one knee. Gripping his sword in one hand and bracing the weight of the weapon in his other palm, he rammed his sword upwards into Sebastian's mouth, shattering his palette and entering his brain. The end of the blade stuttered when it scraped along the inside of Sebastian's skull, then Connor released his grip and it slid out again.

Sebastian's eyes snapped open in shocked surprise. Connor stayed down on one knee and dropped his head forward, absorbing the impact as Sebastian's sword fell heavily from his slack fingers and came to rest in the cradle between Connor's shoulder blades. Sebastian's body keeled over backwards, his eyes staring up into the heavens. The ethereal light in the hall reflected in them, draping a filigree of frost over the dead orbs.

Connor rose to his feet and stared down at his vanquished enemy. The echoes of clashing blades reverberated like the dying note of a tuning fork. Connor's silver-stained body drew every eye as the air swelled with stunned disbelief that the duel was over.

Julian raised a hand and announced, "Doctor Connor is the victor.

Connor suddenly moved in the blur of a silver bullet, lifting the spell as he darted across the arena, vaulted over the hoarding, and joined Julian on his observation deck.

In a lightning-quick manouver, Connor pulled Captain Gerrard's hand gun from it's holster, walked over to the nearby marksman, pressed the barrel to his eye socket, and pulled the trigger. The vampire hit the floor with the bullet bouncing around inside his skull sounding like a wooden spoon stirring custard.

Julian stared into Connor's frosty glare, darting a look at Charles and the lights on the console.

Connor said, "No, I'm not in grave sleep. I'm just really pissed off." He lanced a look over Julian's shoulder to pin Captain Gerrard in his sights. "You're very lucky. I like you."

"Jesus, Connor." Julian breathed as he broke out into a smile.

Fire and Ice: Survival

Chapter 32

Connor stood naked under the needle-sharp spray of boiling water in the wet room. The familiarity of the surgical wing of the hospital drained the residual tension from his limbs as he planted his hands on the smooth tiles in front of him, hung his head, and watched the whirling pool of lead-colored oil and grease washing away beneath his feet.

When the water ran clean, he turned and stepped back into the deluge with his chin raised, raking his hands through his hair. Sweeping his palms down over his chest and sluicing the water from his skin, his questing fingers explored the wounds chiseled into his hard flesh.

Anthony did a good job. The opaque snail trails of glue stood proud, but would wear flat with time.

The sliced cut into his tricep and the eight inch incision Sebastian's shield had made into the flesh over his hip glistened as they undulated across contours of muscles carved in polished quartz.

The scorched trough gouged out of his thigh by the bullet casing had oxidized silver paint into the muscle and would stay there as a permanent reminder of the battle; the badge of a warrior. The gray areas of vampire bruising marking Connor's body bore testament to the force of Sebastian's blows. Their impact had shunted congealed blood back along veins until they collapsed, and so they would remain until he next fed and they were rehydrated once more.

Connor cut off the water and stepped from the shower. He grimaced as rubbing a towel briskly over his ridged abdomen covered it in a generous sprinkling of glittering silver paint flecks. *Going to take a while to get rid of them.* He grunted. *Romantic sparkles are just not me.*

He pulled on tailored pants the color of ash, pushed his arms into a coal-black shirt, and ran a comb through wet black hair which glinted with petrol-blue highlights. He looked in the mirror and, for a moment, he caught a glimpse of the ghostly features with eyes sockets darkened with intent that had haunted his childhood nightmares. He dragged his hands over his face. *Am I a monster?*

He thought of Sebastian and of Rebekah's bruised flesh at *that* monster's hand, and he knew. *No, the killing I did today was deserved.* He just wished he had not enjoyed it so much.

Connor grabbed his jacket and left the room. Walking with forceful assurance through the hospital corridors, he pushed the heavy glass doors aside as though they were made of plastic, bounded down the steps and hit the street running. *I want to see Rebekah and Seren, but they are safe. First, I want answers.*

Connor remembered a conversation he had overheard in Vietnam; a salty NCO setting his squad straight. *"You don't have a life expectancy in combat. If you find yourself under fire, either you started it – in which case the gooks die – or they started it, in which case you die. We don't make mistakes. We don't let them start fights."* A sly smile came over Connor's face. "Well, they started it. I wonder how they feel now?"

When he pushed open the heavy oak doors of the council building, the corridors were deserted. Connor headed straight for Julian's chambers and stepped inside without knocking.

Dressed in his principal garb, Julian was tying his white cravat. Meeting Connor's intense gaze in the mirror, he jerked his chin in greeting.

Captain Gerrard was standing, facing the door expectantly. "Doctor Connor," he said, in a guarded tone.

"Where are they?" Connor's lip curled. "And what the hell happened in there?"

"They are in a holding cell. Anthony's with them and they are awaiting your interrogation." Julian quietly rattled off the situation as he turned and took a step to cross the room.

Connor nodded sharply. "Let's go," he barked and disappeared through the door, leaving it swinging on its hinges.

Julian and the captain caught up four seconds and two hundred yards later. As Connor entered the holding cell, he scanned the room, taking in the two stainless steel coffin shells resting on trestle tables. Anthony stood in between them, his narrowed eyes glued to

Fire and Ice: Survival

his charges. His closed features radiated the disgust the muscles twitching in his folded arms seemed anxious to express.

The two marksmen were presented in profile, standing to attention with their eyes focused front and center as though they were trying to burn a hole in the smooth wooden paneling.

Connor walked up to the first one and intercepted the tractor beam of his gaze. "Guardsman, why did you fail to follow a direct order?"

"Sergeant Burton gave us a direct order. Acquire the target and hold fire until he gave the signal."

"That would be *dead* Sergeant Burton, *headless* Sergeant Burton?" snarled Connor into the guardsman's face. "Captain Gerrard gave you a direct order."

"Sergeant Burton is our squad leader- was." The guardsman's voice was flat with resignation. His eyes suddenly zeroed in on Connor. "I am sorry, Doctor Connor. He fired on you. That was over the line."

Connor looked from one guardsman to the other, digesting their stiff faces. *They watched Captain Laurence die, at least they still knew there was a line*. Connor nodded sharply, turned towards the door and left.

Julian matched his pace as they headed for the council hearing. "Well?"

"Let them sweat awhile, then send them back to barracks." Connor's hard features creased into a grim smile.

Julian's brows climbed in surprise.

"Vietnam. The average life expectancy of a 1st lieutenant in a hot LZ was sixteen minutes. Well, slight exaggeration maybe, but, you get the gist. But I know the impact of living through that, I zipped up the body bags." Connor stopped and looked Julian in the eye. "As a private first class, it was your sergeant who kept you alive. With Captain Laurence gone." Connor shot an apologetic glance at Captain Gerrard and shrugged.

Julian nodded slowly as Connor suddenly set off again, changing pace physically and mentally. "Is Serge expecting me?"

"No. He was confined to the council anteroom for the duration of the duel and he has no idea of the outcome. He's in the courtroom, pacing." Julian smiled with genuine amusement. "He knows he faces exile if Sebastian loses. He doesn't yet know that his plant, Sebastian's second, failed."

"Definitely down to Serge, then?" Connor glowered.

"Yes, Marius recognized the body as one of Serge's recruits. He was only sixteen turned and the guardsmen underestimated him. He was there to *fix* things."

Connor stopped abruptly outside the courtroom door. He straightened his jacket and a smile glittered in the depths of his gray eyes. "Showtime," he said quietly. "After you, Principal Julian."

Connor watched Julian disappear into the door marked, 'Jurors. Private: No Entry', and continued down the hallway and placed his hand on the handle of the courtroom door. The pounding of a gavel on the bench was followed by Julian's strident call to order.

Connor walked into the room.

Serge was standing in the dock. His dry skin crackled as tension sucked his cheeks into hollows and he swung around to see Connor's stony face. Bitterness stirred the disappointment in his eyes as his chin went up in defiance. "Doctor Connor, I'd like to say I am pleased to see you-"

"I know. Annoying, isn't it?"

Connor took in every detail of Serge's repugnance, filling his lungs with the councilor's peculiar odor. *What is that smell?* He wondered if Serge's drab olive-green coat had ever been a good fit for his scrawny shoulders. *Vampires are immortal, sure, but bad maintenance leads to wear and tear. Serge is the worst example I've seen outside of storage facility eight.*

Serge's trembling anger rippled the fabric of his empty coat sleeve. "There is no justice here," he spat vehemently.

"No, you are right." A feral expression clung to Connor's features as he said, "Justice would be *you* lying dead in the arena with a sword buried in *your* brain, or-" His gray eyes clouded with an avalanche of ice as he glared. "A blade between the eyes, like your accomplice."

Fire and Ice: Survival

Serge's gaze skittered around the courtroom, catching sight of Julian's closed expression.

"Save your breath, Councilor Serge," Julian said quietly, "We have always known what you are, and no one is happier than I that you've signed your own death warrant."

Serge choked on his own saliva as he spluttered, "Death."

Connor grinned. "Anything less *would* be an injustice."

"But exile." Serge's eyes stretched wide above slack cheeks as he pleaded. "Surely, Principal Julian, exile-"

"It is not my decision. Your forfeit is in Doctor Connor's hands." Julian pretended to be apologetic.

"Perhaps exile would be more fitting." Connor rubbed his jaw in dark contemplation. "I hear a space has opened up in the Loch Glascarnoch hive." At Serge's blank look, Connor added, "It's in the Highlands of Scotland. Coldest place in Britain at -15 degrees centigrade."

Julian's confusion showed on his face.

"Cold is not exactly a problem for us," said Marius.

"To *us*, no. But the only animals are scrawny goats, and their human farm calls for perpetual hard graft by the vampires to maintain it." Connor smiled as his meaning sank in. "Short rations of blood and no time to yourself, Serge. You could call it a living hell."

Julian laughed softly. "That sounds perfect."

Serge's jaw snapped shut, his eyes glazed with hatred.

Julian lingered over his smile a little longer before he banged the gavel and, peering around the courtroom, said, "Doctor Connor has a declaration to make to the hive."

Connor dominated the space.

The weight of his cold stare dragged across each face in the gallery like fingers of frost over stone as he committed each one to memory.

"You all know me, and that I have fathered a child." Connor's deep inhalation pulled his black shirt taut across his chest and thickened the column of his throat in a display of the raw power of an alpha male. "None of us know where this may lead, but-" He pierced the core of each vampire with a daggered look. "Any vampire who means to harm my daughter will meet the same end as Sebastian." He closed his right hand into a fist, pounding it once upon his chest, over his heart. "That, I can promise you."

Chapter 33

The air inside the soundproofed room at Julian's house was drenched in a bouquet of adrenalin and nervous perspiration.

A battery-powered lantern cast a fuzzy-edged circle over the thick carpet, leaving most of the room in deep shadow. A keen eye would have picked out the makeshift crib of an oak dresser drawer set down on the floor in the corner of the room. The tumble of white linen which filled it stirred with every wriggle of Seren's delicate limbs as she exercised tiny muscles and discovered how movement felt.

The only other sounds disturbing the cloying silence were the scratching of a pencil lead across paper and the whispering of vellum sheets slipping through agitated human fingers.

'How long?', was printed halfway down the page, forming part of the rambling transcript of their thoughts. The white paper caught the lamplight and appeared to float across the space between the two shadowed figures like a prop in a magician's illusion.

Rebekah's intense features emerged from the shadows as she leaned forward to spill her fears out onto the page. 'About nine hours!!!'. She pushed a feathered tress of blond hair back from her brow, and huffed in frustration. 'How much longer? Is he alright? Did he have to fight? Did he win? No, of course he won. WHEN WILL HE COME FOR US?'. Pacing the floor was a luxury she could not afford, so the scribbling continued.

When settling them in, Anthony had taken his escort duties very seriously, taking time to add an extra layer of cloth to the table tops and a thick scatter cushion to each of the armchairs. His frown of serious intent still sprinkled goosebumps over her arms when Rebekah allowed herself to dwell on it.

"You must be silent. Your life depends upon it," was his parting shot, and then he left them in the dark. *In every sense.*

Rebekah's body felt surprisingly pain free. *Vampire post-operative procedures makes human methods seem like the Dark Ages.* Her C-section site had been stitched with an intricacy which only preternatural skill could accomplish. Her brain, however, was screaming in agony.

"Shh." Leizle puffed air between her teeth in a gentle reminder. Her worried green eyes held golden nuggets of the reflected lamplight in their depths.

Rebekah tried to smile as tension crawled under her skin and the hairs on her nape stiffened. An icy chill caressed her face, and she trapped a gasp inside her chest as, darting a sharp glance at Leizle, she caught her attention by gripping her arm. She watched as Leizle's concerned look sharpened to anxiety and, finally, she got it.

Someone's in here.

The chuckle vibrating in his throat, and resonating as a warm rumble through his chest, died as Rebekah's gaze found his face. Even though he stood in the darkest corner, she had his height pegged perfectly.

The spark of alarm stirring diamond fragments in her brown eyes entranced Connor. He dipped his knees and braced his body as she shot up from her chair and flew across the room, knowing that he would catch her.

He pushed himself into revival sleep. Gauging her speed and tempering his strength, he gathered her fragile frame into his arms when she collided with his body. The feel of her heart fluttering in her chest was like a hummingbird's wings beating inside a birdcage. He absorbed the impact and straightened, feeling her soft muscles mold to his. He ran his palm smoothly down the back of her denim-clad thighs and lifted her to cradle his hips, creating a space to keep her still tender incision free from pressure.

"Careful, honey." His voice was rough with concern. "You might feel okay, but you must be careful."

He buried his face in her neck as her excitement stirred the jewels of her blood cells into a fragrant turbulent frenzy. *Ah, that pain.* Familiar hunger unfurled inside his gut and her scent lacerated his throat. *Bliss.*

"Your painkiller is an implant, honey, but be careful." Connor looked into her upturned face, his own features trapped between joy

Fire and Ice: Survival

and lust as his hand pressed firmly down the seam running along the back of her jeans.

He smiled as her heart rate clattered an agitated echo inside her ribcage and a shower of firework embers warmed her blood. An answering heat flushed her cheeks and then dropped like a stone through the center of her body to warm his palms and pulse against his fingers.

"I missed you." She smiled ruefully, and reached up to tangle her fingers in his hair. She tugged at his bottom lip with hers, and filled his mouth with a sigh of need.

"I missed you, too," he said, his palm gently framing her nape as he sank into her kiss and tantalized a thirst which would take a thousand years to slake. Her pulse danced through his body in an earthquake of enticing rhythms, and a purr vibrated his vocal chords as her hands pulled hard on his hair.

"Ahem," spluttered Julian with pretended indignation. "Get a room, you two."

Connor smiled against Rebekah's lips, his words riding the wave of a deep-throated chuckle. "Spoilsport."

"Not at all." Julian strode over to Leizle's side and laced his fingers carefully though hers. "However, the clock is ticking," he murmured in a distracted tone as his gaze dragged a flush over Leizle's cheekbones and his eyes locked onto hers. "Hey there, Red," he said. He drifted closer to taste her delicate flavor, and his lips clung to hers. His thumb stroked over the pulse thundering in her throat as he deepened the kiss, letting her scent drift like mist inside him and tighten his body with the yearning for more.

Connor's cough grated with amusement. "Clock ticking, did you say?"

A few minutes later, with Seren folded securely into Connor's chest, the four of them walked the length of Julian's house and emerged into the damp night air.

Pausing on the top step, Rebekah raised an eyebrow as she scanned the gravel driveway. "A car? Can't we walk faster than you drive that thing?"

Connor smiled, reached out to wind a strand of her hair around his finger, and tugged it gently. "Funny."

"Seriously, though, is it safe?"

Connor's attention wandered and he was lost in admiring the blend of colors in the silky tress. The filaments reflected with a rainbow of gold to his vampire sight – a couple of black, and then every shade of yellow, with a few platinum strands thrown in for good measure.

"Marius has declared the court hearing a closed session. No one leaves until he gives permission, so we have the time to travel by more conventional and comfortable means," said Julian as he elbowed Connor sharply in the ribs.

It was Rebekah's turn to become entranced when moonlight broke from behind a cloud and dressed Connor's skin in silver flecks. Rebekah hitched a gasp which drew his gaze as she breathed, "You get more beautiful every day."

When his lips bowed in amusement, she said with a sheepish smile, "I said that out loud, didn't I?"

"Afraid so," said Connor as he tapped a fingertip on her upturned nose. "We should get moving. I'll be happier when we have you settled back in the eco-shelter."

"But, we'll be alone," Leizle whispered with concern.

"Not for long. Anthony has Oscar and Greg's scent. He's bringing them back," Julian replied.

"Scent?" asked Leizle.

Julian shrugged. "It's been a long time since he was at the eco-shelter. It is just a precaution for both sides. A point of contact."

Connor seamlessly jumped in to finish the thought. "Anthony has the password 'the kitchen is empty', so Oscar will know that we sent him. The eco-shelter will be home again in no time. It remains the safest place for you and Seren, for now, at least." Connor held out his hand to Rebekah. "Let's go. The good news is I can drive as fast as I want."

Rebekah grimaced. "Just don't make Seren sick. I have enough trouble getting the milk into her with that metal feeding contraption you came up with, without it coming back up again."

Her frown, accompanied by a stamped foot, made Connor laugh with genuine delight as he saluted in mock obedience, and said, "Yes ma'am." Gliding down the steps he opened the car door and stood to attention with an arched look that said, 'Are you coming?'.

Epilogue

A month had passed since he killed Sebastian, and Connor was back in harness. His reinstatement to the hospital was unconditional; however, Connor was not a fool. *Dedication to a common cause is not natural for vampires. We aren't herd animals, and the temptation to serve our own interests will always lie just below the surface.* Therefore, enforcing the protected status of the eco-community would be a constant challenge.

Connor paused outside the hospital and took a deep breath of the cool night air. He had been released from a cadaver drawer half an hour ago. His muscles hummed with the purr of rehydration, and he was the human equivalent of being well-fed and rested. He had drunk his full quota of human blood before taking grave sleep, so he was as safe as a fox in the chicken coop *could* be.

He dallied inside the shelter of the stone porch. The light pouring through the aqua-tinted glass doors at his back cast his shadow in a crooked carpet of black. It zigzagged down over the marble steps, tugging at his feet, calling to him to follow, race, and plow through the terrain, until he was once again at Rebekah's side and holding Seren.

Spring is in the air. The thought flirted with a smile which did not quite blossom. The burgeoning flora in Hyde Park was a fragrant bouquet in the concrete vase of this London suburb. The moist atmosphere was laden with promise.

A frown darkened Connor's face as the cold emanating from the granite walls at his shoulders smothered spring's tentative touch with a shadow of foreboding. As eddying gusts of air snatched at the fabric of his pants, he adopted the human display of preparing to brave the elements by buttoning up his greatcoat against the chill, except, the cold resided inside his chest.

The heavy glass door behind him whipped open, and the feeling of foreboding took the tangible form of Juror Marius.

Fire and Ice: Survival

He stopped at Connor's side. "The guardsman is back with the first report on how Serge is faring in Scotland," he said, deliberately.

Connor's look penetrated Marius' nonchalant facade. *Bad news, then. Never a dull moment.* "Oh? What news?"

Marius' silence was heavy with calculation, and Connor fancied he could hear the cogs turning inside the vampire's meticulous brain.

"Just say it, Marius. We're not in court, now, I won't hold you to anything."

"News of the vampire birth has reached the Midland Hive." Marius paused and, for the first time in their acquaintance he laid a hand on Connor, gripping his shoulder. "I'm afraid we will attract the interest of outsiders before long."

Connor looked up towards the black sky where gray clouds had devoured all the stars and billowed with an ill wind. "Not a big surprise."

"Have you worked it out yet. How?"

"The conception?" Connor shook his head. "Not yet. A complete mystery, still."

Marius' dropped his hand down to his side as he said, "Ah, well. It will come to you, I'm sure." The obsidian depths of his gaze glittered with intelligence. "We've waited a decade, a little longer is of no consequence."

He knows I'm lying. Connor cleared his throat, flipped up his coat collar, and prepared to move as he said, "I'll give Julian the heads-up that the secret is out."

"Ah, yes. He tells us that we can expect a weekly update in council? Principal Julian, Surgical Officer Anthony, or you, yourself, will keep us informed on Seren's growth and development. That's acceptable to you?"

"Provided the hive members honor the twenty-mile exclusion zone around the eco-home, then yes." Connor's words were uncompromising. "Any vampire breaking it signs his own death warrant, and Rebekah and Seren will disappear." Without looking back, he descended the steps and raced his shadow along the dark wet streets leaving Marius to digest the ultimatum.

The whisper of Connor's preternatural stride rebounded from the white marble facades lining the route, and the rapt attention of the gnarled gargoyles and blind statues seemed to ridicule his hopes of a peaceful existence.

He breathed easier when he raced along the Embankment, tracking the River Thames. The wind whistled through the trees and shredded the skin of the water, chasing foaming ripples from one river bank to the other. The buffeting gusts swelled to a howl and chased him over Vauxhall Bridge, and Connor outraced them as if the Devil's hordes were clawing at his heels.

With the passing of each mile of the thirty he covered through the Kent countryside, his certainty emerged as a beacon of assurance – he would hold on to everything that now gave his life meaning.

His destination in sight, Connor hunkered down in the woods on the edge of the clearing, looking out over the eco-shelter. His contemplations carved a ruthless expression in the chiseled quartz of his features.

Moonlight slipped through the canopy overhead and slices of deep shadow cut across the ethereal glow of his skin.

The undergrowth moved, and Anthony arrived beside him. "You left without me." A smile colored his tone. "You were in a hurry, I guess."

"I have to be back at the hospital tomorrow. You can't blame me for making the most of every moment." Connor smiled as he rose to his feet, relieved of his vigil. "Julian is here tonight, too. I need you to run the perimeter at twenty miles out. There are eight humans in there, now. I know the jurors and Captain Gerrard are looking after things in London, but-" Connor glanced at Anthony's massive chest and thick biceps. "If you catch a vampire within twenty miles, finish him. I'm not going through the circus of fighting in the arena every time a vampire crosses the line. Just crush their skulls and let's be done with it."

Fire and Ice: Survival

They both knew Anthony would be breaking a host of unwritten rules, and a few written ones, too. *But, exceptional times call for exceptional measures. I'm not going to lose sleep over it.*

Anthony smiled grimly and nodded. "You've got it." Turning on his heel, he disappeared to thread his way through the woodland. His broad, solid frame stirred a surprisingly gentle wake.

Connor set off for the eco-shelter, crossing the meadow and descending into the dark throat of the access tunnel. Moving beyond the heavy sackcloth curtain, he filled his lungs with the rich cocktail of human scents. It felt like coming home.

He scanned the tunnels ahead. His vampire senses constructed a three dimensional image of the descending levels, locating each human by their deliciously wet heartbeat. His mouth flooded with citrus-accented venom, and he clamped his throat closed as Rebekah's honey scent seemed to seek him out and fill his mind with the perfection of her face.

Brushing his hair back from his brow, he realized the moist night air had settled on his skin as frost. *I better warm up before I give them both hypothermia.* He whisked silently down to the lower level, swerved left and powered through the dining cavern.

As Connor entered the kitchen, Oscar looked up from his food preparation, raising a carving knife aloft.

Connor held up his hands as if his life was in danger, pretending he could not easily read Oscar's calm features and the thick steady pulse.

However, *another* pulse rate in the room accelerated abruptly to a thundering, rolling drum beat as her cheeks flushed and a wash of panic covered her skin in a cold sweat.

Connor's gray eyes settled on the middle-aged, flushed female face and he raised an eyebrow. "Oscar, you have a new friend?"

"This is my Evie," he spluttered. "This is Evie," he corrected hastily, a ruddy tide coursing up his thick neck. "Seth said she could visit. She fancied a change of scene."

Connor smothered his smile as speculation pushed his eyebrows to comic heights. The stuttering rhythm of Evie's heart began to stabilize as she moved closer to Oscar and took his hand. Her grip tightened on his fingers and the breath left Oscar's chest in a whoosh of embarrassment. "She cooks," he added lamely, and Connor's chuckle filled the air.

"Welcome, Oscar's friend, Evie," he teased as he crossed the kitchen and disappeared into the laundry room. He mentally added Evie to the eco-shelter family. *Clearly they are smitten.*

Four seconds later, trailing a shower of droplets like a dog after a dip in the lake, Connor passed back through the kitchen leaving Oscar and Evie staring after him.

His skin was warm from his plunge into the hot Jacuzzi pool, and he had left his greatcoat, jacket and shirt there, hanging on a peg. His drenched pants clung to his thighs, and he left a meandering trail of water as he slowed to human walking pace. He could hear the murmur of Rebekah's voice and he closed his eyes for a moment to absorb her lilting tones. *She's talking to Julian.*

Connor moved deliberately through the tunnels to Rebekah's small cave and paused just outside the doorway to eavesdrop shamelessly. *Julian knows I'm here, he'll have heard me arrive.* But, Rebekah was oblivious and if he leaned against the wall in the dark shadow, he could add to his treasure trove of her expressions and gestures and lock them away inside his heart.

Sure enough, Julian shot a lightning bolt of speculation into the dark space, finding the spot where Connor rested, before continuing on as though nothing had disturbed the thread of his thoughts.

"It was her eighteenth. That is still an important birthday?" Julian tilted his head.

"Julian." Rebekah's persuasive tone was punctuated by a frown. "She just wants you. No frills. No grand gestures. Just your love, and for you to finally make her yours."

Rebekah grinned at Julian's poker faced expression; love and lust were clearly written there, despite himself.

Connor watched Rebekah, and the fluid language of her body as it swayed in and out of his line of sight, tantalized his vision. Julian formed the other half of this banquet of revelation – he had no idea his eyes were alive with a maelstrom of emotion.

It helped Connor to push the bleaker elements of this soapbox drama to the back of his mind, where pathos was the bedrock lurking beneath the ocean of optimism.

"It may not be a hundred years, but she has waited a long time to feel like this. She wants to know that you are serious, that's all. And now, there's nothing to stop you, mmm?" Rebekah shrugged eloquently.

"So-" Julian's voice grated through tight vocal chords. "An uninterrupted night alone, in a rustic cottage with a burning log fire? Would that be fitting?"

The delicate arch of her brows rose. "I'm impressed, you have been giving this some thought."

"I've thought of little else," Julian said quietly.

Wistful joy flushed Rebekah's cheeks and filled Connor's dead heart with a moment of sorrow. Their love had been the hurtling adrenalin rush of a white water ride through the rapids of passion, always fraught with danger. *She knows I love her, but we have had little time to savor it.*

The tangible proof of this thought made itself known, when a demanding mewling noise erupted from Seren's crib.

Julian turned to look at the rattling cradle, saying in a decisive tone, "I'll get going. I'm sure Connor will be along shortly. It's past midnight."

In the tunnel outside the cave, Julian halted in front of Connor, his crooked smile daring him to comment.

Connor raised a hand in mock surrender. Jerking his head, he moved away from the doorway of the cave until he was certain Rebekah would not hear them.

Running his fingers over a lump of rock protruding from the tunnel wall, Connor gouged it out and held it in his palm. He polished its surface with his thumb as he said thoughtfully, "Marius says news of Seren's birth is out, and to expect outsiders to visit the hive."

Watching Connor's pale fingers eroding the hard stone to a handful of gravel, Julian said, "So soon? News travels fast." His green eyes sparked with disappointment. "Not entirely unexpected, although, a little more time would have been good."

"Greg and Oscar have the evacuation drill down pat. The panic room is hidden behind a false wall, and once they are inside, even the keenest vampire senses will not detect them." Connor's narrowed eyes glittered in the dim light. "Seren is developing fast, perhaps three times faster than a human child, and I would prefer to wait until she is full grown before we are forced to leave London."

Julian nodded sharply. He was fiercely protective of his little devil-daughter, as he affectionately called Seren. Somehow, God-daughter did not seem appropriate. "We have that time, I am sure of it. Your display in the arena won you the unconditional support of Captain Gerrard and the guardsmen. I believe London is the safest place for Seren, right now."

"Marius gave me an easy time of it when I dodged the question of conception. He and Alexander have come down on our side, it would seem." The handful of gravel fell in a controlled shower onto the ground, punctuating Connor's thoughts. "You know, when I found Rebekah dying of hypothermia, desperation drove me to bathe in boiling water, anything to save her."

The ghosts cluttered his gaze as he looked Julian in the eye.

"We will find a way," Julian said firmly.

"I have no intention of becoming Frankenstein, Julian. It may sound ridiculous, but I cannot get the image of oven-baked vampires, and deep-frozen humans out of my mind. I will not let that happen."

"Even if nothing really changes," Julian said, "and our efforts center on fending off hostile interest in the eco-shelter and safeguarding Seren, it is pretty much where we were before. Business as usual." His grin rode a wave of sudden exhilaration. "But, as *you* once said, I'd swap a hundred years of boredom for one moment of this feeling, in a heartbeat, if I had one."

"You're right. We'll find a way."

"For me, this feeling," Julian ruefully acknowledged, "has more to do with Leizle, than anything else." He assessed the solid wall of

Connor's naked chest and the puddle of water forming at his friend's feet, and said, "For now, at least, I think we both have better places to be than here." As he turned away, the bulkhead lamp lit up Julian's sudden smile. "I'll catch up with you at the hospital tomorrow."

Connor returned to the cavern, and stopped on the threshold. Rebekah was feeding Seren, whose teeth grated over the metal collar of the bottle as her strong tongue worked to fill her throat with blood.

"You're here," Rebekah said softly. "I've missed you."

"I love you," he said simply, and the sun rose for him, right there, in that moment. Her smile washed over him, and the dread he had been holding onto fell away. He crossed to her side, sank to his knees beside her, and leaned over to steal Rebekah's smile with a deep kiss. A laugh vibrated in his throat as Seren kicked him firmly in the gut. "Getting stronger every day," he murmured against Rebekah's lips, closing his eyes and resting his forehead gently to hers.

"Getting bigger every day, too" she whispered, placing the spent bottle on a side table.

As his palm moved to cover Rebekah's cheek, Connor pulled back to look into her eyes. The sadness in their depths was not unexpected, but he asked anyway. "Uncle Harry?"

She swallowed noisily. "Oscar says he's not coming."

Connor was not surprised, because he had visited the man himself. Uncle Harry was a scientist, first and foremost. While he was genuinely pleased to know Rebekah was happy, he was also a coward, and facing his culpability was something he chose not to do. Instead, he had embraced the new challenges of helping Seth's community, deciding to stay and help them improve their environment.

"He'll come around, honey," Connor said gently, "He's just having a hard time dealing with his own guilt."

Rebekah was surprised at Connor's empathy for Harry. "Hey, who's the human, here?"

He grinned, "What can I say? I have everything I need, right here." He embraced her carefully. "I guess I can afford to be generous." Connor looked down into the slate gray eyes of his daughter. "Isn't that right, Seren?"

Rebekah laughed gently as Seren gripped Connor's hand and smiled back at him.

"Why don't you go and have a bath, I got this," he said as he scooped Seren up in one arm, rose fluidly to his feet, and helped Rebekah up out of the chair. "I'll settle her down. I think she may need human sleep tonight."

Rebekah frowned. "You've been here five seconds. How can you know?"

Connor pretended to frown as he said in a dark, mysterious tone, "I can read her thoughts." As Rebekah's jaw dropped open, he reached out a fingertip to close it. "Well, her brain waves, anyway, now, go."

He watched her graceful stride until she disappeared, and then he gazed down at Seren. "Well, kiddo. How about giving me and your mama a bit of alone time?"

Seren obligingly fluttered her eyelids until they closed, and Connor was left to wonder. *Does she understand my speech, is she reading my mood... or?*

Seren was perfect. Her black hair and porcelain skin had the dramatic, vampiric contrast of her father, but her face flushed to pink when she cried. Her sleep pattern was not yet established. It was not every night, and it was apparent by the way she fell asleep suddenly, as though her consciousness stepped over a precipice and into the abyss, that she could not do without it. *Sleep deprivation in humans leads to hallucinations and can culminate in death. So, it looks like Seren has human sleep to juggle as well as the vampire sleep centers, but, we know nothing yet for sure.*

An hour later, Seren was asleep, and Connor and Rebekah were alone. She was where she wanted to be, in Connor's arms, and as always, she was in heaven and he was in hell.

Lying out on his back with Rebekah tucked into his side, her palm laying on his abdomen made concentrating on anything else impossible. Connor wrestled with his darkest desires. He was happy they had found the solution to Seren's conception, but he still had irrational fears about putting Rebekah through it again.

He slowly infused his lungs and the core of his being with her scent, drowning in the storm of electrical impulses firing inside her head like a firework display which ionized the air, and he knew. *She's up to something.*

Lying with him now, Rebekah was a woman with something on her mind; her plan, to assault Connor's virtue. Her fingers twirled the dark, downy hair dusting his stomach, following the trail downward. Although his body remained stone still, he began to pant, and she smiled as she pressed her lips to the wall of taut muscles.

"It's been almost two months." She rested her chin on his chest to look up at him, and his hooded gray gaze burned into her softly pleading eyes. "Please, Connor."

A growl rumbled through him. "But, what if we're wrong?" He knew he was just playing for time, not wanting to hurt her. As a clinician, the facts confirmed the melding of their core body temperatures as the answer. But, the man, the lover in him, was superstitiously cautious about loving her before she had recovered physically. *I could not bear it if I hurt her.*

"Don't stay, then, just love me a little." Rebekah moved over him, trailing kisses up to his throat, and settling her thighs over his hips. She took his still face in her palms, staring deep into his eyes, feeling that she was winning as his black pupils ate the gray away to silver threads. "Please, Connor."

Her tongue snaked into his softened mouth, and his body braced beneath her.

Connor knew she had him; her honeyed scent tore him open, and even in deep revival sleep, his hunger was burning out of control. "I'm sorry," he murmured.

Defeat settled on her face for one heartbreaking moment, until, on a deep inhalation which filled his lungs with her scorching aroma, he sat up slowly. Lacing his fingers into her hair at her nape, he firmly grasped her hip and lowered her onto his urgent body, groaning as he felt her melt around him, and his gaze locked to hers.

"Sorry?" she husked as his arousal chased the breath from her body.

"Mmm," he murmured, his voice deep with testosterone-washed desire. "I was thinking about the bruises you're going to have in the morning. As you say, it's been a long time, honey." Ecstasy stirred a turbulent current in the depths of his ice-gray eyes. As she began to move, he filled his hungry heart with the vision of her naked perfection. Molding his hands to span her waist, he muttered hoarsely, almost to himself, "I'll try to be careful."

Rebekah was exactly where she wanted to be – Connor making love to her, his obvious rapture swelling her with deep satisfaction, her daughter sleeping, safe and sound, and so, for now, nothing else mattered.

THE END

Fire and Ice: Survival

With Seren's birth, a grudging state of status quo exists, but for how long?

Can Connor and Rebekah hope to keep Seren safe?
One thing is for sure, Connor will lay down his life if he has to.

Their battle continues in

Fire and Ice Book 3: Earth Walker

Out on Amazon Kindle and in paperback, Autumn 2018

Watch out for the Prequel to the Fire & Ice Series

OUT NOW

Death of Connor Sanderson

How did Doctor Connor become a vampire?

It all began in **London, in 1910...**

Fire and Ice: Survival

Lightning Source UK Ltd.
Milton Keynes UK
UKHW04f0736170818
327398UK00001B/159/P